My Life with Michael

A Novel of Sex, Beer and Middle Age

LORI L. SCHAFER

This book is a work of fiction. Names, characters, places and incidents are products of the author's imagination or are used fictitiously. Any resemblance to actual events or locales or persons, living or dead, is entirely coincidental.

This work of fiction contains explicit sexual scenarios and is therefore inappropriate for readers under the age of eighteen. All characters depicted are eighteen years of age or older.

First Edition

ISBN-10: 1942170157
ISBN-13: 978-1-942170-15-0

DEDICATION

To Michael – my unwitting, unwilling inspiration.

CONTENTS

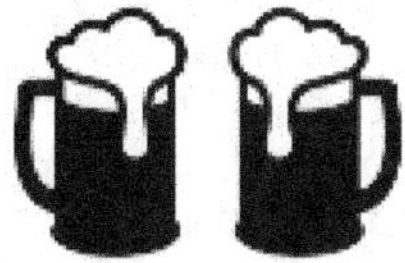

PREFACE

Several years ago, I found myself hopelessly attracted to a man who was married. I had no intention of ever even trying to pursue a real-life relationship with him, sexual or otherwise, and my imaginary affair, existing as it did solely within the confines of my own mind, seemed perfectly harmless. But I did catch myself thinking about it – more often, perhaps, than I would have liked – and one day it occurred to me to stop and truly consider why. Ordinarily marriage is a pretty big turnoff for me. I find it difficult to be seriously attracted to a man who is so clearly unavailable, because having a crush is only fun if you can pretend to yourself that it could actually happen. Yet the feelings didn't pass, and eventually, I began to wonder – was the attraction really about him, or was it about me? Was he truly that special, or did he merely speak to a need that I didn't know that I had?

I didn't know the answers to my own questions. And one day I began to run through it, in the riskless realm of my own imagination, to pretend that the impossible could become real. What would it be like, if we had an affair?

It sounds terrible, doesn't it? Even assuming you were comfortable with cheating yourself, how would you approach a man who belonged to another without feeling like dirt? Under what circumstances would you be able to persuade yourself that it was okay, that your feelings and actions were justified, that you didn't need to care about who might get hurt? How would you feel about having sex with one man and then going to bed with another? How would you deal with all of the lying, all of the deception that goes into seeing someone else on the side? It's easy to see how any of us might slip and succumb to a fling or a one-time encounter. But an actual affair requires commitment and planning, a studied effort to carry out and pursue. You must not ever be able fully to put the guilt out of your mind, because it's not a past sin for which you've already earned forgiveness, but a current and ongoing one that you have no intention of stopping. I would imagine that it must be a very difficult way for an otherwise good person to live.

Yet it happens. Every day it happens, and not just to sleazebags and immoral, loose women, but to real people who are not all that different from anyone else. And because it does happen, and happen so often, I imagine that adulterers must find ways to justify their behavior in their own eyes; there must be circumstances in which they are able to overlook the wrong and focus only on the reward – such as it is. Because, of course the true irony of having a long-term affair that was initially inspired by sexual desire is that eventually you must end up in the same place you are with your spouse – comfortable, secure, possibly even happy, but undoubtedly lacking the red-hot passion that once drove you screaming into the arms of your lover. Even the best possible scenario doesn't end in orgasmic fantasy-land. It ends with a relationship like any other.

This was the scenario I decided to explore in this novel. Most stories of adultery end in disaster, but that, too, is not true to life. Many affairs end in forgiveness, many are never uncovered, some, even, are revealed and accepted. What happens to those people whose lives are not forever destroyed by their own or their partner's infidelity? The experience must still change them, but, perhaps, in ways no one would have expected.

Stories about adultery can be tough to read because it's difficult for those who are basically romantics at heart to feel sympathy for men and women who cheat, and I would certainly not recommend this book to anyone who finds this type of situation inherently repugnant, because you will not enjoy it. But for those of you who don't mind pretending, those who can see some value in living vicariously, in thinking hard about infidelity and what it actually means to the individuals involved, I encourage you to walk with me through the story of fantasy me and fantasy Michael and just see where it takes you.

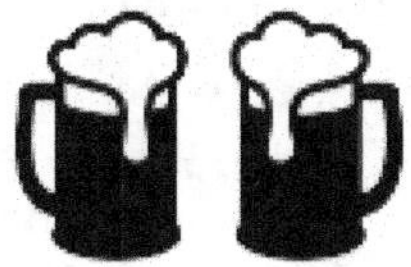

CHAPTER 1

I was thirty-nine years old when I first met Michael. At the time, I was happily cohabitating with my boyfriend of the past four years. Oh, we had our problems, of course, but not many, and for the most part, we were well contented with each other. We had no intention of ever getting married, and neither of us wanted children, so you might say that we were as committed as we were going to get. Nonetheless, by this time I was fairly convinced that I wanted to spend the rest of my life with him, and I'm comfortable saying that he felt the same way about me.

Everyone said we were a terrific couple. They were right. We were both very busy with work and our own projects, so we didn't always spend a lot of time together, but we really enjoyed each other's company when we did. I couldn't have counted the number of late nights we stayed up just talking, or the number of groggy mornings I spent wishing that we didn't always seem to find so many new things to talk about. He was an excellent companion, definitely not someone you'd get sick of in a hurry, and even though we never travelled or really did anything more exciting than sharing a beer at a local pub, I loved being with him. And I had definitely reached a stage in my life in which I was more interested in companionship than sex. Not that sex was a problem – in fact, he was a swell fucker – but I could safely envision still wanting to be with him even if that changed. Although I'd never been in a relationship that had lasted this long before, I assumed that eventually bedtime would become routine and monotonous, just as asking and hearing about the other person's day must ultimately lose its power to enchant.

But as I'd moved through my late thirties, I'd stopped worrying so much about whether our sex life would remain novel and exciting because, frankly, my own drive seemed to be diminishing slightly with each passing year. I still needed frequent fucking, but the strength of my desire for it had lessened, and I didn't always want to make a big production out of it, if you know what I mean. It was similar to the way I felt about breakfast. When I was single, I rarely bothered eating breakfast. Now I cooked breakfast for us every day, and I usually made a bigger fuss over it than was strictly necessary, because I figured if I was going to go to the trouble of fixing food, I might as well make something I really wanted to eat. Yet some days, preparing a three-course meal and washing pots and pans seemed like more hassle than it was worth, when boring old cold cereal would fill us up equally as well as eggs and potatoes. And sometimes I'd even forget for a little while how much more satisfying it was to have a big fancy morning meal until something or someone prompted me into that recollection and I'd remember how awesome bacon made the house smell or how much I enjoyed the confluence of flavors in Eggs Benedict. I only hoped that the day would never come in which I decided to skip breakfast entirely because I'd rather stay in bed and sleep late.

But if that day was lumbering on some far-distant horizon, it hadn't arrived yet, and in the meantime, there was Tom, and that guy wasn't only sexy, he was gorgeous. He wasn't the chiseled, clothes-model type, nor the handsome, dreamy sort, either; he was more like that cute boy who lived next door when you were a teenager who you secretly hoped was watching when you undressed in front of the window, but who you knew never would because he wasn't that kind. He had a real, down-home boyish kind of charm that was practically irresistible, and I never could understand why he wasn't constantly crawling with women, although I suspected it had something to do with the jealous old lady on his arm. Even had he not been beautiful, I would have found him appealing because he was exactly my type, and I mean, exactly, as in, if I were describing my ideal man he would have fit the bill without having to shift a molecule. He had slightly wavy brown hair that he wore a little long, warm brown eyes, and a modest beard and mustache that he never quite managed to keep trimmed. I loved the soft scruffy bristles he grew between shaves, and never tired of rubbing his cheeks. He wore glasses. I've yet to meet the man who was not more attractive to me with glasses than without them. He had a great build, too. A couple of inches shy of six feet, just the right height for smooching, and muscular; once when I'd sprained my ankle out on the front sidewalk, he'd carried me in his arms up the stairs and into the house as if I were a child. Yet he was soft in the belly, which is where I like men to be soft. He had a wonderful deep voice, and a great hearty laugh, and huge smile lines radiating outward from his eyes in a purely adorable and not an old, wrinkled kind of way. Nothing about him struck you as old. There was not one gray hair in that man's head, and I should know; I searched frequently and enviously through every lock and never found one. He was only three years younger than me, but could and did pass for much less. I never told him this, but I harbored a secret fear that one day we'd be out together and someone would mistake me for his mother!

Not that I was so bad to look at either. I'd always been cute more than pretty, and that doesn't come off so well when you get older, but I didn't think I'd gotten a bad deal all around. I had fair skin that was just beginning to get blotchy, unimpressive brown hair that I wore short and plain because it looked even worse long and styled, and rather lovely green eyes that were becoming less lovely as the skin around them sagged and puckered. My mother had been the same way. She used to forewarn me that one day I'd be sorry my face was shaped like hers; that I would grow to despise those pouches and dark circles, and boy, was she right. I wasn't sure whether I should be grateful or regretful that I had no daughter to inherit this precious family trait.

I was surprisingly satisfied with my body, however. I'd always liked my height; at five foot six, I was neither too short nor too tall, and I had a large frame that could carry quite a few extra pounds with some success. Although I'd never been particularly heavy, I'd always had to monitor my weight closely to keep it under control, and when I'd moved in with Tom, the additional meals and sharp increase in beer intake rapidly robbed me of dominion over it. I put on twenty pounds in two months, so fast that I didn't even have time to shop for fat clothes. It took almost two years, but somehow through rigorous exercise and severe alcohol restrictions, I lost the twenty pounds I'd gained and another twenty besides, and for the first time in my life I could actually be described as thin. People did, in fact, refer to me that way, usually with unmistakable envy. But naturally I never understood that, because I still couldn't see anything but the bulges. I'd be willing to bet you could walk up to the skinniest woman in any room and ask her how she felt about her figure, and she'd find an inch to pinch somewhere and tell you she wished she was ten pounds lighter. Anyway, the one saving grace of my aging body was that I finally had a rather nice figure, except for my thighs and butt, which were both disproportionately large, and my breasts, which were decidedly not. That last was the one thing I missed about my old body. Although I wasn't well-endowed even at my heaviest, I'd at least had respectable boobs. Now, even on my considerably smaller frame, they seemed depressingly tiny. Of course, I wasn't sure how much of that was because they had shrunk, and how much because they were simply spreading out over a larger area. In fact, I grew less annoyed by my wee breasts as I approached middle age and gravity began exacting its vengeance on me for defying it by spending so much time upright. I took some small comfort in the assurance that my boobs could never possibly reach my waist, no matter how hard they tried.

Michael, on the other hand, was not at all the kind of guy I would ordinarily have perceived as attractive. In fact, he was almost the opposite of everything I find physically appealing in a man. He had coppery-red hair, which I have never particularly cared for, pale, almost icy blue eyes, and a foot-long beard that I always thought was just ridiculous. This narrowly pointed monstrosity grew almost down to his chest, like a goatee run hideously amuck; a chin-decoration that would have sent even its four-legged namesake scurrying for shame into solitary abandon, but which Michael seemed to wear with pride, stroking it often as if for ideas or luck. I've never understood that about brewers; they all seem to be walking around with piles of crazy facial hair. If you don't believe me, take a look at the faces surrounding you the next time you're at a beer festival and you'll see what I mean. I've often wondered if they incorporate that into some bizarre secret handshake or something. Anyway, he certainly was not a man I would have spotted from across a room and thought, Oh, I want a piece of that! Up close he did have a pretty nice body, though, rather to my taste. Not quite as tall as Tom, and definitely a little rounder. I can still picture that growing beer belly stretching out his T-shirt, and my eyes helplessly watching my own hands reaching out to rub it, without even asking my brain for permission.

But nothing could have been further from my mind than the idea of changing partners on that first unexpected evening when Michael came do-si-do-ing into my life.

"You gotta come see this, Tom!" A largish, nondescript fellow in a navy brewer's shirt was tugging impatiently on my boyfriend's arm. I'd never been able to keep track of all of Tom's many friends, but I was pretty sure he was one of them.

Tom looked at me inquiringly. I shrugged. "I'll be right back," he promised, pecking my cheek and following his buddy down a long steel staircase into the hidden depths of the brewery. I stood awkwardly holding my taster cup, trying to pretend that I was perfectly at home in a room full of strangers and desperately seeking anyone with whom I could fake making intelligent or even somewhat lame conversation.

I should have just tagged along like I usually do, I thought irritably as the seconds stretched into minutes, clutching at my beer as though it were a crutch, and leaning as awkwardly against the wall as if I really had broken something. You weren't invited, I reminded myself, wishing that I could remember Tom's friend's name so I could curse it properly.

I'm sure old what's-his-face didn't mean it personally, I admonished myself, returning to the tasting-room bar to top off my glass, my last sample having mysteriously evaporated more rapidly than usual. He was only an assistant brewer, and evidently a new one at that; probably didn't want to be seen traipsing through the private rooms with an entourage. And you couldn't blame Tom for wanting to go and see whatever the secret treasure was, either. Beer is a big deal where we live, and Tom was unquestionably even more passionate about it than most; he'd often expressed curiosity about what went on behind the scenes.

But, but being a wise and understanding man, he'd never deserted me like this before, and as the minutes passed and people continued to stroll by me, half-smiling in alcohol's comfortable glow, I became more anxious to find someone, anyone to talk to; something to look at besides the tiny cylindrical glass I kept emptying for lack of anything else to do.

And that was when I spotted him. Also alone; also staring at his beer as if debating whether to strike up a conversation with it before someone came along and rudely interrupted. Although I was never very good with faces, I was fairly certain I'd seen this guy around. In addition to being regulars on what you might call the "festival circuit," Tom and I often also made the rounds of the local breweries, most of which, like this one, had tasting rooms where you could sample the new varieties as well as the old favorites. Likely he was a regular, too. It wasn't much of an opening, but I snatched at it like a hound-dog after supper's last bone.

I marched. I was never very subtle. Walked right over and stood close beside him until he turned to look at me, perhaps slightly surprised to find a not-unattractive if no-longer-young woman at his elbow, sipping a beer and not offering the slightest pretense of nonchalance.

"I think I've seen you around," I said bluntly.

"I think I've seen you around, too," he answered, his lips twitching slightly as if uncertain whether they ought to surrender to a smile.

Now if you're a young person, you may be astonished by the boldness of my approach, because if a young woman walked randomly up to some male stranger and struck up a conversation, he'd likely interpret that as a signal, one utterly inappropriate for someone who is happily attached. But when you get to be thirty-nine, you don't worry about that anymore. One, because you're no longer hot and you can't make the assumption that almost any man you meet is going to want to sleep with you if you merely look at him cross-eyed. And two, because if he's roughly your age, as this man was, then both you and he know that at least one of you is bound to be married. In other words, it suddenly becomes possible to be friendly to a member of the opposite sex without it being misconstrued as meaning anything more than that, which is certainly not the case among younger people. It's the one teeny consolation you get for no longer being perceived as a sex object.

"How's your beer?" I inquired, infusing the question with as much sincerity of interest as I could muster. It was one of the few phrases in my very limited array of conversation-sparking techniques that was guaranteed to generate an enthusiastic response among members of the beer crowd, and I wasn't too proud to latch onto it if it kept me from having to talk.

I can't transcribe the answer he gave me, but it sounded very technical; too technical for someone who was not a devotee to attempt to understand. I listened closely to the lecture on fermentation temperatures, but gave up trying when he reached the part about the fruity esters.

"Uh-huh," I answered, nodding my head as if I'd written the book on fruity esters and looking around to see if there was another novice I could talk to instead.

"How's yours?" he asked, nudging my attention back to him.

"Yummy!" I said with conviction. "Must be them fruity whatchamacallits."

He laughed good-naturedly. "That's a stout."

"For your information, Mister whatever-your-name is," I replied with assumed haughtiness, "It's a blend. Unlike you obvious laypersons, we true connoisseurs aren't afraid to mix!"

He laughed again, his eye-wrinkles crinkling in a manner that reminded me of my own.

"Actually, esters or no esters, I really like the beers here," I confided, deciding to give Mr. Expert another chance. At least he had a sense of humor; was less of a beer snob than some others I had met.

"So what's your favorite?" he replied, warming to a subject that was clearly close to his heart.

I told him, and then noticed that I'd polished off my two ounces of beer again. It sure went fast in those tiny cups.

"Your beer's empty," he said, frowning as if I'd been downgraded to critical condition while the doctor was out taking a smoke break. "Here, I'll get you a new one."

Had I still been a young woman, naturally I would have interpreted this gracious act of kindness as an attempt on the part of this man I'd just met to get me drunk in the hopes of having his filthy bar-guy way with me. But being closer to the mature side of life, it was only my innate sense of feminist independence that was offended.

"I'll get it," I objected as he magically transferred my taster cup from my hand to his in one deft, seamless motion, as if he'd had a lot of experience with manipulating glassware. But then I saw that he had ducked the line and was stepping behind the bar to fill my glass with my designated favorite.

"Thanks," I said, clinking my cup against his and taking a small sip. "Do you work here or are you just really obnoxious?'

"Guilty on both counts," he answered, grinning. "Actually, that's my beer you're drinking. All of us worked on it together, course," he clarified. "But it was basically my recipe."

"Nice job!" I said, taking another sip and scrutinizing my new acquaintance with greater respect.

"Glad you think so. My wife says it had better be good for all the extra hours I put into making it."

"Married, huh?" Told ya. "Any kids?" I inquired politely.

"Three."

"Holy cow!" I was always a little stunned to learn of the existence of other people's offspring, especially when it came to people my own age. In my mind, I still thought of grownups as creatures from my parents' generation.

He chuckled, evidently unoffended by my consternation. "You?"

"Nope, no children. That I know of," I qualified. He tilted an eyebrow at me and I knew my little joke had fallen flat. No one understood my sense of humor, I fretted with a sigh. "Uh, no husband, either," I hurriedly continued, by way of dispelling the awkwardness.

"That you know of?" he smirked.

"Right," I agreed. "Although I did go to Vegas last year, so I suppose it's possible. Of course, my boyfriend probably would have noticed if I had married a lion-tamer or something while we were down there. Seems like he would have mentioned it."

"Probably just being polite," he contended. "Doesn't want to embarrass you over not remembering. Besides," he continued, leaning in closer and whispering conspiratorially, "It's not wise to mess with the wife of a lion-tamer. They're very ferocious in defending their territory."

"And how exactly did you become such an expert on lion-tamers?" I queried bemusedly.

"Family tradition," he shot back without hesitation. "My father was terribly disappointed that I was unable to carry on our generations-old trade."

"Just couldn't keep the lions tame, huh?"

"On the contrary. I made them too tame. The audience got bored watching them just sitting and purring; rolling over with their legs in the air until I rubbed their bellies. One even insisted on brushing his teeth – and flossing – before I put my head in his mouth!"

"Thank you, thank you," he said, bowing as I dissolved into a fit of giggles. "May I refill your beer, Miss…?"

"Kate," I answered. "Yes, please, Mr…?

"Michael."

"Ah! One of my favorite names," I said, oddly pleased with the moniker although for some unfathomable reason it didn't quite seem to fit the man.

"Really?" he inquired curiously, cupping my empty glass in his palm. "How come?"

"No idea," I shrugged. "Maybe because I've never known anyone irritating by that name."

"There's still time!" he reassured me seriously, vanishing again behind the bar and reemerging a moment later with two beers and an amiable smile.

And we were off. It turned out we actually had quite a few things in common, me and this heretofore unknown brewer-man. He was three years older than me and, like me, had attended a private university and started down the path to becoming an engineer before shifting into an entirely different career. He'd also moved around quite a bit like I had, and it was refreshing to have a conversation with someone who hadn't been born in the area and lived there his whole life, like practically everyone else I knew. Maybe it was only because we did have so many things in common, but I found him easy to talk to; not once did I sense my brain struggling to come up with what I was going to say next, as it normally spent so much of its time doing in social situations. Anyway, we chatted about this and that and I don't remember what all for probably a whole hour before Tom finally reappeared.

"I am so sorry!" he declared penitently, bursting free of the milling crowd and landing with an audible plop at my feet. "Dave gave me the whole tour; he wouldn't stop showing me... Hey, aren't you a brewer here?" he exclaimed, suddenly noticing my companion.

I introduced them.

"Really nice to meet you," Tom said, in that friendly but not phony way he had with new acquaintances. "I wish I'd brought that beer with me," he added wistfully. "I'm a homebrewer," he explained in response to Michael's questioning look. "A new one; this is only my second batch. You could probably tell me what's wrong with it."

It was too bad, really; the first batch had turned out amazing, I thought, but the second had a powerful off-flavor and an odd smell, like rotting rubber. Tom had blanched when he'd tasted it and was dispirited and heartbroken for about five minutes, which was about as long as he was ever dispirited or heartbroken.

"This is great!" he'd declared at last. "I'm only going to get better if things go wrong, right?"

Sometimes I envied his optimism and even keel. In my universe both good things and bad happened randomly and without warning, and I was rarely able to maintain the smooth, unruffled calm that he so effortlessly achieved.

"Be happy to," Michael said encouragingly. "Bring it by some time. I got started as a homebrewer myself. Sometimes the troubleshooting is tough."

"Thanks!" Tom answered. "I'll do that. But we should probably get going," he said, turning back to me. "I quit a while ago but I shouldn't drink anymore if I'm going to drive."

"Yeah, sure," I said. Tom always drove when we went out, so I never argued when he wanted to leave. He was good at knowing when to quit. Driving after drinking made me very nervous, even if I'd only had one beer; I always worried that maybe I was too tipsy to know I was tipsy.

"Well, it was nice talking to you," Michael said, extending a firm hand for me to shake.

"Yeah, you, too," I answered, clasping the proffered handhold gratefully in farewell and following Tom to the door without looking back.

"I didn't know you knew that guy," Tom remarked as we were climbing into the car.

"I don't," I answered. "I just needed someone to talk to. He looked vaguely familiar, so I went over to him."

He smiled apologetically. "I really am sorry. I know you're not comfortable being alone in that kind of situation."

"Actually, it was fine. Really!" I assured him in answer to his skeptical glance. "Believe it or not, I had a good time."

I think Tom was as startled as I was to hear me say that, me not being a big fan of chit-chat under the best of circumstances, let alone when I've been abandoned in an unfamiliar setting and have no place else to go. In fact, had this happened ten years earlier, when I'd still been painfully shy and reserved, rather than only somewhat so, I probably would have fled the building and started skating the miles across the slippery, icy sidewalks back to our house rather than endure the agony of random discourse with a real live human being. But nowadays my sense of self-consciousness outweighed my shyness; I hated being stared at more than I dreaded making small talk, and trust me, people do stare when you're standing all by yourself in a crowd. Whether it's out of pity or scorn doesn't matter; no one wants to be the subject of either.

"You're sure you're not mad at me?" Tom asked as he hopped energetically into bed. He scootched over to my side, wrapped his arm around my shoulder, and pressed his chest close against mine, a very effective method of attracting my attention as well as my forgiveness.

"You're lucky I had what's-his-name to keep me amused," I answered with mock severity. "And to get me beer!"

"I bring you beer all the time!" he objected, withdrawing slightly from my embrace to look me defiantly in the eye.

"I know you do, sweetie," I conceded, drawing him towards me again. "That's what I keep you for," I joked, planting a hoppy kiss on those warm, soft lips and following it up with more until he took the hint and undressed me.

And I didn't give Michael another thought until the end of April when we ran into one another at the Spring Festival, one of the major events that all of the beer fanatics attended, and my personal favorite. Joyously is not a word I would typically use to describe how I anticipated most of the days of my life, but for that festival, it fits. I looked forward to it for weeks in advance. It was held at this large pub downtown, and although it was tricky, it was possible to get there and back via public transit so that neither Tom nor I had to worry about driving, which was both nice and necessary. Maybe other people were able to attend that festival and drive safely home afterwards, but we were not they. Actually, I always thought that anyone who could wasn't doing the festival right. There were so many delicious beers to taste that we usually found ourselves hanging on until the bitter end, cleaning up the dregs even as the servers were threatening to wheel the last kegs away, which was probably a little silly because after the first ten or twenty samples, they all began to taste alike anyway. But it was always a great time, and I liked the pub itself, too; it had a neat design. An enormous shiny wooden bar had been constructed in a rectangle around the center of the main room. Inside the bar, well protected from inebriated patrons, a mass of bartenders resolutely guarded the dozens of kegs they routinely kept on tap, as well as the hundreds of glasses they kept in stock in valiant defense against continual breakage. Apart from the scores of swiveling barstools, numerous small tables were scattered about where you could sit and listen to the local bands that would play on the raised stage opposite the front door. On festival days they lined the walls with kegs, too, so that it was wall-to-wall beer and people for hours on end, but no brawls ever broke out, the participants were always friendly and polite, and by the end of the day even the servers were loaded, but no one, including the bar owners, ever seemed to care. To me it was the grandest event of the whole year, and from the crowd that always turned out for it, it was apparent that I wasn't the only one who thought so.

"Well, hello there!"

I turned. Michael was standing by my elbow, smiling sideways at me and holding out a hand for Tom to shake.

"Nice to see you, Michael!" I said, reeling him into half a hug and smiling back.

"Oh, yeah, I'm really glad you're here!" Tom said eagerly. "See, I've been having this problem with my mash…"

I nodded politely as they launched into their long-awaited discussion of homebrewing techniques. I people-watched while I pretended to listen – I had rapidly grown accustomed to ignoring a lot of beer talk – and every so often I slipped away to fetch a new taster and pretended to listen some more while I sampled it.

"Would you excuse me a minute?" Tom said abruptly, handing me his taster cup. "I gotta visit the Port-A-John."

"Oh, okay," I said. I had that uncomfortable feeling in my gut again, the one I always got when I was left alone to chat it up with someone I didn't know very well.

"I'll be right back," he promised, hurrying towards the exit.

It's only for a few minutes, I thought to myself, glancing out the window at the long bathroom line. Besides, you got along fine the last time, didn't you?

I sighed a little as I watched him go. And then I turned to Michael, feeling squeamish and wondering what to say next.

"So what's your favorite so far?" he said. Was he ever at a loss for words? "I've been so busy chatting I haven't gotten many samples in."

"Well, let's fix that right this minute!" I replied, steering him by the elbow towards the nearest keg, relieved to have something to do.

In no time we were talking and laughing like old friends, and when Tom reappeared, he found us standing side by side with our arms around each other like it was the most natural thing in the world. I am not generally flirtatious, and rarely am I physically affectionate with anyone who is not my boyfriend – in fact, I think it's rude to fondle someone other than the someone you're attached to – but although Tom eyed me a little peculiarly, he didn't comment.

We were ready to leave not long after that, and in a kinder world that might have been the end of it. Except that as we neared the exit, we heard a voice calling out, "Is that you, Tom?"

"Oh, hi!" he shouted back, waving at an older woman sitting on a bench by the door. "That's a friend of my mom's," he said to me, his eyes glassy. "I'll just go say hello."

Well, I simply could not face having a mom-friend conversation after what seemed like fifty beers even if it was actually only forty, so I went back inside and found Michael again. He was chatting animatedly with someone else, but I unabashedly poked him on the shoulder, past the point of caring whether it was rude to interrupt.

"I thought you were leaving," he said, shooting me half a smile that might have meant anything.

"Not until you hug me goodbye again," I said, throwing my arms wide.

I didn't mean anything by it – at least, I don't think I did – but I guess it was a pretty transparent move because he looked at me kindly, and then put his arms around me and squeezed me so tightly I shook.

"Hey, you're a beautiful girl," he said, pushing me gently away. "But…" And at that moment, Tom came back and found me so I never got to hear what the "but" was. But as I pulled away from him our eyes met for a second, and maybe I was just loaded, but it felt as if we shared a flash of, I don't know what you'd call it. Mutual understanding? Well, maybe understanding isn't the right word, but there was a connection and I felt it even if I couldn't define it. The image that sprang to my mind was that of a circuit being closed. There's a snap of wires and suddenly you have electricity where there was none before. It was so well-defined that it was almost physical. It was a look that bound me somehow.

But in the morning I woke uneasy, and as the day wore on and my hangover wore off, I conceded that it wasn't only the excess of alcohol that was upsetting my stomach. I kept mulling over what had happened, and by early afternoon I was thoroughly disgusted with myself. It was that last comment he'd made that disturbed me most.

"You're a beautiful girl, but…"

Who could have guessed that an unfinished remark could be so devastating? It so clearly implied that he thought I was coming on to him, which I really wasn't. Okay, maybe it was conceivable that there was a fleeting attraction there, but it wasn't as if I intended for anything to come of it. I was a good woman, a fine woman, trustworthy and loyal, and he was merely some dude I'd met once or twice. I loved my Tom, and that made me invulnerable to such frivolous temptations, I was sure. But now I worried, too, with cause, that I had been disrespectful of Tom. I certainly didn't want his countless friends and acquaintances thinking that his girlfriend went around flirting and making moves on other men. I sure as hell would have been pissed off had it been him instead of me. Plus, this guy was married, for God's sake, and married men had always been strictly taboo in my reckoning. The end result was, that although technically I hadn't done anything wrong, the more critically I examined my behavior, the more like a lowlife I felt.

Of course, although I couldn't admit it to myself at the time, I might not have felt quite so rotten about it were it not for the implied rejection. Whether he'd misjudged me or not, I'd still had to swallow his polite, No, thank you, which was a little insulting, even if it was the proper response for a dedicated husband and father of three. Of course, it wasn't logically possible for him to reject me if I wasn't after him, was it? So said the irrational part of my brain, pretending to act rationally and doing a poor job of it. But there may have been a tiny bit of hurt mixed in with my guilt. Maybe it even intensified it slightly. I was almost old, after all. I had no business expecting anybody to give me a second glance, which was all the more reason why I should be thankful that I already had a great boyfriend who still thought I was sexy. So on top of misbehaving, I'd probably made a complete fool of myself flirting with someone who couldn't possibly conceive of little ol' me as an object of desire anyway. By the end of the day, I was so unhappy and ashamed that I resolved to apologize for my behavior and keep a polite distance in future. But there was something about Michael that somehow always managed to unravel my most earnest resolve.

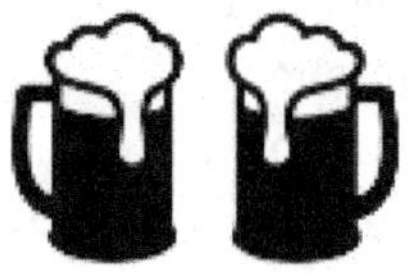

CHAPTER 2

We saw Michael again about a month later at his brewery. I embarrassed myself so badly that I'm not even going to tell you the whole story. I will tell you that I did, in fact, make my apologies, and reassured him that I wasn't really making a move on him, which, in retrospect, as any sane person could have guessed, made a big deal out of a minor drunken incident that otherwise would quickly have been forgotten. I don't know what he thought about my speech because he didn't say anything when it was over, but I felt painfully awkward and drank faster than usual the whole rest of the evening, which was blissfully short because we were not very politely asked to leave when it became obvious that I'd had several too many.

Perhaps I should interject at this point to tell you something about my relationship with alcohol. I'd had my first drink (first through eighth, I should say) at my best friend's parents' house when I was sixteen, unfortunately in concert with some chocolate cake which I promptly regurgitated all over their lovely cream-colored furniture and carpet. My friends were thoughtful enough to tape-record what happened afterwards, and watching the home video of me passed out in half my nightgown while my friends are scrubbing the rug and making snide remarks at the camera did not make my very first hangover any less painful. My second inebriation occasion took place at a party at another friend's house while his parents were out of town. My mom dropped me off early, and he immediately handed me one of those big red plastic tumblers filled to the brim with Southern Comfort and I drank it in about half an hour. I think I passed out before anyone else arrived and woke up on the bathroom floor at three o'clock in the morning, having missed the whole party. I don't remember who brought me home or what my mom said when I finally stumbled through our front door. Good times.

I did survive that phase, though, and once I grew up, alcohol and I got along tolerably well. I mostly stayed away from the hard stuff, and although I enjoyed having a beer or two somewhat regularly, it wasn't until I started dating Tom that I really became a beer drinker. He introduced me to all these styles I'd never heard of, like imperial stout and double IPA, strong, high-alcohol beers, and then he'd take me to these festivals where you'd be drinking all day long, and me, even though I was a sipper and not a chugger, I was shocked to discover that yes, indeed, I could get drunk on beer if I really worked at it. Plus, I think the twenty pounds I'd lost used to contribute to storing some of that alcohol, and I wasn't quite accustomed to my smaller size yet. In any case, it did occasionally happen that drinking got away from me, especially if I hadn't eaten, and although most of the time I was careful not to overindulge, every once in a while I did find myself unexpectedly intoxicated. These rare and unusual occurrences didn't generally end well, as this history will undoubtedly make plain.

And so back to Michael and one of the most embarrassing nights of my life. If I'd thought I'd felt bad before, it was nothing compared to how I felt now. In the morning – oh, awakening, the drinker's nightmare – it was excruciatingly clear to me that I needed to avoid him all together. I didn't know what it was about him that made me prone to such egregious misconduct, but the humiliation was certainly more than I could bear.

And I kept my resolve, too, for quite some time. The next time we ran into Michael and he and Tom started talking, I simply walked away and stayed away until Tom rejoined me, and then I hid out in a corner on the opposite side of the room from Michael until he'd left. Several months later, at the Winter Beer Festival, I looked up and spotted him standing not five feet away from us. That made it harder to ignore him but, by making a studied effort, I succeeded. A few minutes later he casually strolled right by us and did a kind of double-take, as if he hadn't noticed that we were there before.

"Well, hello there!" he said warmly, his eyes glancing off mine and heading straight for the safety of Tom's. "How long have you two been here?"

It was utterly transparent – possibly even more transparent than my feigned ignorance of his presence. I took a sip of my beer to cover up the smile that was tickling my lips, absolutely certain that he'd been on the lookout for us, but not knowing quite what to make of it.

Huh, I speculated as he and Tom chatted, neither of them seeming to suffer from even the slightest discomfort. Maybe this is his way of showing he's willing to forgive and forget. Maybe I should, too?

With a concerted effort I dipped into my arsenal of social weaponry and pulled out my trusty polite nod. I guess it was effective, because as long as I took a swing with it every so often, I was able to dodge the battery of friendly conversation that kept threatening to head in my direction, without being forced to retreat altogether.

And when the Spring Festival finally came around again, I guess I was feeling tipsy and benevolent because when our paths crossed late in the afternoon, I walked right up to Michael and gave him a big hug.

"Michael!" I exclaimed happily, as though he were a long-lost friend. "How're you doing?!"

This was another of the tremendously clever lines I often utilized as a conversation-starter, which may go a long way towards explaining why I'm more of a social moth than butterfly. But fortunately he didn't seem to notice, possibly because his own speeches on this occasion weren't especially brilliant, either.

"I'm good… good!" he assured me, gazing jovially into my eyes with more warmth than I'd ever seen them show. He gently patted the hand I'd rested lightly on his arm in utter forgetfulness of my vow of maintaining a polite distance, which presumably out to have ruled out casual physical contact. "Does this mean you're talking to me again?"

"Oh, well, you know…" I stuttered, startled and oddly impressed by his unexpected directness. "You know, I mean, what the hell, right? You know what I mean?" I babbled inanely.

"You know what? I think I do," he smiled. "After a while you get – past – things, right?"

Maybe it wasn't just me; maybe there was a little bit of magic in the Spring Festival after all.

"I'm glad we're on speaking terms again," I grinned, letting go of him with a modicum of effort and retrieving my glass from the bar.

"Hey, your beer's empty!" he cried, pointing at it as if expecting it to refill itself on command. "Where's your boyfriend? Hey, Tom!" he called, causing Tom to abandon his intensive study of the mile-long beer list. "Come and have a beer!"

Somehow the three of us ended up spending the remainder of the evening together, and it was after that that the fantasies started.

I've always had a very active fantasy life. Maybe everybody does, but it's hard to compare when no one talks about it much. I don't think you can help it; you're sitting in traffic or waiting in line at the bank or the grocery store, and your mind needs to go somewhere. Me, I'd been so busy the last several years that most of my waiting-around time was occupied with planning the rest of my day. This is how many hours I have left, I'm now this far behind schedule, and this is when I need to be at my next appointment, so these are the things that are not going to get done today and have to be squeezed into tomorrow or the weekend or next week. But when I wasn't doing that, or when I couldn't stand to do it anymore, I frequently found myself falling into daydreams, some of which were pretty elaborate. The duller my real life was, the more intense my fantasy life became. And my life at this time, satisfactory as it was, was actually pretty boring. I loved Tom, I really did, but there was little to no excitement in our coexistence, ninety percent of which was work, anyway.

Tom, characteristically enough, seemed perfectly happy with this arrangement. Mind you, an auto mechanic is an incredibly useful thing to have around the house, so I couldn't complain about him constantly sharpening his skills, but sometimes maybe I got a little lonely with him always staying late at the shop and going in on weekends to fool around with some special project or other while I plodded through my own seemingly endless stack of manila folders and spreadsheets. Not that I didn't like being an accountant; I did. But in spite of its complexity, sometimes it seemed as if the vast majority of my job consisted of typing the same documents and the same transactions into my computer over and over again, and well, I guess anything gets dull and repetitive if you do it enough times.

And the reality was, apart from the everyday stuff, Tom and I didn't really have very much in common. I mean, we were great at sharing meals and drinking beer and going to bed; the things most people would get bored silly of doing with the same person each and every day. But we'd never once taken a vacation together, unless it was for a family affair; had never visited a historical monument; never gone for a hike, or, for that matter, even a walk. While it seemed easy enough for us to squeeze in countless beer events, somehow it was always too much trouble to do the kinds of things I liked to do. If I wanted to get out of town for the weekend, I went alone, bringing my work along for company instead of my boyfriend. I liked to relax in the sun or the tub and read a good book. His idea of relaxation was throwing his butt down on the couch and flipping through channels on the television set until eleven o'clock. I, by contrast, wanted to smash in the TV at ten o'clock and fuck so I could get my five or six hours of sleep in before I woke before dawn. And I had to have something to fill the time I spent in bed not sleeping.

Sexual fantasies had always occupied the primary position in my imaginary world, and they were rich and varied and featured a rather insatiable me acting in ways I would never have dreamed of behaving in real life. There were strangers, there were multiple partners of both sexes, there were older men and younger men alike, and sometimes there were exceptionally dirty fantasies that I won't tell you about because they repelled even me in my regular life. But somehow even the raunchiest ideas became acceptable, even appealing, once I got my hands on my pussy. I liked masturbating. I mean, I haven't taken a poll, so I can't be sure, but I think I liked it more than most. Oddly enough, it also gave me a fascinating objective gauge of my progress towards middle age. At this time I was doing it approximately every other day, depending on my work schedule. This was one of the reasons I suspected that I was starting to lose my sex drive, because not very many years before, I'd whacked off every day without exception and sometimes more than once. In either case, it had very little to do with whether I was getting fucked adequately or not. In fact, sometimes it seemed as if the more action I got, the more I wanted.

Why am I not doing this all the time? I would wonder, patting myself between my thighs and pondering whether there was any feeling in the world greater than arousal. I read some book many years ago about a study done on monkeys in which the scientists wired up a button via electrodes to the pleasure center in the monkeys' brains, and if the monkey pushed the button it would have an orgasm. The monkeys stopped eating and drinking and, in the absence of the scientists' intervention, were seemingly prepared to just keep pushing the orgasm button until they died. I guess that's why you don't want to make orgasms too easy to achieve. No one would get anything else done.

Anyway, although I wasn't really hung over the day after the festival, I hadn't slept well and got groggy about midday, so I lay down for a quick nap. Tom was out in the garage, tinkering with the new homebrew system he'd set up. I don't know that I was particularly in the mood, but I had a lot of work still to do that day, and since I didn't fall asleep right away, I figured I'd better hurry things along. The less obvious benefit of masturbating for me was that it generally did a pretty reliable job of knocking me out for about fifteen minutes afterward. Most days I had a hard time getting through the whole afternoon without a quick nap, and I knew from abundant experience that it was much more pleasant to wake up warm and relaxed in bed than face-down on my desk. Anyway, most often for a quickie like that I would stay dressed and merely slide my hands in under my panties and whatever else I was wearing to get to the good stuff, but maybe my bottoms were too tight because it wasn't quite working for me that day, and finally I slid my leggings and underwear down to my knees. Something about the feel of my naked butt and bush right against the cool sheets made me feel dirty and vaguely exposed, and the fact that I was actually only half-naked made it even better for some unfathomable reason that I'll let the sexologists try to explain. Somehow this prompted me into an uncomplicated fantasy about meeting some random guy on the street who had pulled down my pants halfway and was going to fuck me hard and then pull my pants back up and be on his way.

"Well, hello there!" he said, grasping me by my bottom and yanking me up to his waist.

Somewhere in my mind I glanced up, startled. Since when was there talking in fantasy-land? And when I looked at the man's face I saw that it was not a stranger after all; it was Michael.

Even in the moment, I was surprised. I rarely have sexual fantasies about people I know. I find it distracting because there's always some kind of emotional involvement; I mean, you can't quite concentrate on the sex itself because subconsciously you're counting up all the things you have in common, or pondering whether you would actually get along in real life, or thinking about how sweet he was to you the last time you saw him, and debating whether that meant anything. It takes me a lot longer to finish with those kinds of fantasies, so unless I've got an unusually large amount of time to kill, I typically keep my imaginary partners anonymous and faceless. But now here was Michael, and although I kept trying to nudge him out, he didn't seem to be willing to go anywhere, and finally I just let it ride. When I was done, I fell asleep for my requisite quarter of an hour and then woke up thinking about him. Was I really attracted to him after all? After that, it seemed foolish to deny it, but the idea was disquieting. I already had this great guy who was smart, good-looking, and loyal, and if merely looking at someone else felt like a betrayal, leering and fantasizing were surely unacceptable.

I didn't know quite what to make of it. Did it happen to everybody after a certain number of years? Your passion for your mate wears off, and you start craving someone else? But I supposed there was no real harm in it. I mean, I'd known him for over a year, and had only even seen him maybe half a dozen times, so it wasn't as though anything were likely ever to come of it. And, of course, he'd never expressed the slightest interest in me, which naturally did little to elevate him in my opinion, and furthermore increased my desire to keep my desire a secret, insofar as that was possible. It was a harmless crush, I assured myself. It would pass.

And eventually it did pass. The lust for him lingered in the back of my mind and on the sidelines of my fantasies for about two weeks before it faded and I was my normal self again. Normal! That's misleading. The truth was, I was having a difficult spring. In fact, Michael or no Michael, I was a tight little ball of hormones coiled up and waiting for an opportunity to explode all over anyone who happened to cross my particular horny minefield. I'd been like that ever since I was a teenager. Every May it hit me like a wrecking ball, knocking me flat and breathless, and more often than not, flat on my back and breathy. When I was in a relationship, I rarely got the urge to stray, but when I did, that was when it happened. I'd never had it as bad as I did that year, though. Night after night I lured Tom away from his TV and beer and into my nightgown; I was so riled up that my daytime playtime wasn't sufficient to carry me through the evening. We fucked and fucked and fucked but it wasn't enough, still not nearly enough. I wondered if he wondered why.

And then one Saturday night we went out for beer, I had one more than usual, and when we got into bed with our nightcaps, out it all came.

"Tom?" I said, swirling the contents of my glass with my hand and frowning at the resultant lack of foam.

"Kate," he answered sleepily.

"Tom," I repeated. "Tom, lately… lately I've been having some trouble."

"What kind of trouble?" he asked, perking up slightly. That was one of the things I loved about him. Not only did he never walk away during an argument, he never went to sleep when I needed to talk, either.

"Trouble with this, all of this," I said, gesturing vaguely about with my hands like an actor who has forgotten his lines.

"You mean the house?" he asked, puzzled.

"All of it!" I exclaimed, slapping my beer down on the nightstand with an audible thunk. "The house, the job, the suburbs, the whole damned routine, and you, even you."

"Are you unhappy with me?" he inquired gravely, the corners of his mustache drooping like unwatered flowers.

"No, no, I'm very happy with you, still very happy; it's the whole monogamy thing, I'm not sure I can do it anymore."

He paused and I thought I heard him swallow in the silence. "Is there someone else?"

"No, of course not. I mean, I've been good – so far – I'm just not sure I can keep it up for the next thirty or forty years."

I suppose it was a stupid thing to do, telling him that. If it had come from him rather than me, I don't think I would have wanted to hear it. But I've always believed that if you can't talk to the one you love about the things that are really bothering you, then maybe you shouldn't be with that person.

He was still staring blankly at me, fully awake now, and I knew I needed to try harder to explain. "Lately…" I began, taking a large gulp of my beer as if it were truth-telling serum, "Lately, I feel totally out of control of my body, you know what I mean?"

He shook his head.

"Like I have all of this pent-up desire, that needs to be let out, somewhere, on someone, before I explode." I hesitated. "It's not that I want to be unfaithful, but I'm really not sure I can be trusted anymore. I'm inclined to suspect that if the right opportunity came along, I might not be able to stop myself from taking advantage of it."

"Huh," he replied, plucking a feather out of a pinhole in our comforter and staring at it quizzically.

He was clearly confused and I began to wonder whether what I thought was a well-organized speech was coming out as blithering babble. But I was so far into it now that I figured I'd better take another shot at making myself understood.

"I don't know if it's just because I'm getting older or what, but I'm starting to feel like – like my sex life is almost over, you know? Like if I'm going to do – oh, I don't know – any kind of – experimenting, or be with anyone new, that it has to be now, before it's too late. Before I lose the desire altogether."

"Okay," he said, his brow wrinkling as if he were attempting to solve the peculiar riddle that was me. "So what does that mean?"

"Well, I don't know. I thought I was ready to settle down, I really did, and it's not that I don't still find you incredibly sexy, because I do, but, you know, when we got together, I didn't know it would last like this. Maybe I wasn't really prepared to spend the rest of my life with just one person, you know what I mean?"

"I guess I don't."

"Don't you ever feel that way? I mean, you're still young; don't you have any wild oats left to sow?"

"Not really," he said, shaking his head again. "No, I don't think so."

"Because, you know, if you wanted to, say, take some time off…"

He shrugged. "Not really my thing, I guess." And he scooted over closer to me, and circled his arm about my waist, and kissed me on the cheek, and said, "I think we're going to be okay."

And then I didn't know what to say. I wasn't sorry I'd told him. Maybe I'd felt it was the right thing to do. And I guess I knew he could handle it; he didn't take it personally, and although he couldn't understand how I felt, he didn't judge me for it. That was part of the magic that was Tom. And on some level I was pleased, pleased with him for being better than me, proud to have that kind of a man by my side, someone I could rely on, someone I trusted. And when it came right down to it, after all this time with him, maybe I wasn't entirely convinced that I was prepared to be naked with anyone else. Maybe I just needed to be reassured that it was okay to think about it once in a while. Besides, as it turned out, Tom had a pretty decent solution to my problem. He fucked me twice and we went to sleep and never spoke of it again.

I wasn't really all that surprised by his lack of comprehension of my lusty inner struggle. Tom was not the most romantic guy; no question about it. He'd never once brought me flowers or chocolate; had never subjected me to a romantic poem or serenade or dazzled me with declarations of undying love. But he was not the straying kind. The fact was, his apathy towards marriage notwithstanding, he was a committer, pure and simple. He committed himself wholeheartedly to everything of importance in his life: his work, his hobbies, even me. He'd introduced me to his friends as his girlfriend on our second date, and had asked me to move in with him after only three months. It was all or nothing with him. He didn't seem to be able to operate in any other way.

Even our home was a testament to his constitutional constancy. He'd spent his whole life in the house we lived in now, and would gladly spend the rest of it there as well. It had originally belonged to his father's parents, and after Grandma died and Grandpa moved to Florida, Tom's parents had decided to rent it from him and, assuming, since Tom's dad was an only child, that the house would one day be theirs anyway, had ensconced themselves accordingly. But when Tom was nineteen, Grandpa's mind started to go, and his folks decided to up and move down south themselves to keep an eye on him. Tom, who had always rather admired Grandpa, did not feel the need to go to Florida to watch over him, so he assumed the rental, taking on a succession of roommates to help cover the expense. Grandpa, of course, being of hale and hearty stock, lived on another fifteen years, and was apparently sharper than anyone had given him credit for, because when he died it became known that he'd borrowed large sums of money on the house, allegedly to pay off some outrageous gambling debts he'd incurred on floating casinos on the Mississippi river, and had managed to keep this a secret from both his son and his daughter-in-law. The upshot was, a couple of years before, the property had had to be sold, and Tom and I had bought it, so that now Tom could rest comfortably assured of never having to move at all.

In general I found it encouraging that he was so little in need of change – I thought it boded well for the relationship that he valued the familiar and well-worn. Even if I couldn't understand his way of thinking any more than he understood mine, in my heart I was honored that he'd so heartily arranged a place for me in his otherwise invariable environs. And maybe this reminder of his stability did help to soothe my unwieldy desires, because I was a little better after letting loose with those foolhardy revelations that would have sent a lesser man lurching for his little black book. Still, some sense of urgency continued to lap at the edges of my brain. There was just so much I hadn't done. I'd never been with a woman, for instance, except for that lesbian with the big full breasts who'd kissed and fondled me for a moment in the pool on a girls' night out ten years before. I'd never had a threesome of either kind. I'd never made love on the beach in the sunshine. And up until now I'd never been in a particular hurry to do any of those things because it had always seemed as though there was plenty of time if ever I felt so inclined. But now, now I was old, or was going to be old any minute, and time was slipping away from me so fast that I was never going to get the chance to do anything fun because soon I would be too hideous for anyone even to want to do.

I was forty years old now. The milestone didn't offend me, but the reality did. I found myself looking in the mirror much more often these days. Sometimes it took courage. One morning I caught a glimpse of my face in the bathroom mirror after my half-a-night's sleep and thought, "God, I look like shit today."

The next morning I looked again, and it was even worse.

"God, I really look like shit today," I thought, flinching with horror and dimming the fluorescent lights until I nearly vanished into the pre-dawn darkness.

After about three months of that, it came over me that it had nothing to do with the day. This was just what I looked like now. It was very depressing and humbling. Never the flamboyant sort, I now found myself avoiding the eyes of men entirely – I didn't want to be the flirtatious middle-aged fool who doesn't know she's no longer good-looking – and I simply couldn't be certain anymore whether their stares were of appreciation or repulsion. Yet the voices in my mind persisted, whispering, "All the more reason to hurry… not much time left…"

And sometimes I wondered if it even had anything to do with Michael. Were my hormones in a rage because I was attracted to him, or was I attracted to him because my hormones were raging? The latter would have made more sense. There was no logical reason for me to be attracted to him at all. The only basis for my intermittent lust was one look and a few half-remembered conversations. But then why him at all, if it wasn't about him? Why not choose another crush, preferably someone who was not married and actually liked me back? That certainly would have provided for more gratifying fantasies.

I saw him again in August at an outdoor beer festival that we sometimes attended in one of the outlying suburbs. The beer selection couldn't compare with that at the other festivals, but the event was held in a pretty park encompassing an undersized lake, and it was neat to hang out in the sun and sip a beer and go wading in the cool water. I had wandered away from our group to go and fill my glass, and Michael was walking across the grass towards me holding a beer and chatting with a man I didn't know.

"Hi, Michael!" I called out, slackening my pace as I passed him. "Beautiful day for a beer festival, isn't it?"

He muttered something indistinctly in response. I slowed down further, bringing us nearly next to each other.

"Huh?" I said.

He didn't answer. Instead he shot me this weirdly hostile look, and then shoved me lightly on the shoulder as if to push me off in the opposite direction. A flick, as if I were an annoying insect that was pestering him. I was stunned and stung and for a long, cold minute, I hated him. Then I decided that he wasn't worth hating because that would mean I'd have to think about him, and he clearly wasn't going to be giving me a second thought.

Where the hell did he get off treating me like some pathetic groupie? I thought with indignation. One gesture, and I was done with him, really done this time. I let myself hurt for a moment, and then rejoined our friends and drank my beer and forced it out of my mind for the rest of the day.

But in the morning, I had that nasty, uncomfortable feeling in my stomach again that I knew didn't have anything to do with the alcohol. He was a jerk and I was better off without him. He was a jerk and I hoped I'd never see him again. He was a jerk and I was sorry I'd ever done him the honor of picturing him naked. He was a jerk because he obviously just didn't like me very much, and I was an idiot for ever speculating that he might. That last didn't sit too well with me, but that's really what it was about, wasn't it? The rejection. Maybe he wasn't the jerk at all; maybe I was. Maybe I'd been making a fool of myself all along. He knew I liked him, after all; he'd picked up on it right away, and maybe I was just so old and ugly that it was actually ridiculous and sad for me to be flirting with anyone at all. Maybe it was actually a kindness, brushing me off like that. At least it prevented me from humiliating myself in public any more than I already had. How could I have thought even for a minute that anyone might want me? I was useless and pathetic.

I worked myself up so effectively that I couldn't stop the tears from forming and then falling one by one down my cheeks and onto my pillow, uncomfortably wetting my neck and chin. I hadn't felt this low in a long time. Tom was still snoring next to me and I felt grateful again for his love and wholly undeserving of it. I needed to cry harder, and I didn't want to wake him, so I got up quietly and went into the kitchen and started my coffee and blew my nose repeatedly and felt even sorrier for myself.

I guess you could say I'd never been particularly well-stocked with self-esteem. Even though I was smart and efficient and healthy and reasonably attractive, I'd never been very adept at social interactions. I was very shy when I wasn't drinking and an ass when I was, and the few friends I had before Tom had all moved out of town or been left behind in some other town when I'd moved away myself. Although I'd run with a large crowd when I was younger, since then I'd become something of a loner, although, frankly, most of the time I didn't want a lot of company, anyway. Having a boyfriend was usually adequate to fulfill my need for society. One person to give my time to and who doubled as a sex partner was enough. But before Tom, I'd been single for a solid five years and was so lonely that sometimes late at night I didn't care if I lived or died. Sometimes I was even somewhat partial to the latter. But he'd pulled me out of that, and now I had him and his crowd besides, and even though his friends were his and not mine, it sure was nice having a group to hang out with again. I'd almost even begun to enjoy being sociable from time to time. Sometimes I actually wanted to go out and be with people instead of sitting home by myself with my classic books and classic movies. I had not felt that way for a long time.

I'd almost fallen in with a crowd of my own in my early thirties. Through some miracle of planetary alignment, I'd made a few new friends, and through them I met this boy. He hurt me. Not incidentally, intentionally. Or so it seemed. It was so devastating that I've never even told Tom about it. Suffice it to say that I liked him, and rather than telling me to get lost, he instead told everyone in the group but me his dozens of reasons for not liking me back. Without ever letting on to me that he found me objectionable in any way. Naturally, because humiliating me behind my back was apparently his idea of fun, and that would have ruined it. I have caused my fair share of pain to others, I'm sure, but it's always been through thoughtlessness or selfishness, never out of cruelty or downright meanness. But what really wrecked me was that I was utterly oblivious to it until it was too late. He didn't have to like me, I could have dealt with that, but being publicly mortified I simply could not handle.

Now, to be fair, one might argue that I'd brought it on myself. I hadn't been coy, or played the game, or kept my feelings to myself until I was sure they'd be returned, and besides that, I'd been foolish and trusting enough to believe what I was told, without wondering whether his niceties were concealing an underlying attempt to blow me off. And I did learn my lesson, to a point. After that I had trouble believing that anyone could actually like me, and if someone seemed to, I feared that it was a pretense put on to my face to cover the snickering that was surely going on when my back was turned. I knew it was a stupid way to feel, but I couldn't shake it; I was too afraid of being made a fool of again. So I moved a ways out of town for a while and shut myself up in my apartment and didn't look at other people unless it was for work. I sank into myself so far that I'm not sure how Tom found me in there, or even why he'd bothered to look. Some of my self-confidence had returned since I'd been with him, but I still had plenty of low moments. I fought them, though. If there was one thing I'd learned from social drinking, it was how to face people in front of whom I'd completely humiliated myself. I derived a grim satisfaction from having the courage to walk into a room with my head held high, when what I really wanted was to plaster my body into a dim corner and never be seen by anyone ever again. Besides, if I had to stop going places where I'd embarrassed myself, I'd never be able to leave the house. Aw, hell, even the house would be off limits.

Before now, I couldn't have guessed what Michael really thought of me. Our friendship, such as it was, had at times been so awkward and agonizing that I wouldn't have blamed him if he'd wanted nothing to do with me. Yet he'd never avoided me, had never refused my company, had even sometimes seemed to seek it out, albeit in a roundabout way. And the last time I'd seen him I was sure he'd even treated me like a friend. But maybe that was just a matter of convenience. Our first meeting all over again, in which neither of us had had anyone better to keep us company. How foolish I had been to take that at face value, as if it meant more than it did. How stupid I had been not to suspect what I should have suspected all along; should never have forgotten to suspect of a stranger. He didn't like me; of course he didn't. At best, he was flattered by the attention. And at worst, at worst he might see me just like that other boy did, and who knew what he'd said to his friend or colleague about me that Tom or I might one day have to hear through the beer crowd's grapevine. I couldn't stand it, couldn't risk another incident like that; my ego simply wouldn't survive it. He had to be out of my life for good now, and that was that.

"You sleep okay?" Tom asked me over breakfast, watching me unenthusiastically pushing my scrambled eggs around my plate with my toast.

"Fine," I answered. I always answered "fine" even though it was rarely true.

"Your eyes look puffier than usual," he remarked, scrutinizing me through a forkful of sausage.

"Too much beer," I grunted, reaching for the paper and burying my face in the sports section.

"Huh," he grunted back, evidently unwilling to question my sudden inexplicable interest in baseball.

He looked and smelled especially good that day, and I hugged and kissed him longer than usual before we went our separate ways. I spent most of the day working, and although I couldn't quite snap out of my melancholy, I knew it would pass. And sure enough, by the next morning, I was only a little more downhearted than usual.

"You look like you're feeling better," Tom observed as I walked him to the door.

"No more beer festivals!" I threatened for the hundredth time, reeling him into my arms.

"You don't mean that!" he teased, sliding his hands down over my rump for one of his magical buttcheek squeezes.

"Mmm!" I protested, feeling that familiar warmth spreading through my loins. "Now why would I want to go to a beer festival when I could just stay home with you?"

"Beer festivals last longer," he joked.

"Not by much!" I kidded him back.

I waved him goodbye, fully expecting the desire to drain away as it often did nowadays after he'd left me. But twenty minutes later I was still horny. Distractedly so.

Oh, why not? I thought as I climbed back under the covers again.

I couldn't land on the right fantasy, though. I tried this and that and nothing was working for me, and I was starting to get warm under there because the sun was coming out and shining in through the bedroom window. And then I was lying prone on a sandy beach in my hot pink bathing suit, and there was a gentle breeze blowing, but the sun was warming my body and it felt good. There was no one around, so I dropped my top off and basked my naked breasts in the sun, and then I glanced down and my unshaven pubic hairs were peeking coyly over the top of the bottom half of my bikini and for some reason that aroused me. It was a string bikini, and I found myself loosening the side ties, so that the upper half separated from the lower and I was one sudden movement away from hardcore nudity. Just as I was beginning to wonder when someone was going to come along and play with me, a man crested a nearby dune and then stumbled awkwardly down through the sand towards me.

It was Michael. Of course it was.

"Go away," I said disgustedly. "I don't like you anymore."

He seemed genuinely contrite. "I'm sorry about the other day. Let me make it up to you."

"No. I just want you to go away," I repeated.

"Even if I lick your pussy?" he offered, lying down in the sand and tugging gently at my bikini bottom until my vagina was exposed. Without waiting for an answer, he put his hands on my thighs and kissed my clitoris long and slow.

"Uhhh…" I said, less resolutely. It was awfully hard to turn down.

I had a sudden inspiration. "Darn right you're going to lick my pussy. You'll lick it all day long; I don't care how tired your tongue gets. That'll be your punishment for being such a jerk!"

He dug in and I was quickly done, and after that I slept for a little bit, and then bade him eat me until I came again, which took much longer this time. When I finally got up to go to work, the sheets were soaked with sweat and smelled of pussy juice, and I thought that fantasy Michael was much better than the real Michael anyway.

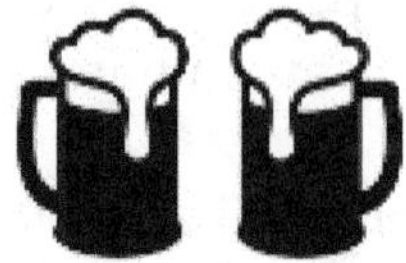

CHAPTER 3

"So what do you say we go down to the brewery where your friend Michael works tonight?" Tom suggested one evening some weeks later. "We haven't been there in a while."

"Uh, he's your friend, not mine," I snapped back, more angrily than I intended.

"What makes you say that?" Tom replied, surprised. "I thought you guys got along great."

"Oh… oh, I don't know," I answered, tossing the dinner dishes into the sink with more violence than usual. "The two of you have much more in common."

"But you don't mind going there, right?"

"No!" I said loudly, plunging my fist into a pint glass and imagining Michael's head at the bottom of it.

Oh, fuck him, I thought as Tom stared back at me uncertainly. I'll be damned if I'm going to go out of my way to keep away from him. He isn't worth the effort of rearranging my life over. Let him avoid me if he wants to so badly.

"No," I said again, more calmly. "I don't mind going there."

As my luck would have it, he was there and wandering about. At one point he walked right by me, close enough for me to spit at. I refrained, and he went on by as if I didn't exist. I didn't buy that for a second. But I wasn't sure what kind of point he was trying to make. Was he proving that he was ignoring me, or waiting to see if I would accost him if given the opportunity? Well, I knew what my point was, and it was to prove that I was in fact ignoring him, so I let him pass without a word. This was all very childish, and I knew it, but I was determined to make it clear that there was no way I was going to speak to him again if I had to go out of my way to see him and snub him fifty times to do so. No, the irony of that was not lost on me.

And the next time I masturbated he was in my fantasy again, and I was still mad. I got him tied to the bed and completely at my mercy. I'm afraid I was very selfish, and not all that nice about it either.

I barely had time to forget about him again before suddenly it was time for the Winter Festival. I hadn't even recovered from the last sighting, and here was another one approaching already.

Good, I thought viciously. I wasn't convinced he was even aware that I wasn't speaking to him again, and that made it a bit pointless. Deep in my heart I suspected that of course he didn't know. He probably hadn't wasted a second of his time wondering what I was thinking, and even if he had, I doubted that it concerned him. The capricious bastard was probably relieved that I was leaving him alone. I tried to remind myself of that now and again. It was better not to pretend otherwise.

It wasn't the best festival day. I spent most of it trying not to look for Michael and didn't enjoy my beer very much, which was a shame, because there were numerous interesting barrel-aged varieties on tap. And then towards late afternoon, after my hourly stint in the bathroom, I saw him, not from across the room, but right there next to my boyfriend in what should have been my standing space.

I swore mentally and ground my feet to a halt several steps away from them. I didn't know what to do. I couldn't forbid Tom to talk to him, nor would I have wanted to explain the reason behind the stricture had I been willing to make it. And I certainly couldn't give Michael the satisfaction of thinking I was unable to face him. I wanted him to know how irrelevant he was in my world, even if that was bullshit. So after a brief pause, I resumed my place next to Tom as if Michael wasn't even there, crestfallen to realize that we were suddenly right back where we'd been a year before.

In silence I let them continue their conversation. I didn't even feign interest by nodding along. Not once did I speak to Michael, nor he to me. I did peek at him out of the corner of my eye, though, and I was pleased to see that he wasn't looking all that great. Funny, but I'd never noticed how puffy the bags under his eyes were. In fact, his were even worse than mine, but of course, he was older than me. He was wearing a shapeless black polo shirt, which made him look pallid and rather square. His voice seemed a bit hoarse, too, but I thought that it had probably always sounded like that, and I'd just never noticed it before. I couldn't look or listen any more closely without appearing as if I cared, but that didn't faze me because for once I didn't feel like I was missing much.

And for the first time, I began to believe that my infatuation had died at last. It wasn't merely my anger getting in the way; I truly wasn't attracted to him now. I never should have been. It was a fluke, a temporary addlement of my brain and body. I'd never understood the feelings he'd triggered in me, and now I knew that the reason it made no sense to me was that there was no sense in it. It was ludicrous from start to finish, and it was about time I reached the finish.

"Well, so long, Tom," I heard Michael saying as he ambled away, to all appearances, still oblivious to my existence.

"So long, Michael," Tom repeated, giving him a friendly little wave. I said nothing.

And the next time I perused the crowd to see if he was still around, I couldn't find him and I relaxed a bit. The rest of the festival passed pleasantly enough, and by the time we got home I was really glad that it was Tom who was crawling into bed with me and I didn't wish even for a second to have it any other way.

But as I lay awake after my three a.m. pee, I started to wonder if maybe there was something I just didn't understand about Michael. If he was actually intent on shunning me, as he had seemed to be that day at Lakeside, then why would he come over and talk to Tom when he would have known I couldn't be far away? It wasn't as if he and Tom were close, either; they were merely festival acquaintances, too. Come to think of it, his behavior was often inconsistent. Sometimes he was very friendly, and other times he appeared to be avoiding us. God knows I'd given him plenty of reason to stay away from me. But maybe there was some other cause for his aloofness that I simply didn't comprehend. What if it did have something to do with me, but not in the horribly insulting way that I thought? I'd certainly been guilty of sometimes being a little too friendly with him, and in certain environments, that might lead to gossip. It was an interesting possibility. What if he merely didn't want to be seen with me by the wrong people? That was a self-flattering delusion and I knew it, but it made me think more kindly of Michael. Perhaps I had been too hard on him. And if I'd really gotten over it, why couldn't I accept him on those terms? Let him have his way. Whatever his motivation was for staying away sometimes, I could wait. He could come to me. And if he didn't, I would accept that, too.

I wouldn't claim that my new strategy was successful, exactly, but I did at least achieve mental peace in my relationship with Michael. It probably helped that the conflict was all in my head and he knew nothing about it. I saw him a few times over the next six months, but I refrained from touching him even lightly, and I never spoke to him unless he spoke to me, which he did more than once, furrowing his brow as if it required considerable effort. Still, by the time the Spring Festival rolled around again, I had learned to relax a little around him. And by the time the festival was over, I knew that I'd learned to relax too much.

This is how it went. Tom and I worked our usual Saturday morning shifts, and at noon we headed down to the bar. A number of our friends came and went while we courageously plodded on through. Around five o'clock, we decided we'd better eat something, and four of us headed over to a nearby hamburger joint. Tom and I shared a beer and a meal there, watching while one of our friends kept trying and failing to fall off her stool. Finally her husband decided he'd better get her home, and we finished our burger and headed back to the festival. Coming in the door, I collided with Michael as he was attempting to walk out of it. I guess I must have passed the point of only slight inebriation, because once again I up and hugged him like there'd never been an uncomfortable moment between us.

"Congratulations!" I said, leaning in close to him and fingering the new medal he was wearing. "I'm sorry we missed the awards ceremony," I added wistfully.

"Thank you!" he said, reaching down to touch the medal, too, and accidentally brushing his fingers against mine. "But don't worry about it; it wasn't much of a speech."

"I doubt that," I said, placing my hand on his chest and spotting Tom standing beside us out of the corner of my eye. "Look who won, Tom!" I said.

"Congratulations, Michael!" he said sincerely. "How about a beer?"

Then it's black.

Now the three of us are sitting at a table drinking beer and Tom and Michael are talking intently about something, probably beer, but I'm not paying attention to any of it because I'm too busy thinking about the pressure and warmth of Michael's leg against mine under the table. I'm pushing up firmly against him and although he's not pushing back, he isn't pulling away, either. Interesting.

Then more blackness.

There's live music and I've gotten up and I'm dancing, which I ordinarily never do except at weddings, when it's required. I'm neither coordinated nor graceful and I generally avoid dancing in public, but today the mood has stricken me and I can't stop myself. I beckon Tom over during a slow song and he comes and tucks his hands into my back pockets and rotates me slowly around. Michael is watching, and I'm certain it's not out of appreciation of my nonexistent dancing skills. I can't really interpret his expression, but I think he's looking at me in a new way. And even more, I think I like it.

The next memory is gray. It seems to me that perhaps Michael and I are alone for a minute, and I can picture him looking at me and he's still wearing that look and now I'm pretty sure I should be flattered by it. What I'm not sure of is whether I actually reached under the table with my hand and felt him up or if I was just thinking about doing that.

Black again.

I'm standing up to hug him goodbye and somehow a beer spills on me and a glass is breaking, and I'm thinking that I may have kissed him on the neck while I was hugging him.

Then comes the final blackness.

When I come out of it again, it's about ten o'clock and I'm staggering down the street with Tom trying to make our way to the bus stop. I've gone over to the bad place, and am sobbing and expounding upon how he's ruined my life. It's a very long ride home.

"Some festival, huh?" Tom said over breakfast the next morning, a wonderful greasy bacon-pancake concoction guaranteed to soak up any remnants of beer still lingering tenaciously in our otherwise empty stomachs.

"If you say so," I answered vaguely, not quite looking him in the eye and nervously waiting for the other shoe to drop.

"You feel all right?" he asked innocently.

Was he toying with me? I wondered. "I think I'm okay, actually. Lucky I had that hour and a half on the way home to sober up."

He cleared his throat and nearly chuckled with amusement. "It was not our smoothest trip home, no."

I glanced hurriedly up from my plate and he was smiling slightly; apparently neither angry nor upset and that seemed strange, given that what I did remember about my behavior the previous evening was bad enough, and that what I didn't was probably worse.

Maybe I shouldn't have brought it up, but I had to; I needed to know.

"It's all that Michael's fault," I grumbled irritably, peering intently at Tom as I said it. "We always end up staying out too late when we hang out with him. He's a bad influence."

Tom being the mild-mannered guy he was, I wasn't expecting an outburst of jealousy or rage. I had, however, at least prepared myself for a strict admonishment. I didn't get it.

"Yeah, and I'm pretty sure it was his fault your glass got broken."

"Right," I agreed sarcastically. "Because I've never broken a glass on my own before."

Actually, I hadn't broken a keepsake taster glass since my very first festival, six or so years before, not long after Tom and I had first started going out. I'd actually gotten pretty good at the festival thing in the interim; hardly ever over-drank at them anymore. Except, of course, when Michael was involved.

Tom laughed. "Well, we made it home, anyway. No harm done."

Maybe no harm had been done after all, I thought, amazed at such an unlikely prospect. But we finished breakfast without his breaking any major newsflashes, and I could only assume that if there was a story there, he wasn't telling it.

He set down his juice glass. "You still mad at me for ruining your life?" he prodded gently, leaning towards me with his breath smelling sweetly of citrus.

"You didn't, sweetie," I answered, rising from my chair and balancing my butt precariously on his lap. "I was just in a mood, I guess."

"I know how you get," he said, cupping a supporting hand under my ass and succeeding in turning me on in spite of too much beer and not enough sleep. "A couple of beers and all of the things you're secretly mad at me about come tumbling out!"

"A couple!" I snorted, doubting I'd said anything during our argument that he hadn't heard before. I wasn't exactly the keep-it-to-yourself type. Except, I hoped, when it came to Michael.

Yet he seemingly had nothing to say about him, and I might have been relieved had I not been so confused. Was there really nothing more to tell? Because some idea, some clue as to what might have happened, something that I probably needed to know about, was nagging at the back edges of my brain, and finally, the next day, it hit me what it was. At some point at least once in the latter part of the evening, Tom must have gotten up to go to the bathroom, which would have left Michael and me alone for a few minutes. That must have been my gray memory – it was real after all, or at least partially so. So now the question was, What the hell did I say to or do with Michael while Tom was out of the room?

I couldn't answer that question. I tried and tried to reconstruct the scene, but drew only blanks. Naturally I couldn't ask Michael, and Tom wouldn't have been able to tell me even had I dared to question him about it. Maybe there wasn't anything to be worried about. Maybe after coming on so strong, I had chosen that particular moment to be shy and demure, and hadn't embarrassed myself any worse than I remembered. It drove me crazy not knowing, but there was nothing I could do about it. I would have to wait until I saw Michael again, and the way he behaved toward me would tell me if I needed to break out the paper bag with the eyeholes.

You might be wondering why I wasn't also struggling to remember why I'd been so upset with Tom. Even though I didn't recall the beginning of our argument, I could guess well enough what had triggered it. It wasn't the first time we'd had this particular fight, either. Several years earlier, I'd decided to go back to school to get a Master's in Taxation. I was already doing bookkeeping and accounting and some tax work, but I found the tax preparation aspect most interesting, and thought it would be useful to have a formal education and maybe some initials after my name besides.

So I'd quit my regular job and taken on a number of part-time bookkeeping clients instead, which, although it was virtually the same amount of work, gave me the flexibility of working whatever hours I chose so that I'd be free to attend classes. I still retained those clients year-round, which was more than enough to keep me busy, and after I finished school and expanded into doing tax preparation professionally, I already had a captive market of clients who were pleased with my financial accounting, and brought me their tax returns to do as well. In fact, I had enough work that I turned away potential clients the first year. Frankly, I was still tired from the effort of completing my degree in a year and half while still working almost-full weeks, and was hoping to have some time to myself again for a while. But the mortgage we acquired when we bought the house was considerably higher than the family-rate rent we'd been paying, and the downpayment had utterly wiped out the savings I'd spent years struggling to accumulate. Tom, tireless worker that he was, had never been very responsible with money, and, never forgetting the severe poverty of my early life, I'd taken on numerous additional clients so I could be sure we'd have enough cash coming in to keep us solvent. So now I was overworked even in the off-season, and during tax time it was crazy, absolutely crazy; I was so busy that I sometimes forgot that I actually enjoyed tax law.

Now, before Tom this might not have been a problem. I'd almost always had more than one job, or work and school or school and work, and I was well-accustomed to busting my ass most of the time. But the only person I had to clean up after then was myself, and it was doing laundry once or twice a week and not every day, and cleaning one bathroom instead of three, and eating my meals out while I read a book or studied instead of cooking breakfast and dinner and washing dishes twice a day, and doing the grocery shopping that made that possible. And then in addition I had many more checks to write, and someone else's money to manage, so that sometimes it was like having another client, except this one didn't pay me. Maybe it doesn't sound like much, but when I added it all up, it totaled two hours of my life every day that I spent taking care of someone else. And we didn't even have children!

It was a ludicrous state of affairs. I was just as intelligent as he was, better educated, and made more money on an hourly basis, so there was no logic in me being the one to enjoy the dubious honor of being solely responsible for housework. But I knew those everyday necessities of running a household simply wouldn't get done if I didn't do them, and I couldn't live like that. I knew it wasn't his fault that I'd become a glorified housewife. These were not things he'd asked or demanded that I do in order to keep him, so to speak; he was perfectly content to leave the floors unswept, the toilets unscrubbed, the mail unopened, and the laundry unwashed, and would not have faulted me in the slightest for operating in exactly the same way. And, in his defense, being adept with tools and mechanical concepts, he would tackle household repairs without complaint, albeit substantially long after they required prompt attention. But the reality still stood that the majority of the time, when he came home from work, he got to play around with his hobbies or sprawl out on the couch watching television while I was occupied with chores until nine or ten o'clock every night, and was usually up and working again at least a full hour before his alarm even sounded. He worked hard, too, no question about it, and he undoubtedly deserved leisure time as much as I did. But he got his at my expense, and of course I resented that.

The even more depressing aspect of it was that I'd never wanted to buy our house in the first place. I mean, I'd wanted to buy a house, was even willing to buy a house with him, but not this one. For one thing, it was much too big for only the two of us. Having an extra bedroom was nice, because we'd been able to convert a spare room into my home office. But having three extra bedrooms only meant more floors to polish, windows to shine, and spider colonies to expunge. The semi-finished basement, also great. Tom stored all of his tools and spare parts down there, along with an old VW engine he was working on rebuilding. He'd also transferred his homebrew supplies downstairs the previous fall, when we'd wanted to move our cars back into the garage before the snows came. But now the basement floor was a sticky mess, the shelves were constantly covered in dust from cracking grain, and the countertops were spotted with piles of mysterious ingredients from where he'd spilled and done a poor job of cleaning up, if he'd even made an attempt. When flies began aerially invading the ground floor, I knew it was time to head downstairs with my swatter and gas mask and power wash everything. Not that he wouldn't do it himself, if asked. He certainly never intended to burden me with such chores. But it would be a month later before he got around to it, and there would already be growths and insects and one time, a family of mice, and my patience ran out long before his did. And then there were the three toilets to scrub, and the two tiled showers, which Tom admired the look of, but of course it's much easier to appreciate that when you're not the one who has to scrape the grout. With the house we'd also "inherited" a lot of furniture, which was wonderful because it meant that we didn't have to buy any. But I had to dust often, and that in itself was no mean feat. It took an entire can of furniture polish to do the whole house, which should give you an idea of the scope of that project.

And, of course, the crowning joy of living with an auto mechanic who is not particularly tidy or conscientious about personal hygiene was the way you found greasy fingerprints everywhere: on the sinks, on the counters, on the door handles, on the end tables, everywhere he might have walked or sat or stood or skipped in the interval between coming home from work and hopping in the shower. There were occasions on which I was touched to find these oily little reminders of my sweetie all over the house. But those were very rare, and I had to be having a damned good day.

I might still have been happy with the purchase if the house had only had the one thing I'd always wanted, a nice big backyard. I know, those require maintenance too, but my desire for private property had always hinged on having real outdoor space of my own. To be able to be outside and still have privacy, you know? Instead we had a teeny little yard that you could maybe prop a chair up in if you pushed aside all the junk that Tom had dragged home and hadn't put away yet. But even if you did that, it was positioned behind the house in such a way that it only got sun for about an hour a day even in summer, and was bordered by a hedge that as yet was only about two feet tall, so it still wasn't suitable for sunbathing in the nude.

But the worst part, the absolutely worst part of all of it, was that I was working my ass off for the privilege of a possessing partial ownership interest in a piece of property that would be completely useless to me if something were to happen to Tom, or to Tom and me. My name may have been on the title, but historically it was his house, and if we split up, it was obvious that I would have to be the one to move. He wouldn't be able to afford to buy me out, so I supposed I would be forced either to find him a new live-in girlfriend, or continue paying the mortgage for the balance of the remaining thirty years until it was paid off, or face foreclosure. And it was the last place I'd want to live if he were to die before me. Lumbering around that gigantic place all by myself with mementos of him everywhere? I would envy him his demise. I wouldn't even be able to get the hell out of town like I would want to, because it would take months to clear the piles of crap from the shelves and cabinets and closets to get it ready to sell. I couldn't even imagine how depressing a task that would be.

In terms of the human condition, these weren't real problems; I know they weren't. Plenty of people would give up every minute of their spare time to have too much work and a home of their own. Hell, plenty of people would do it just to have food money. I knew all about it; I'd been there. But I don't know that admonishing yourself that others are worse off than you has ever made anyone feel better about his or her own problems. Mostly I think it just makes you feel bad about complaining. But I did try not to complain. I knew I should be thankful to have someone that I wanted to buy a house with, and do housework for, and come home to after a long day at work, and most of the time I was. But after a while, it wore on me. Tom hadn't really ruined my life, of course he hadn't; in most ways he'd made it much, much better. But I never forgot that being with me had made his life a lot easier, while being with him had made mine harder, and it was unfair and that made me angry sometimes.

But I wasn't thinking about any of that now, because today I had a new problem that completely overshadowed the annoying minor details of my life with Tom. I could no longer kid myself. I was back on Michael in a big way. The months of pretending that I was through with him had, in my mind, already been relegated to the distant past. I'd never been sure what it meant, the nonchalance with which he sometimes treated me, but now it was forgotten, because of one fact that was irrefutable. He hadn't pulled away when I'd snuggled up against him. The impropriety of my behavior had been unmistakable. A hug, by contrast, is always open to interpretation. You might judge it by its duration, its pressure, the position of the hands on the other's body, whether only the chests collide or if pelvises touch, too, and whether the parties involved look each other in the eye before, during, or after, and how. You can always argue to yourself or others that it was just a hug or that it wasn't just a hug, depending on how you were motivated to read it or to have it read. But nobody, nobody shoves their thigh up against someone else's underneath a table without it being some sort of come-on.

Why did I do that? I thought, laughing at myself. What was it about him that made me act that way? It had to be chemical, I thought. I'd read somewhere once that there had been a study done in which women were given men's sweaty shirts to sniff, and that the scents the subjects found most attractive were the excretions from men who carried different immunities from them. Maybe my body knew something my brain didn't.

And maybe that was all. Maybe he had some hidden quality that would be biologically beneficial to our potential offspring, and that was why I always found myself touching him when I knew I shouldn't. But that wasn't new. What was new was the fact that he hadn't objected, hadn't pulled away, hadn't gotten up and left, hadn't tried to stop me in even the most offhand way. Even if he wasn't the aggressor, he still really ought to have put up some sort of resistance. He was a married man, after all, and he had his own obligations, even if I was tempted to disregard mine.

You might be thinking from the way I'm talking that I had little sense of morality, but that's not true. I was a good person, indeed, one of the most moral people I knew. I was principled, trustworthy, and honest. I wasn't a cheater, and I wasn't a thief, either. I respected commitment and the obligations implicit in it, and, at any other time in my life, I would have ended a relationship before I seriously contemplated straying from it. And I never wanted to be the one to get in the way of someone else's happy coupledom, either. There were plenty of fish in the sea, right? Why try to snag a fish from someone else's line?

But there was only one Michael, and I wanted him. I confessed it to myself freely now. I wanted him, wanted him, wanted him. I shamelessly cast aside all the guilty thoughts I might have had in regards to his wife and children. I would lead him down the path of vice and let him dally in the valley of my sin and never ever regret wanting it or thinking it or doing it. I shoved Tom onto the sidelines in my mind and told him he could get back in the game when I was done playing with Michael, whenever that might be. I recklessly abandoned all hopes of trying to behave myself because I knew now, oh, I knew that if Michael were to cave, I would cave, too, without even pausing to reconsider whether I really ought to reconsider. And if there were anything I could do to help him along to the point of caving, I wouldn't hesitate to do that, either.

It was a sorry state to be in, but I was giddy, giddy because for the first time, I began to suspect that there might be the tiniest shred of hope. My idle fantasies took on the force of conviction, blurring into alternate future realities and leaving me foolishly attempting to guess which ones would really happen and when. I was masturbating every day now, sometimes two or three times if I was doing an efficient job of it. Tom would leave for work, I'd lapse into thinking about Michael, feel my temperature rise and find myself going back to bed, oh, just for a minute, and then it would be two hours later, and I'd still want to go at it just one more time. I'd fall into sleepy daydreams at my desk and would open my eyes astonished to find that it was bedtime, and I still hadn't gotten my work done. On the plus side, I don't think I've ever felt more rested and cheerful.

But after about a week of this, I'd fallen so far behind on work that I knew I had to force myself out of this lust-induced stupor or spend the rest of the year paying the price for my laziness. I couldn't concentrate, so I set aside the difficult jobs and instead urged myself into performing my easiest, most mechanical tasks, while in the back of my mind I replayed fantasies about Michael. I went to the office earlier so that when I got the itch, I had to play with myself quickly and furtively in the bathroom, and couldn't be tempted to go back to sleep. I tackled housework with relish because it left my mind free to wander through my fresh fleshy fields, and if Tom thought it strange that I didn't listen to the TV or to music anymore when I was cleaning or cooking or folding laundry, I didn't care. It wasn't as luxuriously lovely as reclining in bed with my fantasies, but at least I was getting something productive done. I got so wrapped up in my wonderful dream world that it became hard to snap out of it even when Tom was around. Sometimes I was almost irritated that he was around – it was as if he was continually interrupting me when I was trying to watch a movie.

After about three weeks, the intensity of my desire finally began to ease up, and that was when I saw Michael again. Tom and I had stepped out for a beer at an out-of-the-way local pub, so running into him there was a complete surprise. I had the impression that he didn't go out to bars much. But when his eyes met mine, I saw something in them that thrilled me to my core. I knew instantly that I'd been right, that he was indeed looking at me in a new way, and there was only one word to describe the expression that transformed his face when he saw me. Lust. There was no doubt about it. If you've been fortunate enough to have someone look at you in that purely impure, unadulterated fashion, you know what I mean. I could almost see the hard-on in his eyes.

"Fancy meeting you here!" Tom exclaimed, holding out his free hand for a shake.

"Mmph," Michael answered, still staring at me as if utterly unaware that Tom was there.

"You come here often?" Tom continued while I stood paralyzed by Michael's gaze. I had never been more grateful for Tom's gift for making small talk; without it, I think I would have fallen over on the spot.

Abruptly Michael jerked his eyes away from mine and turned to Tom.

"No," he said finally, grabbing half of Tom's wrist and then letting it drop a second later. "I'm sorry, I've really gotta run."

He turned back towards me.

"Kate," he murmured, his eyes focused on a spot over my shoulder.

I suppose I must have stuttered some kind of greeting in return, but I couldn't tell you whether it made sense or not because I was too busy pondering that look and hoping he'd direct it at me again. He didn't. Instead he hugged me much too briefly, and then all I could see was his backside as he vanished through the front door like he'd just remembered that he'd left six gallons of chocolate ice cream melting in the car.

I was almost glad he was gone. I wanted to bounce all over the room, I was so excited. Because rapid departure or no, this settled it beyond any reasonable doubt. It was not my imagination. There was hope after all. Not that I was hoping, of course. Even now I was unwilling to admit that somewhere deep inside me I might really be considering what I knew it was awful of me to even lightly consider. But even if nothing ever came of it – and I knew I shouldn't, couldn't really want anything ever to come of it – it was almost enough to know that he was thinking about it, too. Of course, it might not even be personal. Maybe it was simply difficult to resist the charms of a woman who came on as strong as I apparently did. What the hell had I done at the festival to provoke that kind of reaction? The possibilities made me shudder and smile. I didn't know what I'd done, or how I'd done it, but I was pleased with myself in a rather disgusting way. And on top of it all, I was tremendously flattered. I didn't catch men looking at me like that very often anymore, and the fact that it was coming from someone I was so inexplicably nuts about made it all the sweeter. Even the bathroom mirror was my friend now.

You're not old yet! it seemed to say, especially if I examined my reflection in the late afternoon, when the light was dim and golden and particularly kind to my face.

I know I sound like a silly schoolgirl talking about this, and at the time I felt like one, too. I should have been asking myself sensible, grown-up questions like, what about your boyfriend, and loyalty and faithfulness, and would you really want to ruin the life you have planned for yourself over some guy you barely know? But I didn't. Instead I was all hyped up with wondering, does he really like me, and do I think he's going to ask me out, and do I really want to go all the way? And I didn't care about the consequences, either; I barely even acknowledged that there might be any. It was, in fact, exactly like being a teenager all over again. My brain had stepped aside and left the hormones completely in charge. I wondered if that was normal; if, at the end of your fertile years, you behaved just as ridiculously as you had at the beginning. It was an intriguing idea, and I would have liked to look into it, but I didn't have time for homework because I was much too busy trying to figure out what I was going to do the next time I saw Michael.

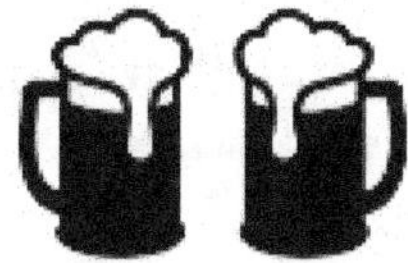

CHAPTER 4

But fortunately for the state of my morality, our paths didn't cross again for some time, and, impatient as I was to see where our next encounter would or wouldn't lead, I had no alternative but to wait. This depressed me for two reasons. One, because even though I was sure he had no intention of ever doing anything about it, I was desperate to know if that look he'd given me was anything more than a passing fancy for an otherwise nice woman who had tackled and flattered him into temporary arousal. And two, because even if I was feeling pretty good about myself right now, there was no doubt I'd already begun my descent down the hill, and if I only saw Michael a few times a year I was rapidly going to age myself past the point where he'd want to look at me, anyway.

That realization deflated my burgeoning hopes somewhat. It's just as well, I told myself. This'll force you to be good, and maybe that's what you need right now. It was spring again, and if I'd thought my sex drive had been out of control the year before, this year had to be measured on a different scale entirely. Last year I'd had a vague feeling of restlessness and dissatisfaction and a passing urge to stray. Now I had a strong feeling of restlessness and dissatisfaction, and I was convinced that straying with Michael was the key to making me rested and satisfied.

He was in all of my fantasies now, every last one. I'd be playing around with some juicy long-haired brunette with firm breasts and a tireless tongue, and suddenly he'd be joining us on the bed. That sounded pretty good until I caught him looking at the other girl and had to eject her bodily from the room. You would think that under such limiting conditions my imagination would start to lack for variety, but it never did. I invented a thousand new ways of humping him and they were all unbelievably fun. The only scenario I refrained from thinking about too much about was our "first" time. If we ever did surrender to sweet temptation, I didn't want to ruin it by having a lot of preconceived notions about how it would go. I thought this was both highly pragmatic and uncharacteristically optimistic of me. It's not going to happen! I shouted at myself. But it might, I whispered back.

Somewhere within myself, I turned a corner that summer. Michael or no Michael, I'd decided it was time for a change, and I worked out little ways of bringing greater happiness into my life. I quit work early most afternoons and sat on the grass in the park in the sunshine and read for an hour before getting up to do my exercise. I got through more books in those three months than I had in the previous five years combined. My joints were deteriorating and my doctor didn't want me running every day anymore, so when I finished my reading I'd do my stretching right there on the grass, and then take a long brisk walk under the trees and hum along to the music playing on my Walkman, and disregard the curious stares of the young people passing by who had never seen a Walkman. I compensated for this time off by working extra hours in the evenings and early mornings in my home office, which was all right because those were the times of day I felt more like sitting quietly at my desk than being up and about anyway.

Perhaps most importantly, I spent a number of precious hours drawing up an annual schedule for housecleaning with a daily chore on it. It rotated through a variety of tasks at varying frequencies, so while I cleaned all of the floors every month, I swept more often than I mopped or vacuumed, and because it was the most used, the master bath toilet got sanitized more often than the basement one, and so on. It's sad how much that schedule changed my life. But I found it was much easier to keep up with a list of assigned tasks than to try to clean the house when it needed it, which was always. Scrubbing, dusting, mopping, vacuuming, sweeping, polishing the furniture – everything had its place and time, and I truly believe that organizing it into manageable chunks cut my housework load in half.

Tom was getting a little chubby, so I decreased the fat in our diet and replaced it with fruit and lost another two pounds myself even though I wasn't running as much. We still did little that was fun, and nothing that was special, but I felt more contented with my lot in life. Forty, forty-one, it wasn't over yet. No, not yet.

And somewhere in the back of my mind, I happily anticipated seeing Michael again.

But as the weeks passed, it became apparent that my wait might be lengthier than I'd thought. I talked Tom into going down to the brewery for tastings not long after we'd seen him last, but Michael wasn't around, and I cursed my bad timing with especial virulence. That meant my next probable chance of running into him again was at Lakeside, that same outdoor festival he'd cut me at the year before. The superstitious part of my brain, which was quite small, and ordinarily very quiet and well-behaved, nagged me gently but persistently about avoiding him there. It would be bad luck to even approach him in that venue, it insisted. It was not a good place for us; it would ruin everything. The logical portion of my mind agreed, and its arguments were far more convincing. Whatever his reason had been for acting the way he had, I had to assume he'd be off limits again. Until I knew what that reason was, I could take no chances.

I don't know whether it was the time delay or the unpleasant reminder of that painful incident, but I finally found the attraction fading. How could it not? Even a cherished fantasy cannot survive on its own without some feedings of encouragement. And eventually it became harder to maintain than merely to give up. I'd wake in the middle of the night and engage my standard procedure: launching a daydream to half-occupy my mind while I sought to relax back into sleep. But when it came to Michael, I was finding that it felt forced. The truth was, now that it had been a few months since I'd seen him, I could hardly even picture what he looked like anymore. In my mind he was more an assemblage of qualities than a man: coppery-red hair and pale blue eyes and a beard I didn't like. It became far more soothing to think of Tom, and how sweet he'd been the second time we'd made love, or how he threw his head back and laughed when he was telling a funny story, or how good his arms felt around me when he was hugging me hello or goodbye, or how his rough fingers dug into my skin when he was caressing me.

But I was sad about it, too. I missed my fantasy life; it was half the fun of my infatuation with Michael. It wasn't only that I liked him – I liked liking him. Having a crush on Michael had become my primary source of entertainment. I enjoyed the excitement of it, of looking forward to seeing him again, of wondering what he was thinking when he said this or did that, because each time I acquired a tiny piece of the puzzle that was Michael and could pass my idle moments until I saw him again trying to figure out where it fit. Each encounter was electrifying because it meant that something might happen, and when nothing did, it didn't matter very much because there was always the next time. And with every delay I was rewarded with more prolonged anticipation, which was almost as thrilling as having the real thing happen, and was guilt-free besides. Even the setbacks had no lasting effect on my fun because I could almost always fix things inside my head, which was where the results mattered most anyway. And much as I wanted to see my dirty plans through to their natural and very real conclusion, I could be content with the fantasy if that was all I was going to get. But I had to at least see him every once in a while. I needed the occasional booster of whatever it was that drew me to him to keep it going.

And by the time Lakeside rolled around again, it had worn off to such an extent that I was no longer prepared to hump him against the nearest tree if he would only just ask me. Now I was going to take convincing.

I found out early that he was not going to attempt to convince me.

"Good to see you, Tom," he said, standing up politely when we came over to the booth where he was serving. "Kate," he nodded, meeting my eye without a hint of emotion, as if we were merely acquaintances saying hello. "What can I get you?"

He poured us each a beer and handed them across the table.

"Thank you," I said, refraining from brushing my fingers against his as I took back my taster glass. He nodded again in return.

"See you around," Tom said. He nudged my arm and we turned away.

And that was it. Without so much as a furtive glance or pointed phrase passing between us, the long-awaited encounter was over.

See? I told you so, I told myself so. The look I'd found so inviting and promising was gone; the moment had passed for him, too. It was already too late. I walked off with Tom, disappointed, but again feeling grateful that he was mine and that I had not failed him as a girlfriend, even if I didn't deserve the credit for that.

The afternoon passed cheerfully enough despite the lack of any real excitement, and apart from the occasional bout of cursing my luck, I mostly forgot about Michael until rather later in the day when, to my very great surprise, I saw him wandering towards the edge of the lake where we were standing.

My interest was immediately aroused. This seemed promising, didn't it?

"They finally let you off duty, huh?" I heard myself calling out. I cringed, cursing my speech-censor for napping on the job again. I was still half-convinced I was forbidden to speak to Michael at this festival, and the last thing I wanted to do was give him a reason to repeat his prior year's performance.

But he didn't seem offended. "For a little while," he said, smiling slightly. "How are you guys enjoying the festival?" he continued, turning to Tom.

Thank heavens, I thought, listening to Tom prattling on about Belgian Dark Strongs while I watched the staggerers lurching by and the birds hopping about snatching up the scattered leavings of drunk people's lunches.

"Oh, be right back," Tom said suddenly, casually waving his empty cup at me and meandering off to get a beer, utterly oblivious to the fact that my heart had just stopped.

Michael and I were alone again. It would be rude not to speak to him now, I supposed as I peeked at him furtively sideways. Still, it wasn't easy, what with the wind having abruptly vacated my lungs and all.

"So…" I began at last, "How've you been?" A brilliant beginning, I thought. No one had ever used that line before.

"Good, real good. You?"

"Oh, you know, same old same old. Can't complain."

This was already the worst conversation ever, and we were only three lines into it. Why again had I thought I had something special with this guy? Apparently I couldn't talk to him any more than I could anyone else. To me, that's the real essence of shyness; they ought to rename it oraphobia. You can fake being comfortable around people as long as they're doing all the chattering and all you have to do is listen and nod along. But when the other person stops talking, and you know you have to come up with something clever to say yourself and you just can't, it's awful. If there were a hell for shy people, its main form of torture would undoubtedly entail being forced to make conversation in a public venue with someone you don't know very well for all eternity.

And so I found myself nodding blankly about nothing and not really looking at him. His head was oscillating around as if he hoped that someone who was moderately more intriguing than a turnip would stray across his field of vision. That pigeon by the elm tree appeared unusually intelligent; for that matter, the tree was outranking me in entertainment value at the moment. I felt the beginnings of panic stirring in my stomach. I was going to lose him. My brain was churning almost as fast as my gut, and with equal futility. I had no news about work, which was the same as always; I wasn't planning a trip or just returning from one; I hadn't taken up a new hobby and was still barely finding time for my old ones. I glanced apprehensively over at him and he was opening his mouth as if he was about to say he'd see me around and then walk away, and that's when it hit me, the one thing I really, truly wanted to talk to Michael about.

"What happened at the Spring Festival?" I blurted out.

"What?!" he returned with apparent surprise, but that dirty look I had found so auspicious had flashed across his face for a second, and I knew I'd said the right thing.

"What happened at the Spring Festival?" I repeated.

"You don't remember?"

"Off and on," I clarified.

"Oh." We were looking each other in the eyes now, and there was a bit of a sparkle in his that I would guarantee paled by comparison to the twinkling in mine.

Ha! I thought. And now it was his job to talk. But I was still plenty nervous, so I followed up my query with a comment that was guaranteed to keep his attention where it belonged.

"My beer's empty," I announced, lifting my vacant glass, so he took me lightly by the arm and we proceeded down the gravel walkway for refills. I glanced around for Tom, but didn't see him coming. I figured he must have run into some of the many people he knew at the festival and would be back eventually.

Michael still didn't answer, but hemmed and hawed as if he was thinking it over. The noise level by the pouring stations drowned out all attempts at human speech, but through a complex series of hand and foot gestures we were finally able to communicate to each other that we'd already had all of the beers near at hand. We walked a ways down the aisle before stopping for a pour, and then began strolling casually through the grass on a diagonal back towards our standing spot by the lake. I tried not to think about the last time I'd seen him on this grass. He evidently wasn't thinking about it.

"So what do you remember?" he wanted to know.

I longed to put it back on him, but of course his way made more sense. I'd reveal what I recalled, and he'd fill in the blanks. I decided not to bother trying to rationalize it. "Tell me your side first."

"Um, okay." He chuckled a little. "Well, my team won an award. We drank a bunch of beer. Tom and I talked a lot about beer. You danced. Then we went home."

"That's it?" I said. "Sounds pretty dull." I was trying to use my eyes to bore into his skull in order to find out what was locked up in there, but apparently I wasn't much of a safecracker.

"Oh, no, it wasn't, not at all," he contradicted me.

"So what else then?"

He attempted unconvincingly to look as if there was nothing more. "Nothing else in particular."

"Uh-huh," I said. I paused, uncertain whether I should say it. Oh, what the hell, I thought. I really wanted to know. "Did I behave myself?"

And suddenly there it was, out in the open, and he was laughing unabashedly at me and I was smiling sideways at him and I wasn't even really embarrassed, although I knew I should be.

"Not very well," he admitted.

"So on the scale of impropriety, what are we talking here? Two? Four? Nine? Should I leave town or will a public lashing do?"

"No, no, nothing like that. Let's call it a three. Maybe a five if you consider the fact that your boyfriend was only about a foot away."

"Sorry about that." I was still grinning, and I seriously doubted that I sounded sorry when I said it.

"You don't look very sorry!"

"Well, I'm sorry I'm not all that sorry, then!" I huffed. But he didn't seem terribly upset, either. "From what I recall, you weren't exactly doing the best job of resisting, yourself!"

"I'm afraid I don't know what you're talking about," he pronounced with dignity. "I'm a happily married man. I would never permit a strange woman to feel me up at a beer festival no matter how pretty she was." But his face lit up a little as he said it, and he had put his arm around my waist and I pivoted slightly towards him so that we were almost facing each other, our glasses in our outer hands, our bodies in our inner ones. We stood there smiling for a minute and then someone coughed loudly nearby and Michael jumped and let go of me, and the moment was gone.

He turned back to me deliberately. "My wife is a wonderful woman," he said.

That was unexpected. I nodded.

"I would never want to do anything to hurt her."

"Of course not."

He cleared his throat. "I mean, I don't intend to."

"Of course not," I said again. I didn't like the direction this conversation was taking. I'd been so happy just a minute before, and now I felt like a foul temptress receiving a lecture from one of her intended victims.

"So, you know . . ." He drifted off and seemed to be staring at something perplexing over my shoulder. I turned to see what it was.

It was Tom, and he was making out with some girl up against the side wall of the visitor's center.

I have to tell you, I was stunned. Simply stunned. Stunned more than hurt, even. I felt my jaw hanging open and I knew I must look stupid so I closed it. I couldn't believe it. My Tom? My solid, faithful, unchanging Tom? Who hardly ever even made out with me in public?

They parted a bit for air for a second and I caught a glimpse of the woman's face. It was worse. I knew that girl. She was also a homebrewer, but what really offended me about her was that she was maybe twenty-nine and super perky and cute. I had always hated her on principle, although in reality she was actually very nice. Or so I'd thought!

My eyes focused back on Michael. His face had set into a sober expression and he was resting his hand on my forearm in a friendly, comforting fashion. Did I even have a right to be mad about this? I wondered. Considering my present company and the thoughts I'd been having about him? Wouldn't I have taken my chance had it been offered to me? Hell, for that matter I probably would have made out with the girl myself if the opportunity had come along. She was awfully cute.

Yeah, except I hadn't gotten mine and he had gotten his, and even if my intentions could hardly be called pure, it still didn't seem fair somehow. Especially when I was pretty confident that I wanted it more. I rotated back toward Tom and his partner but they had vanished.

"You know what really stinks about this?" I spluttered. "Tom finally gives me a solid excuse for having a fling and the only man I would want isn't available!"

A second later my brain absorbed the implications of what I'd said. Michael was studying me with one of his inscrutable expressions, and I couldn't take that, not now. I whirled around and stalked off with as much speed as I could muster in my sandals, finally settling my butt down on a curb near the park exit after refilling my beer once more. I sat quietly and drank and wept a little bit and felt sorry for myself. Even Tom didn't want me anymore, I thought. And Michael didn't want me, either. Apparently no one did. That sensation of being old and useless began to wash over me again but I knew I couldn't let it take hold just now; couldn't break down out here in public where anyone might see. I straightened my spine and was instantly several inches taller in both body and spirit. I am woman, roaring. Rrrr.

I snickered a little at the feebleness of my roar and that made me feel better. After a few minutes, the rational part of my nature began to assume control again. What was I going to do now? Forgive him? Did I have a choice? Find out what really happened first, I thought. Can't dump the guy just for smooching. That wasn't what I wanted, anyway. I sighed. The bottom line was, I understood. I of all people did understand.

There was a rustle behind me, and before I could object that I wanted to be left alone, someone was joining me on the curb.

"You okay?" he said.

I shrugged.

"Anything I can do?"

I shrugged again. I was afraid I might cry if I tried to talk, and I reasoned that if I said nothing that he would go. But minutes passed and his butt was still warming the concrete so I figured I should say something.

"You on your way out?" I asked.

"Soon," he said vaguely. "How are you getting home?"

"How can I go home?" I retorted bitterly. I thought about that a while. It hadn't occurred to me before that home was the last place I wanted to be right now. Yet I had no place else to go. Michael was sitting very close to me. I could feel the cloth of his canvas shorts rubbing against mine, and I was sorry I was in a bad temper because I probably would have immensely enjoyed that under other circumstances. "I guess I have to eventually."

"What are you going to do?" he queried.

"See what he says, I guess. I don't think anything like this has ever happened before, but I guess I'll never be sure now. I'll never be sure of him again." And that was when the impact of what he had done finally hit me. This was the reality behind it, of what I'd hoped to have for myself all these months, of what it would do to one's partner. It was less fun from this perspective.

"But who am I to judge?" I said aloud. "I'm not much better." I stared at my feet, wanting to smash them against the asphalt.

"You didn't do anything to deserve this," he responded in turn.

I thought of the Spring Festival, and how Michael hadn't given me a straight answer about what had happened there. "Maybe," I said.

"Definitely not," he said, taking my hand and cupping it in his.

I squeezed back. I guess I still liked him.

Another question popped into my head, a very personal one, and I wanted to ask it although it really wasn't any of my business. I compromised and posed it timidly, as if that would make it more polite. "Have you and your wife ever had this kind of problem?"

"No," he answered, after a pause. "I mean, not that I know of." It seemed a cynical thing to say, but I didn't comment. We sipped our beers and were quiet for a minute before he continued. "Actually, we haven't slept together in nearly a year."

That got my attention. "Really?!!"

"Nope."

I didn't know what to say. "How come?" I finally asked, now painfully aware that this was none of my business. Why was he telling me this?

He shrugged. "I don't know exactly. She's just never in the mood anymore, and the last few times we tried, it was sort of obvious she wasn't into it." Now he was staring at his feet, too, and he looked just as miserable as I felt. I can honestly say that I forgot my own problems for a time. Catching your boyfriend making out with someone else was upsetting, but it didn't compare to the awfulness of no sex at all.

"Have you talked to her about it?" I knew that his wife was a few years older than he was, and I could think of numerous reasons why her sex drive might have declined that had nothing to do with him.

"I've tried, but she always just says she's too tired, and then if I want to talk about it, I'm being selfish for keeping her up."

That was the kind of thing I would say. Suddenly I felt a great deal of sympathy for his wife. Was she suffering the effects of aging as much as I was?

"Well, I think you need to find out what the deal is," I replied. "There might be any number of reasons why. It's probably not that she's lost interest in you or that she's into someone else. It's much more likely that there's another cause. I mean, I know it's none of my business, but say, if she's put on weight or is getting gray or wrinkled she just might not feel very sexy anymore. Also, people take more medications as they age, and if she's started taking a new drug or stopped taking an old one, it could be a side effect." Talking about this was actually making me feel better. And strangely enough, I seemed to be able to come up with a lot of solid reasons why a woman might lose interest in sex. "Or maybe, like the rest of us, she's just getting older and her hormones are behaving differently. Or maybe it's physical, because I've heard that eventually you get, sort of, you know, um, dry, and doing it isn't really comfortable anymore." I was uncomfortable myself saying that last bit – I'd already started to notice a reduction in my own flow, and I didn't want him thinking I knew too much about it – so I rushed forward. "So I think you need to see if you can figure it out because it might actually be a problem you can solve. But what you need to do is bring it up when you're not in bed together, because otherwise it sounds like you're complaining about not getting any, or worse, trying to pressure her into giving you some. If you want my advice, I'd say take a walk and then you can have a serious conversation about it without the distraction of lying down together."

I was not in the habit of giving romantic counsel, and you can see why. But for some inexplicable reason it was important to me that he resolve this with his wife. I knew that was foolish because the worse things were between them, the better they boded for me. Was I really that unselfish? I didn't think so. Maybe I just didn't want him if I had to get him that way. That was equally stupid because what way could there possibly be that wasn't slimy and underhanded?

"Huh," he answered, and then nothing more, making my long speech seem even longer.

In the sudden silence, I noticed that the festival was shutting down around us. That got us moving. The proprietors of the nearest booths were starting to pack up and close. I jumped up to top off my beer once more before it was over. Michael followed suit.

"I should go and help clean up," he said, facing me.

"Yeah," I agreed.

"You gonna be okay?"

I shrugged. Did I have a choice?

"How are you getting home?" he asked again.

"I'll figure something out."

He pulled out his phone. "What's your number?" he asked. I told him and he dialed it and let it ring until my voicemail picked up. "Now you have my number, too," he said. "Call or text me when you get home so I know you made it okay. Okay?"

"Okay," I agreed. That was sweet, I thought. For a moment it almost felt like we were friends and that heartened me.

And when he took me in his arms and hugged me, I tried very hard to think of him as a friend and nothing more. But I couldn't help it; I wanted it to be more. And I tried to hide it; I did try. I might even have gotten by with it had I not made the mistake of looking into his face as I pulled away from him. His eyes showed clearly that he could see what was lurking in the depths of mine.

He looked straight back at me, though, and putting his hands on my shoulders and gazing steadily into my eyes, said quietly, "You wouldn't really want to, would you? I mean, if I were…?"

I was taken aback. Again I hadn't expected him to be so direct and it threw me. Like that night under the table; all at once we were treating one another as much more intimate acquaintances than we were.

What was the right answer here? I wondered. It was probably too late to pretend that I didn't like him, so I decided I'd have to settle for the truth.

"I like to think that if it actually came down to it, that I wouldn't," I answered. He nodded. "But in reality, I probably would."

He didn't smile, exactly, but the corners of his eyes crinkled up a little like he was thinking about it. "Good to know," he said, and squeezing my shoulders one last time, he dissolved into the thickening dusk.

I sat down with my beer again and mulled over the day's events. This is it, I thought. I'm never coming to this festival again.

I dislodged my phone from my jacket pocket. Aside from the call from Michael, Tom had called five times. He was probably looking for me. Fuck him, I thought.

Let him worry.

The phone vibrated again while I was holding it. Tom again. I was just irritated enough to answer.

"Where are you?!"

Fuck you, I thought again. But I told him.

"Wait there," he said. "I'll come get you."

A few minutes later, there he was before me, looking just as gorgeous as ever, and possibly even more so with that hangdog expression drooping all over his face.

"I tried calling you five times," he said defiantly, as if it was my fault.

"You know I never answer my phone," I reminded him. This was true – unless I was specifically expecting a call I usually kept it on vibrate in my coat pocket, where I rarely felt it go off.

"What have you been doing for the last hour?"

"Kept myself amused," I said.

He didn't know it yet, but this was a test. If he told me voluntarily what had happened, I could forgive it. If not, I wouldn't be able to trust him again. I might be willing to overlook the indiscretion, but I wasn't going to be played for a fool. It was funny; I'd always thought I was the one who was more likely to slip, but also the more likely to confess if I did. Tom, I believed, was much less likely to slip, but more likely to cover it up if he did. I'd never caught him in a lie, exactly, but every so often he'd say something that I knew wasn't strictly true, but was obviously what he thought I wanted to hear. So although I believed he was fundamentally honest, I had never deceived myself into thinking he told me everything. Unlike me, who eventually spilled my guts on almost every subject. Almost.

"Okay," he said. He knew me well enough not to bother trying to get information out of me if I didn't feel like giving it. "Shall we go?"

And so we went. He'd sobered up so he could drive, but I watched the road carefully, too. It gave me an excuse for not looking at him.

"Did you have fun at the festival?" I said evenly after a while.

"It was all right," he replied. "You?"

"All right," I said. "You know I don't like that one as much as the others."

Was he going to tell me or not? I was getting impatient and wanted to prompt him somehow, but that would have defeated the purpose of waiting to see if he'd confess on his own.

We didn't talk any more on the ride home. When we got back to the house, I grabbed another beer and my nightie and went into the bathroom to pee and change. Although I was making a concerted effort to act normally, I couldn't quite stomach the thought of undressing in front of him. For a second I thought of Michael and mentally yelled Ha! Two can play at that game, buddy. Which reminded me, I'd said I would let him know when I got home. I made it a quick text, "Home now." I didn't want him to worry that I might abuse his number. A minute later it buzzed back, "G'night then." Funny guy, that Michael.

When I emerged from the bathroom, Tom was already lying in bed, looking expectantly in my direction. It was still summer-warm and stuffy in the house, and I opened the window wide before going over and plunking down on the far side of the bed. I sipped my beer. I'd sobered up considerably near the end of the festival, and I was afraid that I might not be able to sleep. I took another sip and slipped in under the sheet. Tom flicked off the light, and I rolled over onto my side away from him. I always slept on that side, but not usually so close to the edge of the bed.

He scooted over and put his arm around me. I didn't try to stop it, but I didn't respond with my usual half-aroused warmth, either. He raised himself up on his elbow and tried to curl up and over my body, but I merely lay there. If he tried to get frisky with me tonight, I thought, I would beat him senseless.

"You okay in there?" he finally said, withdrawing his arm.

"Yup," I replied.

"You sure?"

"Yes."

"Are you mad at me?"

"Should I be?" I said vaguely.

He rolled back over to his side and lay there silently for a while.

"You know, don't you?" he said at last.

"I know what?"

"About what happened?"

"What happened?" I wasn't going to make it easy.

"Between me and Tammy, I mean."

"I only know what I saw. I don't know what happened, exactly."

He started to tell me, and suddenly I didn't want to hear it.

"Let's just go to sleep, Tom. We'll talk about it in the morning."

He rolled over abruptly and lay still, facing away from me. Not wanting to talk about something right away was a sure sign that I was really, really upset.

But at the moment I wasn't all that bothered, I thought as I sipped my beer again. I was too busy thinking about Michael and how sweet and kind he'd been.

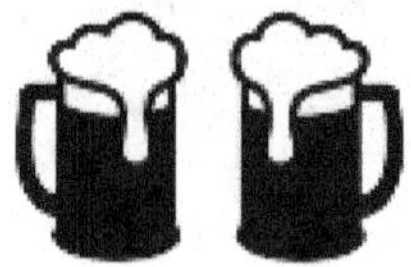

CHAPTER 5

In the morning we were polite and civil to one another, always a dire warning of impending doom for a happy couple. I laid out a nice breakfast, as I always did. But an expert in human behavior wouldn't have failed to notice that the pepperjack cheese that Tom was so fond of was mysteriously missing from our omelet and had been replaced with the provolone I liked, and that for once he got the breakfast pork chop with all the bone in it, as well as the imperfectly trimmed cantaloupe slices with the slightly green edges. When breakfast was over, I refilled my coffee and sat back down next to him right there at the table where we ate together twice a day and said coolly, "So. Why don't you tell me what happened?"

It was brutal, if I do say so myself. I asked a lot of embarrassing questions.

"What do you mean, you suddenly just started making out? What started it? Who started it? You expect me to believe that? And where did you touch her while you were kissing? How can you not remember? Or has this happened so many times since you've been with me that you can't keep all of them straight? Okay, so did you touch her tits, then? Over or under the shirt? Were they better than mine? Where did she touch you? Did you have a hard-on? What made you stop? What kind of interruption? Well, why didn't you start up again after that? Do you wish you had? Are you going to see her again?"

When that interrogation was over, the accusations began. "You should have told me you were tired of me. If you're not attracted to me anymore, let's just split up, then. You'd rather be with Tammy, be my guest. Oh wait, of course, you've probably already been seeing her behind my back. You wouldn't even have told me about this if it hadn't been obvious that I already knew." And so on. Even I didn't believe half of what I was saying, but I rather sadistically enjoyed making him defend himself anyway, particularly against my increasingly outlandish assertions, the last of which was that he was only staying with me because I owned half of his house and he was too polite to ask me to move.

But finally the dreaded talk was done. I was adequately reassured that he still loved me, wanted me, needed me, and that what had happened was a fluke instance, a momentary lapse that was not indicative of our relationship being in jeopardy. Then it was my turn to make demands. Was it wrong that I'd been looking forward to this?

"All right, Tom," I said sternly. "This is how it's going to be. A year ago I told you that I was really tempted to have a fling. I thought I might be too tempted to be able to control myself. I even offered you some time off in turn. You didn't want it. Now here we are, and it turns out you did want it after all. And in the meantime, I've done nothing wrong. So fine. You have yours, and I intend to take mine. Understood?"

He nodded glumly, his head sinking nearly down to his chest.

"And do you still want to be with me under these conditions?"

He nodded again.

"All right," I said, getting up from the table and heading over to the sink, where the tower of dishes was still threatening to topple onto the floor. "Now I have things to do."

He got up, too, and went about his day. I tried to work for a while, but he was shuffling pitifully around the house and it was driving me crazy so finally I went for a drive.

I took the highway east. Driving calmed me; it always did. There was something serene about the unchanging character of the roadway as the miles slipped beneath you: the telephone poles swishing by one by one, the cars flashing past in the opposite direction, the regularity of the exits promising gas and food and shelter to the hungry or weary traveler. Even though I'd decided to let the incident go, I was still upset. I wasn't really angry. It was more that my self-confidence was shaken. If this had happened six months earlier, it would have been utterly devastating. It would have meant that I really wasn't attractive at all anymore, not even to the man who was supposed to love me. Or at least that's how I would have interpreted it. But now, because of Michael, it wasn't quite so bad, because I didn't feel unattractive. It wasn't necessarily even about me, I thought logically. It was probably more about us. Maybe Tom was getting a little bored, too.

An hour later I had to get rid of my coffee so I pulled over at a convenient rest area to pee. There were only a few other cars there, and none of their owners were in sight, so I climbed up onto one of the stone picnic tables and sat for a while surveying the view. It wasn't much to look at, just flat asphalt in front and flat lawn behind, but it was a gorgeous day, sunny and green everywhere, with a light breeze tippling through the treetops. I was glad I had come.

After a while I took to the road again. A little further, I thought, and then I'll turn around. The sun streaming through the window was making me very warm. Very warm, and a little horny. Make that, a little warm and very horny. And suddenly I couldn't hold it back anymore, I whooped for joy because now I was free, free, I could have Michael if he only just wanted me and that was so much closer than I'd ever thought we'd be that I was almost glad, almost thankful to Tom for fooling around with that girl because if that was what I would have to suffer through to allow me to have Michael, it was so, so worth it. And I thought of him like I hadn't in months, without prohibition or inhibition, and I yanked down my tube top so that my breasts were bare and I twiddled my nipples between my fingers and when I chanced upon a secluded straightaway I even strained my neck down and licked the little tips, which were all that I could reach. Then I was passing a town and the highway crowded up slightly, so I pulled my top back up and drew my panties down from under my skirt instead. Unabashedly I lifted my skirt up from under my butt so I was sitting there bare-assed, and I wondered if truckers going by were looking and if they could see if they did, but as long as no one stopped me I didn't particularly care. I spread my legs apart and reached in to rub my clitoris with two fingers of my right hand while steering with my left and every so often I would take those fingers and penetrate my pussy with them and I felt so good that I didn't even need a fantasy to help finish me off, it just happened and I shook because it was the best orgasm I'd given myself in some time.

I got off at the next exit and turned around and started heading back, my mind overflowing with pleasantly dirty thoughts. Half an hour had passed when I spotted a hitchhiker on the side of the road with his thumb out. Although I was feeling downright cheerful now, I still had no intention of stopping. I'd picked up a hitcher once when I was about twenty; had even hitchhiked myself once or twice when I was in Alaska where everyone did it, but I'd heard too many horror stories and seen too many movies since then to consider it now. Besides, I wasn't particularly interested in having company right then. My underwear was still dangling from the seat next to me and my skirt remained crumpled about my thighs. But as I overtook the hitcher I was shocked to realize that I knew him. Even at full speed, I couldn't miss that foot-long beard or that glowing red hair. What was he doing here?

I veered the car onto the shoulder and jerked it to a halt. Hurriedly I straightened my skirt and watched the man in my rear-view mirror as he ran up. It was definitely Michael. I couldn't believe my luck.

I popped the passenger door open, and as he bent over to thank me he recognized me, too. "What are you doing all the way out here?!" we both exclaimed. He got in the car and told me his reason, and I told him mine.

"Whoops, sorry," he said. "I seem to be sitting on something." He hoisted his butt and reached underneath it and extracted the ball of cotton that was my panties. He looked at me inquiringly.

"Just playing a little game," I said coyly.

He let out a whistle. "Must have been a fun game!" he concluded.

We drove on for a while, and he began twirling my underpants around his finger like you would a Frisbee or a yo-yo, slowly at first, then faster and faster. It was uncharacteristically juvenile and oddly hypnotizing. I couldn't concentrate on driving.

"Stop playing with my underwear!" I finally shouted.

"Hey, you were playing a game with them first!" he retorted.

"The game was not with them," I clarified. "I had to remove them in order to, um, play."

"I see," he said softly. "So how did it go? Something like this, maybe?" And he reached over and pulled down my tube top so that my breasts were exposed again and then his lips were on my right nipple and his fingers were squeezing my left. I had to yank the wheel to miss a truck that had just swerved in the slow lane on our right. I could see the driver's face in his side mirror. He was definitely staring.

"This is not safe," I observed reluctantly. "Get back under your seatbelt." He'd removed the shoulder strap so that he could reach me.

He retreated back to his seat, but in another moment I felt a hand on my thigh, and as it crept its way up into the space between my legs, I lost my disdain for distracted driving. I scooted my pelvis forward and bunched my skirt up out of the way again. The vinyl of my seat stuck to my naked thighs but I didn't mind. And then he was touching me, touching me there and I had waited so long for this that I couldn't stand it anymore, I needed him inside me, I wanted to swallow him whole, to be utterly subsumed by his flesh, his body, his being.

We were approaching the rest area on the opposite side of the highway now, and I gunned it toward the exit, trembling. He let me alone for a minute so I could park. I chose the most isolated corner and then scrambled quickly into the back seat. He followed close behind. My top was still down and my bottoms were still up and I pushed him out of the way so I could lie down. "I want you on top of me," I said.

"Okay," He struggled awkwardly out of his pants and then lay astride me.

"Up here," I said.

He gazed at me uncertainly and then shifted his pelvis forward so that he was straddling my ribs.

"No, further." He brought his thighs up over my breasts, and that still wasn't what I wanted, but now I could reach his butt so I took hold of it with both hands and pulled it hard towards my face. He sat up straight and didn't argue. I fixed his pelvis directly over my chin and stuffed his dick all the way into my open mouth, all at once. His belly blocked my nose and for a second I couldn't breathe so I pushed him back just the tiniest bit and then drew him in again. His cock filled my mouth and throat and I was actually doing it, I was going to swallow him whole, and I was so excited by that that I was thrusting his entire body in and out of my mouth, all the time thinking, Fuck my face, Michael, that's it, Fuck my face. His body filled all of the air around me and I was surrounded by him, full of him, and somehow I felt much nearer to him this way than if he'd plunged his dick into my pussy and been stuck way down there instead of up here with me. And it didn't matter if I hadn't gotten mine yet because now the line had been crossed and we would have plenty of time for everything, as much time as we wanted, and we could do dirty things, the dirtiest things to each other over and over, once or twice or dozens or hundreds of times until it was all burnt out and we didn't want to anymore.

But then it seemed that we were in fact out of time because here was my exit and I had to get my clothes back in order because someone might recognize me here in my own neighborhood, and somehow it sounded a good deal worse to me to have to explain to people that no, I hadn't been playing around, I'd just been playing with myself.

And then I waited. I waited for Michael. I knew I might be waiting indefinitely, that it was possible, perhaps even likely, that he would never come to me at all. I had every intention of carrying out my threat to Tom, with or without Michael, but without him the proposition held no pleasure for me. I couldn't even consider any alternatives because they all left me cold. There literally wasn't another man in the world I wanted to fuck right then, even if I'd had free reign over them all.

I still couldn't explain it. It had never happened to me like this before, the way it was with Michael. I wasn't ordinarily prone to unreasoning desire. I'd never fallen in love at first sight; had never seen a man from across a crowded room and wanted to get to know him better; never gotten hot and bothered over a pretty face merely because it was pretty. I'd never even had a crush on a celebrity, be he actor or musician or athlete. Much as I've gone on about how gorgeous Tom was, I'd had ugly boyfriends, too, and the fact was, looks had never really been very important to me. Although I was perfectly capable of recognizing when a man was attractive, objectively speaking, that never triggered the wanting-to-fuck response in me any more than a beautiful sunset would. I was much more likely to be turned on by an attitude, or a depth in the eyes, or the tenderness of a touch, or the qualities that gradually reveal themselves as you get to know a person and make you see him in a new light. But with Michael it had been immediate, unmanageable, insurmountable, incomprehensible. I liked him better than he deserved, much better, given how little I knew him. It was almost as if I liked him based on what I suspected he might be, rather than on what I knew he was. And somehow my addled brain had translated that into wanting to fuck him. Nonstop. For maybe a month. Two, perhaps, if it went well. But even once would do. If only I could have that once.

The situation at home remained strained at best. Logically you would think that the tension between Tom and me would ease up as time passed, that we would settle back into our normal relations as the memory of what had happened faded. Instead I became conspicuously more irritated with him with each passing day. I knew it might be months before I saw Michael again, and perhaps months more before he succumbed to my dubitable charms, if he ever succumbed at all, and I endured the minutes and hours and days with diminishing patience and an ever-increasing sense of foreboding. And each day I waited reminded me of what Tom had done and how I wished it had been me who had done it, and, crazy as it sounds, I resented him for getting there first. I wanted my turn.

Twenty absurdly long days after the festival, I received a text message that shocked me more than if I'd met a family of pumas riding a carousel.

"Going to convention in city in two weeks do you want to come?"

Luckily Tom was out in the garage, so he missed seeing me drop to my knees like the world's worst sinner on the Day of Judgment. This couldn't really be happening, could it?

I read the message again. My head began to spin and I wondered whether I'd lost it at last. Maybe my fantasy world had finally taken over my brain. Get out, stupid, boring reality, it said, hitting the trespasser with a swift kick to the groin. You're no longer wanted here.

It sure seemed real, though, I thought as the digital characters swam in pretty circles around my eyes. Maybe if I just went over it once more, I'd snap back to my senses.

It was fortunate that it was only a text message, because I must have read it thirty times. Then I still didn't believe it was from Michael so I checked the number five times and read the message again. Did I want to come?

Such a simple question. Such a complicated answer.

Possible answer number one: Yes, of course I want to come, you nitwit, only can't you make it happen any sooner?

Possibility number two: I'm offended and appalled that you think I'm the kind of girl you can proposition with a text message. Now go away, I never want to see you again!

Number three: Yes, I would like to come, but I wouldn't feel right deceiving my boyfriend about it. Do you mind if I tell him? He'll be cool.

Or four: I have mixed feelings about this. On the one hand, I would be gratified to finally satiate the sexual desire I've felt towards you for so long, and I now feel perfectly justified in doing so. However, I'm worried that intercourse with you, whether prompted by lust, revenge, or both, will permanently damage the relationship I have with the man with whom I've chosen to spend my life. How will I be able to go home to him after having been in bed with you? Furthermore, I'm afraid of what it might do to you and your relationship with your family, and I'm not sure I want to be responsible for that. I think we should get together and talk this over in depth so that we can arrive at an informed, well-considered decision that will ensure the best possible outcome for all parties concerned.

That would have been a long text message, and doubtless would have had the effect of making him sorry he'd even asked.

Finally, there was my personal favorite, possible answer number five: Conventions are boring. I'll pass!

But of course I wasn't going to pass, was I? I mean, how could I even pretend that I might not go through with it? It was all I'd been dreaming about for months. Yet, scowling over at Tom during dinner, sipping on the beer he'd brought me, letting him wash the dishes because he was trying extra hard to be considerate these days, I did feel bad. This wasn't the way to heal the relationship. Or was it? Maybe it would actually be a good thing. I would get Michael out of my system and re-devote myself to my man. We'd start fresh and even, as if we were having our first date over again. I would probably even appreciate sex with my sweetie more after letting myself be groped by a near-stranger who didn't know me or my body at all. All in all, this was probably a great step forward in our relationship!

I was glad that neither Tom nor Michael could hear me wrestling with my inner scruples over this, because most of my arguments were unbelievably idiotic. But by four o'clock the next morning, I had finally arrived at the conclusion that it was not my code of ethics holding me back, but my desire to pretend to myself that I was a good person who would at least hesitate before jumping into bed with a married man, especially when I was already attached myself. I didn't know why he'd changed his mind and I didn't want to know. My conscience might not approve, and I wasn't in the mood to think about morals and virtue and the feelings of others. I wasn't even moved by the vision of my sweetheart, lying there beside me so blissfully asleep, so peacefully unaware of the filthy antics I was plotting, and if that didn't choke me up, nothing would. The debate wasn't real. I wasn't having a crisis of conscience; I was just bullshitting myself. Of course I would go.

It was a Saturday, and, having been up most of the night, I slept later than usual, until about seven o'clock. When I finally rose, there was another message from Michael. Again I almost lapsed into convulsions. What if he's changed his mind? I gulped. But no, it said, "Did you get my last message?"

He was wondering why it was taking me so long to answer.

"Yes, I was just thinking about it." I sent back.

His response was immediate. "And?"

"Yes," I wrote back.

And that was it. I was headed down the path of transgression. And I couldn't wait.

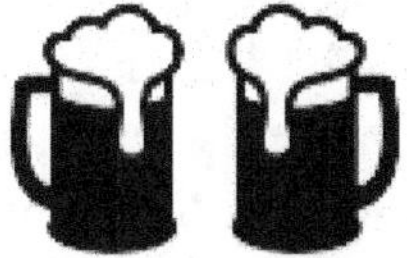

CHAPTER 6

Yet I didn't even enjoy the next two weeks. I had praised the joys of anticipation, but now that it was so very close to real, I couldn't anticipate anymore. It was actually going to happen, and I was so ecstatic and horrified that I didn't know what to do. I couldn't think about him, couldn't fantasize about him, and when I dared to think of sex at all, I felt a powerful urge to cover up my body, as if afraid that if someone saw my raunchier parts, they would know what I was planning. On top of that I had moments of pure panic in which I was petrified that he'd change his mind. I didn't think I could handle that particular disappointment, and as the appointed day drew near, I caught myself quite unintentionally leaving my phone at home or at the office, or letting its battery run dry, and if I had new messages they wouldn't come through until at last, when curiosity conquered my resistance, I would pounce, frantic, to look at the list and not see his number on it and then breathe again while the bluish tint faded from my face. It was the most wretched transcendent bliss I've ever known.

We worked out the details. This was not a conversation I could conceive of stuttering through with him by phone, and I vowed to dispatch an expensive and well-deserved thank-you gift to the inventor of text-messaging as soon as I learned his or her secret identity. He was leaving that Friday morning. I would meet him at his hotel on Saturday afternoon. I told him I couldn't miss an extra day of work, which I really couldn't. But in truth, I was also afraid that two days might be too much. We barely knew each other, after all. What would we talk about during all that time? But he didn't object to that arrangement, and in any case he would have brewing events to attend so he wouldn't be bored without me or anything.

Right, I thought. He'll probably be more bored with me than at the convention. Now I had that to worry about, too. Up to that point, I'd only been concerned as to whether my less-than-bodacious body would pass muster. Tom had watched it dilapidate gradually, so he probably didn't notice all the telltale signs of aging like a first-time viewer would. Wasn't that why people committed in the first place? To make getting old seem less objectionable? In any case, I'd begun to feel self-conscious about it. First of all, I hadn't been with anyone else in six years, and the idea of being naked in front of someone who was not Tom didn't sit quite right in my belly. Second, this wasn't a meaningless fling or a one-night stand; I actually liked this guy, in my way. I cared what he thought about me, and I had to care, because after it was over we'd still be running into one another every now and again. What if it was a letdown? Or, more candidly speaking, what if I was a letdown?

I didn't have any particular confidence in my skills at lovemaking. I knew what I liked, but as far as boys were concerned, I really had no idea. I mean, it always seemed to go over fine, but no one had ever said to me, "Oh, that's the best thing that's ever been done to me," or, "That's great, but I'd really enjoy it more if you would do this." And if I asked, "Do you like that?" the only answer I ever got was "Yes." Which made sense, given the question. Come to think of it, that was a pretty silly way to try to get information out of somebody. Of course you're going to say you like whatever it is unless you actually dislike it, and half the time most people will say they like something, even if they don't, just to be polite. But that doesn't help the other person figure out what you prefer, and in any case saying yes or no isn't the same as expressing degrees of appreciation. Of course, I was generally equally uninformative in that regard, although I'd gotten a little more vocal about that kind of thing as I'd gotten older. Why is sex so difficult to talk about when we spend so much time thinking about it?

Anyway, the only real definitive feedback I'd ever received was from a boy in high school who complained that I was squeezing it too hard. I've been told dozens of times since that I have a very firm handshake, and I've unintentionally caused new acquaintances to cry out in pain during an introduction on more than one occasion. My grip must be stronger than I think. But to this day, I am unable to hold a cock sturdily in my hand, and I still feel ill-at-ease trying to give a handjob. I always worry that it'll hurt, so I'll barely wrap my hand around it and don't rub too hard, which is probably equally futile as far as giving pleasure is concerned. Amazing how those little things stick with you. Here I'd been permanently scarred by one comment from an otherwise very sweet boy who undoubtedly hadn't intended any harm. He'd just been honest, and hell, you know, I was fifteen, I needed to learn.

Actually, I'm wrong – there was one other time in which I got a second opinion on an aspect of my lovemaking. In my early twenties, from a thirty-something-year-old man I was dating. Once, midway through what turned out to be a very short relationship, he abruptly halted in the middle of going down on me and said, "I'm glad you're enjoying this, but every time you move like that, you squish my nose." I guess I'd been writhing a bit. But I never forgot that either and since then I'd always been very careful not to move if I was getting head. It was actually good advice, but I never did quite get past it as far as he was concerned. From then on, all I could think about when we were having oral sex was keeping still, and that instantly and permanently destroyed his ability to give me orgasms, which he found unbearably insulting. In fact, I would say it was a major contributing factor in ending the relationship. These are the kinds of things they should really teach in health class. Keep your teeth off the cock. A neck will bruise if you suck on it hard enough, as will boobies. Long fingernails generally do not feel good inside a pussy. And watch how you criticize the someone you're lucky enough to have playing with you because you can really fuck them up even when you're only trying to help.

So, in essence, when I thought I couldn't have Michael, I was confident, horny, and cheerful, and he was the greatest thing since sliced bread. Now that it seemed I was going to have him, I was apprehensive, self-conscious and miserable, and he had transformed into a vicious monster who would mock and condemn me and leave me in tears on the floor.

And then finally the day had arrived, and reluctantly I prepared to trot off to my imminent doom. My enthusiasm for this venture had subsided into a barely perceptible undercurrent that sparked my interest only in miniscule surges that quickly waned into nothingness, as undetectable as muddy ripples on a murky, algae-covered pond and not nearly as appetizing. I had already told Tom I was going out of town for the weekend. Since I often went away by myself for a night or two, he didn't raise an eyebrow. I was glad of that. Although technically I had permission, it still wasn't the kind of thing I wanted to rub in his face. "This is the weekend I'm having my fling, so ha!" Since I'd heard from Michael, I'd gone easier on him. And by now I was such a wreck that I was almost wishing I could stay home with my agreeable and familiar Tom and let that awful Michael find some more brazen female to take to his convention.

It was only a couple of hours with traffic from where we lived, so I didn't want to leave too early. Michael had events all afternoon, and there was some dinner we were expected to attend in the evening. The plan was for me to arrive in between the two, around five o'clock, when he would be back at the hotel for the unofficial "nap time." All morning I waited expectantly for him to call and cancel, and I couldn't decide if that would make me feel better or worse. It was the longest day I ever killed. For a time I kept busy with cooking and cleaning and packing, but the morning was interminable, and worse, I couldn't very well hang around the house all day when I'd told Tom I was going away, so by eleven o'clock I found myself out on the street with my bag. I was at a loss. What did I do now?

I barricaded myself in my car. It was a station wagon. I knew it wasn't cool to drive a wagon anymore but I didn't care; I found it comforting. The first car I remember my mom driving was a Ford station wagon. It was yellow and decorated with that fake wood paneling that was popular once and I loved sitting in the rear facing backwards and pretending we were racing the car behind us. And my first car, the one I'd run away from home in and lived in for several months, was a station wagon, too. Ever since, I had only purchased vehicles that were large enough to sleep me comfortably. Much of my young adulthood would have been very unhappy if I were six feet tall.

After the poor wagon broke an axle and was ceremoniously buried in an Alaskan graveyard, where it might still be rusting today, I bought a twenty-year-old Dodge cargo van and tooled around in that for several years. People thought I was nuts. "You can't drive that thing cross-country," they argued indignantly. It had two hundred thousand miles on it, which was absurd for a vehicle of its vintage. But they were wrong, just like they'd been wrong about the station wagon, because that battered, decrepit machine eventually dragged me from coast to coast not once, but three times, not to mention the north-south trips I squeezed out of it. It got lousy mileage, but the next time I ended up homeless I was really grateful for all the space.

It was truly one of the best places I've ever lived, although, paradoxically enough, I changed my address nightly. I always parked in the crappy neighborhoods where the residents were more likely to be sympathetic to the homeless teenager and less likely to call the police. I felt more at ease among the poor, anyway; back then, people who had money were like foreigners to me; they spoke another language and had an entirely different culture. I concealed my living space with black cloth curtains I made out of some old sheets I'd brought from home, and I'd duck oh-so-subtly into the back and cover up the windows and light a couple of candles while I studied and did my homework. I loved that van like it was my first-born. I never let anyone else sleep in it, either, so it remained pure until the end. I think I would have kept that ol' Dodge forever except that finally it needed a part that could not be procured from any salvage yard in the state and I was forced to junk it. I wept without shame when they came to take it away. I can only hope that its good organs went to extend the life of some other Dodge van that was loved and cared for as much as mine had been. I'm sorry I don't believe in heaven, because if I did, I'd sure look forward to being reunited with my old Dodge.

After the van, I drove a Ford pickup truck for a long time. I installed one of those flat shells on its rear and I slept in it when I travelled, which was still often back then. I'd kept my handmade black curtains, but they didn't hang as neatly in the truck as they had in the van, and when I lit candles back there I found that the ceiling of the shell overhead got all sticky, as if it was melting. It also wasn't as spacious, naturally, but the mileage was considerably better, and since I was done with college and had a real job, I'd bought it new and it remained worry-free for a long time. It never came to mean as much to me as the van had, but I still developed a great deal of affection for it. I think I'm just that way with cars. I have more fond recollections of vehicles I've owned than of people I've known. I guess it's the same way some people think of their pets – you feed it, you take it places, you clean up its messes, and in return you get unconditional love.

I'd bought the station wagon after the truck was totaled in a non-injury accident one wet winter night. I'd moved in with Tom by then, was tied down to my work as well as my man, and wasn't travelling much anymore, so I probably could have gotten by with something more economical. But somehow I just wasn't ready to give up the old, young me yet so I'd bought the wagon and although I'd only slept in it a few times, it gave me peace of mind to know that it was there if I needed it.

And so it was now. It bore me smoothly out of town, obeyed my requests, listened respectfully to my misgivings, and calmed my nerves. I arrived in the city well ahead of the appointed time, and, having nothing else to do, I went shopping. Before I'd left the house I'd donned what I liked to call my driving dress. It was short, not prone to wrinkling, and so flexible that when my butt started falling asleep on lengthy trips I could literally hoist my clutch foot up onto the dashboard and be perfectly at ease. But it was nearly ten years old and getting frayed and threadbare, so I thought perhaps I should purchase a new one in honor of the occasion. My heart wasn't in it, though, and before long I was back in the wagon cruising around town searching for a place to take a walk. Fortunately there were lots of parks there, and I felt much more at ease among the trees and flowers and sunshine than I had among the display windows and fluorescent lights.

I couldn't tell you how many times I checked the clock. I'm sure you know how it went, anyway. You look at the clock and it's only two minutes later than it was the last time you looked. Next time you check it's only been three more minutes. The next time you hold out as long as you possibly can until you're sure it's been at least twenty minutes, and then you look and it's still only been five. And then finally you start thinking about something else and you don't look at the time and suddenly it's been an hour and if you don't hurry up, you're going to be late. So rather sooner than I expected, it was after four and I still had to find the hotel, so I decided I'd better get going. I hastened back to the car, and it was almost a relief to be rushing around because if I instead had to think about what was going to happen in less than an hour from now, I was worried that my brain might implode and I would have come all this way for nothing.

I must have made half-a-dozen wrong turns on my way to the hotel. I'd always had a lousy sense of direction, but this was unusually bad, even for me. I was downtown, and each misstep resulted in an eternity of turning around or circling the block and waiting for traffic lights and pedestrians. By the last time, I was half-convinced I was trying to get lost on purpose. But then I realized that if that happened, I'd have to call and tell him, and having that particular phone conversation sounded even more unendurable than seeing him in person. And when I crept around the next corner, fingers clenched to the steering wheel as if it were a life preserver, the street sign told me it was the right one and there I was, driving into the hotel parking lot at last. I still had twenty minutes to spare. Why wasn't it over yet?!

I sat absolutely still for five of those minutes, mentally commanding my heart to cease its infernal yammering. I spent the next five gathering up my things and checking to make sure that all of the windows and doors were locked and the parking brake was set six or seven times. And then it was ten till and I still had to get to the tenth floor and I figured I'd better hurry because I didn't want to be late. What was this, a job interview?

Contempt for my own foolishness finally got me going. I made it through the lobby and all the way up the stairs to the tenth floor without hesitating, and then I was in his hallway and the room was right there, but I was panting and sweating and I couldn't go in just yet. Unless I was going up to the thirty-eighth floor or I had a lot of baggage or companions, I always took the stairs, and now I regretted that age-old resolve on my part because I was a mess and even worse, I'd lost my physical momentum and had started thinking again about what was going to happen here. Big mistake.

The hallway was high-ceilinged and dim. Phony candle-type lanterns hung in iron brackets every ten feet along the walls, spilling what little there was of their eerie light onto the blood-red carpet. The only windows to the outside were at the very ends of the protracted hallways; I could barely make out the tiny breaks they carved into the pervasive gloom. I wondered whether they were large enough for me to jump through. Hoping for respite from the strangling sensation that clutched at my throat, I craned my neck skyward. The ceiling was decorated with some sort of bronze gilded pattern, and where a moment before it had given the impression of loftiness, now it seemed to be pressing down, ever closer to my unprotected skull, and the gilding wasn't an artistic design, it was a web of interlocking chains poised to drop down and trap me there, where Michael would undoubtedly find me the next morning, huddled in a whimpering ball and ready for the insane asylum. I peeked reluctantly back towards his door. It stood tall and ominous, a large black iron knocker dead in its center. "Boom! Boom! Boom!" I seemed to hear it clamor, surely in order to summon the damned spirits within. "Boom! Boom! Boom!" And then there was a slow creaking sound, like that of a poorly oiled door or the gates of hell opening, and I leapt into the air and from that elevated vantage point finally saw that there was a visitor entering another room down at the other end of the hall.

I exhaled. Somewhere in my head I heard chicken noises and that was annoying so I ran a brush through my now mostly dry hair, resettled my bag on my shoulder, and took a fortifying deep breath that I wished was a beer. I took the teeniest hold possible of that big black knocker and gave it the most timid tap I could muster. "Boom!" it resounded. I heard movement inside the room, and then a chasm was opening before my eyes, threatening to swallow me up, and I held my breath as the door separated slowly from its jamb. I don't mind telling you that in that moment I was scared out of my wits and not in the least bit horny. And when he finally appeared in the doorway the expression on his face told me that he felt about the same way.

"Hi," I said. As usual I'd chosen the best moment to show off my quick wit and brilliant conversational skills.

"Hi," he answered back, with equally impressive eloquence.

And then we stared at each other, motionless with fear.

"Can I come in?" I asked finally, speculating with some justification that the answer might be no.

"Oh, of course." He moved aside about three inches, and I wiggled my way out of the hallway and into the room.

He closed the door behind him. We were standing in the foyer. There was more staring.

There was no magic in the way our eyes met.

Had this been a mistake? I wondered. There was still time to back out of it. Maybe the idea of being with him was more appealing in theory than in reality. I couldn't remember ever enduring so much anguish over something as ordinary as spending the night with someone. And, of course, advance planning was bound to ruin anything that should have happened spontaneously. But of course, that pleasure was reserved for people who got together legitimately, who didn't have to figure out where and when, and how to keep their significant others from finding out. We were jeopardizing the relationships we had with people we loved, and for what? One night that was bound to be a disappointment for us both.

I can't begin to guess what he was thinking while I was preoccupied with these melancholy reflections, because he simply stood there wearing one of those inscrutable expressions I found impossible to interpret. The tension continued to build until at last, I couldn't stand to look at his face anymore. I gazed down at my trusty feet instead, the visual refuge of the abject, the afflicted, the abashed. They were wholly uninspiring. Yet, slowly, gradually, in spite of myself, I began to sense a change in me, something jolting my nerves and flowing through my veins and arteries, a kind of warmth that I can't describe. That familiar effect he had on me when he was near me was taking control, that undefined quality he had that made me utterly unable to stop touching him, the chemical reaction or whatever it was that unexpectedly transformed him from not-my-type into sexiest-man-alive. I raised my head a little, and my eyes were met by the propitious onset of what would someday be a nice round beer belly. I thought of how pleasantly it would fill the space between my legs and felt my cheeks flush. I looked up into his face again and he was smiling almost imperceptibly, more with his eyes than with his mouth. I noticed that in the last minute I had involuntarily drawn several inches nearer to him, so that we were nearly skin to skin. And then I laughed and reached up and fixed my arms about his neck.

"Maybe we're both a little nervous?" I suggested, pulling in closer.

"Maybe," he conceded, settling his hands on my hips. They were very warm.

I brought my arms down to his waist and drew him to me, my body flush against his, chest to chest, belly to belly. We stood holding each other like that for several minutes.

"That dinner is in an hour," I finally heard him say from where his chin was resting on my shoulder. "We should get ready to leave pretty soon."

"In a minute," I replied. I was squeezing him just above the butt so that our pelvic regions were temptingly close. His hands had moved from my waist down to the outer parts of my thighs, and he was gently rubbing the soft skin just beneath the hem of my sundress. I pushed my breasts harder into his chest.

"Ow!" we said together. My dress closed with a long row of hard round buttons right down the middle and they were pressing uncomfortably against my chest and his as I held him against me. He drew back a little.

"That dress is dangerous," he observed. I could feel the rise and fall of the hem now as his hands made the journey from my thighs all the way up to my naked hips and back. He wasn't quite touching either my ass or my pussy and that made my nether regions deliciously tense.

"We could probably fix that," I murmured, glancing up at him again.

"Yeah?" he said, removing his hands from my legs and reaching for the first button.

"No, no, you keep doing that!" I interrupted, grabbing his hands and repositioning them back on my thighs. He laughed, fortunately unoffended by my rudeness. "I'll take care of this." I reached back and loosened the drawstring cinched tight about my waist, and in seconds I had shimmied out of that dress as it was, buttons and all.

"Impressive!" he asserted. I didn't know if he meant my maneuver or my now nearly-naked body. I hoped it was the latter. And, in fact, he had stepped back and was examining me as if I was a painting or a sculpture by some historically underrated artist. He didn't seem displeased. I was glad I was facing him – I still looked pretty good from the front, not so much from the rear. Plus, I was still wearing my bra, so my middle-aged boobs would remain perky a moment longer. He scrutinized me for what seemed like an eternity of self-consciousness, but somehow being checked out like that also aroused me, as if I were proud to put my nakedness on display.

"Very impressive," he said again after a moment, and this time it was clear what he meant. I felt myself glowing. Even though I knew the unspoken part of the compliment was "for a woman your age."

"Why don't you come inside?" he prompted. We were still standing in the foyer. He clasped me by both arms and guided me over to the bed. He sat down on the edge and I stood close before him. My breasts were in his face and I suddenly wanted them in his mouth so I reached back and unclasped my bra, dropped it down off my shoulders, and not very subtly aimed my left nipple towards his lips. He sealed them around it, licking with his tongue and sucking with his lips. Suddenly his mouth opened wide and most of my breast vanished into it and for a moment I was almost glad I was not stacked because then I could not have known how awesome that would feel. My other breast was getting jealous so I nudged it over in his direction and he gave it the same treatment. Then I found myself leaning full against his face while he sucked my tits in turn, so hard that it almost hurt but just gently enough that it didn't. I climbed up onto the bed, my knees straddling his, keeping us both in a sitting position. His hands travelled softly over my backside for a moment, and then he grabbed two giant fistfuls of my ass and squeezed hard. I could have done just that all day and been completely satisfied, but I knew I only had one chance at this, so I slid further up until I could feel his penis, solid, under the lips of my vagina. He was still fully dressed, but while he continued to fondle my ass I rubbed my pussy over and over that spot until his pants were wet with my moisture.

"Get up for a second," he said at last. I rolled sideways and lay on my back and watched him tear off his shirt and then reach for his belt. I had never noticed before that he wore belts, but I was glad to see it now. I've always found something highly erotic about a man when he's removing his belt – it's as if he's undoing the chain that lets you have access to the good stuff. He pulled it tight, unbuckled it, and gave his pants and underwear a tug, but of course they didn't drop because they got hung up on his tentpole of a penis. He grinned a bit sheepishly and tried again, more forcefully, and suddenly there he was, all naked before me. I smiled broadly and so did he, but he didn't return to the bed; he moved towards the nightstand instead and I realized that he must be getting prepared and I was glad that I hadn't had to be the one to bring it up. So I just lay there quietly for a moment and when he came back and got on top of me I pretended there had been no delay because the time for delaying was over and he had already pushed my legs apart and was inside me. For a moment I was full, completely full of him and my pussy was on fire and then I felt that sudden stiffening of his cock that told me he was about to come and he groaned loudly several times and then lay his head down on my chest in an almost apologetic fashion.

"Did you time that?" he asked after a long pause. "Because I think it might have been a speed record!"

I laughed. "Michael," I said, "After all this anticipation, I would have been insulted if it had taken any longer!" And I meant it.

He started to get up and I hoped he wasn't actually perturbed by the quickness of our quickie because I sure wasn't but then I saw that he had just gone to dispose of the condom and was now coming to a halt near the foot of the bed with his face between my half-parted legs and was extending his tongue to lick my pussy. I opened up so fast I nearly kicked him in the head, but he graciously brushed that off and slid his rough wet tongue flatly over my clitoris one, two, three times and that beard, that damn foot-long beard was tickling my asshole and my pussyhole all at once and it felt so stupendously amazing that I was already screaming and shoving him away because I couldn't take any more.

He surfaced and clambered up and plopped down next to me, settling his arm gently around my stomach as I lay there, still panting and sweating.

"Now who's fast?" he demanded, grinning.

"Don't get your hopes up!" I retorted. "I'm never that quick!"

"Don't worry, it's all right. I would have been insulted if it had taken any longer!"

I punched him softly on the arm. He was propped up on one elbow, beaming down at me, and when our eyes met, all the awkwardness of my arrival was gone, we were good together again, and I was as happy being naked with him as I had ever hoped to be. I guess maybe he was thinking something similar because suddenly he leaned down and kissed me firmly but gently on the lips. It was everything a first kiss should be.

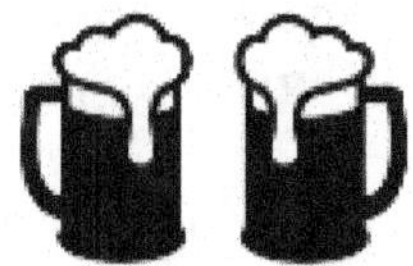

CHAPTER 7

After a few minutes we got up to get ready to go to the dinner. We stood on opposite sides of the room and watched each other dress, like teenagers who aren't quite sure what the protocol is after you've had sex for the first time, but who don't want to miss out on any of the good stuff either. I slipped shyly into my best dress, a simple, neither formal nor casual brushed cotton affair that didn't seem in the least bit sexy but which was so flattering on me that even I thought I still looked hot in it. It was royal blue, knee-length, sleeveless with thick straps, cut low enough for even me to show some cleavage, and tight around the ribcage and flared about the hips so that wearing it I almost really had an hourglass shape. Michael whistled when he saw me, which may have been overdoing it, but I decided to buy it anyway.

"Thank you!" I beamed. "You won't be embarrassed to be seen with me?"

"Not at all! Will you be embarrassed to be seen with me?" he inquired, gesturing towards his slightly wrinkled button-up shirt and casual slacks.

"Go naked for all I care!" I answered. "Come to think of it," I pondered as I sidled up to him and fondled his crotch, "That sounds like a pretty good idea…"

It had been a good twenty minutes so I was in the mood again and was also hungry, so I wrapped my free arm around his neck, gently brought his face down to mine, and kissed him once in a nice sort of way before I let my tongue take over his mouth entirely. Every time I sensed he was going to attempt to withdraw, I sucked harder on his tongue so he couldn't quite break free. Plus I could feel his cock hardening under my hand, so I figured if I could just keep it going a few more minutes, I was bound to get lucky again. Finally he made a noise like "mmphrysigl" so I reluctantly let him up for air for a second.

"We have to go," he said. "We're going to be late."

"We're already late. What's a few more minutes?"

"I'm supposed to be giving a speech. I can't miss that."

"Oh," I said. "Well, I suppose that's pretty important. We'd better go." Who knew there were going to be speeches at this thing?

"I can't go right this second. I have to wait for that to go away," he explained, pointing toward his trousers. "So you have to behave for a few minutes!"

"I can do that," I vowed bravely. "At least, I'll try." He frowned at me with mock severity. "I'll try really hard!"

"Speaking of which, we'd better be on our best behavior tonight. You're just supposed to be my companion for the evening, only a friend coming along for the ride. You know how people talk. So no hanky-panky, okay?"

"Does that mean I should put some underwear on?" I inquired innocently.

"Hey, I'm trying to lose a hard-on here!"

So I considerately went to pee, and by the time I re-emerged from the bathroom he was all better and we headed out on our very first date. I wondered what you were supposed to call it if you had sex before your first date. I didn't know, but I was sure it wasn't very nice.

The walk from our hotel was not long. One of the fancier downtown hotels near the convention center was hosting the event. You proceeded into this massive structure through tall arched wooden doors and inside, the scenery stunned you with its opulence, the heavy linens draped over the furniture and scented candles burning everywhere and professional servers bustling about in black tie. The dinner was one of those pairing deals where they cook with beer and serve specific dishes that are supposed to be coupled with specially-selected varieties of beer. Me, I've never been particularly impressed with the ones I've attended. I mean, I like the food and I like the beer, but I don't know that my palate is sophisticated enough to be able to tell which should go with which, or even to appreciate it much if someone tells me what I'm supposed to think. But everything was yummy and mostly I just tried not to eat too much so I wouldn't be overstuffed for later.

I did a darn good job of behaving myself, too. For once I didn't sit too close to Michael, didn't touch him, barely even spoke to him, in fact, but instead chatted with my neighbors, which was pretty difficult because naturally a lot of it was brewing tech talk, which left me with not much to contribute. Still, I think I did a decent job of being personable. In some ways it was easier talking to complete strangers. Since you knew nothing about them, you could always start with asking where they were from, and where they'd gone to school, and what they did for a living, and how they'd met their spouse, and so on; with people you'd met before it was actually harder because you'd already covered the main points and had to come up with new angles to keep the conversation going. But here we were all strangers, and in that company I wasn't significantly worse at making conversation than anyone else. I didn't even get flustered when someone asked me the worst of all possible questions.

"So how long have you two been married?" my neighbor said, craning his neck around me to get a good look at Michael. You know how it is, once you get to be a certain age, people just assume.

"Oh, we're not married," I responded matter-of-factly, dismissing the ridiculous idea with a careless wave of my hand. "Just friends. I happened to be in town for a conference, too, so we decided to come together. While we're out partying, his poor wife is at home minding the children," I said sadly.

My neighbor clucked sympathetically. "Mine is, too. The sacrifices married people make, eh?"

I'd been about to deliver a long speech on my aversion to marriage, which would positively have confirmed the forever-after nature of my singledom to anyone who was listening. But since it seemed there were people there who actually were married, some of them perhaps happily so, I politely refrained.

"And how gladly they make them," I answered gravely, diving back into my salad with a zeal that precluded further conversation on the subject.

If anything, Michael was the one comporting himself suspiciously. When he wasn't talking, he'd turn to shoot me an indisputably lascivious leer, and once I even had to shoo him away when I felt his hand caressing my thigh. Fortunately, he spent most of his time talking, especially after his speech, which was a big hit. He was really, really on that night. It wasn't just that he had a lot of intelligent things to say about brewing, he had engrossing and entertaining things to say about absolutely everything. And then I recalled with some surprise that it was talking that had gotten me interested in him in the first place. The attraction had so long ago transformed into something so thoroughly sexual that I'd forgotten that at one time I'd actually enjoyed his company for its own sake.

After dinner, a number of the attendees were heading over to a nearby brewpub. Michael disengaged me from the exiting crowd and asked if I wanted to go.

Of course not, I thought, I want to take you home and rip your clothes off. But what I said was, "Do you want to go?"

"I don't want to be out all night," he answered. "Maybe we could just go and put in an appearance and go home early?" I really liked that guy.

I said that was fine with me, and I went and peed for the tenth time that night and then rejoined him on the sidewalk much more at ease. By now, most of the teetering crowd had dissipated or pulled ahead, and we ambled along in a leisurely fashion so that it was almost as if we were alone for a spell after all. Although I was still trying to behave, I was several beers in now and found myself walking very close to him, so that every time I turned to say something my nearest breast brushed up against his arm or his chest. I guess he must have noticed because he gave me an odd, almost amused look whenever it happened. We walked more and more slowly, and then finally stalled in the middle of the sidewalk.

"Are you sure you wouldn't rather skip the pub and go back to the hotel?" he said.

"Nah," I replied. "You should go and do your group thing. I mean, that's why you're here, right?"

"Yeah, I guess." He didn't look that thrilled by the prospect either. We were passing an oversized parking garage that towered countless stories above us. At its base was a metal door that emptied onto the street and which presumably led to a staircase that climbed up to the higher levels. Someone had propped it open with a brick. Hoodlums, I thought to myself, or no-good punk kids. We had walked another twenty feet before I halted abruptly and grabbed Michael by the arm and began towing him towards that open door.

"What are you doing?!" he asked, alarmed, but allowing me to lead him along.

"You'll see."

It was a stairway, a real enclosed one with concrete steps, not one of those big open shafts with suspended metal stairs and landings that you often find in parking structures. It blocked out the noise from the street, and you would hear it if someone entered either above or below you once you were in there. I dragged him up three flights before I was satisfied. We took a moment to catch our breath.

"What are we doing here?" he asked finally.

"This," I responded. Feeling like a no-good punk kid, I knelt down on the concrete and started unbuckling his belt.

"Oh, shit," he said.

I loosened the belt and pulled his pants down.

"Oh, shit," he said again.

I could have left him in his boxers and just worked around them, I suppose, which would have been safer, but somehow that didn't sound like as much fun. Down they went.

"Oh shit, oh shit!"

I went for the balls first. One at a time, I very carefully rolled them softly in my mouth, then got my tongue between them and licked him there, too. I tilted my head up to look at him and found myself with a face full of balls and I wanted to giggle but my mouth was full so I choked it back. I bent to face forward again and started running my tongue up and down the length of his cock, which was quite hard now. I used my tongue to tickle his head under its chin and then took just the head into my mouth and sucked it hard. I glanced up towards his face and he was gazing down at me mouthing something that looked suspiciously like "oh, shit," so I figured that was okay. Then I lifted my head up higher and opened my mouth and helped myself to all of it at once, closing my lips when I reached the base of the shaft and sucking in my cheeks like I was trying to remove all of the juice from his cock, which of course I was. I felt his hands come to rest on the back of my head and as I pushed his penis in and out of my mouth he grabbed a couple of fistfuls of my hair so that my scalp was stretched tight with every inward motion. I liked that. I lunged harder, trying to swallow and suck some last millimeter I might have missed before. I grabbed his ass with both hands and yanked him closer to me, forcing his penis into my throat. He moaned loudly, and I kept still a moment and held his dick fast where it was at its deepest until I couldn't hold it there anymore. I made a move to pull back but he clenched his hands on my head and with one final thrust spewed what seemed like an enormous load all over the inside of my mouth and into my throat. I didn't think I was going to be able to swallow it all but pride demanded that I try, and after I felt the first wad trickling smooth and warm down my gullet I knew I was going to make it.

I let his cock slip out of my mouth, then took it gently back in, not sucking now but merely closing my lips and tongue around it. He shuddered slightly, so I gave it another pass, then two more to make sure he was spotless. I brought up the boxers and the pants, and then rebuckled the belt so his goodies were again all wrapped up in a neat package that I hoped I would get to reopen later. Finally I stood up and he enveloped me in a rather sweet hug and then kissed me on the mouth and didn't even seem to mind that I smelled and tasted like a gallon of semen mixed with half a gallon of beer.

"Shall we go?" I said, getting abreast of him and crooking my arm about his.

We descended the stairs. "You know, we're really lucky no one saw us," he commented.

"That's why I went for the third floor. I figured most people would probably take the elevator if they were up more than two floors, and anyway we'd at least have some warning if someone did come."

He looked impressed by my foresight.

I pointed at the top of my head. "Not just a hat rack!" I said.

We made our way to the bar and oh, I was so glad we went. We were at least a beer behind everyone else and they were all having a fantastic time and soon we were, too. You know how it is with beer drinkers, after a few, everyone's your best friend, and we had important, meaningful conversations we'd forget before morning, and embraced all the strangers we'd never see again, which was just as well because we'd never remember their names anyway. Michael was in high spirits and so was I but 'round about midnight the crowd started to thin out and some one-on-one time sounded awfully good to me again. I moseyed up to within a few inches of him, cocked my head and shot him a look that I hoped was easy to interpret. "Time to go!" he announced. I always had been rather an open book. We said our last goodbyes and made our getaway back to the hotel.

"We can take a cab if you want," he offered.

"I like walking," I answered. "It's only about a mile, anyway, I think. Besides, we could probably use the time to sober up!"

"I can't argue with that!" he agreed.

The streets were much emptier now, and he circled his arm around my waist and I put mine around his and we stumbled along together, bumping into each other with every step. It prolonged the trip, but I didn't mind. Halfway there we passed the parking garage we had stopped at on the way down. I grinned involuntarily. If the reminiscent look on his face was any indication, Michael had noticed it, too. The brick still had a foothold in the door at street level.

Suddenly he was dragging me across the sidewalk towards the opening. "What are you doing?!" I cried.

"Just come here a minute," he responded, tugging on both my arms.

"No, no, Michael, you're pushing our luck. People are heading home now – we'll get caught for sure!" I tried to plant my feet on the sidewalk but my sandals didn't give me much grip and in any case he was too powerful for me to withstand for long. Before I knew it he had scooped me up in one arm and was hauling me over the threshold, nearly crushing my leg in the door as it slammed behind us.

In an instant he was all seriousness. "Are you all right?" he said, setting me down carefully while I rubbed my thigh.

"Fine," I answered. "The brick was in the way; it barely smushed me."

"You're sure?"

I nodded.

His expression of concern reverted to a leer and the game was on again. He anchored me by one arm, reached backwards with the other and drew the brick inside. The door snapped shut. I took advantage of those few seconds of comparative freedom of movement to position my body against the base of the middle stair railing, such that my back was propped up against it. I spread my legs wide for maximum stability and planted my feet on the non-slip coating that lined the stairwell. He seemed startled when he turned back and saw me with my defenses up.

"All right, buster!" I exclaimed. "Let's see you move me now!"

It turned out that he was too smart to try.

In a flash he had squatted down, lifted up my dress, and buried his face in my pussy.

"Oh, shit!!" I shouted.

I quickly forgot all about getting caught. At that point I didn't even care if someone came, as long as I did.

His tongue was working my clit just the way I like it, sort of slow but steady, neither too rough nor too smooth, and not too hard or too soft either. Consistency always helps me concentrate on the raw feeling – methodological changes are distracting. I couldn't really take the time to explain that in the moment, and I hoped my "ohhhhhhhs" would get the message across. I took hold of my dress and flattened the skirt up against my body so that I could see him. When he glanced up in turn he was still wearing that dirty look and that pleased me immensely. The tension was rising within me and I thought I might be getting close, though that was difficult to believe after so many beers. I let my hands rest on his head and resisted the urge to push, but he was a good sport and voluntarily nudged in a little deeper, clutching my butt cheeks for balance. I felt my core temperature rising. His tongue was warm and moist and he was eating my pussy and I was butt naked in a public stairway and now I was sure I was going to come, I just needed a few more seconds.

And then the door opened one floor above us and I glanced up and a small group of twenty-somethings had appeared on the landing and were heading down the stairs. They stopped dead when they saw us, but Michael didn't stop and me, it was too late for me to stop, there was no stopping it now, so I just shut my eyes and let it happen. My climaxing scream reverberated throughout the stairway and the echoes seemed to last for minutes. I jumped as Michael gave me one last intense lick and then he was standing beside me and smoothing down my dress and the three guys were descending the stairs again and he played it cool as a cucumber as they passed us one by one in the narrow passageway. "How's it going?" he said to one and "Have a nice evening!" to another and "Already got mine, thanks for asking," to the last one who obnoxiously shot out, "When's your turn, dude?" as he was exiting.

When our audience had gone, I turned to Michael and threw my arms around him and kissed him on the neck and we laughed and laughed.

"You told me so!" he declared.

"I wasn't going to say it!"

"Well, you were right and I should have listened to you. I'm very sorry for putting you through all that. It will never happen again," He bowed his head solemnly.

"Now, now, let's not be hasty!" I countered. "After all, it wasn't all bad!"

And so we bantered all the way back to the hotel, where we had another beer at the bar and then returned to our room. We were all smiles as we undressed each other by the lamplight, and I concentrated on memorizing the look and feel of his naked body so I could keep it with me after this was over. Earlier I had paid no attention to the room itself, but I did now, and I wanted to remember that, too. It's stayed with me, and it's mostly how I picture Michael now, against that backdrop. It was white, sparkling white, the walls and the carpet and the sheets and the blankets on the king-sized bed, a clean, bright, fluffy kind of white that gave you the sensation of being at a spa or in a commercial for some really awesome laundry detergent. The windows were draped with white curtains and sheers, which I loved in a hotel because you could have privacy but still let sunlight into the room. There was a dark wooden dresser with a large mirror on top of it and from where we standing I could see Michael's butt reflected in it. I felt very sneaky checking him out behind his back until I realized that he had probably been peeking at mine in the same way that afternoon. We were on the tenth floor, and between the two windows stood a sliding glass door which led out onto a small balcony. The city looked pretty from that vantage point, as cities always do at night. And Michael, oh, Michael looked pretty too, all redheaded in white and against the twinkling lights of the city night.

I think we knew we were both done for the night but we went for it anyway, and I felt spectacular with him inside me and it felt like it would never end and never should although I knew it must, and soon. When it was over I snuggled up next to him and simply enjoyed the feel of his warm sweaty skin against mine and went peacefully to sleep.

In the morning I woke as early as usual. The sun had just cleared the horizon, and its light was filtering delicately through the sheers as I had hoped it would. I eased my way out from under Michael's arm, which was still holding me, slid out of bed, donned my little silk bathrobe and very, very slowly and quietly slid open the sliding glass door and nudged my way out onto the balcony. It was still quite warm and I was comfortable even though I was barely dressed. I sat down in the metal chair the hotel had so thoughtfully provided and enjoyed the view for a while and re-played the previous night in my head. It was much, much more satisfying than re-playing my own fantasies in my head. I felt perfectly, perfectly content except that I wished I had a cup of coffee. There was coffee and a coffeemaker in the room, but I didn't want to wake Michael so I toughed it out. The sun was really rising now; the sky was glowing with all sorts of colors, and the reflections off the windows of the other highrises were amazing, and for a moment I thought perhaps I should wake him after all, but I figured that was too corny, making him watch the sunrise with me. Then there was a noise behind me, and the slider was opening and out came Michael with the coffee I'd been craving. I took it gratefully.

"Do you always get up this early?" I asked him.

"Not unless I have to," he replied. "I must have sensed you'd gotten out of bed."

"I'm sorry; I was trying not to wake you."

"It's okay." He sat down in the other chair. "I can't remember the last time I saw a sunrise."

We didn't hold hands or gaze meaningfully into one another's eyes or anything goofy like that, just sat and watched the sky change while I drank my coffee. I knew our time was almost up but I was determined not to think about it any sooner than necessary. Finally I had to ask. "When do you need to be back at your convention?"

"Nine o'clock." His eyes were focused far away, somewhere out over the balcony railing, as if his mind was elsewhere. "Actually, I think I'll go and shower now so I'll be ready." He turned and left, and as the sliding glass door closed behind him I felt like I wanted to cry.

He was going to go and shower now? He didn't even want to take advantage of the little bit that was left of our time? Maybe he'd been expecting it to be over already and was getting impatient for me to leave.

By the time he emerged from the bathroom I was packed, dressed, and ready to go. After all that time I'd spent packing, I'd somehow forgotten to bring an extra outfit for the morning and I'd had to put on the same damn dress I'd worn the night before, so now I looked as stupid as I felt. I studied my reflection in the mirror while I was brushing my hair, and considered the possibility that I was overreacting, reading too much into a man's natural desire to take a shower, especially after so much sweating the night before. But then I noticed how puffy my under-eyes were, and how saggy my eyelids, and remembered that morning, like daylight, was no longer my friend. Maybe he actually was in a hurry, to get away from my morning-after ugliness; or at least to get a beer in to make it more palatable.

I decided it didn't matter. I couldn't afford to take chances here. Better to be safe than to risk overstaying my welcome. Maybe this was it for us, but I still didn't want him to think of me afterwards as that annoying woman who couldn't take a hint and go home when her company was no longer wanted. I heard the shower valve clinking to a halt and Michael whistling off-key as he dried himself, probably celebrating my imminent departure. And then the water was gurgling noisily down the drain, taking the brief resurgence of self-confidence I'd experienced the prior evening with it.

He seemed surprised when he saw me standing there, tapping my impatient toes against the carpet as if I couldn't wait to get the hell out of there. I supposed he'd assumed he'd have to force me out kicking and screaming.

"You're leaving now?" he said, lurching a bit clumsily as if caught in one of his double-takes.

"Well, I've got things to do . . . you've got things to do . . . figured I might as well get an early start," I finished lamely.

"Okay," he said, and that was all. He looked awfully cute with a fluffy white towel cinched around his waist, but I tried not to notice. It was a replica of the moment when I'd first arrived, painful and awkward, and I was horrified that this was going to be the last memory I would have of him.

"So, I guess I'll see you around," I said briskly, having nothing else to say.

"I guess so." Apparently he had nothing else to say either.

I hoisted my bag to my shoulder and headed for the door. The knob was in my hand, I was turning it, the door was opening, and then I was back in that miserable hallway again and it came over me that I simply could not stand to let it end like this. I caught the knob just before the door slammed to and marched back into the room. I had made a fool of myself with this guy so many times already that surely once more couldn't hurt?

He was sprawled out on the bed, still wrapped in the towel, staring blankly up at the ceiling. I had no clue what he was thinking. I wondered if he regretted what we'd done. I shook my head vigorously to clear it. I couldn't worry about that right now. I dropped my bag loudly to the floor and he looked over at me but his expression didn't change, so that didn't help me. I mustered up my courage, anyway, strode over to the bed, and clambered right up on top of him again. "Michael," I said, "I had a really good time last night."

He smiled unexpectedly and everything was right between us again. "Me too." He pulled my face down towards his and kissed me firmly on the mouth. I leaned in and kissed him back. That was a much better ending and I was happy with it. I started to get up to go again, but he resisted my motion, fixing his arms around my back to keep me straddling him. I took the hint and kissed him again. I put some tongue into it this time, and he gave me some back. We continued the lip and tongue play while he slid his hands almost up to my armpits and began caressing my nipples with his thumbs. When I looked down, I could see them becoming erect through the thin material of my dress. I guess he could, too, because he lifted his head and took one gently between his teeth right through the fabric and gave it a tug. I groaned appreciatively and he did the same to the other side. I felt his hands moving up along my backside and finally landing on the zipper that travelled almost the full length of my back, and I was so very glad he was going to let me out of that dress because my breasts were swelling so much that it was tightening uncomfortably across my chest. He took his time bringing me out of it, but link by link, my torso gradually exposed itself until I was naked to the waist. I lifted my hips and wriggled out of the rest, discarding my panties along the way. Michael was prone beneath me and the towel was still tied around his waist, but his cock had poked its way out from between the folds below the knot and was standing there as if in salutation. I laughed and so did he and then I untied the towel and let it drop off to his sides so that we could both be naked. I climbed up higher along his body so I could reach the nightstand, and while I was attending to necessities he stroked my ass with one hand and my tits with the other, and by the time I'd gotten him ready I was plenty ready too.

I was still leaning over him and he kept me in close while I reached underneath me and guided his penis into my vagina. I pushed my pelvis forward and took him all the way in, and then raised my ass up and accidentally let him out again.

"Whoops," I said. I tried again and got two thrusts in before I let him slip out this time. "Urgh!" I took hold of his cock one more time and very firmly directed it into my now rather anxious pussy. "You stay there!" I ordered, and that seemed to do the trick, because now I was able to move it in and out without losing my grip. Not too fast, just up and down in a steady rhythm while he fondled my ass and I thought about the mounting pressure on my clitoris as his cock rubbed against it. When my cheeks tired, I leaned back so that I was perpendicular to him. His cock was still angled inside me and up and down didn't work anymore, it was more back and forth, me thrusting my hips forward over and over on his cock while he jerked his hips in response and held me upright by my breasts. He plunged into me faster and faster and I tried not to look at his face when he came but I couldn't resist. His eyes were half-closed and his mouth was open and his whole face tightened up as he forced himself in further for those last few thrusts before letting it all out with one loud moan. I slowed almost to a stop but kept him moving inside me as long as I could, until he began to soften up and I had to get up to dispose of the condom before it was worthless. And then I came right back and climbed on top of him again.

"I can't go again that fast!" he protested.

"I know!" But I settled down on top of him just the same and started sliding my pussy back and forth against his penis. There was still plenty of wet and it felt really good even without the hard-on. I was leaning over him again, my face against his neck, so I was surprised when he tapped me gently on the shoulder and said, "Roll over a minute, will you?"

I rolled over onto my backside next to him. He rolled me back toward him a little so that I was lying sideways facing him. "Open your legs, please," he continued politely, emphasizing his intent by pushing against my upper knee. I spread them halfway. "Wider." I opened up entirely so that my pussy was completely exposed, and again I felt that odd sense of prideful arousal in showing off my goodies. As he snuggled up closer to me, I felt something travelling between my thighs and then his finger was stroking my clit, but it was so much better than when I did it that there was really no comparison. Crazy thoughts flew through my head, thoughts about opening up my pussy to be played with, except that wasn't crazy, pussies were meant to be played with, and mine surely deserved it as much as anyone else's and I hoped he would go on playing with it because it felt so fantastic that I was going to come and then I was coming and I had to tell him to stop before he broke me.

I closed my knees and eyes and I guess I went back to sleep because when I lifted my eyelids again Michael was sleeping next to me and the clock read eight forty-five and now it really was time to go. In five minutes he was ready to leave but there wasn't much time for a proper goodbye, which was probably just as well because I wasn't one for sentimental speeches anyway. One strong hug, one final kiss, and he was heading down the hall towards the elevator. I surveyed the room one last time, saving it in my mind. Our room, I heard myself calling it. Not one for sentimental speeches, my ass, I thought to myself, and chuckled. And then I gathered my things and made my way home.

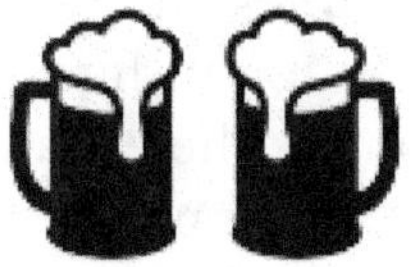

CHAPTER 8

Many weeks passed before I saw Michael again. The night we'd spent together was a pleasant dream that I'd relived many, many times in my mind, but I knew that was the end of it. I had to live in my real world now; the fantasy one was gone. Sometimes I did miss him a little, though. Maybe we hadn't been friends, exactly, but I had enjoyed bumping into him every now and again. Even that part of it was over and I tried hard to accept that. I'd decided to avoid visiting his brewery, too. Since I'd resolved to stay with Tom, going with him to the workplace of the man who'd been my partner in unfaithfulness would have been like revisiting the scene of a crime or something. But the chilly autumn evenings continually reminded me that the Winter Festival was approaching and I knew there was an excellent chance that we'd run into him there. I braced myself for that. After all, Tom had no reason to avoid Michael, and would surely want to say hello if we saw him.

Tom and I were doing all right. Things still weren't what they once were, but officially speaking, I was no longer carrying a grudge. Finally having Michael after wanting him for so long had, in a strange way, relieved a lot of the pressure I'd been feeling about my relationship with Tom. I hadn't fully grasped the impact of it at the time, but Michael had come between Tom and me long before we'd done anything about it. I'd gradually grown more interested in my crush than my boyfriend, and that was bound to have hurt us in some way. Sometimes I even wondered if my fascination with Michael had somehow indirectly created the rift that opened the way for what happened between Tom and Tammy. (Tom and Tammy. Isn't that just too cute?) But I thought it was more likely that the rift was already there, and that she had managed to sidle her way into it, just as Michael had unintentionally done with me. But either way, now that the deed was done and it was finished between Michael and me, I felt closer to Tom again. It's hard to explain.

Incidentally, we bumped into Tammy at a pub a couple of months after the Lakeside incident. She stumbled when she spotted us approaching, clearly at a loss as to what to do, but I nodded civilly and she warmed up a bit after that. But after a couple of minutes of casual conversation she patted Tom on the arm and I instantly shot her my "stop touching my man" look. I've never been on the receiving end of this look, but I know that mine must be very powerful because I've watched many a strong, confident woman crumble under its ferocity, and she was no exception. The little flirt was flustered, speechless, and tripping backwards out the door before Tom even got the chance to work up an appetite. I knew I would probably see her at the festival, too, but on the discomfort scale, that didn't even register next to the thought of seeing Michael again. Unless she was with him! I had to shut that thought down quickly because it filled me with such burning rage that I really thought she might get hurt if I saw them together. Even now I was a lot bigger than her.

Festival day finally arrived. I hadn't even been able to look forward to it. Plus it was super-cold and wet, and we'd have a long trek there and back, so I had to bundle up in a sweater and one of those loathsome turtlenecks that keep themselves amused all day trying to strangle you, and then I plastered my long-johns on underneath my fat jeans and prodded my feet into some rancid rubber galoshes, perfecting the picture of my hideousness. I told myself it didn't matter. I wasn't trying to seduce him, right? Who cared what I looked like? I sighed internally. I was strong enough to be practical enough not to wear some cute skimpy outfit and be miserable the whole day, but not strong enough not to be depressed about it. I am woman, roaring. Rrrr.

I tried not to look for him. Much. I drank my beers and hung out with Tom and his beer buddies and periodically scanned the crowd in what I hoped was a nonchalant manner. It was late in the day when I finally glimpsed him through the crowd. It was hard to miss that bright red hair and chest-length beard. It was even harder to miss the attractive young blonde he was hugging when I saw him. Unfortunately for me, Tom spotted him at almost the same moment.

"There's Michael," he said, "Late as usual. Let's go say hi?"

I hesitated. "It looks like he's with someone, Tom," I said, giving the floor a savage kick and cracking off a splinter. "Maybe we should just leave him alone."

"She looks familiar," he replied, oblivious to the damage I'd inflicted on the hardwood. "I think she might work at the brewery."

Even worse, I thought. She has access to him eight hours a day; probably after-hours, too. I only get to see him once every few months, and I'm getting older by the minute. How can I possibly compete? I felt a jealous rage swelling within me, and impulsively I wanted to smack the little tramp out of the way. Fortunately, the logical part of my brain kicked back in and I caught myself. I breathed deeply. It was not a competition. For what it was worth, I'd already had Michael. I had no right to expect him not to move on to someone else. It wasn't her fault, and it wasn't his either. I could be a grownup about this, couldn't I?

"Well, I suppose it would be rude not to say hello, at least," I conceded. Tom meandered over to where they stood, not thirty feet away, and I trudged along behind him, feeling enormous, ugly, and ancient. The blonde was scrutinizing me with pity. It'll happen to you! I wanted to yell, but she was already walking away, leaving Tom and me alone with Michael. Tom shook Michael's hand, but I merely nodded and averted my eyes, my brief dream of behaving rationally fading quickly in his suddenly very tangible presence. They talked about beer while I seethed silently, excoriated myself for even caring, then seethed silently some more. I couldn't tell if Michael was even aware of that, because I wouldn't look at him. He doesn't care, I reminded myself viciously. He never did. He was just using you to – to get his feet wet, I thought, among other things. He was probably picking up chicks left and right now. Who knew what number blondie even was? I was well shut of him. I had refilled my taster twice while the boys were chatting, and I was so consumed with brooding that I didn't even notice when Tom stepped away to fill his.

"How've you been?" Michael was saying, reaching out to touch my arm. I jumped. Then I realized who was talking to me and I pulled out my best contemptuous sneer.

"Fine, thank you, and yourself?" I answered coldly, jerking away from his touch.

"Wow!" he exclaimed. "What did I do?"

His ignorance of his wrongdoing incensed me even more. Not even the smallest part of my irrational fury was mollified by the look of kind concern he was directing at me.

"Who's the blonde?" I spat it out like a curse.

"Excuse me?" he said with affected innocence.

"You heard me. How long have you been seeing her?"

"You mean – you mean the blonde I was talking to a little while ago?"

"You seeing some other blondes, too?"

"She works at the brewery," he said calmly.

"You're screwing someone you work with now?" I snapped scathingly. "That sounds smart."

"I'm not 'screwing' her," he reiterated firmly. "She works at the brewery; that's how I know her."

"Oh." I was still too mad to be embarrassed, but I could sense that that was about to change. Although I'd already stripped off my jacket, I was growing uncomfortably warm in my remaining layers, and beginning to wish I'd worn that skimpy outfit after all. I figured I'd better backtrack fast before he started thinking I liked him or something. But it's hard to backpedal when you've got your foot in your mouth.

"I'm sorry," I said coolly. "It's really none of my business. I just don't want to see you ruin your reputation." Really? I confronted my addled brain. That was the best you could do? I thought you were supposed to be smart. But it was out and I would have to stick to it now.

He didn't buy it anyway. "In case you're wondering, I haven't been with anyone since you."

I knew it might be just a line but it sure didn't sound like one and his expression was sincere and his eyes were maybe even a little sad and I was suddenly aware that he was standing very close to me and then Tom came back with his beer and I needed one. When I returned, Tom and Michael were still talking their dull beer talk but I was happy again and it was almost like old times, before that night, only more so because I could do a much better job of picturing Michael naked now. And if I hadn't known it was finished between him and me, I might have believed that the anticipation was starting all over again, the wonderful wondering of what just maybe could possibly happen if the planets were aligned just right, a feeling I had sorely missed these last months. Michael was ready to leave before Tom and I were, and we exchanged our farewells in a simple, direct fashion, without hidden meanings cloaked in clever words or a grandiose embrace. Yet when his eyes met mine, I knew that I still liked him as much as I ever had, and that that wasn't going to go away just because we'd had sex once or twice.

And when he was gone, it came over me that it wasn't over between him and me; wasn't even close to over. So when I received a text from him a few days later asking if I wanted to meet him for a beer, I was barely even surprised. I was surprised, however, when we bumped into each other in the municipal parking lot before our scheduled drink and within seconds were getting it on in the frigid backseat of my station wagon. I was even more surprised when through the open window, which we'd cracked slightly to release some of the steam, I heard some teenagers snickering, "Don't come-a-knockin' when the station wagon's rockin'!" I wondered briefly how obvious it had been; then decided I didn't want to know.

"Let's pick a more private spot next time," he suggested drily, as we struggled, sitting, back into our clothes. It was still the best beer date I'd ever had.

The following week we rendezvoused at one of the less-popular local parks. I parked my wagon in a corner spot and he parked next to me so at least we were only exposed on one side. I'd worn a long skirt and leggings to work, so before we climbed into the backseat I slipped out of my undergarments, and presto, easy access. He didn't undress me or himself, just slipped his pants down as little as necessary, got on top of me, and began to slide very slowly and quietly into me in a studied effort to avoid rocking the car. After the first few minutes my pussy was still only half-full, and I was not feeling very optimistic about getting it topped off.

"Maybe we should try my car," he suggested. "I think it has better suspension."

"The car you drive your kids around in?"

"Ew, right." He pondered for a moment. "You get on top," he said finally.

"But I thought we agreed that would be worse. I need to be up higher to get a good angle, which means boobies in the window."

"No, you get on top, and turn around," he clarified. I got it then. We awkwardly switched positions and then I reversed myself so that my vagina was suspended over his face. I hiked my skirt up to my waist but I refrained from dropping my pelvis down to his level. It just seemed rude, somehow. Instead I leaned forward and took his cock into my mouth and began sucking on it vigorously. I could feel little flicks of his tongue on my vagina, and I started to worry that he would strain his neck trying to reach it from all the way down there, so I finally relented and lowered my pussy very delicately towards his mouth. I mean, he didn't seem to mind, so who was I to object? Momentarily I was too busy enjoying eating and being eaten to fret over it anymore, and by the time I finished, I had also forgotten that we were in a public parking lot and I think I yelled loud enough to be heard halfway to downtown. He let himself go shortly after I did, and in the sudden silence that followed, I overheard a dessicated elderly woman's voice tittering, "It was a bloodcurdling scream, truly it was. Could you send a squad car right away?"

After that we gave in and rented a sublet near the University. Apparently the poor kid had finally told his parents he was flunking out, and was going home halfway through a six-month lease. It was perfect, Michael and I agreed. Three months was plenty of time. After that, we could end it with no regrets.

The apartment was small, but suitable for our purposes. It was a fairly standard starter apartment – the living room was minimal, the bath fixtures were cracked and broken, and the kitchenette barely had room for my coffeepot, but the bedroom was large and sunny and featured a big bay window, which I dearly loved. The student had left behind most of his furniture, so we didn't have to buy much to furnish the place, although I did pick up some towels and washcloths and sheets and a thick comforter for the bed to get us through the winter. I didn't explain to Michael why I bought everything in the purest white.

The building was full of college students who were still passing, and on the rare occasions we spent the night there they would keep us up with their loud music, which was incredibly annoying, or their quiet fucking, which was slightly less so. You wouldn't hear even a whisper of a voice, not the rumble of a laugh or the tone of a word spoken, just the timid squeak, squeak, of an innerspring mattress, or maybe the slightly bolder thump, thump, of a headboard on a wall, and the sound would be faint but regular, and then it would get faster and faster and then stop suddenly and the silence would again be complete, and that's how you knew someone had been fucking nearby. "Amateurs!" we sneered. Sometimes I wondered if they ever heard us fucking and what they thought about those old folks in 201 who even did it in the daytime!

The nicest thing about this place was that it was the corner apartment on the second floor on the rear side of a two-story building and there was no other building behind it, so we could walk around naked or screw with the curtains open with relative impunity. Since our neighbors were all half our age, there wasn't much chance that anyone would see us there who shouldn't. This was fortunate because outside the apartment, we devoted a substantial amount of time to avoiding being seen. The University quarter was pretty far from where either of us lived or worked, but you never knew what might bring someone you knew down there, and then you'd have to come up with a plausible reason why you were there yourself. I worried mostly about getting caught physically entering the building, because how the hell would I ever explain that? It seemed unlikely that I could have a client there, although I supposed that would do for an excuse in a pinch. Still, I always made the turn into the parking lot at record speed, and I took to wearing a hat and scarf to hide my face, although those were garments I normally shunned in all but the bitterest weather. It was worse for Michael because with that crimson mane and chest-length beard he was much more recognizable, even at a distance, and, especially since he'd been promoted to Head Brewer a couple of months before, he was also better known. But I joked that it was no problem for him because people would simply assume he was doing some college girl and would be impressed. Doing some forty-one-year-old, now, that was just bizarre. No one would believe it even if he told them the truth.

On the other hand, in a way the sneaking around sometimes made it even more fun, like we were teenagers trying to get away with something, and I relished the sensation of youthfulness that imparted to me. Again it struck me that life really had come full circle. In the early years of my womanhood, I'd lost control of my hormones and snuck out of the house to see my boyfriends. And now at the end of my child-bearing years, it was the same thing all over again. Maybe that was how it worked – at each transition your passion overflowed the confines of your life and body, because at the first, love and sex were novel and enchanting, and at the last, they were again, because you knew you would never experience them again in the manner of a young person.

My heart was light that winter, light as the snow that dusted the trees outside our window and Michael's beard when he came to me during a storm. His lips would be cold and his hair would be frosted and I'd make a fuss over how he needed to get directly into bed to warm up. I'd strip off his wet clothes and snuggle him hard and close until our temperatures had equalized, and then he'd unwrap me from the warm fluffy robe I'd bought specially for the apartment and fuck me in a way that always felt fresh and pure as the newfallen snow. Since my work hours were flexible and his were erratic, we met randomly, two or three, maybe four times a week, sometimes at lunchtime and sometimes later in the day, if he was able to get off work early. But my favorite times were the early mornings. Once in a while I stayed at the apartment by myself, and since I slept later in the winter when the morning darkness lasted longer, sometimes I'd wake up to find him crawling into bed with me. We'd cuddle and do our thing, and then he'd tuck me back in under the covers and leave me with a final squeeze and a kiss on the forehead. I'd go back to sleep for a while and wake up again all cozy and warm and feeling a little bad that I got to stay in bed while he went off to work after getting up super-early in the cold and dark to come and see me. But of course I never felt guilty enough to want it otherwise. A handful of times in those three months Michael was able to get away from his family for a night – I never asked him what excuses he made – and we spent the whole night together, which was wonderful because it meant I saw him both before and after sleep and sex. Those occasions were so infrequent that it was almost a treat for me to wake up in the middle of the night during one because it meant I got to catch him sleeping. I knew it was silly, so I never told him how cute and funny he looked when he was breathing deeply, his elongated beard stirring in the breeze created by his exhalations.

You might think from the way I'm talking about Michael that I'd fallen in love with him, but I hadn't. It's true, I'd been almost half in love with him from the day we met, but the fraction was only slightly higher now, and I didn't foresee anything occurring that would permanently tip the scales in his favor. I was completely enamored of him, obsessed and fascinated by every aspect of his being, but I wasn't foolish enough to believe that he should be my mate. Tom was my sweetie, and no matter what happened outside our home, I never forgot that. I didn't try to justify my going back to Michael. There was no justification for it and I knew it. It was wrong, pure and simple. I just didn't care enough to want to stop it. I couldn't. Knowing that there was no future in it didn't keep me from wanting him. I wanted him even knowing that having him might destroy the future I did have, had planned to have, with Tom.

It wasn't as easy as it sounds, splitting my affections that way. I'd thought that if I ever slipped in the adultery department, that I wouldn't be able to deceive my boyfriend about it. But here we were, and somehow I did it. I'd be surprised if I did a good job – I'm really not much of a liar – but if Tom ever suspected anything, he didn't mention it. Ironically, the sex was the hardest part. Imagine being with one man at seven o'clock in the evening, and getting into bed with another a few hours later. Maybe that doesn't faze you if you've already given up on one of them, but sleeping with the one you don't love and not with the one you do simply doesn't work over an extended period. So at first it felt… well, to use the technical term, icky. I couldn't be with Tom in that way if I'd just been with Michael, and vice versa. This wasn't like a fantasy in which I could have had two strange men in a row or at the same time or along with numerous other people and still found it perfectly palatable. These were real people, people I cared about, and I couldn't overlook that entirely. And, to be blunt, although I've always found the idea of being fondled by two men simultaneously incredibly appealing, I absolutely could not put those particular two together in my mind in that way. Perhaps inevitably, the idea popped into my head one day early on while I was jerking off and even then, at the height of my filthiest thinking, it turned my stomach. Feelings, they always get in the way of treating people like sex objects!

It would have been easier if Tom and I simply weren't sleeping together anymore. But I still loved him, he was still hot, and you'll probably think it makes me a terrible slut, but I still wanted to fuck him, too. Okay, maybe I was more intensely interested in fucking Michael for the present, but that certainly didn't mean I'd stopped being attracted to Tom. After a while it became clear to me that my tolerance for switching partners was largely dependent on the passage of a particular length of time. If I'd been with Michael in the evening, I was not going to be sleeping with Tom that night. If I was going to see Michael at noon, I knew I'd better not fool around with Tom in the morning, because that would be too close for my sexual comfort. But if Tom and I fucked in the evening and I saw Michael the following afternoon with a night of sleeping in between, that became acceptable to me. I couldn't rationalize my own stance on this, myself. I'm not sure it was rational. Perhaps it had something to do with the smell of one being off me before I moved on to the other.

I don't mean to suggest with all the ongoing sex talk that everything was peachy-keen between Tom and me again. Our attitudes towards one another had perceptibly changed since Lakeside, and even though we were theoretically back on solid ground, I think we both sensed that something was still a little off. Before Michael, I would have talked to him about it. With Michael in the picture, I simply did not want to bring it into the open; it would have drawn attention to too many things I didn't want to discuss. You could argue that technically I hadn't done anything wrong. I'd declared my intentions to Tom after the incident and he'd accepted my conditions for us staying together. But that was nearly half a year ago now, and in my months of infidelity I had surely been more than compensated for his one five-minute make-out session with someone else. I still wouldn't say I felt guilty about it, but I started to think that maybe I should.

But soon it would be irrelevant, because two months had passed in less time than it took me to count them, and the final one was gone before I even flipped the page on my calendar, and suddenly we had to be out of the apartment in a week. I couldn't believe it. I avoided mentioning it to Michael, but finally I knew I had to because moving day was hastening toward us like a pack of puppies after a stinky pile of freshly worn shoes. I guess he must have been aware of it, too, though, because he made a point of arranging a meeting every day that final week.

"I'm almost done with the cleaning," I announced when he arrived on the next-to-last day, wrenching off my rubber gloves. We'd spent so little time there that there wasn't much to do, just mopping and vacuuming and scrubbing the tub and toilet. "But I don't know what to do with the linens." Somehow the idea of bringing them home wasn't very appealing. How could I ever use them there?

He leaned in the bathroom doorway and looked contemplative for a moment, his beard wagging slightly as he nodded in thought. "Don't you have someplace you could store them? I mean, they might be useful to have someday."

"The comforter's the big problem; it's huge folded." I had no spare bed to lay it on, and although we had plenty of space at home, it would be hard to hide a heretofore unseen, enormous and gleaming white bedcover. But my logistical difficulties began to fade in importance in Michael's palpable presence. I finished washing and drying my hands and went over to him with arms outstretched. He circled his arms around my waist, pulled me close and held me tightly.

"Michael?" I proffered tentatively, raising my face from where it lay buried in his shoulder.

"What is it, Kate?" he answered, brushing his scruffy cheek against mine as he turned kind eyes toward me.

"Are we done yet?"

He didn't answer, just stood there silently embracing me for a long while. Finally he said, "Come here," and led me into the bedroom and drew me up onto the bed after him. We lay close together, facing each other, arms and legs intertwined. His hair looked especially red against the white of the pillowcase that day, and it struck me how attached I'd grown to that color combination.

"This was what we said, right? Three months and that was it?" He had reached up with one hand and was gently stroking my hair.

"That's what we said." Damn, I thought. He was ready to go. I wasn't.

"We can't go on like this forever."

"No, I suppose not."

He was really going to let it end, then. I felt the threat of tears coming on, and I pulled closer to him so I could hide my face against his chest. I tried desperately to think of something else. His beard was tickling my cheek, and I gathered it up with my free hand and tugged it gently. That was all I had to hold him by, one wispy handful of hair and when I released it he'd be gone. The lump in my throat grew bigger and I swallowed forcefully. I would not cry. I fought it hard. He was kind enough not to say anything else so I didn't have to talk and I guess eventually I must have fallen asleep because the next thing I knew he was waking me and saying he had to go. We hadn't even had sex.

"When are you meeting the landlord tomorrow?" he wanted to know.

"At ten."

"Do you want me to help you with the towels and bedding and stuff?"

"Nah," I said. "I'll wash everything before I leave."

"Okay."

He paused and made a face as if he was about to deliver a speech and I didn't think I could stand that so I cut him off abruptly, saying, "Let's not make a big thing, okay?"

He nodded.

A kiss, a hug, and he was gone again.

I hated saying goodbye to that guy.

I hated him, too, for making me.

I stayed up late. I stripped the bed and washed the sheets and towels and cleaned the floors and still had energy left over so I decided to wash the windows, too. When that was done, I noticed that the shelves were dusty so I went after them with a damp cloth, and if I was doing shelving, I figured I ought to be thorough and wipe down the crown molding as well. The refrigerator wasn't very dirty, but I gave it a once-over anyway, and I scrubbed the kitchen sink, and then broke out the furniture polish and shined up the coffee table, desk, and dresser the student had left behind although they would probably get parked out by the dumpster come morning. While I was cleaning, I turned the radio up loud enough to force the downstairs neighbors to bang on the ceiling until I lowered the volume, and I drank the last several beers he had left me and tried not to think about who had brought them. It was after one o'clock when I finally dropped, fully dressed, onto the bed, exhausted. Since the sheets were already clean and folded, I simply kicked off my shoes and wrapped myself up in that snow-white comforter, and the only thing I recall thinking before I passed out was that maybe I should keep the comforter in the trunk of my car for emergencies because it didn't matter anymore if it got dirty.

I awoke around four, my mouth tasting strongly of stale beer. Snow was falling outside the undraped bedroom window. The sky was that murky orange it gets when it's packed with snow clouds, but for once I didn't think that was neat; it made me feel cold and lonely. Tomorrow night I would be with Tom, and knowing that lifted my spirits slightly. I didn't really need Michael, after all. I had a perfectly satisfactory life without him. Maybe it would be duller, emptier now. It was even possible that I was less sad about losing him than I was about not being able to look forward to seeing him again. That and the fucking. I would definitely miss the fucking. I thought back to the first night we'd spent together, and I couldn't help it, soon I found myself reaching down into my underwear and between my legs. I hadn't masturbated in quite a while. Somehow I'd gotten it into my head that it was more fun to conserve my sexual energy when I was obliged to share so much of it these days. But I supposed I would be keeping more of it to myself now and should stay in practice. It felt pretty good – not as good as Michael – but before I got very far along, I had drifted back into sleep.

When I woke again it was quite late, nearly half past eight. I was still facing the window and I could see that although the snow had stopped, the sky remained heavy with clouds, which imbued the air with a dusky quality. And on my other side, Michael was crawling into bed with me. I rolled over to face him.

"You smell like beer," he commented.

"I decided that drinking it was the easiest way to move it." I looked at him hard. What was he doing here?

"What are you doing here?" I said. I'd wanted to phrase it a little more gently, but I was still groggy, and that was the best I could do.

"What do you think about trying to find another sublet?" he proposed, his eyes bright. I heard the words, but my brain wasn't absorbing their meaning. "A few more months would be nice, don't you think?"

I didn't answer. I didn't know what to say.

He faded a little. "You don't want to."

And then I finally understood what was happening, and I burst into a huge grin and cried out, "Yes, yes! I want, I want!" I might have gone on like that for some time, but he smothered my mouth with his and dug me out of the wrinkled clothes I had slept in and fucked me extra, extra good like I really deserved it. And then it was almost time to meet the landlord and I shooed him off to work so I could get ready. As I was bundling up the comforter I detected wetness and noted that there were fresh sex-juice drippings on it, and I found that charmingly obscene. And when I got home after work and looked in the mirror I discovered two new smile lines on my face and realized that I must have had a very, very good day.

CHAPTER 9

Finding a new place wasn't as simple as it sounded, though. The ones I saw advertised were all either too expensive or too close to where one of us lived or worked. And then tax season was in full swing, and I had no more time to spend searching for apartments. Michael kept trying, but he had no more luck than I'd had.

It was just as well, I thought as I headed home at nine-thirty at night. It was too late for me to see him now even if we had someplace to go, just as it had been the night before and would be again the following night. In the mornings I went to the office early, and even if he'd been able to come and see me on the weekend, I usually had to work straight through anyway. He sent me a message the first week of March wanting to know if we could just get together for a beer, but I had client meetings that evening and couldn't get away. By then it had already been more than a month since we'd seen each other. I didn't hear from him again during the weeks that followed, and I was so overwhelmed that I confess I made no effort to contact him, either. Then finally, finally, it came, the tax practitioner's most sacred and blessed day, April the sixteenth. Just minutes before I'd still been transmitting files, but now it was after midnight and everything had been sent that was going to get sent and the extensions were done and I could be human again.

I drove home and crawled into bed. Tom was sleeping soundly. Normally he waited up for me and we had a beer together before going to sleep, but I'd forewarned him that I'd be extra late that night. I didn't care. I slept, too. In the morning when I rose, I felt twenty years younger and twenty pounds lighter, as if someone had finally brought in that pack mule I'd been asking for to help carry some of my burden. Then I consulted my list of daily chores and discovered I was six weeks behind. I groaned. I hadn't even done a load of laundry all week, and it was overflowing the hampers. I tackled that as soon as breakfast was over. Unfortunately, there was already a stiff wet load sitting in the washer. I couldn't even guess how long it had been there, so I ran it through again while I read my personal email, which I had also neglected for some time. When the washer buzzed, I moved its contents over to the dryer and filled it up again. Then I went back to the computer and finished sorting through my pages of messages. By the time that was done, my first load was ready to come out of the dryer, so I moved the next one in and started the whole cycle over again from the remaining pile of clothes.

While I was folding, I took a stab at planning the rest of my day. I knew I'd pay dearly for it tomorrow if I didn't go to work at all today, but maybe I could see him afterwards. It was already after nine now, and he would likely be at work himself. I wanted more than anything to haul my ass down there right then and make him do me in his office, but that wasn't advisable if we were trying to keep things quiet, so instead I sent him a message that read "How soon can I see you?"

One, two, three hours passed and I got no answer. I went to work and kept busy organizing the piles of miscellaneous garbage that had sprung up like shantytowns around my office over the last couple of months. But as the hours ticked by, there was still no word from Michael, and I began to get panicky. What if I had waited too long? What if he had given up on me all together and was with someone else now? What if something terrible had happened to him and I didn't even know about it because I'd been out of touch for so long? By the time five o'clock rolled around, I was in such a state that I was reconsidering going down to the brewery after all.

At a quarter past six, I finally got my answer. It consisted of an address and three words: "Whenever you're ready." I didn't even pause to look up directions; I knew where that street was and I was sure I could find it. I was moderately surprised that he hadn't told me he'd found something. We'd had such a difficult time of it that we'd agreed that it would be okay to grab a good place if one came along without waiting for the other to approve, but it seemed strange that he hadn't even mentioned it to me. If nothing else, I should have put up my share. It was easier for me because I kept my finances totally separate from Tom's. Since I paid his bills, he didn't have a bank or credit card transaction that I didn't know about, yet, for his part, he had no idea how much money I had or how I spent it, nor, I assumed, did he much care. But Michael's wife would surely notice if hundreds of dollars went missing all at once without any explanation. I wondered how he'd covered it.

But as I neared the address I'd been given, I expelled those thoughts from my mind. I could ask about that later. Right now all that mattered was being with him. I needed that very, very badly. I'd been so busy I hadn't realized how much the months of stress and waiting had really gotten to me and I was anxious for it to be over. And now that I was free, most compelling was my overpowering need to be fucked by him.

Yes, fucking Michael was something else. I truly got a thrill out of the way he did me. Part of that, I'm sure, was because sex with him was still a novelty; probably being with anyone new would have been exciting in some way, at least at first. But there was no doubt in my mind that even without that, he was one of the best lovers I'd ever had. I never have orgasms during intercourse. There have been a few times when I thought, well, maybe, but I've never actually been able to bring it off. I've also never appreciated being made to feel like a failure on that account. I mean, if I'm already suffering because of it, do I need to be made to feel bad on top of that? It's not as if it's my fault. I stay in shape. I do my Kegels. God knows I'm not a prude in any respect. But I can't change the way my body functions, and for whatever reason it simply doesn't do that. And I'm sure I'm not the only woman on earth who's like that. I am perfectly capable of having an orgasm, but I require supplemental manual or oral stimulation to make it happen and I've never felt comfortable having to prompt someone into doing that. If the man doesn't volunteer, I feel as if I'm asking him to perform some chore just when he's ready to go to sleep and that seems selfish. Or, if he only does it because I asked, I'm aware that it's a chore for him, and then it's hard for me to just relax and enjoy it and I won't finish anyway. Even worse, if you ask a couple of times and are refused, it becomes too embarrassing even to mention again.

And to me it never seemed like this was a job I should have to have approved by a committee in order to get it done. If the garbage is full, you take it out; if you dirty dishes, you wash them; if you've gotten yours, give her hers, too. Yet in most of my relationships, I'd had to do all of the chores, and that was a sore spot sometimes. The men who'd made me feel like pleasing me was too much work to bother with because I couldn't finish like they did made me reluctant to even broach the subject with anyone new. I'm sure there were boys who would have been delighted to give me what I needed if I'd only told them what that was. Take care how you treat your partner. I'd spent much of my adulthood being not-quite-satisfied because a handful of otherwise perfectly nice, hardworking fellows had been too lazy to take a few minutes to bring me home, and too self-centered to realize how that would permanently affect my ability to relate to men.

Of course, this had changed some as I'd gotten older and bolder. I was still much more comfortable doing sex than talking about it, but with the right person and in the right mood I could sometimes say I like this, or would you please do that, or may I have just a few moments of undivided attention so I can get to where you're at. What was rare and wonderful about Michael was that with him I didn't have to ask. It wasn't every time, of course, because who has time for that, and even with him I couldn't always pull it off. But it was regular, and more important was his attitude about it. He never made me feel like finishing me off when he was already done was a chore. To him, I don't think it was. It was maybe more a normal part of his routine. Routine sounds bad, I know, but it's precisely what I mean. It just went with the territory for him. He saw dirt on the floor and rather than waiting for someone else to come along and clean it up he got out the broom and the dustpan and did it himself. I absolutely always enjoy fucking and being fucked, and having an orgasm was secondary to that. The clitoris is a wonderful invention, but it's not a substitute for the high-quality relief you get all over from deep-down penetration. But with Michael I got plenty of both types of stimulation, and although that wasn't why I liked him, it sure didn't hurt.

But at this rate I was never going to get any kind of stimulation, because I couldn't find the right address. Fuck, I thought, Fuck, fuck, fuck, I must be in the wrong part of town. There were no apartment buildings here, only hotels. I passed a number that came after the one I was seeking, so I swung a U-turn and retraced my path so slowly that the traffic in my lane screeched to a loud and angry halt behind me. Cars were honking and their drivers were swearing as they swerved around me, but I paid them no attention because I'd finally found it. From this side it was easier to spot because the street number of the property was posted in small digits on a sign by the road. It was a hotel after all. It was set back from the road a ways at the end of a long driveway, so you wouldn't see it unless you knew it was there. There was a liveried valet out front but I averted my eyes from his come-hither stare, passed him by, and drove my car straight to the parking area in the rear of the building.

It wasn't a large hotel, maybe five stories, but it looked really nice from the outside. Maybe too nice, I thought as I approached the entrance, examining the heavily ornamented façade and the multi-colored rosebushes that lined the walkway. A pale-faced doorman parted the etched glass panels for me, and once I was inside, a bellhop in a scarlet uniform with golden fringed epaulets appeared as if from behind a magic curtain and then vanished with equal alacrity, disappointed in being unable to carry my bags because I had none. I crossed the lobby and marveled at the posh upholstered furniture, the marble floors and columns, and the giant sculptured stone fountain that guarded the space beneath an equally gigantic crystal chandelier. I felt hopelessly underdressed in my cheapest business suit; this setting demanded an evening gown. As the elevator operator escorted me up to the fifth floor, I thought, This place is surely out of our price range, and I wondered how many of the tax returns I'd worn myself thin preparing would have to contribute to covering my half.

When I reached 502 I knocked and heard a masculine voice respond, "Come in!" Just as I was pondering how to do that without a key, I observed to my surprise that the door sported an old-fashioned keyhole drilled into a metal plate rather than a magnetic card reader. It was obviously unlocked from the inside, because it opened at my touch, and I entered what seemed to be a full suite of rooms. I was standing in what appeared to be the main room, which was in itself larger than any hotel room I'd ever occupied, and in addition there were three other doors leading out of it. Thick drapes lined the wood-sashed windows, deep pile carpet cushioned my heels, and a gas fireplace opposite me crackled merrily with glowing orange heat and light. Michael was nowhere in sight, and I seriously considered the possibility that I was in the wrong place. I didn't have any idea how much money he or his wife made, but with three underage kids and a mortgage, I was sure it wasn't enough to support this kind of lifestyle, even for one night. I drew out my phone and double-checked the address. This was definitely what he had told me.

I decided that maybe I should just look around very quietly first, so I didn't call out to him, but tiptoed over to the first door and peeked inside. It was a combination kitchen area and bar, fully stocked with bottles of liquor that were too expensive for me to buy even at my local liquor store, let alone at some hotel's marked-up rate. And not a beer in sight, which didn't bode well for my finding Michael anywhere nearby. But lacking proof, I stroked my chest softly in an effort to calm my erratically thumping heart, pretended I was a high-society cat burglar, and padded my way noiselessly towards the next door. It opened onto a bedroom that surpassed the size of our last apartment, the bed tucked away under a satiny canopy and framed by what looked like mahogany head and foot boards. A larger door led off of that, presumably into a walk-in closet. I returned to the main room and inspected the final door, which was sealed shut. I gulped, then took hold of the handle and swung it open as cautiously as if I expected to encounter a family of rabid skunks on the other side.

I'd found Michael at last. He was reclining in a jade-colored hot tub big enough for three or four people. On the granite countertop beside it stood a crystal ice bucket with four twenty-twos of his brewery's beer in it. Underneath his head sat some kind of plastic-wrapped bath pillow and he was lying quietly with his eyes closed. Although I could have sworn he'd yelled to me to come in just a few minutes before, now I wondered if he'd fallen asleep while I'd been investigating the suite. It made a funny picture. He'd never struck me as a relaxing-in-the-tub kind of guy.

"Michael!" I whispered, but bubbles were burbling softly up all around him, and I wasn't sure if he'd have heard me even if he was awake. So I quietly sidled my way over to the ice bucket, pulled out a handy opener from a notch in its side, and cracked open a bottle. His eyes popped open instantly.

"Aha!" he cried. "Caught you, beer thief!"

"What are you going to do about it, wet naked boy?" I retorted.

He responded by splashing soapy water at me. "Hey, watch it!" I yelled. "Can't you see I'm trying to drink a beer here?"

He splashed some more and I set the bottle down on the floor, walked around the tub behind him and splashed him back, full in the face.

"I'll teach you!" He lurched up onto his knees, turned sideways, grabbed me under both arms and dragged me, fully clothed, into the tub. My hair was half-wet, my skirt and jacket were billowing and floating about me, and water was dripping from my lips from where it had crashed up into my face when I'd landed. Fortunately, my suit was wash and wear. I glared at him.

"Happy end of tax season?!" he suggested.

"I'll give you end-of-tax-season!" I repeated nonsensically, scrambling over to board his naked body with my soggily attired one, and slapping his chest with my soaked sleeve.

"Really, you'll feel so much better once you get out of these wet clothes," he assured me as he untucked my shirttails. I permitted him to yank my blouse off over my head, but when he reached for my bra, I leaned haughtily away from him.

"I don't think so," I scoffed.

"You don't want to celebrate?" he said, instead reaching down for my skirt and forcing it in one motion almost up to my waist.

"I have my beer," I answered, entwining my legs around his and squeezing tightly.

"Yahhh!" he yelled. I pressed harder.

"Fine then," he said sulkily. "If that's the way you feel, then why don't you just go home?"

"Okay, I will," I replied. I stood up carefully, turning slightly and extending my posterior so I could be sure he had a good view of my naked ass poised above my thigh-highs while I did so. He reached out and smacked it, hard.

Something must have shown in my face, because he spanked me again, harder, sending a spray of water droplets flying off my bare skin. I moaned a little in spite of myself.

"You like that?" he said, his eyes crinkling like he was amused.

"Um, I don't know," I answered, shrugging with apparent indifference, and feeling myself blushing as I did so.

"You do like that!" he exclaimed, slapping my ass again while I spluttered something incoherent in response.

I felt a hand tugging at my wrist, and abruptly he got up, sat down on the flat edge of the tub, and plunked me face down on his lap, my belly flat across his knees, my oversized butt gloriously exposed to the steamy, open air. He whacked me again, and a peculiar, tense, excited feeling began to radiate in both directions between my ass cheeks and my loins.

I turned to look up at his face and he said playfully, "Have you been very bad?"

"Oh, god, yes," I answered, and he spanked my ass over and over, each blow rapidly succeeding the last, until I could feel the heat rising all over my cheeks and running through the rest of my body and I yelled because it hurt oh so good and as long as no one called the cops I didn't care if the neighbors heard or what they might think was going on in here.

Finally he released me, but not for long, because he pushed me up against the side of the tub on my knees, my arms hanging over its edge, my stinging bottom facing him above the level of the water. He pulled back on my hips so that my hindquarters formed a tall tight frame around my vagina, which was twitching tensely in anticipation of the cock that was about to be inserted. Yet the cock was withheld, and I wiggled my butt in what I hoped was a friendly, inviting fashion while the water swished in waves around me. But still the cock did not come, and I looked back and saw that Michael was leaning over the edge of the tub reaching for something.

"You're looking a bit red in the fanny," he said, and before I could protest he had grabbed some body lotion and was rubbing it in slow circles over every inch of my ass in a way that was so erotic I thought I was going to lose my shit right then.

Then I felt his hands grasping my cheeks and spreading them apart so that my pussy opened up and finally it came, the eagerly awaited cock. He teased me, giving it to me with agonizing slowness, and when I attempted to speed things up by rocking back into it, he thwarted my efforts by placing his hands firmly around my waist and across my back and gently forcing me back into my assigned and rather helpless position. He was definitely in charge today.

He leaned forward and cupped my breasts in his hands and I felt the angle of his still-stroking penis inside me change and intensify and it was almost too much, too much cock for my poor little pussy. I guess he felt it, too, or heard it in my moans, because after a moment he leaned back again, then grabbed my cheeks and began pounding me so forcefully and fast that the water was splashing all around us and I could feel his balls slapping hard against my genitals with every thrust. He was grunting loudly and so was I and then he came and we relaxed and I lowered my pelvis back down into the comfortably warm water for a while, and enjoyed the bubbles nudging their way up through my pubic hairs from a jet right below us while his penis gradually softened and finally fell out of me.

It wasn't until we got out of the tub that we noticed the box of condoms he'd had the foresight to stash away on a shelf built for drinks alongside the Jacuzzi. And then I felt something warm and gooey oozing down my thigh, and then I smelled it and boy did it smell good, but the fact that I could smell it was bad, very, very bad.

"Whoops," I whispered.

"Yeah," he agreed. He looked thoughtful, and I wondered what he was thinking, but I didn't dare to ask.

"Well," I continued evenly, "Nothing we can do about it now. No sense in letting it ruin the rest of the evening."

"Right," he said, gathering me up in a fluffy white towel and turning me about to buff my back and legs dry.

"Really the amazing thing is that it's never happened before," I said. I had a knot in my stomach and I hoped that talking about it might make it go away.

"Uh-huh," was his telling reply. Well, at least that was two syllables.

"I'm sure there's nothing to worry about, anyway," I resumed. Perhaps I thought saying it might make it so.

He brought me about to face him again and kissed me on the mouth. "If only you were a little older!" he said.

I laughed wholeheartedly. "Michael, that is probably the nicest thing anyone's ever said to me!"

He spent the night and I was grateful for that. I'd already texted Tom an excuse about working late again and I didn't feel like going home to him anyway. I didn't want to be alone because I didn't want to think, but when I woke in the wee hours as I nearly always did, I couldn't help thinking about it; I had nothing else to do.

I was forty-two now. My biological clock was no longer ticking, it was winding down. I knew this for a fact because my menstrual cycle had changed to the extent that there was really no question about it anymore. I hadn't missed any periods yet, but in the last couple of years they'd gotten shorter and closer together. My always-quick three day period every four weeks had become a two-day period every three weeks. At first I'd thought it was my imagination. They seemed to be coming around so fast that I'd barely finish one before I had those premenstrual munchies again. So I'd finally started tracking the timing and duration and sure enough, it was real. I didn't know exactly how the biology worked on this, but I personally suspected that it was my body's stealthy way of giving me extra chances at ovulation in case I changed my mind about making babies before it was too late. I hadn't, but now here we were and I couldn't help considering the possibility, however slim the odds were.

What would I do? I'd asked myself that question every time in my life I'd had a scare because I was late or had lost a condom mid-stream, but had never come up with a satisfactory answer. And with Tom it had stopped being an issue because he'd had a vasectomy several years before. So if I was knocked up and decided to keep the baby, that would certainly be the end of him and me. He'd know damn well it wasn't his, and even if he was willing to accept that, I couldn't imagine that he'd be willing to take on the responsibility of raising someone else's child with me, especially when he didn't want kids either. On the other hand, I had a hard time picturing myself having a baby and then giving it up for someone else to raise. I didn't know if I'd ever be able to forget that this piece of me was wandering around somewhere and that I'd neglected my duty to it. As to the final option, although I wasn't opposed to abortion in principle, I wasn't sure I could stomach having one myself. I got a funny feeling in my guts whenever I thought about getting rid of an unwanted child like it was a pest and not a kid. My kid. I'd think you'd get attached to the little bugger lounging around inside you pretty quickly. I wondered how long it took to forget something like that. I'd always hoped I would never have to know.

And, of course, if I were pregnant, this was probably my last chance at doing the whole offspring thing. Would I take getting knocked up as a sign that I should have a baby? I didn't believe in signs, of course, but it would be tempting to view such a happenstance as a final opportunity to do one of the big things in life I was never going to do otherwise. I'd always wondered if one day after it was too late I'd wake up and be sorry I hadn't had children. That day had not yet come, and I was pretty confident now that my opinion on the subject was not going to change.

What would Michael want? I wondered. He already had a wife and family, and even if he hardly ever spoke of them when he was with me, I knew he valued that tremendously. Would he want another child, especially one who had to be kept secret from its near relations, and which would be raised in seclusion by some "other" woman? It seemed unlikely. But you never knew. Maybe he'd be as crazy about and committed to our child as his other children. Maybe he'd even be the one who'd be adamant about keeping it, if it existed. For that matter, I didn't know what his stance on abortion even was. Come to think of it, there was an awful lot I didn't know about Michael.

I rotated my chest in his direction and leant up on my elbow to look at him. He immediately rolled over onto his other side, almost as if he knew I was looking and didn't feel like being stared at just then. So I scrutinized the broad back bent toward me and felt amused by the irony of the position he'd assumed just as I was pondering how little I knew him. I knew the main facts. I knew where he'd grown up and gone to school and what jobs he'd had before his current one. I understood his sense of humor and his commitment to his career and his biggest pet peeves. But I didn't know how long he'd been married or what his children were like, and worse, I didn't know how to ask him about those kinds of things without discomfiting him. I didn't know what kind of relationship he had with his parents or whether he was jealous of his older brother or if he'd ever secretly wanted to be a rock star, and again, those questions seemed out of place in a relationship like ours. I didn't know the first thing about his religion or politics and I supposed he didn't know that I had neither. For that matter, we'd never even talked about "us" like new couples usually do. I don't mean those unendurable conversations you're supposed to have about your feelings; I mean the silly things like, when did you first notice me, and what made you decide to ask me out, and what were you thinking about on our fifth date?

And for me, too, there were huge parts of my life that I purposely excluded from my conversations with him. I would never have mentioned, for instance, perimenopause or its symptoms, not because I didn't think he could handle it, but because I never wanted him to think of me as aging. It was different with Tom; he had signed on to grow old with me. Michael and I, we were temporary, had to be; it was the very nature of the beast, and maybe that prevented us from taking each other too seriously as mates no matter how good a time we had together or how much we fucked.

The connection I thought Michael and I had when we first met, it wasn't grounded in any kind of reality of life or living. I didn't believe in the concept of a soulmate, but even if I had, I wouldn't have thought he was mine. I believed that inside we were very much alike, but it was more that I felt we were cut from the same cloth, if you will, than that we were meant to be together. Who wanted to be with someone just like themselves? That was bound to get old. Through all that had happened, I still thought of Tom as my sweetie for life. It may be hard to understand how I could think of him that way even as I was studying the other man I was lying in bed with, but that's how it was. I couldn't imagine anyone better suited to spending the remainder of my years with me. We may have had superficial, day-to-day things in common, but on the inside we were very different people, and that's what kept it interesting. I liked Michael, I liked him very much, but once the sex died, as it inevitably must, I wasn't sure there would be much left for us in being together. While I looked at him, I'd unknowingly drawn my chest up against his back and was resting one hand on his butt while he slept. Even now, I had no control over my desire to be near him. But it wasn't love, it wasn't meant to be forever, and it certainly wasn't the kind of relationship in which a child would be a welcome addition.

The light from a streetlamp trickled in through the bed and window curtains I'd intentionally drawn and I watched it for a while before I finally felt myself drifting off again. My troubled thoughts expunged, my dreams were benign and I slept straight through until morning.

CHAPTER 10

His side of the bed was vacant when I awoke, and I was alarmed. It was rare for me to wake up in an empty bed; I was always first to get up. But then I heard a flush and Michael came out of the bathroom and crawled back in under the covers in refuge from the still-chilly early spring air. I wrapped my arms and legs tightly around him until we were both warm again, and then I felt his hardening cock burrowing into my bare pussy and I thought of the night before.

He must have been thinking of it, too, because he angled his pelvis away from mine. "We don't want another accident," he said. His face tensed up like he was preparing to say something else, and I waited, but when nothing more came, I plunged ahead.

"What made you change your mind about me?" I blurted out. I don't know why that was the question I started with, but there it was.

"What?"

"What made you change your mind about me?" I repeated.

"About you how?" He was clearly confused and I supposed I couldn't blame him; of course he didn't know what I was talking about.

"About being with me, I mean? You know, that day at the festival I didn't think there was any chance it could happen."

"Oh," he said, obviously still surprised by the question. "Well, I took your advice. I talked to my wife."

"Oh!"

"You sort of guessed it right. She's a few years older than me, you know, and I guess when her, you know, system, uh, started to change, her interest in sex just dried up. It stopped being fun, and after a while she just didn't want to bother anymore. I guess she experimented with hormonal remedies but they had unpleasant side effects so she finally gave up."

"Oh!" I said again. I thought about it for a moment. "But you still seem to be interested in sex," I said, nuzzling him gently. "How were you supposed to remain celibate for the next thirty or forty years?"

"Well, once I brought it up it turned out she didn't expect me to. She'd never said anything because she wasn't comfortable talking about it, any more than I was, I guess. But she said she still wanted to be with me, wanted to keep our family together, but if I – how did she put it – if I wanted to take a lover she would understand. She said she just wanted me to come home at night and never wanted to know about it," he finished.

"So what do you tell her when you do stay over?" I was hoping his excuses were less flimsy than mine.

"Beer festivals and competitions, mostly. There are a lot of them."

"Huh," I said.

"Huh what?"

"I can't believe I didn't know all of that."

He shifted a little. "We haven't really spent much time talking, I guess." He grinned shyly as he said it.

I smiled, too. "We've been having other kinds of fun." I tugged gently on his beard. "I'm glad to know now, though. I've always felt very guilty about them. I mean, your wife and family."

"Really?"

"Yeah. Even before – you know – I hoped I would never meet her. I always felt terrible about having dirty thoughts about her husband."

"Interesting," he said, furrowing his brow as if it really was interesting and he intended to reflect on it further. He paused. "What about Tom? Or has he been…was that day at the festival the only time he…?"

I broke in, "As far as I know it was. I got him back in an extreme way, I guess." I shook my head guiltily. "He really is a good guy, you know? I'm the bad one."

"You feel bad about – about this?"

"When I'm with you, no, not at all. Not so much when I'm with him either, really. It's when I'm alone that it gets to me."

I didn't feel like talking about that anymore, and my body was too warm now to take the heat of his naked skin against mine, so I rolled back over onto my side of the bed. There was a sparrow on the windowsill and I watched it flit about in a seemingly random way. I was sure it must have some purpose, but whatever it was, was lost on me.

I changed the subject. "What do I owe you?" I asked him.

"For what?"

"This, all this," I said.

"Are you paying me for sex now? Because I could really use the money…"

I elbowed him in the ribs. "For the suite, silly."

"Nothing."

"Nothing?" I repeated. "Don't we always split costs?" I liked to refer to such expenses as "the costs of us doing our business."

"Called in a favor from a friend. He's a night manager here. We couldn't afford the going rate otherwise, or even half of it, for that matter. He mentioned this place a while ago so I checked it out. Thought it would do in a pinch. I had to wait all afternoon to see if they'd have a vacancy we could squat in. Do you like it?"

My eyes circled the premises. Funny how I hadn't noticed that everything in it – the sheets, the linens, the drapes, the carpet – were all crisply, cleanly white.

"It's beautiful," I replied. Maybe Michael knew me a little better than I'd thought.

"I thought you would," he said. "It reminds me of the place we stayed in our first night together. All the white . . ." he gestured.

I smiled. He actually was a pretty nice guy.

He smiled back and squeezed my hand.

"Didn't you want to get back to the office early?" he reminded me.

"I suppose so," I answered. "I've still got a pile of crap to put away."

"Then get going, lazybones!" He pushed me toward the edge of the bed and whacked me on the tush. That brought back the memory of the prior evening and I blushed and he grinned and pulled me back towards him and held me close.

"No," he said after a time, finally finishing a conversation we'd started months before, "I don't think we're done yet." And he kissed me.

After that, we gave up on the idea of a sublet and rented a regular apartment. You might be wondering why we even bothered with apartments when we could have simply stayed in motels when we wanted to get together. Well, for one thing, it was a heck of a lot more convenient having a place waiting for us when we wanted it; no scrambling around trying to figure out where to go in the event of a sudden urge. Second, it would be bad enough to be seen coming out of a strange apartment, but to be seen leaving a local motel would absolutely scream of an affair to even the most uninterested observer. And third, economically speaking, there actually wasn't that much difference between the two options. I know this isn't true everywhere, but if you stay out of the high-rent districts where we live, you can actually find a passable place for about four hundred bucks a month if you're not particular about location or quality. By contrast, even a cheap motel will run you forty bucks a night before taxes, so unless you're meeting very irregularly, it's not much more expensive to rent something semi-permanent. It felt a lot less sleazy, too, and although I knew that didn't change the reality of what we were doing, I was happier to have a set space in which to do it.

Our new place wasn't actually an apartment, though; it was an in-law cottage, a separate structure with its own bath and kitchenette in the backyard of a house in a suburb of our city. The owner was a middle-aged single guy with thinning hair and a severe limp he'd acquired in some unspecified on-the-job injury. Since his career as a carpenter had come to an untimely end, he was living on disability payments alone, and had decided to rent out the unit to supplement his income. He had originally built it for his aged mother, who had passed the previous winter.

"You seem like a nice couple," he commented approvingly when he saw us. "There've been a lot of students and young people over here looking at the place, but I don't really want parties going on back here."

"You won't have to worry about that with us," I assured him.

"Isn't it a little small for the two of you, though?" he remarked.

"We travel a lot for work," Michael answered. "We won't even be here very often; we just need a place to stop at when we're in town."

The man's eyes travelled down over Michael's hands, and then over mine. "I see how it is," he said slowly.

One with ring, one without. Hmm, maybe we weren't such a nice couple, after all.

I was about to make up an excuse to get us the hell out of there, but then he resumed talking, in only a slightly forced manner. "The rent's fixed," he said, "Includes utilities because you won't use much in a place this small and I'm not set up to track it separately anyway. No lease, but I'll need first and last up front. Cash or money order is fine if you don't want to write a check," he finished slyly.

"No putting anything over on that guy!" Michael commented as we were leaving.

"You don't suppose we're that obvious to everybody, do you?" I wondered anxiously.

"Well, maybe if you hadn't had your hand on my ass the whole time we were walking up to the door, he would have believed we were a real married couple!" he retorted.

"Har, har, har," I snorted. "Actually, I feel bad for him. Still single and now that mom's gone, he's all alone and can't even work anymore. We're probably the most exciting thing that's happened to the old guy in a long time!"

"The old guy?" said Michael, emphasizing the adjective.

"Well, not old, I guess, just older."

"I think he's about my age, actually." Michael was forty-five now.

"I don't think so," I laughed.

"No, really. While you were in the bathroom he mentioned graduating from high school in the same year I did."

That didn't seem possible. This guy was middle-aged, and Michael, well, Michael looked the same as when I'd met him what, three or four years ago now? Oh, maybe there were a few more white hairs mixed in with the red, and maybe he did occasionally make an "oomph" noise when getting out of bed, but I was the same way, and I certainly wasn't middle-aged!

When I got home, I consulted the bathroom mirror. Not the casual glance I usually gave it these days, but a line-by-line examination. I hadn't done that in a long while, and now I realized that I'd mostly stopped worrying about my aging face and body in the time I'd been with Michael. I always felt attractive when I was with him, so there was never any need to look. Or maybe I simply didn't want to know about it if there was anything I didn't want to see. But now here was my reflection staring back at me, and you know what, I looked fine. I'd started dyeing my hair a couple of years before, so that was basically the same, although I had yet to pick out the right color. Every few months I became a slightly different shade of brunette. And maybe my complexion was getting uneven, and my face was becoming dotted with odd white bumps and mysterious brown spots, but my wrinkles were not appreciably deeper. In fact, they almost seemed smoother and softer than the last time I'd scrutinized them closely. My whole face was rather soft around the edges, actually, as if the mirror was an old-time movie lens coated with Vaseline. I leaned in nearer to the glass and discovered that I couldn't quite focus. It wasn't just my face; everything was a little blurry.

Damn, I thought, my eyes are going. I frowned. I looked terrible in glasses. Plus this probably meant I actually looked much worse than I thought I did. Of course, Michael's eyes were probably failing, too. I'd noticed him squinting at the fine print on the labels on the beer he sometimes brought over. Tom had worn glasses since he was a kid so he was bound to be getting fuzzier, too. Ha, I thought. You're never too old as long as everyone else is getting old with you. That cheered me up considerably.

We moved in on the first of May. I was so excited I had to smother my face with my pillow to keep from telling Tom about it. I dug out the sheets and towels I'd tucked away in the back of a closet, and dislodged the fluffy down comforter that was still lining the trunk of my car. I had to soak and wash it three times to get the stains off, but I wouldn't give up. It still reminded me of happy times, and I guess the superstitious part of me maybe believed it was good luck. As long as I kept that comforter, I would keep Michael, I thought. And then hit myself on the side of the head for being a moron.

But I was happier that day, that week, that month than I had been in all of the last year. I loved, loved, loved moving, I loved deciding what to bring, and setting up the new space, and figuring out how to make all the things fit in there that I wanted to fit in there. Before Tom, I had moved all the time, nearly every year, when my lease was up. Since Tom I hadn't moved once, and I only got that thrill if I took a long trip out of town and had to settle myself into a motel for a while. But this was so much better, because it wasn't a hotel or a sublet; this was a semi-permanent home, and I wanted it to be just right.

It was a big job, too, because the place was as tiny as its rent suggested it should be. When you entered through the front door you found yourself in a very short foyer. Immediately to your left was the so-called kitchen, which consisted of a countertop with a microwave on a shelf underneath it, and a hot plate on top of it. I doubted seriously that this arrangement was up to code. Next to the hot plate, a small but new-looking stainless steel sink had been inserted into the countertop, underneath which there was room for a wastebasket and some cleaning supplies. Directly across from the kitchen area stood a door that led to the bathroom. I was pleased that there was a full door and not merely a curtain, although it was a pretty hollow-sounding door. The toilet and sink were crammed into one corner while a square shower enclosure occupied two of the others. There was a little medicine cabinet with a mirror over the sink, and a small cabinet beneath it where we could store the spare toilet paper and the emergency supply of feminine necessities of which I had less and less need.

You took one step away from the kitchen and bath areas, and you were in the main room. A solid wall stood directly in front of you, but fair-sized windows were cut in to each of the other two sides. A long but shallow closet had been framed in next to one of the windows, and next to the other stood a shelf that was obviously intended to hold a television set. The windows helped greatly to conceal the smallness of the room, which measured perhaps ten feet by twelve. The driveway didn't extend up to our front door, which was probably twenty yards from the backside of the main house, but the owner had put down sufficient gravel to make it passable. I thought for sure we would have trouble shoveling it if we were still together come winter, but Michael and I agreed that it would be worth doing if it meant being able to keep our cars off the street. As it turned out, our landlord had a neighborhood kid who handled those kinds of chores for him, and it wasn't our problem. A small hedge had been planted alongside the window that faced the main house, the tendrils of which were just tall enough to clear the windowsill. The rest of the yard was spotted with trees so that when you walked across it, you felt almost as if you were in a suburban park. I got a real kick out of gazing out the window that faced away from the house and pretending we were log-cabin pioneers roughing it in the woods.

Fortunately, we didn't need to keep much there in the way of home furnishings, but I wanted some clothes and dishes and bathroom stuff so we could be prepared to spend the night at the last minute if the opportunity came along. We also had to buy a bed because there wasn't one provided. We both hated to spend money on that on top of the rent, but it was the one thing we couldn't do without. It was also extremely awkward because going shopping together – especially for something as telltale as bedroom furniture – seemed incredibly risky. In the end, we went separately to one of those discount chain stores and picked out mattresses we liked, and then I went to the local one later on and paid for the selection we'd agreed on and had it delivered. We also bought a simple boxspring and laid it directly on the floor so we wouldn't have to fork over any additional cash for a bedframe. I told Michael it would actually be better this way, because we could leave the drapes drawn and still not have our butts show in the windows when we were fucking. In most positions, anyway.

I worked hard on that little apartment. I went down on Michael very enthusiastically against the back side of the front door on the day we moved in, and then didn't let him back into the place until three weeks later when I was done cleaning and arranging it. I made him close his eyes at the threshold and steered him in proudly, feeling peculiarly like a bride presenting her new husband with their first home-cooked meal.

"What do you think?" I inquired nervously.

"It looks good," he confirmed, nodding.

It was obvious he didn't know why he was supposed to be impressed.

So I guided him through it, the whole shebang, including the reasoning behind each one of my decisions. I'd placed the mattress in the center of the far wall – not in the corner – so that no one would have to crawl over or be crawled over to get to the bathroom. I'd found some carpet remnants and put those on either side of the bed over the hardwood floor so we could get out of bed comfortably in winter. There wasn't much room for nightstands, and standard ones would have been a bit tall for our short bed anyway, so I'd bought some stand-alone shelves designed for shoes, tucked our slippers inside, and laid mats on their tops to hold our beer, water, and other necessities of life. I'd redesigned the configuration on the dinky little fridge so that it would hold twenty-twos as well as breakfast food for those rare meals we had together. I had installed a larger towel rack in the bathroom area so we'd have space for two towels, and spent about two hours scrubbing the grout until it finally passed for something in the neighborhood of clean. There was no coat closet, so I attached some wire shelving across the top of the shower enclosure to hang our wet jackets from in rainy or snowy weather, so that we wouldn't ruin the floors which I had so assiduously polished. I had split the closet into his and hers sections with hangers for our spare clothes, and had stocked mine with a variety of outfits. Since there was no room in the place for a dresser, I also positioned two nightstands with drawers on the floor of the closet so we could have storage for underwear and such.

I'm more about organization than decoration – you'll rarely find knickknacks in any place I more than casually inhabit – but I did at least bring a neat little wrought-iron candelabra that I'd had buried in the depths of my home office and the candles that went with it. I liked the idea of lying with Michael in the candlelight in the winter when it got dark early and light late. I thought I'd probably look more alluring by candlelight, too. On the TV shelf I placed a small boombox I'd been lugging around since the nineties and a handful of my favorite CDs. The walls had been freshly painted after Mom had passed, but I cleaned the windows inside and out until the room itself seemed to shine. Our landlord had apparently not noticed that the overhead light fixtures were full of dead bugs so I scraped those out, and also brought over a spare gooseneck desk lamp to place by the bed so that we wouldn't have to get up to turn off the lights. I stocked one of the two tiny kitchen cabinets with two plates, two bowls, a skillet, and a mixing bowl, and the other with cereal, baking mix, and my precious coffee. The silverware and utensils had to go in a tray on top of the microwave because that was the only spot for them, but there was just enough clearance for it between that and the cabinets, so at least it was a good use of space.

Michael oohed and aahed in all the right places, which I appreciated. I could tell that he didn't really care about this kind of thing, but he was looking at me in an amused way as if he thought it was funny that I did, and that was good enough for me. Unfortunately, I'd wasted most of our evening on the tour, and when it was over, there was only enough time for a quickie before he had to go. I was watching him rebuckle his belt – it still turned me on – when he abruptly ceased cinching halfway and plopped back down on the bed, such as it was. Unsure of what was coming next, I scooted my naked body over next to him and let him wrap his arm around me.

"Remember that, um, accident we had at the hotel?" he said.

I had to think about it for a minute before I understood what he meant. "Oh, of course!"

"Do we have a verdict on that yet?" he inquired enigmatically.

In the excitement of moving I'd forgotten all about it. "Yes! Well, I mean, no. Had my period two weeks ago," I clarified. It was odd, but I felt a little peculiar telling him that, like it was a dirty secret or something. "Sorry to have worried you."

"I wasn't worried," he replied unconvincingly, heaving a heavy sigh of relief. "All this… I wondered if maybe you were, like, nesting or something." He seemed disquieted by the term. I know I was. I'd never seen myself as the maternal sort.

But I laughed as if it were a natural if erroneous assumption. "Nah, I just like moving!"

But as long as we were on the subject, there was more that I wanted to say, and this seemed like the time to say it. "Michael?" I proffered tentatively, and immediately wished I could take it back. Only silly girls asked the question I was thinking of asking, not mature adult women.

He turned to me obediently, but it was obvious that he was dreading what was coming next. He knew what my question was going to be, too.

Feeling like a silly girl, I asked it anyway. "What would you have wanted to do? I mean, if I had been, you know?" How stupid was it that I couldn't say it? This man knew almost every inch of almost every crevice of my body, but I couldn't utter the word "pregnant" to him.

There was a very long pause in which neither of us spoke and the laminate flooring received a very thorough visual examination.

"I'm glad I didn't have to decide what I wanted," he finally said. And I knew that that was the best answer I was going to get.

But it was his next statement that threw me completely. "I thought maybe you had stopped having them."

Now it was my turn to be confused. What the hell was he talking about? He thought I'd stopped having kids? When had I started?

"Or not every month, I mean."

I got it then. "You mean periods. You thought maybe I'd stopped having periods every month." I said it more for my own benefit than for his.

He nodded.

"No, I haven't. Not yet."

"Well, I would have thought it was too soon, but you never seem to have them when we're together." He wasn't quite looking at me when he said it.

"No, I guess not." I knew I should be able to talk to him about this, and I hated feeling like I'd lifted my skirt and shaken my goodies in front of a stranger. I cleared my throat. "They're really short now. Usually not more than two days. But they're more frequent. I guess the timing has just worked out." Actually, I generally avoided sex during my periods nowadays. Although they were shorter, the flow was also much heavier, and that didn't set the stage for the best lovemaking. Plus, two days simply wasn't very long to wait.

He nodded again. His expression was hard to read.

"I'm getting old, too, Michael," I said, not quite looking at him either.

He opened his mouth like he was considering denying it, but then seemed to realize that was pointless and shut it again.

"It's okay," he said instead. I wasn't sure if that was supposed to be comforting or not.

"I know we won't be lovers forever," I continued, deliberately keeping my voice even.

"Forever is a long time."

I knew what I had to say next and I didn't want to say it, but I knew it might be my only chance to say it while I could still be rational about it, so I let the words fall gently, not accusatorily, from my mouth. "You'll let me know when you're ready to move on?"

He pulled me closer with the one arm he still had about my waist, and for a fleeting second that familiar dirty look flickered across his face.

"Not even close to ready yet," he said.

And in that moment, I did love him, I was wild, crazy in love with him, always had been, couldn't possibly think of anyone else; he was the man for me, I was the woman for him, and we were meant to be, we should be we.

But then I thought of Tom waiting patiently at home, and of the way Michael never spoke of his wife to me, and I knew it was just a dream, and I shut my eyes and let the feeling wash over me until I was cleansed of it. And then I opened my eyes and kissed him sweetly on the lips and sent him on his way. I was not upset to see him go. The sun was still streaming in through the open window and I sat naked on the bed and gazed around our little shack and thought fondly of the first place of my own that I'd ever had. It had been about half this size. Of course, I hadn't had to share it! And by the time I got up and got dressed and headed home, I was again at peace with my world and Michael's place in it.

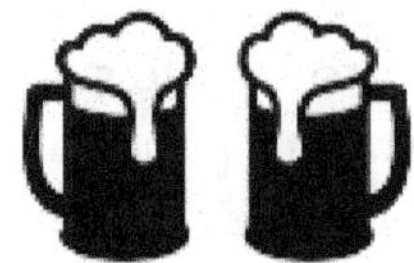

CHAPTER 11

We met at the cottage two or sometimes three times a week. It was farther out than the sublet we'd taken in the student quarter, so it wasn't terribly convenient to get to, and often we'd have to cut our time short in order for him to get home at an acceptable hour. I never raised a fuss, though. I knew he had obligations, and I was plenty satisfied with the time I got. And on the plus side, being so far away from our homes and offices, we gradually began to feel relatively safe and secure about not being seen. Every once in a while we even dared to go out together for a drink or a snack or a walk. I was fond of joking with him about that.

"Uh-oh, Michael," I said one night when we were out at a local restaurant, "I think this might be our third actual date. Better watch it or I might try to get frisky with you!"

He reached under the table and fondled me between my legs. Instantly I parted them, feeling the color rising in my cheeks and the blood flowing to my loins. But then the server came over and asked what we wanted and I started to say "Michael's cock" but he glared at me so I settled for a beer instead and had to wait until we got home to get any action.

I'll never forget that first summer at the cottage. At the time I didn't realize how nearly perfect it was, but it was, nearly perfect. I'd internally resolved to get to know Michael better. I wasn't quite sure why I thought that was necessary after all this time. I mean, we were still fucking plenty, so why worry about squeezing in more conversation? The truth was, I was developing a strong curiosity about what was going on inside his head; maybe I thought that if I dug around in there I'd figure out why it was I'd always liked him so much. All I knew for sure was that there was a man behind the penis, and I wanted to know more about him.

I began by asking questions about the children. This was embarrassing. I couldn't even remember how old they were, if, indeed, I had ever known. The one daughter, Meghan, was coming up on her junior year in high school. She got along fine with her dad, but was at an age at which everything her mother did was either annoying or embarrassing. Mom, no doubt, construed her daughter's behavior in roughly the same way. Meghan had an artistic bent, and appeared to possess some talent for drawing and painting, but was so undisciplined that she rarely completed her assignments even for her art classes, and in her core subjects was barely getting by, no matter how strictly the homework rule was enforced. Michael's older son, Brett, who would be starting high school in the fall, was doing exceedingly well academically; in fact, Michael hoped he might even be a good candidate for college scholarships by the time he graduated. However, for some elusive reason that Brett seemed reluctant to disclose, he was constantly getting into fistfights with the other children, mostly, it appeared, at his own instigation. This was troubling and Michael couldn't understand it; he was such an even-tempered kid with his family, yet it seemed that he was coming home with a black eye at least once a month. Michael hoped this would change once he got into a new school and some of the kids he'd antagonized were gone. Christopher, his youngest, was a cheerful, popular child, a good if not exceptional student, helpful around the house, well-behaved, and respectful of both his mother and father. But he was the one Michael was concerned about most. "It's not natural," he said, shaking his head. "I think he feels obligated to be perfect because his brother and sister aren't." This insight surprised me; I wouldn't have suspected Michael of being so perceptive about people. But once he started, he actually seemed to enjoy talking about his children – it brought a glow to his face that you didn't see at any other time. He was clearly a very devoted father, and although I had no experience with children of my own, I admired that.

Talking about his wife Miranda was more difficult. I totally understood that. Although I knew it wasn't logical, I often felt as if my behavior would somehow be less adulterous if I pretended as if Tom didn't exist when I was with Michael. Of course, this pretense was flawed at bottom because Michael already knew Tom, and even still bumped into us occasionally when we were together, although I'd noticed that their interactions had become quite brief in recent months. But other than that I spoke of him rarely, and then it was only to divulge innocuous information like "I can't see you tomorrow because Tom and I are going to such and such a place." Anyway, eventually I did get him to tell me how he and his wife had met, how he had proposed, and what their marriage had been like so far. But he still never talked about her as a person; whether she had an outgoing personality, or if she was a good mom, or whether she had a strange sense of humor, or even if he loved her. I thought maybe he needed to keep that part of her to himself, and I didn't push it.

I learned other things about him that summer, too. He was as irreligious as I was, and viewed politics as skeptically as he did religion. He didn't read much, but could recite entire passages from the books he had read. Most of these were unfortunately about brewing, which took much of the fun out of that otherwise astonishing skill. He did not enjoy board games but liked mathematical puzzles, and had always regretted not learning a foreign language. Like me, he was also enthusiastic about both running and hiking, but did both of those things less these days because of his work schedule. This was perhaps just as well, because although it would have been neat for us to have activities besides sex to share, arthritis and allergies were forcing me indoors more and more often these days, and I wasn't quite up to admitting how old I was getting yet.

But I talked, too, that summer, and I was amazed at how little he knew about me, either, even of the most noteworthy points of my life. Like how I'd once gone three weeks without eating because I had no money and then one day had found a five-dollar bill on the sidewalk and how I cried and then promptly threw up the food I bought with it. Or that although my mother had been married four times, I had no relationship with any of my fathers. Or the fact that I'd almost gotten married myself once and was almost prepared to thank the God I wasn't sure I believed in for making me change my mind because the guy turned out to be kind of a jerk.

There was nothing unusual about it – it was a process common to just about every couple on the planet. Yet to me it was almost as thrilling as starting a new relationship, when everything about the other person is still novel and intriguing. We'd already spent copious amounts of time delving into one another's bodies, but all this conversation opened up a new realm of exploration for us. There were sides to Michael of which I was completely ignorant, and vice versa. And it was fun, surprisingly fun. Not more stimulating than sex, maybe, but you can't fuck all the time. He'd come in and we'd screw first and then lie around talking and cuddling until suddenly it would be twilight which, since it was summer, meant it was quite late. And he'd scramble to get dressed, and I'd scramble, too, because it wasn't nearly as pleasant being in our place by myself when it was dark, and I generally preferred to leave with him if I could.

The one thing that made me less happy than I could have been was that he never stopped by in the mornings anymore. Not only was the new place farther away, the morning traffic on the highway you took to get there was simply awful; the road crawled right through the heart of the manufacturing district. It simply wasn't feasible for him to get out of the house and come to see me before he needed to be at work. I really missed those mornings we'd had at the sublet, and one day I told him so.

"Miranda is taking the kids up to visit her sister next weekend, Friday through Monday," he said. "I can't miss that much work right now, so they're going without me."

I couldn't see my own face, of course, but I'm pretty sure it lit up like a Christmas tree. It had been a long time since we'd spent a whole night together. "Does that mean what I think it means??!!" I said excitedly. "When can you get here?"

"Actually, I was thinking maybe we could go away for the weekend. Or, the night, at least," he qualified it.

"You mean, like, a trip somewhere?" I said, my joy turning to trepidation.

"Well, nowhere far."

"Still, that's almost like a vacation. It's very, sort of, I don't know, couple-y."

"How long have we been seeing each other?" he prodded.

"I don't know," I answered. "Close to a year, I guess?"

"Then I think we can handle one night away together," he reassured me.

Logically I supposed I had to agree, but I was still plenty nervous when I met him at the apartment the following Saturday. The last time we'd been out of town together had been our first time, and that had almost been disastrous. Although I knew it was silly, I couldn't help fearing this would end badly. What would we talk about for a whole day and a half? I wondered. What if we got sick of each other and had to come home early? It was horrifying to me to take such chances on what had been a perfectly satisfying relationship.

But, of course, my fears were all for naught. We chatted plenty during the drive, and when we weren't talking we cranked up the stereo, and that wasn't uncomfortable, either. I learned that he liked symphonic music and electronic fusion, and he learned, to his never-ending dismay, that I could and would sing along, note for note and word for word, with practically any song from the '60s, '70s, or '80s that might chance to be played on the radio.

It was a short trip, and by early afternoon we had checked into our cabin. I couldn't tell you what it was like because it was August and frightfully hot and we barely glanced at it as we changed into our swimsuits and then hurried down towards the semi-private beach.

I was sweating uncontrollably and was elated to be out of my clothes, but in minutes even my bathing suit was wet with a sticky combination of perspiration and sunscreen. From our door, the lake had appeared cool, restful, and inviting. As we drew nearer, it actually seemed to be steaming in the sun. Given the heat, I was almost glad I wasn't at home this weekend. Tom was at that fateful outdoor beer festival at Lakeside. He'd looked very sad when I'd told him that I'd already planned on being out of town for the weekend and couldn't go. I hoped he'd found someone else to go with him. During the past few years, most of our mutual friends had begun the gradual process of converting into old fuddy-duddies, and were much less likely to come out for a beer even on special occasions. Poor Tom, I thought. What would he do in his old age if I were gone? But I shoved the image of his downcast face out of my mind and tried to focus on Michael. He appeared a bit thoughtful, too, so that wasn't terribly effective.

He looked back at me. "What are you thinking?" he said.

"Never you mind," I rejoindered. I always said that – he knew enough not to be offended by it.

He grasped my hand and swung my arm ever so slightly as we walked.

"Were you thinking about Tom?" he asked finally. I guess he must have recognized the face.

I nodded reluctantly. "Beer festival day today," I explained, and then recollected my current company. "Hey, why didn't you go?"

"I've gone every year for the last ten years. I figured someone else could serve for a change."

And for a few minutes he was silent while we walked, and then it was my turn. "What are you thinking?" I asked.

He got as far as "None of your b –" before I shut him up with a kiss.

We had left the shaded area and were baking in the outdoor August oven when Michael finally said, "I can't take any more. Water?"

"Water!" I agreed. We both raced toward it then into it, not slacking up as it climbed past our knees, waists, and chests, and I tried to pretend that it didn't rankle me when he outpaced me.

"I win!" he cried.

"Pshaw!" I answered. "I totally let you win!"

"Oh, you did not!"

"Okay, maybe not," I conceded. "But I bet I can outswim you!"

And then proceeded to prove my point by lying back in the still water and stretching out into my elementary backstroke. I was a very good glider, and in six strokes I had pulled a pool's length away from him.

"Hey!" he yelled. "Where are you going?"

He sounded a little concerned, so I pulled up and began treading water, the way it should be done, not strenuously but real relaxed, languidly stroking with my hands and feet in turn. When he finally came abreast of me, panting heavily, I shot him a glance of superiority and pulled out my sidestroke and executed it in tight circles around him.

"See?" I gloated. "I can swim circles around you!"

Once again he thwarted me through an unfair advantage – he remembered to use his brain instead of his body. When I came around for the next pass, he latched onto my bikini top, and before I knew it, he had jerked on the two strings that untied it, lifted it off my chest, and rendered me topless.

"Hey!" I shouted. "Give that back!"

"Not until you admit I'm a better swimmer than you!"

"Never!!" I yelled defiantly.

He took my top and strung it around his neck, about which it hung limply, emptied of boobies. My breasts were floating comfortably, perkily, even, in the lake water, but I refused to let that arouse me in light of the competition we had going. Two can play at that game, I thought. Without warning I dove down fast and grabbed hold of his swimsuit and yanked it down to his ankles. He was kicking to beat the band but he needed his arms, too, to keep him afloat so he was nearly powerless to stop me. I was almost out of breath when I finally got them off, and with my final stroke, I kicked away from him in order to preserve my freedom of movement. He began paddling towards me as soon as I surfaced, but I frog-kicked away again while debating what to do with his trunks. They wouldn't have fit around my neck even if I'd wanted to store them there, and they wouldn't have stayed put on any other part of my body, so finally I knotted the drawstring to the right cord on my own string bikini, where it flapped eerily against my skin like seaweed or some unseen slimy water creature. Unfortunately, this required a lot of strenuous kicking and most of my attention, and I did not notice that he was drawing nearer to me until he lunged suddenly at my hips and I felt my bottom coming loose and then, horror of horrors, vanishing from between my thighs.

I inhaled sharply and quickly reversed directions, gaping down into the water seeking my lost swimsuit. For a second I thought I spotted a flash of fuchsia and I grabbed for it, but nothing came up in my fingers and then it was gone.

"Gotcha!" he proclaimed triumphantly.

"Got yourself, too!" I sputtered. "Both of our bottoms are gone now!" I explained what had happened.

"Hmm," he said when I was done. "Well, it's only a five-minute walk back to the cabin, so that should be fine, right?"

I pulled my bikini top tight around his neck by the elastic and then let it go.

Thwap!, it resounded as it whacked him on the face and neck. "Oof!" he exclaimed, when I snapped him again, harder.

Gratifying as that was, it didn't solve the problem. We were still mostly naked and had a long walk back. Well, long for naked people, anyway. We swam cautiously close to the shore. I waited for my feet to scrape bottom, and then scuttled along like a crab with my body underwater until I'd reached the shallowest place I could get to and still be covered. Michael followed suit.

I held my breath as we surveyed the scene. I could see no one, not on the beach, not in the water, not among the trees. The landscape appeared devoid of humanity, and in a brief, nonsensical flash, I wondered if we were all that was left and it was up to us to repopulate the earth, which would be unfortunate because at our age I didn't think we would succeed. I tried to prick up my ears to listen, but then remembered my ears didn't do that so I cupped them with my hands instead, listening for laughter, voices, music, any sound that might signify people and not plants or animals. I heard nothing. It was eerily still. How could there be no one else here on such a hot weekend day? Michael was straining his eyes and ears, too, but had apparently also detected nothing to fear, because after a little while he looked at me and nodded. I nodded back.

And then we were standing, rising up from the water, and as the droplets cascaded down my naked body I imagined myself as a mortal and less awe-inspiring version of Aphrodite, and Michael as Poseidon, except with, um, only one prong in his trident. I couldn't recall my mythology well enough to know how closely related that made us, but under the circumstances I decided not to fret over it. The dripping continued as we waded slowly towards shore, trying not to make waves or gurgling noises as we picked our feet up from the muddy lake bottom and set them down again. The coast was still clear as we reached solid ground and, as if by unspoken mutual agreement, we strode quite naturally along, perhaps a little faster than we normally would have in our bare feet. There would be opportunities to slink behind trees and bushes if someone came. But until then we marched erect and proud, unhampered by shame or clothing. Michael looked as handsome as he ever did in the buff, except for that stupid bikini top still dangling from his neck, which clashed horribly with the shade of his hair.

Aha! I thought. We do still have one article of clothing! I reached for it, but he leaned away from my grasp.

"What?" I whispered. "It's mine, isn't it?"

"Sorry," he whispered back. "Wieners are hardcore. I need it more than you."

We had reached the small wooded area between the cabin and the beach. I'd cooled off in the lake, and now the sun was streaming through the trees and it felt pleasantly warm on my body as the water evaporated. There was still no sign of anyone nearby.

"Then why aren't you wearing it?" I muttered.

And with that, he pulled the top up over his head and began attempting to fashion it into some kind of cover for his penis. The first attempt resulted in more of a sling than a cover, and I giggled silently at the sight of his junk swinging along in a hammock as we walked. Next he tied one of the breast-cloths directly over his penis-head, which made it appear to be modeling some hot pink bonnet. I almost couldn't contain my amusement. Finally I got myself under control.

"Here, let me try," I said. We stopped in the middle of a soft sandy patch in the ground so I could take my shot at reconfiguring our one garment. I was just as unsuccessful. I removed the hat and attempted to fashion a coat instead, but it ended up behaving more like a loose scarf. Then I tried wrapping his penis up in the straps, so it became like a highly ornamented barber shop pole. They wouldn't hold, and even worse, he had become erect from all the fiddling, so for the brief moment they did stay in place, it was a very poorly disguised cock indeed inside those spandex ribbons. After that I gave up, unwrapped him, and handed him back the top, which he promptly tossed over his head and at the foot of a large extra-bushy hedge beyond.

"Hey!" I said.

"You ever going to wear that again with the bottoms missing?"

"Probably not," I admitted.

"You don't seem to be missing it much right now," he commented.

He was right. Ever since that hard cock had come out of its pink sleeve I'd been fondling it and was, even now, nearly humping his leg in an effort to wiggle it into my vagina. We were standing facing each other, and we would have had to have been gods to make that work, but my body seemed unwilling to concede defeat as yet.

"That's a really big bush," Michael whispered.

I looked at him quizzically. Was I supposed to be offended or flattered by that remark?

"No, there!" he said, reading my face and then tilting his head back over his shoulder. "That bush is big."

It was big, big enough to conceal two naked adults if someone approached it from the other side. We looked at each other with that unspoken mutual agreement again, and then he pushed me gently down to the ground and silently climbed on top of me. I buried my face in his chest and breathed deeply. God, he smelled good. My legs instinctively spread to admit him. The ground gave little, and I kept my hips down firm against it while he pushed up and into me from his own flattened position, breathing heavily but quietly.

It had only been a moment when we heard them, a multitude of increasingly audible voices that indicated a crowd of people was drawing near. Michael didn't pull out, but merely paused, bringing his face up to mine in a silent query. I shook my head and he jumped right back into it. I took his shoulder between my teeth and used it to muffle my own heavy breathing while I fucked him back and waited apprehensively to see if they would chance upon us. The voices got louder, and finally became so clear that I could understand what they were saying. "Yes, that was a hell of a barbecue," and "I can't believe they invited everyone in the place," and although I was gratified to know why the lake had been so quiet up until now I really, really didn't want "everyone in the place" to interrupt the lovely private moment I'd been having with Michael.

We kept it up for several more minutes, while the whole cavalcade passed right on the other side of the shrubbery, not ten feet from us. Michael held it steady until all we could discern was the distant noise of twigs cracking, and then began pumping me hard and fast, as if he really meant it. I sensed that powerful stiffening inside that meant he was about to come, and I opened my mouth to remind him to pull out, but he was already out and leaning over me, holding his cock in his hand, jerking out every last bit of gizz and spilling it all over my tits until my nipples were white with the stuff. And then we lay there quietly for a while, panting, and I concentrated on the feel of his juice drying on my skin until it almost felt like a garment, and I thought it funny that even without the top, my breasts hadn't ended up naked after all.

We made it the rest of the way back to the cabin without incident and between meals managed to make love thrice more before it was time to go home. Each time Michael came all over my chest and by the time we left the next day, my skin was so tacky that I had trouble slipping into my shirt. I didn't shower for two days after that and at least once an hour when I was alone I would stroke my fingers across my sticky breasts and think of him.

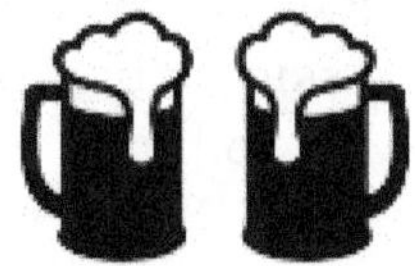

CHAPTER 12

The rest of the summer passed pleasantly. We continued meeting at our little place fairly often, and I was very happy with that. I can't speak for Michael, but I suspected he was, too.

My life with Tom went on essentially as usual, except that my guilt level regarding him had vastly increased as of late. For one thing, we were getting along well, better, in fact, than we had since Lakeside. But even before that incident, there'd been something missing from our relationship. Not that anything was wrong, really, but it wasn't entirely right, either. I believe this is popularly referred to as the boredom phase in a relationship. Not that I was boring or that he was boring, but boy, we sure were boring together. Day in, day out, breakfast, dinner, talking, TV, beer; it never varied. It was a satisfactory life, but gravely lacking in excitement.

We'd gone through some dull dry spells before that had made me wonder if we'd ever be able to stand being retired together. If we weren't always so busy with other things, rather than with each other, how long would we be able to keep monotony at bay? But we'd always gotten past it, and somehow I assumed we always would. And this last time had proved to be no exception. Tom and one of the guys he worked with were considering opening their own shop, so there was plenty of fodder for discussion there. Also, as he increased his homebrew production, we found new entertainment in hosting our own private tastings, just him and me sampling the new beer, and trying to locate the proper descriptors of its flaws and finer points in his reference books. Me, I'd taken on some corporate clients, which made my work considerably more interesting because it required financial accounting in addition to tax accounting. I took a rather nerdy pleasure in yanking out my old textbooks so I could refresh my memory on the proper execution of some standard from near-forgotten days at school. I think I was also just generally happier, and that made my company more desirable, both to me and to him. I tried not to give Michael too much credit for that.

So it was much tougher for me mentally to justify my outside relationship when my inside one was going well, and that grated harshly on my conscience. But don't misunderstand – however remorseful I felt in regards to Tom, I never once, for even a second, considered giving Michael up voluntarily. That I was going to see through to its natural end. But I did have compunctions about the way things were going with him. In particular, incongruous as it sounds, since our little "accident," we'd gotten rather sloppy on using protection all of the time. One of the horrible fears that had always helped to keep me prudishly faithful to my various boyfriends was that I might bring a disease home. Being unfaithful, that was bad enough by itself, but taking the risk of infecting your sweetheart with something you picked up from your lover, that was unconscionable. After the accident, I'd insisted that we both get tested for the usual stuff, which hardly seemed necessary. I'd been certified clean before Tom and I had started dating, and Michael had been married so long that it seemed unlikely that he'd be carrying any sexually transmitted diseases without knowing about it. At our age, and given our respective levels of near-monogamy, it seemed a stupid thing to be concerned about. But I reminded myself that microbes don't practice age discrimination, and at least I felt more comfortable about Tom's potential for exposure afterwards. The unanticipated upshot was that once we had all our papers stamped "negative," it became more difficult to convince ourselves that condoms were strictly necessary. We still used them most of the time, but in special situations – say, the box was empty, or that weekend at the lake when none were handy – we weren't always as diligent about it as we probably should have been. One time without suffering the consequences, and suddenly we were open to taking our chances at any time. Yes, of course, we both knew you could get pregnant even if the man didn't come inside you, but it seemed less risky at our – particularly my – age somehow. Which I suppose is adequate proof that world-wise forty-somethings are just as stupid and ignorant as inexperienced teenagers. Or that people of all ages turn into nimrods when sex is involved.

When September came, I saw much less of Michael. Well, this is it, I thought. He's finally getting tired of me. Was he maybe even seeing someone else? I wondered. I knew I had no right to be jealous, but it was hard not to be, especially when I was incredibly adept at interpreting the lack of evidence of his infidelity as proof of it. In October, he cancelled on me so many times that I only saw him twice, and by the second of those times, I was not very receptive to his embrace.

"What's wrong?" he asked.

"Are you seeing someone else?" I demanded.

"Of course not!"

"Because, you know, you can tell me if you are."

"Okay, but I'm not."

"Are you just sick of me then?" I pressed him further.

"Nope."

"Then what's going on? I hardly see you anymore."

He sighed. "Meghan is still having a lot of trouble in school, and I've been trying to help her more with getting her homework done."

"Is that all?"

"She and her mother still aren't getting along. I mean, at all. Things go much more smoothly when I'm around." He paused. "I haven't been around much in the evenings the last several months."

I knew what he meant, though I thought it was polite of him not to say it outright. I plopped down on the bed, and he sat down next to me, resting his hand proprietarily on my thigh.

"Brett's still getting into fights at school, and when he's not fighting with other kids he's taken to picking on his younger brother."

I waited for the other shoe to drop.

"Miranda thinks I need to spend more time with the children. I agree with her."

My heart sank to my knees. I knew where this had to be going, but what could I say? Of course the children had to come first. They would only be young once, and he had a responsibility to contribute to their care and upbringing.

"I think so, too," I concurred quietly.

Not knowing what to say next or even how to look at him, I took refuge in staring at my trusty feet for a while. They were dangling off the edge of the bed, bare and a bit chilled, but for once I resisted the urge to wedge them under his thighs to warm them.

At length, trying to keep my voice calm, I said, "So should we give notice on this place then?"

Both of his eyebrows leapt skyward in surprise. "Do you want to?"

"Well, there isn't any point in keeping it if we're not going to use it," I answered.

"Whatever you think is best," he replied.

"I can go either way."

"Me, too." He was staring out the window as intently as I'd been staring at my feet. His face was set in an expression that would have been at home on Mt. Rushmore – all stone and silence.

Suddenly I was reminded of the morning after the first night we'd spent together. This was ridiculous, I thought. After all this time, after all the progress we'd made these last months in getting to know each other, we still couldn't simply say what we meant?

I lifted my elbow and poked him in the stomach with it.

"Hey!" he cried. "What was that for?"

"I'm going to keep poking you until you tell me what you really want," I cautioned. A few seconds later I'd carried out my threat. He tried to squirm away, but in that place there wasn't far to go.

"Do you want to stop seeing me or not?" I said, poking him again. "Do you want to stop seeing me or not?!" With each utterance I yelled it louder and poked him more violently.

"No!!" he finally yelled back. He was laughing and clutching his ribcage.

"Was that so hard?" I teased.

"No, but I am," he answered in his most deadpan voice. We both groaned at the terrible tasteless joke, but got undressed and made love anyway.

Afterwards we cuddled quietly, and after a time he spoke again. "Maybe we could get on a more regular schedule."

"How do you mean?" I queried.

"Well, school nights are obviously no good, and my wife expects me home on the weekends. What if we made Friday night our regular night?"

I considered that for a moment. "That could work," I said. "It would actually be more convenient, knowing in advance what the schedule is going to be." That sounded a bit clinical; very much like something an accountant might say. "I mean, it would be nice to have something to look forward to at the end of the week," I added, hoping that softened it up some.

And that was how Michael finally became my Friday night lover.

It actually was much better. He would come by after work, usually sometime between six and eight, and stay through until about nine the next morning. To this day, I have no idea how he arranged that with his wife. He didn't mention what lame excuse he'd made for what he was doing on Friday nights that made him unable to come home, and I decided not to pry. Although we were more intimate now than we had been, I still tried to respect his privacy, especially when it related to his home life. I never forgot that I was an outsider as far as that was concerned, and I certainly didn't want to be an intruder. Besides, whatever he'd told her, she probably didn't buy it anyway. I still didn't know very much about her, but from what I did know, it was apparent that she was not a moron.

For my part, I didn't make any excuses; I merely said that I was going to take Friday evenings off to myself for a while. This worked out well because Tom had taken to brewing on Friday nights after work, so it wasn't as if he would be bored or lonely without me. Plus he was always up late, and naturally I couldn't sleep until he shut everything down and came to bed, which was always after midnight, and more often closer to one or two o'clock in the morning. In fact, even before now, I would have welcomed an excuse to get away on Friday evenings, but paradoxically, I had always felt that I should reserve my "alone time" for when Michael was available. When I told Tom my new plan, he didn't ask any questions, either, but every Friday he would ask me if I was coming home that night, and he always sighed almost imperceptibly when I said I wasn't. I pretended not to notice.

But for Michael and me it was lovely. You might say we'd reached the point in our relationship where we were comfortable enough to be free with each other, but hadn't quite lost all the newness and passion of it yet. In a strange way, I suppose it helped that we saw each other so little. Had our relationship been ordinary, it might have burned out and died in a year; instead it was still growing and developing. We didn't always screw first thing anymore, either. Often we'd go for a walk and talk about our week, and then go back to our little hut and lie around and snuggle for a while before it was time to do the deed and go to sleep. And always, always, maybe even more so because we only had that one night, I found myself in constant contact with him while we slept, my hand on his stomach or my front against his back or my foot on his leg. It had been like that with Tom once, and sometimes it made me sad that it wasn't that way anymore. Which made me all the more grateful to have that, to still want that with Michael.

But surprising as it may sound, I think the Friday night only thing was beneficial for Tom and me, too. I thought I'd always done a fair job of keeping my men separate in my mind, but when I saw Michael every other day, there had been a constant shifting in my focus. Now I concentrated on Tom all week long, and Michael's day was all the more special because there was only one of it. By the time I saw Tom on Saturday night, I was all his again, and I think he sensed that. He would always snuggle me extra hard as if I'd been away, making me feel warm and safe, and each time I remembered how much I still loved him. But not enough to give up Michael; never enough to give up Michael.

Seasons passed. Michael's brewery was expanding and had opened a second location in the next town over, and he was put in charge of getting it up and running. I had taken on even more clients, but I'd also given in and hired an assistant, so my schedule was easier than it had been, and I was earning more besides. And Tom was the same as he had always been, still gorgeous; still working for the same shop, his idea of opening his own place abandoned once we'd run the numbers to see what it would actually cost to maintain; still playing around with engines and homebrewing and his other hobbies and not much else. We still went to beer festivals. We had yet to take a real trip or vacation together. Yet there was peace in our home. The craziness that had possessed me, the powerful desire to get away, to scrap my whole life and start over, had finally passed, and I began to appreciate his comfortable qualities again. The way he looked sunken cozily into our bed when I got up before the sun to cook our breakfast. The way he would get up to bring me a beer when I was sunken cozily into our bed before it was time to sleep. The way he still kissed me a lengthy goodbye before leaving for work, giving my butt a friendly squeeze on his way out. The way he still listened to me babbling on and on after too much beer even when he was fighting to stay awake himself. Even the way he never ever said I love you unless I really, really needed to hear it.

As I moved through my forties, I needed it more often. I knew by definition that I wasn't menopausal yet, but I supposed my hormones were at least in flux because I was often moody for no discernible reason. It was almost like PMS except that it followed no traceable pattern, had irregular ups or downs, and lasted for months. I had spells of worthlessness. I don't mean that I merely felt worthless; I actually had days in which I was utterly useless as a human being. I moped and felt sorry for myself and couldn't get anything done. I cried when I saw children playing, or a dead squirrel lying in the road, or a long line at the grocery store checkout. I loathed myself for falling so far out of control, but I felt powerless to stop it, and that frightened me. I would get angry with Tom over nothing, and although I could see that this baffled him, he never complained and never, ever tried to calm me by telling me it was just my hormones and that I had no real reason to be mad at him. On good days I really appreciated that. It made up for whatever slight offense he might have committed to upset me in the first place.

And worse, I was spending time in front of the mirror again. This did not improve my mood any. I knew it wasn't healthy to dwell on things I couldn't change, but I wasn't feeling healthy. Everywhere I went, it seemed, I was confronted with beautiful young women. No, it wasn't even that; I was constantly confronted with average-looking women who seemed beautiful because they were young, and I was not, and I was jealous, insanely jealous of all of them, and their age, and the time of life that stretched leisurely before them. Maybe there was nothing I could do to stave off my ever-increasing aches and pains, but surely there was something I could do to look better, I thought. I'd seen the multitudes of commercials promising that this or that cream or serum would make me look years younger in two short weeks of regular use. I wasn't greedy. I didn't need to look twenty-five. Thirty-five would be just fine.

And suddenly there I was, skulking through the beauty aisles with all of the other "women of a certain age." I'd never pictured myself here. I'd given up wearing makeup at the age of sixteen because I hadn't wanted to bother spending the time applying it. The only cosmetic I'd ever liked was eyeshadow, anyway. It was fun putting on the different colors, like painting or drawing with charcoal, except that it was such a tiny canvas that it didn't matter much that I wasn't artistic. If I skipped the foundation I already had rosy cheeks and didn't need blush, I never did get the hang of lining my eyes with that stupid pencil, and I would have preferred to remove my lips all together than have to smear them with lipstick every day. Of course, this stance was easier to maintain when I'd looked good without makeup. Now I couldn't make the switch even if I wanted to, because I was afraid people would notice the change and think me vain. It was bad enough I was disappointed in myself for being vain without letting everyone else in on the secret. Besides, I'd worn makeup once half a dozen years earlier when I'd been a member of a bridal party, and I hadn't thought it made me look any better. In fact, the foundation just seemed to cake up in my under-eye wrinkles, which only emphasized them.

I'd always wanted to grow old gracefully. More than that, I believed that I would grow old gracefully. My appearance had never been terribly important to me. I'd never fussed over my hair or my clothes, and I'd always seemed to do just fine in the romance department, so I never saw any point in wasting my time on those superficial things. It had cost me a lot of soul-searching to make the decision to finally start dyeing my hair a few years back. Something other women did as a mere frivolity, yet on me it had a significant impact. It changed who I was; my perception of myself and who I was going to be. At twenty, at thirty, even, I hadn't cared what I looked like. But at forty, when it was too late to care, when there was no longer any point in caring, I couldn't stop worrying about it.

And so I sighed and joined the legions seeking youth in a bottle, and I was stunned by the abundance of those bottles. For your face alone it seemed you needed night creams, day creams, masks to remove impurities and masks to restore minerals, one special serum for your crow's feet and under-eye areas and another to tighten the skin of your eyelids. Until I spotted that last one, it had never even occurred to me that one's eyelids might sag, but if they made a product for it, it must be so. And sure enough, one glance in my rear-view mirror and it was obvious; my eyelids were even saggier than the pouches under my eyes, and I was horrified. I grew so embarrassed by my heretofore unnoticed eyelid-hoods that I took to wearing my bangs longer to cover them up, and immediately after a haircut I felt naked and exposed, as if every flaw in my faulty face was highlighted in thick stripes of neon green.

I couldn't help but wonder what would happen to your skin if you actually used all of these highly recommended products simultaneously. Either they were all the same and combining them neither hurt anything nor did you much good, or they were all different and were bound to cause some unwanted chemical reaction that would sear your skin off. Either way, it sounded like a waste of perfectly good money that might otherwise be spent on beer. And then you had lotions for the rest of your body that proposed to remove stretch marks, cellulite, dark spots, and so on, or at a minimum to give your skin the smooth, silky glow of a freshly shaven young woman with spectacularly shaped legs free of scars and varicose veins. I didn't try them all – that would consume multiple lifetimes for any woman – but I did sample quite a few before accepting the fact that none of them had that grand of an effect on either my face or my body. I finally settled on a simple moisturizer with sunscreen in it and used that daily after showering. The economist in me appreciated the fact that it did double duty, and I was able to kid myself and anyone watching that, being naturally very white, I wasn't concerned about my appearance, but rather about the risks of skin cancer. Moisturizing did actually help, though. It softened my wrinkles and restored a bit of my glow. I hadn't even realized how dry my skin had become until I started wearing it regularly. One of the many joys of getting older. Apparently, like everything else, your skin stops working, too.

But of course, this didn't make a substantial difference in either my appearance or my mood. Although he didn't know it, the melancholy in which I was foundering affected my relationship with Michael, too. He didn't have to deal with my moods much. The worse I felt, the more I looked forward to that one night with him, so most of the time he found me cheerful and welcoming, not depressed and aloof. I felt more like my old self with him. Or perhaps it would be more accurate to say, more like my younger self. But my relationship with him was completely different from my relationship with Tom. Tom was my boyfriend, my mate, my partner in life. Tolerating my getting old was an integral part of that commitment, and it was to be hoped that he loved me enough to want to stick around for that. To Michael, I was supposed to be a sex object, just as he was to me. That was the whole point of our being together. And although he still had the same illogical effect on me he'd always had – because his own aging was not going to change that – I was very rapidly becoming unsexy, and there wasn't much I could do about it. Even the figure I'd worked so hard to achieve and maintain was finally starting to fail me. No amount of pushups and tricep dips was effective in eliminating the turkey waddle that was drooping from beneath my arms, and worse, I was developing an odd paunch in the gut, despite the fact that I hadn't actually gained any weight. But I knew where it came from, nonetheless. It was my very own beer belly. Maybe one day I would be proud to sport such a magnificent trophy of alcohol consumption, but for now it was an unwelcome addition to my wardrobe.

Being with Michael was no longer enough to make me feel desirable. It wasn't his fault. It was nothing he'd said or done; it was simply life progressing. If I had trouble accepting it, it was because of who I was, not because of him. Yet it changed my perception of him nearly as much as it changed my perception of myself. If he looked at me fondly, I wondered if he was examining my flaws. If he dimmed the lights when we were getting romantic, I assumed it was because I was less unattractive in shadow than in light. If he left fifteen minutes earlier one Saturday than he had the last, I interpreted that as an indication that he was becoming bored with me. I recognized how irrational it was to have these thoughts. Even if they'd been true, I had no real cause to think them, because his behavior toward me never altered. And it was tiring, constantly searching for signs of his disapproval, and having to invent them when I could find none. But as much as I tried to logic myself out of my unsupported apprehensions, I could never quite clear my mind of them. I simply couldn't, at heart, believe that he still wanted me, and there was nothing he could have done to change that. There was nothing anyone could have done to change that.

Early one Saturday morning during our second autumn at the cottage, I woke in the night and couldn't get back to sleep. This had become an even more frequent occurrence of late, and it was particularly irritating when it happened when I was with Michael, because I couldn't simply get up and go into my office and work until I was sleepy again. But I slipped into my big fluffy bathrobe and traversed the two steps to the window. A three-quarters moon was illuminating the yard, and I could faintly discern from the shades of gray that the leaves on the trees dotting the lawn were commencing their change. Ordinarily this was the most beautiful thing that happened all year, but that night all it made me think of was death. Death and burial. The leaves would fall to the ground; would crumple and wither and be trampled into bits. They would disintegrate, just as my body, the body I had enjoyed so much, would one day not so far off fall to the ground and shrink and collapse and be forgotten like a bit of dead leaf blown away on the wind. A sob caught in my throat; I'd become a victim of my own morbid monologue. I brought my thick sleeve up to stifle the noise but it was too late; there was someone behind me, and I felt warm reassuring arms circling my waist.

"What's wrong?" a gentle voice murmured.

I merely shook my head. I couldn't speak. He'd never seen me cry before, and I didn't want him to have to listen to my voice all choked up either. But he stood there with me a long while, and I gazed out the window while he rested his chin on my shoulder, and I tried to think about how beautifully radiant the moon was, and not about the ominous shadows the trees cast about the yard and against our cottage. I tried really, really hard, but it was building within me, growing and growing until I could feel the tipping point coming. I thought it was funny how severely bad emotions led to an outburst in much the same way really good ones did, and I hoped that if I had to let it out, that it would give me release in much the same way.

"Please don't leave me," I spluttered at last, grasping his forearms, holding them tight about me, and leaning back against his chest.

"I wasn't planning on it," he answered quietly, squeezing back.

"I need you." I hadn't meant to say it, but there it was. "I really need you." And I knew that I had no right to force my need on him because he wasn't mine to need; my needing him was stupid and inappropriate, and if he had any brains at all he would leave me if for no other reason than because I'd had the gall to say it.

He didn't respond to that, and I was glad. I didn't want to have to explain. After a while he led me gently back to bed and held me while I alternated between crying and blowing my nose. And then I remembered that I'd fallen asleep with a half-empty beer on my shoebox-nightstand, and I drank the warm flat liquid and felt better, and he stayed up with me and finished his, too. We didn't talk, but before I lay back down again I said "Thank you," and kissed him on the forehead and thought once more about how pretty he looked in the moonlight.

By morning I was all right again, but I knew how terrible I looked after crying, and I kept my back to him while we went about our morning routine. When he reached for me, I turned and quickly buried my face in his shoulder.

"Are you okay?" he asked uncertainly, squeezing me tight against his chest.

"Of course!" I answered, patting him awkwardly with one arm while I covered up my eyes with the other.

"Then why won't you look at me?" he prodded gently.

I sighed. Why couldn't I just tell him?

"Because this is what I look like after crying," I said, tilting my face up to his. I knew that my lids of my eyes would be nearly as swollen as the pouches underneath them, the skin so puffy that it would almost swallow my red and bloodshot orbs.

He whistled. "You look like you've been beaten up," he remarked.

I laughed. That was much better than pretending that I looked fine. "It'll take hours to subside."

"Better not let the landlord see you – he'll wonder what I did to you!"

"Well, pretty soon he won't be our landlord anymore, so fuck him."

The day before, he had given us notice that we needed to move. He was selling the house, and the buyers actually wanted to use the in-law unit for an in-law. I guess I was still a little mad that he'd forced us into deciding once again whether we were going to continue on together or not.

He interrupted my thoughts. "That reminds me; I wanted to talk to you about something."

My heart dropped into the pit of my stomach, and I glanced around for the tissue paper, wanting to be prepared if I needed to start crying again.

"Okay," I said.

"Would you mind being in charge of finding us a new place? I've been busting my ass trying to get the new brewery going, and I'm not sure I'll have time to look into it this week."

I peered out at him through the tiny pits that were my eyes. It must have looked odd, because he began backtracking, saying, "If you don't have time either, that's okay; it can wait awhile, I guess." And then, "Why are you looking at me like that?"

Because you just made my whole year, I thought. "No, I'll do it," I said.

I forgot all about my hideous face. I felt beautiful again.

After he left, I tackled the cleaning and packing. We'd probably only have one more Friday before our time was up. It was still unfortunate that we had to go. I'd been very happy here.

I started looking for places as soon as I got home. I felt good for a change, hopeful and optimistic, as if I'd just gotten the news that the sitcom I starred in was being renewed for another season. The glow carried me all the way through that chore and then through the weekend's housework and grocery shopping as well. I was still in a good mood when Tom came home.

"Let's go out tonight," I suggested.

"Okay!" He was rarely a tough sell if there was a promise of beer, and he knew I wouldn't suggest something that didn't somehow involve beer any more than he would. "Where do you want to go?"

"Anywhere," I said, "As long as there's loud music and good beer and we can stay out late."

Tom contacted several of his friends and we somehow managed to get a whole group together for a pub crawl. It was fun to be with a crowd for a change, and even though I thought I talked more than was wise – given all the secrets I was keeping – I didn't believe I'd said anything I shouldn't have.

It was late when we got home, but I was up as early as usual and I'm not sure if maybe I was still a little buzzed or what, but I sure felt great. I checked my email, and I had received some responses to my inquiries about apartments. Thinking about Michael made me even more cheerful until I heard snoring emanating from the bedroom, and I remembered about Tom. My sense of having done wrong began creeping up on my subconscious, but before I could reprimand my weak mind and body, I suddenly perceived the absurdity of my situation and laughed in spite of myself. Normal people didn't live like this, I thought. They get together and either stay together or split up, they don't just indulge on the side indefinitely. I wondered how Michael felt about it. He certainly never seemed torn or in a state of moral upheaval. But he had one relationship with no sex and another that was mostly sex. Strictly speaking, he was monogamous. I was not. And me, I wasn't even sure what the source of my contrition was. Did I feel guilty about being with Michael because of Tom, or did I feel guilty about being with Tom because of Michael?

I shoved these thoughts forcibly away. They were too complicated for my mood. I was not going to let anything ruin this day.

And it seemed that nothing could bring me down now. From then on I was better. Although I still had my lows, it was as if the worst of the crisis had passed, and I began to enjoy more of life again. I found a new apartment for Michael and me. It was a small studio and was on the third floor of a building close, but not too close, to his new brewery location. We would have neighbors again, but that would be all right. It was in a semi-commercial area so there were businesses nearby, which might be useful. I had hoped for a private place again like we'd had, but the few that were available that we could afford were in locations that seemed too risky. And there's something to be said for living around a bunch of other people if you're trying not to stand out. But I hesitated a bit when I called Michael about it. It was right at the top of our price range, which we'd set lower now that Michael's kids were rapidly approaching college age. On top of that, it was run by a property management company, and they wanted a year's lease.

"But it's month-to-month after that," I added quickly.

"That should be fine," he reassured me.

One day, I knew, I would just have to accept the fact that he actually wanted to be with me. Just a few more years, I thought stupidly, and maybe I would be convinced.

Moving in was not nearly as fun or exciting this time, either. Although the studio was larger and more comfortable than the cottage, it didn't feel as homey. Plus, we had almost everything we needed already, so it felt more like transporting a bunch of stuff across town than setting up a new place. This made me a little sad for some inexplicable reason. I kept attempting to redecorate, but it didn't really seem to need doing. Finally I acquiesced and hung a picture on the wall, something I'd never ever done before. It was a photograph of me and Michael from that beer dinner so long ago that someone had taken and sent to him afterwards. As far as I knew, it was the only picture that had ever been taken of us. Somehow looking at that lonely photograph in its thin frame depressed me a little, so I removed it, patched over the nail hole so that no sign of it would remain, tucked it back into a drawer, and left the walls plain.

I had to stare at those bare walls by myself for two consecutive Fridays. Michael had thrown his back out and was stuck at home. I felt as if I should be doing something for him, but what could I do but send good thoughts from afar? The superstitious part of my brain was neither large nor powerful enough to believe that that would be of any use to Michael, so I didn't bother. I didn't want to change my Friday-night routine at home, so I stayed at the apartment alone. I was almost grateful that we had neighbors now; it prevented the silence from ringing too deeply. I guess I got used to it. The first night I read a book in the bathtub and went to sleep early. The second time I read a book in the bathtub, went to bed early, and couldn't sleep, so I got up and drank two beers in quick succession, climbed back into bed with my book, and then fell asleep with it on my lap.

Although I really enjoy reading, it was still a relief when the following Friday arrived and Michael finally came. It was already after nine when a rough thumping noise leaked in from the hallway. I leapt clumsily across the room, landing precariously at the doorstep on one trembling foot, like an uncoordinated kid on a hopscotch board. Breathlessly I yanked at the door and threw it open as wide as the arms with which I planned to greet him. He entered cautiously, holding his body stiffly upright. I'd been prepared to spring as soon as he knocked, but seeing him still hunched painfully over, I caught myself; patted him gently on the shoulder instead.

"Hmph!" he grunted. "You don't have to treat me like an old man!"

"Then you should stop acting like one!" I joked, kissing him wetly on the cheek.

"Says Miss, ehhhh! My knee! And ehhhh! My hip!" he retorted pointedly.

That was the noise I made when my joints hurt. I was making it pretty often these days. On bad days I wondered how old people ever even did it. Sometimes walking seemed like too much effort, let alone all the aerobicized contortionism that went with sex.

"Yeah, yeah, yeah," I said. "I'll still never be as old as you, so there!" I stuck my tongue out at him. He stuck his out back, so I licked it and we both laughed.

"Can I get you a beer?" I offered.

"Oh, God, yes."

I went into the kitchenette, fetched a bottle from the fridge, and divided it between two glasses, humming some stupid romantic ditty softly to myself and grinning at my own cheerful idiocy. Broken or not, I was happy to see him.

He had sat down on the edge of the bed. I handed him his beer and he took it, downing half of it in one draught. He still seemed to be in pain. I fondled the back of his neck sympathetically, my fingers tingling over the swath of razor-trimmed bristles lining the base of his skull.

"This place is all right," he said, glancing around. "It's nice that there's an elevator."

For a moment, I felt oddly disconnected from him, as if he had suddenly become much older in my eyes. I had never yet heard him praise the presence of an elevator, and at our first sublet, he had always accompanied me without complaint up and down the stairs. But, of course, I'd been fortunate enough never to have had a back problem, so I didn't know what it was like. It probably made stairs really hard, old man or young.

"When did you buy the sofa?" he inquired abruptly. I had by ruthless rearrangement carved out a space for a loveseat off in one corner of the main room.

"Someone who was moving out left it behind, so I grabbed it," I replied, perhaps a bit too hastily. It was only partially a lie. I had only paid fifty dollars for it, and the man who was vacating had helped me angle it awkwardly up the stairs.

"And the new bedframe? Did someone leave that behind, too?" he queried suspiciously, his brow creasing into a multi-layered frown as he sampled the cushiness of our new sleeping arrangement with his one free hand.

"No, I bought that," I confessed, blanching under his icy blue gaze. For the first time he reminded me of a warlock with that long pointed beard. I liked it better after that.

"How come?" he demanded, shooting the question at me as if I were a suspect under police interrogation and causing me to glance guiltily away.

"Oh, I just thought it was time we lived like grownups," I said vaguely. "It's hard getting dressed so low to the ground, you know?" I had noticed him having trouble with shoes sometimes. I wasn't sure if it was due to stiffness in his spine, the effort required to bend around his growing gut, or the combination of both.

"What you mean to say," he pronounced with an aura of mature dignity, "Is that you thought that after my back's been out, I might not be able to get up and down off a low bed anymore, isn't that right?"

Damn, he was good! I was extremely impressed with his perceptiveness. I didn't see any way I was going to win this argument. But I had to think for a second before rejoindering excitedly, "Wait until you see how I fixed the toilet!"

He looked horrified, and began struggling to get up. "Kidding! Kidding!" I said, forcing him back down onto the bed with all of the strength it would have required to subdue a newborn kitten.

"You should be nicer to your elders," he said, wincing as he settled back into position.

"I am nice." I took his glass from his hand and set it on the nightstand, then pushed him gently on the chest while supporting him by the shoulders until he was prone on his back on the bed. I lay down beside him and fondled his arm. It seemed the safest place to touch him.

"Listen," he said. "All joking aside, I'm not really sure I'm up to – stuff – today."

"Then why did you come over?" I didn't mean it that way, but now that I'd said it, I let it stand. I was curious. Why had he come over if it wasn't for sex?

"Because it's Friday, of course."

"Just part of the routine, eh?"

"That's right." But he didn't quite meet me eye when he said it.

"You'd better watch it, sweetie," I teased. "I might start to think you actually like me."

"I do like you."

It was the strongest declaration of affection that I'd ever gotten, or ever would get, from Michael.

"Well, in case you're interested, I like you, too," I answered, nodding my head in affirmation.

"That's good."

"I think so."

"Well, all right then."

We were not very good at this kind of stuff. I got up to get us another beer. When I returned he was still lying in the same position, as wretched as a sickly old dog and twice as pitiful.

I set our beers down and sat down next to him on the bed, placing my hand softly on his chest.

"Would you like to just go to sleep now?" I said kindly.

"I'm sorry… I guess I'm not very good company tonight."

"I'm glad you're here," I reassured him. "Want me to help you undress?"

"I can do it!" he responded, disgruntled.

"I know, but it's all romantic and shit if I do it."

So he let me help him out of his shoes and shirt and pants, and then I got myself into a lacy pink chemise that covered up my sagging this and drooping that while he scooted himself awkwardly up into the bed and under the covers. I ducked under the blankets, too, climbed astride him, and drew the comforter over us both. I looked down at him fondly. There was also something appealing about this new, old, fragile Michael. His pelvis was directly underneath mine, and I guess I must have made a telling motion because he said again, "I really don't think I can…"

"I'll be very gentle," I promised. "I'll do all the work. Just tell me if it hurts."

And so I slid him into me, oh, so very slowly and gently, with no sudden or rapid movements, and then, with just the slightest of motions, I gradually let him out, and at length brought him back in again. This went on for a very long time. At long last, I finally felt him tense up, and finish, without hurting anything, and I was immensely pleased, and as we were lying down to sleep, I said to myself, This is how old people do it. Carefully. And I smiled.

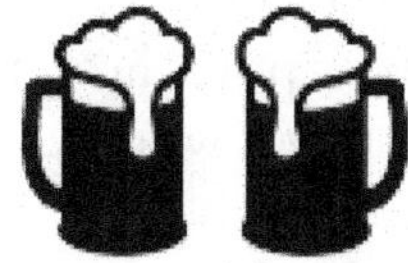

CHAPTER 13

But that winter was rough. I couldn't quite put my finger on it, but something just wasn't right between Michael and me. Although mechanically everything was still working the way it should, he seemed distant and I was – well, maybe I was getting a little bored. Bored isn't even the right word for it. Here was my exciting, illicit lover, yet being with him had become surprisingly routine. It was a routine, after all. Every Friday was the exactly the same as the one before, and I suspected that we were finally losing some of our passion for each other. In fact, although I hated to draw the comparison, my relationship with Michael was becoming strikingly similar to the one I had with Tom, except that it was one day a week instead of six. Irrationally I blamed the apartment. It was dull, and it was making us dull, too. It had never given me that special feeling of being "our place" that I'd had with either the sublet or the cottage. But I would have felt foolish telling Michael I thought we needed to break our lease for the sake of our relationship, so naturally I said nothing about it.

He continued to come on Fridays and I continued to meet him. But he came later, and left earlier, and our lovemaking became largely restricted to the ten minutes immediately before it was time to go to sleep. I was surprisingly okay with that. Much of the sexual urge, or at least the sexual urgency, had passed for me. I still wanted to fuck him, but I didn't really need a make a big to-do about it anymore. I wondered if he felt that way, too. It was certainly how he acted. It was possible that my age, or maybe even his age, had finally caught up with us, but somehow I didn't think that was it. It just wasn't new anymore. Didn't all relationships eventually go this way? Except that you were supposed to be fucking someone you wanted to be with even when you weren't fucking. I almost had that with Michael – but only almost. We were great together before, during, after, and between fucks. I'd once told him that I liked him well enough to do, then hang out with until it was time to do him again. But once you subtracted out the hours for fooling around, that left a lot of empty holes to fill – no pun intended. And somehow we had never reached the point of being able to enjoy each other purely for the company, or at least not for extended periods of time, anyway.

But I couldn't admit to myself that the end might be approaching. In fact, I couldn't even stomach thinking about it. Every time I thought of a life without

Michael, my chest got tight, and my head hurt, and I felt myself turning about mentally, searching for something to cling to and finding only his waiting arms. I knew it was crazy to feel that way, but I did. I had meant it that day in the cottage when I'd said I needed him. I did need him, fully and desperately. He'd been an anchor when I was lost in a stream of runaway emotions and hormones and life changes and I wasn't ready to be set adrift, not yet. Tom may have been my true companion, but Michael was the pivot point around which the rest of my life turned, and I was afraid that if he was gone that I would stop turning all together.

So I said nothing and hoped for the best, but I knew that soon a change would have to come, and I dreaded that day like the collapse of The Milky Way. It was almost a relief when tax season arrived and I could be assured of being too busy to think again. I had informed Michael from the start that I would be hauling work over to the apartment, and he had responded in kind by bringing over recipes to tinker with while I plodded through my data entry. Although the brewery expansion was officially complete, the company was now seeking to augment its variety of brews, and Michael was very creative in that respect. But designing and brewing new beers from scratch was labor-intensive, and he always looked exhausted. Of course, I wasn't sure if that was overwork, or simply because he had natural bags under his eyes like I did, and was more prone to appearing tired as he aged.

But, as plans sometimes do, my scheme to make the most of our now rather empty Friday nights by getting work done had utterly unexpected results. Working side by side transformed my relationship with Michael. I didn't even notice it happening at first, then one Friday afternoon in March I found to my eternal amazement that I was nearly caught up on work for that week. I could even have finished it at the office before heading over to the apartment, but instead I packed up my papers and computer and took them with me. It was only five o'clock when I arrived, and I was astonished to find Michael already there, too, sitting cross-legged on his side of the bed with his own laptop, working on hop bitterness calculations. He was just as surprised to see me.

"Hi!" I exclaimed.

"Hi, yourself!"

"You're early!"

"You are, too!"

"How'd you get off work?" I inquired.

"I was just done with being there," he sighed. "It's more relaxing working here."

He was right. It wasn't only more relaxing; it was more fun, too. I'd set my documents on my nightstand and my computer on my lap and I'd sit very close to him so that our knees or legs were touching, and I'd work for a while and when I had to pause to think I'd glance over at him and he'd be intent and frowning slightly over his own labors. He looked awfully cute like that, and I'd turn his face towards mine and kiss him, or rest my head on his shoulder for a moment and nuzzle him, and it was so much nicer than my sterile office where there were only the marvels and intricacies of tax law to make you feel all warm and cozy inside. He'd kiss me back, or squeeze my thigh with his adjoining hand while he was thinking and not typing, and later in the evening we'd order take-out Chinese food from a place down the street, and one of us would go to retrieve it and we'd take a break from work and talk about our week and crack open a beer. Then we'd reassume our working positions and pretend that we weren't finished being productive, but by the time we poured the second beer the computers would be sitting lonely on our laps, and we'd chat about taxes and brewing until we surrendered and stashed the hardware away, and slid under the covers with our arms around each other without even getting undressed because it was still winter and cold in the apartment.

We'd snuggle for a long time, just talking, telling stories about our lives, things that had happened in high school or elementary school or college, people we used to date, movies we'd seen, places we'd like to visit, trivia we wished we could still remember and wondered if maybe the other one did. And by then we'd be too warm to stay dressed and we'd shimmy out of our clothes, and I'd see him smiling at me by the starlight filtering in through the windows that I still liked to keep uncovered, and I knew that he could see me smiling back, too, and I hoped it made him feel as good all over as I did. Then we'd make love and afterwards I'd kiss him and push my body up against his until it couldn't get any closer, and we'd fall asleep and when it was morning I'd still be smiling, because somehow my coffee tasted especially yummy when I got to drink it with him in our bed.

But it wasn't until that particular Friday that I recognized how much things had changed and that now, rather than skimping on our time together, we were putting more of ourselves into it. And my heart swelled in my chest because I knew now that I would not yet need to ask him again if he was ready to move on because that time had still not come. Knowing that made me feel all funny inside, so I put down my things, relieved him of his, and climbed into his lap and wrapped my arms around his neck and kissed him until he took the hint and made us both naked, even though it was early and that wasn't part of the routine anymore.

For the remainder of tax season, I looked forward to Fridays as much as I ever had. I concluded that it shouldn't bother me if my relationship with Michael paralleled my relationship with Tom. Tom and I had been through these same phases, and we still had a solid relationship. They were very different men, but I, I was one woman, and maybe this was just how I related to the men in my life; perhaps this was a normal progression for me. I had been with Michael longer than I'd ever been with any man besides Tom. Part-time, to be sure, but it was still a landmark. I supposed I didn't really have much experience with the long-term relationship, but then, who did? For most people it was the person you married. There simply wasn't time in a fairly limited youth to be with multiple partners for five or ten years each. Unless, of course, you had them simultaneously, but of course, decent people don't do that. Ahem. Anyway, most people who signed up for the long haul probably either had no idea how it would go and whether the love would last, or had ridiculously high expectations and ended up sorely disappointed when the magic faded and the reality of day-to-day took over.

I asked Michael about that once. I don't recall how I phrased it exactly. I didn't use the words disappointment or disillusionment; I said something to the effect of, had it been everything he hoped it would be. He'd answered that he still loved his wife and had clammed up after that, so I clammed up, too. I sometimes suspected that he felt more ashamed about being with me than I felt about being with him, even though technically he had no cause for remorse. It wasn't solely the vows. It was one of the few ways in which we were conspicuously dissimilar in our construction. Me, I'd never wanted marriage, family, permanence, the same thing every day for all time. I varied the route I took to work; I went to a different supermarket from week to week; every so often I even rearranged the furniture just to change things up. As time had gone on, familiarity and the security that went with it had become more agreeable to me, and I began to appreciate the value of coming home to the same house, the same car, the same man every day. But it didn't come naturally, and I had to fight harder to stay in that place than to stay out of it.

After a while I'd begun to understand that it wasn't so much that I was uncomfortable with commitment; it was more the feeling of being trapped that scared the crap out of me. Before Michael, I'd been perfectly happy just being with Tom, as long as I wasn't stuck with him, if you know what I mean. It wasn't that I had any intention of ever leaving him; it was more the thought of not being able to get away if I wanted to that rattled me. In my mind it was bad enough that we'd bought a house together, and I felt no desire to intertwine our lives any further in the eyes of the law. Yet family, friends, even strangers could never believe that I didn't want to marry him, and I frequently found myself forced into trying to convince people that I preferred things the way they were. It had happened at a party we'd attended recently, even; a young woman I barely knew had accosted me.

"So when are the two of you getting married?" she'd asked.

"Not until death parts us!" I vowed, smacking my hand against my heart.

"Well, you know," she answered grimly, disregarding my obviously failed attempt at humor, "You have to insist or he'll never do it."

This attitude was everywhere, but I couldn't fathom it at all. Why did everyone have to get married? I didn't want to be married. Wasn't this the twenty-first century? Weren't women liberated yet? Why did people assume I wanted to "trap" a man? Couldn't we just be together without having to permanently legalize the union?

Although Tom didn't share my fear or revulsion regarding marriage, he felt that it was an outdated institution that was unnecessary in the modern era. Yet in a way he was actually better suited to it than I was, because he simply didn't take it seriously. It was meaningless to him. To me, those vows were solemn and earnest, much too momentous for me to ever consider rendering myself. And I truly believed that the idea of promising to love and cherish someone else forever was a bit far-fetched. How can you promise that your feelings will never change? It's part of the nature of feelings that you can't control them. If you believe that your love will last forever, you're making a prediction, not a promise. But no one to my knowledge has yet perfected the art of prophecy, and that's an awful lot of future to anticipate.

Take the whole idea of staying together in sickness and in health. A noble vow. You don't abandon your spouse because he or she has a heart attack or becomes a paraplegic. But what if your mate is diagnosed with an untreatable mental illness? The person you thought you would love forever might not even exist anymore. Or what if you yourself suffered a severe trauma, a near-death experience, for instance? Would you be the same person afterwards?

Circumstances change and people change with them. It isn't that I don't believe that forever is possible. I simply think it's overly optimistic to assume that you can know how you'll feel about something or someone in ten, twenty, fifty years. Then again, the majority of people on the planet disagree with me, so maybe they know something I don't. I don't believe that the institution of marriage is bad, merely inherently flawed, which does not mean that it serves no useful purpose in civilized society. Without marriage, people would still certainly couple up; they'd still have children and raise them. But perhaps without that little piece of paper making it legal, they would be less committed to either their partners or their offspring. There must be comfort in having a permanent co-parent for your children, another breadwinner for feeding the family when you lose your job, and a captive caregiver for you in your old age, if you're lucky enough to last that long. But, practically speaking, would our lives be any different without husbands and wives? Would our underlying needs and values change if the institution of marriage did? Or would we continue to mate roughly as humans always have, semi-permanently and semi-monogamously? Would we be happier if we gave up spending our lives seeking out some romantically inspired vision of "the one," about whom we are often wrong, and who may not even exist? I didn't know the answers to these questions. I knew only that it wasn't for me, and I didn't understand why it was for everyone else.

But if I was dysfunctional where the whole wedlock thing was concerned, Michael was not. His marriage hadn't failed, and his family was intact. But perhaps being with me was a constant reminder that his life had not turned out quite the way he'd wanted it to be. I don't suppose any decent guy goes into a marriage figuring on keeping a lover on the side. Forsaking all others. That was a tricky one, too. It didn't allow for the possibility that the sex in a marriage might end before one of the spouses was ready to go without it. I knew I had no excuse for my behavior, but I didn't believe that Michael deserved to feel badly over his.

But married or no, we did appear to have hauled ourselves out of the doldrums before we stifled in them, and as the snow melted in the spring sun, I felt lighthearted and easy. Then one Friday close to the beginning of June, Michael arrived at the apartment with his face shining like he'd just won the Super Bowl. It tickled me just to see him.

"What is it?" I said, half releasing him from the death grip I called a hug.

"I can't see you next Friday," he answered radiantly.

I had a flash in which I wished he didn't look so thrilled about it, but I knew that was only my foolish insecurity surfacing, since he was obviously happy about something utterly unrelated.

"How come?" I demanded.

He paused dramatically. "I have to go to Meghan's graduation!"

"Oh, my god!" I exclaimed. "Congratulations!!"

"Thank you, thank you," he beamed, like the proud father he was.

There had been considerable doubt as to whether she would graduate at all. She seemed to have turned a corner during the past year, and had finally started to get her act together, but she'd had to cram a lot of extra work into her senior year to make up for the years of slacking.

I reeled him back in to my embrace. "I'm very, very happy for you," I said. "Take lots of pictures so I can see, okay?"

I hadn't meant anything by it, but when a shadow flickered across his face, I knew I'd said something wrong.

"I'm sorry you can't come," he said, some of his glow fading.

"Oh no, don't be silly!" I practically shouted. Sorry, why should he be sorry? I wouldn't have even dreamed of considering thinking about going.

"I could see you on Saturday, instead, if you want," he offered.

"No way!" I shook my head vigorously. "It's a very important occasion and you should spend the weekend with your family." I was glad it came out "your family" and not "your real family." I rushed on, "Are you planning a party for her?"

"Yep!" he answered, and as he regaled me with details about the unexpected celebration, his glow returned and disaster was averted.

But I felt bad, nevertheless. Nowadays he generally spoke to me about his home life without much difficulty, but every so often it seemed that some part of his existence with me would cross too close to the line of his life with them, and he would become uneasy. Like now. The idea that one of the most important people in his world had to be excluded from one of the most important occasions of his life, and the reason why I had to be excluded, detracted somehow from his pleasure in the event itself. Not because I couldn't be there, but simply because he had a me who couldn't be there, and that was a scar on the face of an otherwise elated family unit. At least, that's what I thought it was.

"…And her girlfriend from that private school she got thrown out of is coming, too," Michael was saying. "Miranda thinks she was a bad influence, but I figure, well, she's not the one who got booted, you know?"

"Mm-hmm," I assented. "You know, we should celebrate. Do you want to go out tonight?"

"Okay!" he said brightly. "The quiet place or the noisy place?"

"I think this calls for the noisy place!" There were two pubs within walking distance of the apartment that we felt safe frequenting. No one was ever in the quiet place, so it seemed unlikely we'd ever be seen there. The noisy place was always so jam-packed with people that you couldn't see or hear past the neighbors at your elbow. Both of our significant others could be standing in the same room, and the odds of either one of them actually bumping into us were incredibly remote.

He was still going on about the graduation party. I hadn't heard him babble like this since, well, ever. "And I guess we'll have to invite that punk she calls a boyfriend, but I really don't like that guy."

"Well, he can't be all bad," I interjected. "Her grades have gone up since she's been dating him, haven't they?"

"I guess," he grunted grudgingly. "They must actually get some studying done during all those hours in her room with the door closed." He glowered protectively and it was so adorable that I grabbed his hand and swung it while we walked.

It was a lovely evening. We stayed out later than planned, and had maybe one or two pints more than we should have, and when we returned to the apartment, we passed out before even screwing. We both slept late and I panicked when I woke and saw that the clock read eight-fifteen. We never bothered setting the alarm because I always woke up so early, but today Michael had a meeting with his son's prospective new language tutor at nine. I shook him roughly and he groaned.

"Whatcha want?" he mumbled.

"You have to get up," I insisted. "It's quarter after eight."

"You slept late," he remarked.

"You kept me out late!" I rejoindered.

He struggled to rise. He was a mess. His hair was plastered up in numerous different directions, his beard was tangled, and even with his back turned towards me, I could tell that he still reeked of beer. He finally stumbled out of bed and began struggling into his clothes while I powered up the coffeemaker. Then he vanished into the bathroom bearing a grim, determined aspect, but when he emerged minutes later there hadn't been much improvement.

"Ack!" I cried.

"I know," he answered. "But I don't have time to shower."

"You should at least brush your teeth," I said, waving my hand in front of my face as he leaned over to kiss me goodbye.

"I did!"

"Oh. Well, then you'd better do it again!"

He went to give his mouth another round of fluoride while I sought to cover my own terrible tongue-flavor with the pungent tang of coffee. I heard loud, scary belching and hoped that signified the escape of the worst of the beer breath demons.

I subjected him to another sniff test when he returned, and proclaimed him passable. He embraced me and leaned in again for a goodbye kiss, and this time I accepted it.

"Hey, you know what we forgot to do?" he said suddenly.

"I know!" I replied. It was the first time since our last night at the sublet that we'd rendezvoused without having sex.

"No time for it now, I suppose," he continued.

"Maybe it's just as well," I said. "Not sure my stomach's quite up to it yet."

"I know what you mean," he concurred, rubbing his own rumbling belly.

"So I'll see you in two weeks?" I said, feeling a little wistful. We hadn't missed a Friday since he'd injured his back the previous autumn.

"Guess so." He looked a bit glum, himself.

This was rapidly turning into an awfully melancholy leave-taking for such a short separation, and that was so silly that I laughed and he joined me.

"You'd better go," I said.

He nodded.

"Have fun at the graduation."

He nodded again, and turned to go. And then I realized that I wasn't ready, and I pulled him back and drew his face to mine and kissed him like I had not done in ages, long and hard and with lots of probing, prodding, intermingling tongue. He still tasted terrible.

When I released him, he rewarded me with a goofy grin and I gave him one back and said, "Two weeks, then." And as he finally left for his appointment, it was pleasant to me to feel so assured of his coming again, particularly now that I was horny and two weeks sounded like an awfully long time to await his return.

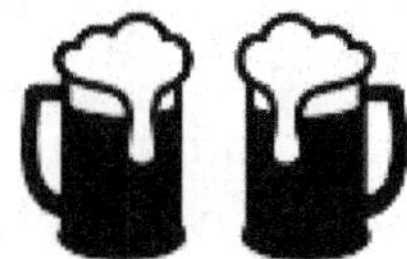

CHAPTER 14

It was a good two weeks, though. On Friday morning, the Friday without Michael, Tom asked me, as usual, if I was planning on coming home that evening. "Actually, if you're not planning on brewing, I was hoping you'd go out with me," I said.

He was stunned. "But it's Friday!" he said.

"I know," I answered. "But I want to go somewhere special."

"Where?"

"The planetarium. They're doing a program for grownups with wine and cheese."

"Wine!" He made a sour face.

"Well, I thought with that barrel project you were thinking about doing, you might actually want to know what some of the vintages taste like." I knew that was a long shot, but it was still my best shot.

"I suppose so." He thought a moment. "Okay, you're on."

We had a blast that night. I hadn't been to the planetarium in years and years, and I'd forgotten how neat that phony night sky looked. The crowd was rowdy and the show got pretty entertaining as the attendees got liquored up. Hecklers shouted out rude remarks over the commentary, the couple sitting two rows in front of us were making out like the deadly asteroid really was about to hit, and I could swear there was some asshole in the back row throwing popcorn because I found several pieces of it in my lap, and we hadn't bought any. We beat it as soon as the program ended, and were vacating the parking lot just as two cruisers were driving into it. I could picture the headline in the local paper: "Twelve Arrested in Planetarium Riot."

Not being fans of wine, we'd both been moderate in our drinking and poured ourselves two full pints of beer when we got home, and then stayed up listening to music while we drank them. 'Round about midnight we decided we should probably toddle off to bed. He looked awfully good as he was undressing, and as we got into bed I thought he smelled awfully good, too. I guess he knew the look, because he didn't hesitate but plunged right in and gave it to me, hard and fast and just the way I liked it, and I loved him as much as I ever had.

In the morning I was bustling about the kitchen, humming a little under my breath, when he came up behind me and reached around to fondle my breasts.

"Mmm!" I said, reaching back in turn and stroking his cock behind me.

After a few minutes I turned off the stove and led him over to the sofa where we fucked some more. It was the best Saturday morning we'd had together in a long time.

After breakfast we went our separate ways, he to his dungeon and me to mine. Michael had texted me a picture of him with his daughter in her cap and gown. He had his arm around her and they were both beaming. I was pleased with the picture and touched that he had sent it. And then Tom came into my office, and I shoved the image guiltily away. I atoned by whipping up a batch of the best brownies ever made, chocolate fudge with a cookie dough topping, which was unusual because I never kept sweets in the house. Somehow it felt like a special occasion to me, too. I worked and Tom tinkered and then we had dinner together and watched TV until I implored him to shut it off so we could make love again.

"What's gotten into you today?" he asked. It had been quite some time since we'd done so much fucking.

"I don't know," I replied. "I just feel – good."

And I did feel good. I felt good about Tom and I felt good about Michael and I wondered what I had done to deserve to have two such terrific men in my life when I was obviously such a wicked, incorrigible woman. I'm sure I would have felt heinous about it if I hadn't felt so incredibly good.

Tom and I spent a lot of time together that week. I was downright jolly and laughed out loud at virtually everything he said. Every night he fell asleep with his hand on my thigh, and every morning we made out at the door before he left for work. Then on Friday morning he asked me again if I was coming home that night.

I was taken aback by the question. "No," I answered, as if it should have been obvious. "It's Friday."

"Oh," he said, disappointed.

"Listen," I continued, determinedly ignoring his dejected expression. "Why don't we plan on doing something together tomorrow night?"

"What did you have in mind?"

"I don't know, I just… I've really had fun hanging out with you this week," I answered.

"Yeah? Me, too."

It was true, it had been fun. Again I thought maybe I liked my boyfriend more when Michael was out of the picture. He was a serious distraction. But that didn't matter now, because it was Friday and I was ready to be distracted again.

I was so excited; it was pathetic how excited I was. You'd think he was returning from a tour of duty overseas for the amount of time I wasted picking out something to wear, then brushing the hair on my head, and removing it from every place else. I was planning on getting to the apartment first, but I got held up at work, and even though it was only six o'clock when I arrived, Michael had still beaten me there. He opened the door before I'd finished fiddling with the lock and had his arms around me before I'd even tucked my keys away. I was glad to see him, too.

He pushed me up against the side of the loveseat, which was near the door, and kissed me forcibly on the lips.

"I missed you!" I breathed between kisses.

"I missed you, too!" he said. And to prove it he set me down on the arm of the loveseat, lifted up my skirt, slid off my panties, and then unbuckled his belt and trousers and gave it to me without further ado. When it was over I let myself fall backwards onto the little sofa with my legs still in the air, fanning them back and forth as if I was trying to air out. I love my pussy, I thought. Love it, love it, love it!

I must have smiled unconsciously, because Michael said, "What are you smiling about?"

"Pussy, pussy, pussy!" I replied. He snickered.

"I agree!" he said.

"You want one, too?"

"Just yours!"

And then I laughed and pulled him down between my legs and on top of me, which was not very comfortable with the arm of the loveseat in the way, so I rolled him slowly off of me and down to the floor instead, where I landed on my knees on top of him.

"Pussy, pussy, pussy!" I said. And he reached down between my legs and stroked it until I came and I was even more grateful to have such a marvelous, wonderful pussy and such a marvelous, wonderful man to play with it.

Later in the evening, he asked me if I still wanted to look for a new apartment when our lease was up.

"I don't know," I said. "This place has kind of grown on me." It had, too. It didn't look any homier, but somehow it felt more like us. I don't know if it was from being empty and locked up all week or what, but somehow it always smelled like sex in there. "We still have nearly three months left on our lease, anyway. We don't need to decide right now. Do we?" I added in response to an unidentifiable something in his face.

He paused. "Meghan wants to attend the junior college over here."

"Oh!" I said. "That's a little close for comfort."

"It's the only one in the area that has this graphic design program she wants to pursue. Plus, since she doesn't have a car, she can ride in with me on my way to work."

"I see." I reflected for a moment, but my brain refused to furnish me with an alternate solution. "Well, we probably should plan on moving, then."

"I thought so, too."

We even saw some of the kids from the college at our pubs from time to time. If she was going to be attending school here, there was no way of knowing if we might run into her, or even a friend of hers who might recognize Michael. I didn't want to ask how he was going to continue meeting me on Fridays if he was providing shuttle service. There was plenty of time still to worry about it. We'd work something out.

"When does she start, around Labor Day?" I inquired.

He shook his head. "Week after next."

"So soon?" I gaped.

"She's still behind on some of the basic requirements. There's an accelerated summer program she can do that will get her caught up by fall if she busts ass on it."

"Oh," I said again. "So . . . does that mean we're on hold for a while?"

"If that's what you want."

It was the kind of thing I would say. Sometimes I wondered if, in his own way, Michael was as insecure and uncertain about my feelings towards him as I was about his towards me. Probably not "as."

"Well, I don't know about you, but I can't afford another rent on top of this one and my mortgage. We're not allowed to offer a sublet here, and it would be tough to do in the summer anyway when all the college kids are trying to rent out their places for a few months."

"Right," he said.

"I suppose we could just be super-careful and take our chances, but that would be nerve-wracking. It's low-rent here – she could meet someone who lives in this very building."

He turned and looked over his shoulder as if the evil fellow-student who would doom us was standing in the doorway. "Uh-huh."

I was about to make it worse. I knew that what I was about to say would cause Michael's face to distort into one of his pained grimaces, but it needed to be said.

"Being caught by your wife, who probably already knows or guesses, would be bad enough. But being caught by your daughter – that would be bloody awful."

"My thoughts exactly," he agreed, flinching only slightly, as if he'd been half-prepared to hear it out loud.

"So, what other choice do we have but to cool it for a few months?"

"Well, I had a thought." He hesitated. "I'm not sure if you're going to like it, though."

"Hit me," I said.

"How do you feel about camping?"

"Camping?" If he'd suggested that we squat in the abandoned gymnasium of the condemned elementary school, I could not have been more surprised.

"Yes, camping. Do you like camping?"

"Well, sure," I said, shrugging. "I mean, I'm not big into it or anything, but I've enjoyed it well enough when I've gone."

He picked his pants up off the floor and dug a brochure out of the back pocket. "See, there's a public campground down by the river. It's far from here, but not too far from where either of us live because it's in the opposite direction. I don't know anyone who goes there, do you?"

"No." I'd never even heard of the place.

"It's cheap to stay there and warm enough now to sleep outdoors."

The idea was becoming more and more appealing to me.

"It'll be mosquito city near the water," he continued, "But at least it won't be as bad as the lake, because it's running and not standing water."

This was true. There was really no escaping the mosquitoes in summer where we lived, anyway.

"So what do you think?" he finished hopefully.

"I – I think it's a great idea."

"Yeah?"

"Yes! It'll be a nice change."

"Getting bored with me, are you?"

"You bet I am!" I cupped his balls in my hand and massaged them fondly. "But how are we going to make Friday nights work if you're going to be chaffeuring Meghan to and from school?"

"Her boyfriend volunteered to come and pick her up on Fridays; he's got a summer job, but that's his day off. Then they can go and do – you know, whatever teenagers do on the weekends in their last summer before college."

"Hmm…" I said thoughtfully. "You know, I don't think I'd want my daughter doing any of the things I did during the summers when I was a teenager."

"Oh, well, I'm sure it's totally different now," he said unconvincingly. "New generation and all. All they think about is schoolwork and finding a career."

"Right," I agreed. "They probably only sneak booze and make out after the library closes."

"Well, if they do, we won't know about it because we'll be off on the other side of town," he replied, crossing his arms defensively and shooting me a look that said I'd better not push my luck when it came to speculating about his daughter's potentially less-than-wholesome activities. "But I think we should make an effort to get down there early before the place fills up – I don't know how crowded it gets in summer."

Evidently it got pretty crowded in summer, as we discovered two weeks later when we arrived around seven o'clock in the evening. It wasn't even dusk yet, and we had to creep past campsite after campsite chock full of people unpacking vehicles, lighting barbecues, and raising tents. We'd taken my wagon and I slumped down in the driver's seat, cringing under the eyes of the other campers, who stared as one unit as we went by like they'd never seen an automobile before. Even worse, every site we passed was occupied already, and I dreaded having to run that gamut all over again so we could go back and try the left-hand fork. Finally we came to the end of the road, we were at the last site, and it, too, already had a trailer parked in it.

"I guess I'll have to find a place to turn around," I sighed. "There's not much room on this road, though."

"That looks like a cul-de-sac up ahead," Michael said, pointing.

I drove forward, then grimly looped the car around, thinking that this camping idea was losing some of its charm.

"Wait! What's that?" I said. A miniature wooden post was protruding at a slant from the ground to my left.

Michael gasped. There, just ahead of us, nearly invisible from the other direction, one tiny little campsite had been tacked on off the edge of the turnabout.

I punched the gas and we lurched up over a mound of gravel at the entrance and down a little hill to a flat space beyond. I parked and we craned our necks in every direction but saw nothing, no one, not even the trailer from the campsite that was closest to us, and we looked at each other and knew that this was the place; this was our home for the summer.

It wasn't much. The site was large enough to hold a two-man tent and our mid-sized cooler and that was about it. But that was a bargain if it meant being shielded from the road, and, there was less likely to be competition for such a little space even if someone else did find it. It was comparatively noisy for a while because other cars kept veering up the road and turning in the cul-de-sac to try their luck elsewhere just like we had. But the light was dimming and not one car crested our little hill, and it seemed that our position was as unnoticeable to everyone else as it almost had been to us. After a while we stopped worrying about having uninvited guests and went about the work of setting up camp. This was mercifully brief. Michael assembled the tent while I fetched us beers from the cooler, laid out the propane stove he had brought, and cooked the bacon and hamburgers because by now we were both starved, and hell, you know, when you're camping, there's not much else to do. By the time he'd finished inflating the air mattress, dinner was ready and we sat side by side on my tailgate, balancing our plates in our laps and our bottles between our legs, and ate and drank and admired the setting sun.

After dinner I had an unpleasant moment when I realized I didn't recall seeing a port-a-john at our end of the campground. I certainly wasn't above peeing in the woods, but if one of us had to take a dump, it could be a momentous problem. So I commandeered the flashlight and we ventured up the road a ways, but there were no facilities in sight. There wasn't much we could do about it now except hope for the best.

It wasn't quite dark yet, so on the return trip we crossed the road and picked our way across a narrow field to the river itself. It was prodigiously wide up close, and its motion seemed deceptively slow, as if it was really roaring past at frightening speed, but silently, like a predator with sharp teeth and soft paws. We could still almost discern the outline of the road from that vantage point, and when we thought we'd come roughly parallel with the cul-de-sac, we prepared to traverse the field again. I shot one last glance downriver and glimpsed a clearing a short distance ahead that looked like it might be a picnic site. I hoisted my flashlight and was elated to perceive an outhouse right there next to the picnic table. It was especially delightful because by then my beer had worked its way through my system, and I really had to go.

Once necessities had been attended to, we made our way back to camp, cracked open fresh beers, lay down on the hood of the station wagon and gazed up at the darkling heavens. It was really quite a lovely campground if you removed all those excess people. Proud evergreens towered all around us, and just beneath the racket the armies of crickets were making, you could hear the faint swishing of the river as it meandered along across the way. There was no moon, and without city lights the stars flashed boldly above and beyond us. How incredibly peaceful and natural it seemed to live summer this way. When the bugs, evidently undaunted by either our citronella candles or the spray in which we'd doused ourselves, became too overwhelming, we seized a couple of spare beers and raced into the tent, unzipping and zipping it up again rapidly, Michael shouting, "Go! Go!" like we were paratroopers on a mission. He'd stuck our bags into the space between the air mattress and the wall of the tent and I unwedged mine and put on an extra long T-shirt and stashed my slip-on sandals by the door for when I had to pee. Michael simply stripped to his boxers, then lay there quite contentedly on his side sipping his beer while I fussed about with folding this and rearranging that. Camping or not, I still liked things neat.

When I was settled in, I lay down on my side next to him and he draped his arm about my waist and cuddled me closely while we reiterated what a treasure we'd found and how we should claim this territory every Friday for the rest of the summer. And then he kissed me and I knew that soon it would be time for sex, and even though I couldn't see his face anymore I suspected he was smiling. I knew I was.

In the morning we packed and slipped away early, mostly to avoid the bulk of the gawping that would inevitably follow our departure. Also, there would be no food for Michael and no coffee for me until we got back to town, and that was another reason to make haste. We'd agreed not to bother with packing provisions for breakfast, since that would mean that by the time we cooked, ate, and cleaned up we'd be late starting for home. Michael had actually told his wife that he was planning on camping on Friday nights for the rest of the summer. That had been the biggest surprise of all.

"I read that the cell reception isn't very good here," he explained. "And you know, they should know where to find me, if something were to happen," he finished ominously.

I eyed him curiously. If something happened to his wife or one of the kids, or if something happened to him? How old was Michael now? Well, I was forty-three, so that would make him forty-six. Not quite old enough to be worried about his health, but almost. For a long moment I felt a vague uneasiness in the pit of my stomach like I always did when I thought of something bad happening to Tom. This happened in phases. Sometimes I'd convince myself that nothing could possibly ever happen to him and that he'd just be there forever, or at least until long after I was dead and gone. But other times I'd get all freaked out imagining he'd have a heart attack and die the following week, probably on a Friday night when I was with Michael. Talk about a shitty way to go, kicking the bucket while your girlfriend's fucking her lover. When that possibility occurred to me, it made me so anxious that I had to shut it out of my mind quickly or I'd find myself dissolving in a gush of tears. Was I going to have to start worrying about both of them now? My life was too complicated for my fragile sensibilities, and although the blame for that was all mine, knowing it did not make it any less upsetting. Maybe I'd get lucky and get run over by a bus walking down the street by myself so I wouldn't have to worry about them anymore, or who I was going to be with when my own end came.

But these gloomy thoughts dissipated after we arrived back in town and I got some coffee percolating through my system. We'd parked his car at my office. I know that sounds foolhardy, but it seemed the safest place to stash it overnight, since it wasn't practical to leave it at the apartment.

"Hey, you know, maybe next time we should take your car," I suggested as I was dropping him off.

"You worried about leaving it here?" he said.

"A little," I admitted. "But also, I was thinking, you know, if someone did come looking for you… I mean, they'd be expecting to find your car, wouldn't they?"

"Good point," he said gruffly. I wondered if he was trying as hard as I was not to formulate a picture in my head of how that particular scene would play out if it happened.

"Anyway, we're not packing so much stuff that we really need the wagon. And it definitely won't look so suspicious if your car isn't here overnight week after week."

So the following week that's the way we did it, and when I climbed in, I felt like the undeserving recipient of some privilege I hadn't really earned. I'd never actually ridden in his car before. Neither Tom nor Michael had been in my car much, the first because he always drove when we went out, and the second because we were almost always meeting someplace in two cars rather than going somewhere together. So I didn't feel as if either of them had dibs on that territory, I guess. But being in Michael's car made me squeamish, as if I was invading his family's space somehow. It was the vehicular equivalent of going over to his own house to fuck him. I eventually adjusted my mind to it, but I never touched him when he was driving, didn't put a hand on his leg or stroke his hair or do anything that even remotely suggested physical contact. All things considered, I knew it was a strange place to draw a moral line, but somehow I respected myself more for respecting his family's space.

Every summer I had with Michael was wonderful, but that summer of Friday night camping was truly something special. I didn't know it then, but those were the last really good times I would have with him. After the first week, we made a point of arriving earlier so we could claim our spot before anyone else uncovered it, and also thereby avoid the crowd. Then the fourth week Michael got stuck at work, and we were very late. We found our area occupied and had to cross over to the other side of the campground, where we landed somewhere in the middle of a field of young screaming children. We tried to make the best of it, but it was a miserable evening and it saddened me that my one night with Michael had been ruined by factors as stupid as work and other people's obnoxious brats. I had grown unreasonably attached to our usual campsite, and I reckoned that we were two of only a handful of people who ever found and used it. One Saturday morning when I got home, I discovered that I had accidentally left my hat behind. The following week I found it, still perched on the tree stump one of us often used as a chair while the other sat on the ice chest. Occasions like that made me feel as if, even if it wasn't much, the place was truly ours. In fact, its meagerness and inconvenience reminded me of almost every place we'd rented together. I guess I had grown to associate cramped living quarters with Michael!

After that week we lost out, I went down to the campground at four o'clock just to ensure that we retrieved our rights to that spot. Around five-thirty, a car crowned the little hill and I caught myself mid-wave when I realized it wasn't Michael, but some other camper trying to steal our space. The driver made a face that said, Sorry!, and reversed carefully back up the driveway, but I already felt as if our home had been invaded. I told Michael about it when he finally arrived forty-five minutes later, and we agreed that from then on we would take turns getting there early if the other was going to need to be late. It was worth the scanty price of admission to squeeze a second vehicle protectively into that driveway. I was always proud when I was the late one and descended the hill to find Michael in a defensive posture, teeth bared, fists clenched, beard wagging, swearing and glaring like a crazy man at the unwelcome visitor until he saw it was me, at which point he would drop his scary stance and smile and wave me in cheerily. The first time I saw that convinced me that anyone who tried to get into that campsite once when Michael was protecting it would never try it again. I was also quite certain that he enjoyed playing the insane hermit for strangers. For my part, I never had to chase anyone away again, and thus was able to sit and read quietly there in the comfortably shady clearing until Michael came.

It was very peaceful. On warm days we waded thigh-deep in the slow sections of the river, and on cool ones we made a game out of jumping from boulder to boulder along the riverbed. When a thunderstorm sprang up we made a mad dash for the car and sat in it, usually already drenched, and sipped beer and waited for it to pass, and when the midsummer air was hot and steamy again we would strip boldly naked in the driveway and don our spare clothes and lay the wet ones out to dry in the open field between us and the river. A little later we would flip them over, and then go and gather them up when they were fully dry, and somehow I enjoyed having that little chore to do; it made me feel homey and domestic out there in the woods. Sometimes after dinner when it was utterly dark and silent, and a bit lonely on our end, we would stroll along the edge of the road back towards the heart of the campground, eavesdropping on the chatter of close-knit families and old couples and groups of young people fooling around and drinking beer as we were; see the light of their fires and the shape of their shadows and then fade quickly into the night if they caught a glimpse of us in turn. And other times we would simply lie down in the mosquito-free tent with the top flap open except for the mesh cover and hold hands and gaze up at the sky, and speak seriously of timeless subjects like man's place in the universe and whether fighting ought to be banned from hockey.

And most often we would, with some difficulty, make love on that bouncy, floppy air mattress, very quietly so that passersby wouldn't hear through the paper-thin walls of the tent. But other times the crisp clean outdoor air would put us to sleep before we got that far, and I wouldn't even know I'd been sleeping until I woke in his arms. I'd lie there quietly as long as I could in the brightening dawn, because there was no method by which a mere mortal might succeed in rising from that mattress without waking the other person. But eventually I wouldn't be able to wait anymore to pay a visit to the outhouse, and I'd throw on my sweatshirt and my sandals and go. When I returned, Michael would be dozing lightly and would wake halfway as I crawled back into bed, and he'd turn over on his side and we'd wrap our arms around each other and nap a little longer. And sometimes I'd remind him that he hadn't done his chores, and he'd tell me to hop on then, and I'd pull down his boxers and clamber on top of him and take the morning wood, my knees pressing awkwardly into the rubbery surface of the mattress, still very quietly, since we could hear the sounds of the rest of the camp stirring as we did it. And although it was wasteful, sometimes I was glad we had our separate automobiles there because it meant I could say goodbye to Michael long and slow there in the privacy of the campsite rather than quickly and furtively in the parking lot of my office.

But soon, oh, too soon, it was September, and there was an early cold snap and by Labor Day we were shivering through the night no matter how closely we snuggled, and we knew it would have to end. Plus, Meghan had successfully finished her summer school program and was rolling right into the fall semester, so I went to the apartment without Michael and cleaned it and packed our things. And then I didn't know what to do. We hadn't found a new place, and truth be told, we hadn't really been looking very hard. I didn't know how it was going to work now. Our long-standing Friday night tradition was over. It was simply too awkward to expect Michael to bring his daughter home from school, and then go out again after dinner and not come back until morning. And frankly, we were in a different place now as far as sex was concerned. More of our time nowadays was spent cuddling rather than screwing, and the idea of meeting up with him just for a quickie now and again sounded weird and would have felt forced. But looking over the furniture and wondering what I was going to do with it, I felt strongly impelled to make a decision. Was this to be the final crossroads?

Money was also becoming a larger and more insurmountable problem. The J.C. wasn't very expensive, but Michael's older son was a sophomore now and was already dreaming about attending a highly competitive private college out of state. He was still having a lot of trouble getting along with the other kids at school, and having a goal seemed to make academic life more tolerable. I felt bad for the kid. I'd never met him, of course, and it was hard to imagine what had transpired in his life to date to make him such an outcast. Of course, it doesn't take much if you stay in one community for your entire youth. Half the people you knew in grammar school are still there with you in high school, and if they didn't like you then, they wouldn't like you now. In any case, Michael had promised him that if he kept out of trouble and was accepted to the expensive university, that he could go. I didn't know how he expected to pay for that, and my guess was, he didn't either. So although he never said so, as our deadline drew nearer I think Michael was a bit relieved at the idea of having a few months rent-free. I understood. Theoretically, of course, because it wasn't encompassed in the realm of my experience. Family had to come first.

Unfortunately, his unwillingness to take a real stand placed the burden squarely on my shoulders, and by the last week of September I was pretty cross with him. I hadn't even seen him in nearly three weeks, and trying to figure out what "we" were going to do about "us" via text message was incredibly irritating. Deep down, of course, I wondered if this was his way of passively ending it. I hoped not. If it was, it was a really chicken-shit way to go, and even if it was over I didn't want to think of Michael like that. Of course, by this time I was so ticked off with him for leaving everything up to me that even I wasn't sure if I cared if we got back together or not.

I'd never really been annoyed with Michael before, not for more than a few minutes, anyway, and I wasn't sure I knew how to handle it. I didn't think there had ever been an angry word spoken between us. I didn't kid myself into believing that that was because we were such an awesome couple who always got along. There's simply no sense in fighting with someone you only see once a week; you brush off the little irritations because it's a waste of your time together to dwell on them. And it's hard to have genuine disagreements when you don't actually share a life together. We weren't a regular couple. We didn't have to work through our differences; we could just go home and fight with our real mates about the things that mattered. What would we have argued over? There were no big questions for us, no, should we buy long-term care insurance, or do you think the kids are old enough to be left home alone, or can we really afford a new car right now. What would our issues have been? Whose turn was it to make the bed? Who was going to mail the rent check? How many beers should we keep in the fridge? Those were all easy questions that we'd settled long ago. He made the bed because he was better at it than I was, he gave me cash and I wrote the rent checks because my bank account was private, and the refrigerator should hold as many beers as would fit inside it. We were logical people who derived rational answers to the questions of daily – or in our case, weekly – life, and without more constant interaction, we were unlikely to come upon any serious stumbling blocks in our relationship.

Yet here we were, and although I was in the mood to fight with him now, I couldn't because we didn't see each other, and fighting with a blank wall is both dissatisfying and painful. In the end I stopped trying to solicit his opinion, and sold the furniture for a hundred bucks to a kid who was moving in and had none. I couldn't bring it home, and it was a better solution than paying to store it until God-knew-when. But I still didn't have the heart to dispose of the linens, and back went the sheets and towels to the hall closet, and the comforter to the trunk of my car. And then the apartment was empty, and for once I didn't stand starry-eyed looking around and remembering all the good times we'd had there; I just closed the place up and turned off the light, and wasn't even sad to unburden myself of the keys.

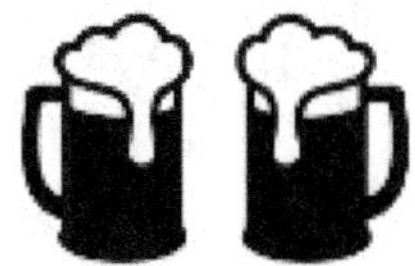

CHAPTER 15

But actually adjusting to a life without Michael was another matter entirely. Until then I had not realized how much of my current pleasure in my existence revolved around that weekly dalliance, and suddenly I had nothing more to look forward to again but work and housework and an occasional beer with Tom, which was all I'd had before Michael and which demonstrably had not been enough. You would think that with Michael absent, I would naturally have turned my excess affections to my legitimate partner. I'd certainly felt sometimes that Tom and I were happier when Michael was not around. But having him vanish from my life permanently was vastly different from our occasional temporary separations. Now I suspected he was never coming back, and I was as irritated with Tom as if it was his own doing. When the following Friday came and he asked me, as always, whether I was coming home that night, I snarled my yes in response, and I think he was even more surprised by my tone than by my answer. It wasn't his fault, of course. He'd been more than tolerably patient with me and my moods and the unexplained absences that few men would have let slide. And I'd been very happy with him – as long as I'd had Michael to round out my entertainment. But now it was just he and I again, and although I was maybe getting closer, I still wasn't quite ready to putter quietly about my half of the house while he puttered quietly about his half until death parted us in a more permanent fashion. And whereas, a few weeks ago, I'd had two men I'd adored to be torn between, now it seemed I had none, and without that I was lost.

The worst part was not knowing what was going on with Michael. I hadn't contacted him since before moving day, and he'd remained silent as well. If it was over between us, it wasn't official, and as the days passed, that rankled me more and more. However, I was grimly determined not to initiate the first contact. In a bittersweet way, that reminded me of how I'd struggled to stay away from him early on in our relationship, before there'd been anything between us. The only difference was that now when I hated him, I knew it was just a cover.

In early October I met with one of my clients who'd been on extension to finalize her tax return. She also had a number of questions regarding the affairs of her father, who was in the advanced stages of emphysema and was not expected to live much longer. He resided out of state and she was taking a leave of absence from work to go and spend his remaining time with him. I explained to her the rules on dependency, claiming the medical expenses of a parent, and so on, and when the discussion was finished and the documents were signed I handed over her bill.

Although it was no more than usual, her cheeks flushed when she looked at it, and I knew what she was going to say next. I decided to let her off the hook.

"You can hold off on paying that if you need to," I said. "I'm sure this thing with your dad is going to be very expensive. We can work it out after you get back."

"Thank you." She smiled gratefully at me. "That reminds me, I also wanted to ask you, what are the tax consequences of renting out my condo?"

I gave her the rundown on that, too, but when I was done she said, "I guess I will try to rent it while I'm gone, but I probably won't be able to, anyway. I mean, who would want to take a place without knowing if they'd be staying for three weeks or three months?"

I opened my mouth to say that Michael and I sure would, but then I remembered that we weren't speaking right now, and I promptly shut it again.

But after she left, my mind was still stuck on him, and I knew I was in trouble because my annoyance was beginning to fade, and fear was replacing it. What if he hadn't been in touch because he'd been in an accident or had thrown his back out again or his wife was in the hospital, and here I was holding a grudge over some stupid quarrel that wasn't even a quarrel? Although I was hurt that he hadn't called, I still didn't believe in my heart of hearts that he would leave me without any explanation; without even saying goodbye. And the longer I thought about it, the more I began to worry that something really had happened to him. It wasn't long before my ill-defined sense of dread grew into full-blown panic, and I knew I had to do something.

Calling or texting was out now, I knew that. What if his wife had found out about me and forbidden him to contact me again? If he actually was in trouble, the last thing I wanted to do was draw attention to myself to whomever had custody of his phone. Come to think of it, I didn't even know if he'd made any sort of effort to cover it up on his end. Did he delete my text messages? Did he use a fake name for me in his contacts? I had a horrifying mental image of Tom finding out about Michael and me via my telephone history after I was gone, which seemed a particularly cruel way for him to acquire that information. Michael was well-hidden in my day-to-day life. But there were a hundred clues that would give us away in the event of my untimely demise, most notable of which were the leases, which I still retained among my financial papers. I couldn't believe this had never occurred to me before. I vowed to destroy everything that was incriminating as soon as I'd checked up on Michael.

What would Michael do if I suddenly vanished? I wondered. I mean, assuming we ended up together again. It would be the same deal, right? One day things are fine, and the next I don't call or show up for our scheduled meeting, and he has no way of determining if something happened to me because we're hardly supposed to even know each other and it's not as if he can just call or drop by the house. So then he has to sit and wonder how long he should wait before calling the hospitals and the jails, and then he's not going to be able to get much information out of those people anyway because we have no recognizable relationship. I supposed if he were really concerned he could drop by my office. My assistant had never met him, naturally; I'd taken care to avoid that, so he could call or visit one time in relative anonymity.

And of course, there was the solution staring me in the face, and I was a moron for not having seen it sooner because no one except for Michael would think twice about it if I simply stopped by the brewery where he worked. Even if I didn't run into him, I was bound to get some information there, and at the very worst, I would come home with some good beer.

Once I had the idea I didn't wait; I went that very afternoon. I left work early, stopped by the house to put on something colorless and nondescript, and then made the long trek across town to the brewery expansion. I had never been there, but Michael had described it to me plenty. He didn't do it justice. It was a massive place, probably the length and width of a city block, and even though real estate wasn't particularly pricy in that industrial area, it still must have cost many arms and legs to lease or buy. I was awed that this down-to-earth guy whom I mostly pictured naked was in some respects in charge of such an enormous enterprise. I drove in through the expansive wrought-iron gates and felt horrendously self-conscious already as I tried to figure out where the visitors' parking area was.

You're just buying a growler, I said to myself over and over; you're just buying a growler; no one will think it's weird at all. Finally I found what I thought was the tasting room, off on one corner of the main building, but when I got out of the car and walked up to it, the door was locked. Either it was closed or I was in the wrong place, and either way my nerve had run out, so I scurried back to the car and sat in it a moment trying to catch my breath. I glanced back up at the building, and although the windows were translucent, I could discern the outlines of gigantic stainless steel fermenters on one side of the warehouse and oak-aging barrels on the other. And then I glanced back at what I'd thought was the tasting room door, and a middle-aged red-headed man was coming out of it.

I should have sat there; I should have stayed quietly in the car until he was gone and he never would have noticed me, but instinct kicked in and I couldn't fight the urge to flee, so I started the engine and let out the clutch too fast and immediately killed the motor like a student driver experimenting with Dad's sports car. The tires squealed as I jerked to a rocky halt, and Michael naturally looked over and it was apparent from his face that he recognized the wagon.

Well, then I didn't know what to do. I was tempted to peal out, let him smell my burnt rubber, and shout out "In your face, Michael!" as he choked on the gassy fumes I would leave in my wake. My other option was to behave like a grownup and wait patiently to see what he would do before I let myself skid into a temper tantrum. Needless to say, I decided to make a break for it. But by then he was already ten feet in front of me and I couldn't have driven off without running him over, which would surely have drawn a lot of unwanted attention to my presence and many witnesses to my impending flight to freedom. So instead I waited while he approached my window and then quickly glanced over his shoulder before signaling to me to roll it down.

"Hi," I said, nodding as if we'd merely passed one another on a crowded street.

"Hi," he answered, scrutinizing me without a blink of those icy blue eyes. "What are you doing here?"

It was neither a friendly nor an unfriendly inquiry, merely matter-of-fact, as if maybe I'd come by on a sales call or for a job interview or even veritably to buy beer. But now that I was seeing him and knew he was fine, I forgot the worries that had brought me down here and started worrying instead that he might think I was spying on him. In that light, I decided that honesty was the safest tactic.

"I haven't heard from you in a while," I explained. "I was worried that maybe something had happened to you."

"Oh," he said, and his eyes softened slightly. "I haven't heard from you in a while either."

"Guess not," I answered. And then there was nothing more to say, and I was uncomfortably aware that there might be people watching from the windows of the upstairs offices so I said, "Well, I'm glad you're all right. I'd better be going."

"It was good seeing you," he said.

"Good seeing you too," I answered automatically.

Without looking back at him, I started the engine again. He stepped away from my window and I drove off so I could get the hell out of there before I started crying because now I knew it really was over, and worse, I still didn't know why and I knew that would torment me.

I remembered, as I left him, that first night we'd spent together in the hotel and how he'd behaved inscrutably the morning after; how badly I'd wanted to walk out except that I couldn't stand to let it end like that. That was how I felt again, and for a moment I wanted to go rushing back and force him to give me, if not an explanation, at least a proper goodbye. But no, I couldn't do that now because here it was years later, and I still didn't know what he was thinking, and anyway I had done enough chasing after him and this was just how it was going to have to be. And then my phone rang and it was Michael and I was grateful, hopelessly and pathetically grateful to him for not letting it end like that when he knew how painful it would be for me, and when he asked if I wanted to go and have a beer with him, of course I said yes.

Ten minutes later I was in his arms again in the parking lot behind the bar we'd chosen and he was rubbing his hands against my back briskly because it was cold, but whether for my benefit or his I couldn't tell. And for once I didn't care that we were out in public or who might see, I kissed him hard on the lips and then he took me tenderly by the arm and we walked inside.

"What happened?" he asked once we had our beers. This particular place sported a bar all along its perimeter, and we'd selected a spot in the back corner away from the door.

I shook my head. "You tell me," I said. "You were being weird and indecisive about the apartment and the furniture, and it was annoying because I didn't know what to do, either." He nodded. "I mean, the scheduling's not going to work out anymore, and it just seems silly for us to shell out that much dough for a place we may not even be able to use."

"Yeah, that's kind of where I was at, too," he confirmed. "I kept wanting to call you but there aren't a lot of places we can go out in public. And it's not the same as being alone together, either."

"Right," I agreed. I tried and failed to mental stock of the options. "So what's the alternative?"

"Well, next summer we can go camping again," he suggested helpfully.

"Uh – I'm not sure I can wait that long!" I replied. Now that he was near me again, the weeks of vexation were fading out of memory, the physical effect of his presence was beginning to take hold of me, and I was already finding myself aching for some alone time. But even so, I was touched that he still planned on being with me next summer.

"Missing my action, are you?" he winked. It was one of his rare uncharacteristically vulgar moments, and I laughed.

"Not in the least!" I said, inserting my cold hand between his legs. It warmed up instantly.

He laughed, too, squeezing his thighs together over my frigid fingers, and then said thoughtfully, "Seriously, though, we don't have to have sex every time we get together." He nearly whispered when he got to the word "sex." "I mean, we can see each other sometimes without that."

I wasn't sure if he was trying to convince himself or me, but it was still a sweet thing to say to the lover you kept mainly for sex.

"I know!" I answered. "But it's sure nice to have the option when you want it."

"Well, it sounds to me like we're stuck in the same boat as a month ago." He sighed. "Well, maybe we'll have to do what all of the other adulterers in the country do, and start going to motels." He whispered again when he got to the word "adulterers." "If we made it a couple of times a month, that wouldn't cost much, split two ways."

I hesitated.

"You don't want to," he said.

"It's just so – so sordid, Michael. I mean, I know that what we do, what we're doing, it's the same no matter where we go, but at a motel, I don't know, it feels icky somehow. That's where people go when they just need a place to fuck. And honestly, we're not spending that much time just fucking anymore, you know what I mean?"

He nodded. "And if we ever get caught, I don't want it to be coming out of a cheap motel. It seems less sleazy when we have our own space."

"Right," I said. "I mean, if we're going to get together just for a quickie, I'd almost rather do you in my car, or at the park, or something."

"Didn't we try that once before?" he said, chuckling.

I could feel my face reddening with the memory. "Oh, right. That didn't really work out so well, did it?"

"Wait!" He brightened suddenly and his eyes twinkled. "What about your office?"

I laughed out loud. I'd had so many fantasies about doing Michael in my office that for a minute it sounded really appealing, and I ran the idea through my head to see if it could really work.

"No," I said at last, disappointed.

"Aww! Why not?"

"Well, it might do in a pinch, but it's not a good long-term solution. For one thing, it wouldn't be very comfortable. If I were still working alone, I could set something up for us in the back room and keep it hidden, but that won't work now that I've got office help. But the bigger problem is that I have a lot of clients from our neighborhood, most of whom drive by my office on their way to and from work. Actually, that's the main reason I chose that location, because not only is it near my house, it's also on that main thoroughfare, and very visible. If my assistant was off, you could come by during the day and maybe no one would notice, because the traffic wouldn't seem unusual, but you're at work then, so it couldn't happen anyway. But you know how that building is set up – the parking lot may be out back, but the entrance is right there in full view of the street. If you were seen coming or going after-hours when there's no one else around, that would be very fishy. It's unfortunate you're so recognizable!" I finished, giving his beard a gentle tug.

"Should I get rid of the beard?" he inquired.

"Would you?" I responded, surprised. It was as if he had asked me if I thought he should chop off his leg because it was ruining the line of his pants.

"Good God, no!" he exclaimed, stroking it roughly and looking more like a wizard than ever.

But I really liked the office idea, and I continued to review it in my mind as if merely thinking about it enough would make it feasible. But then I had a bright idea of my own.

"Let's table the office option for now," I said. "I have another suggestion." And I told him about my client who was going out of town and wanted to rent out her condo until after her father passed.

"She can't afford to pay me," I said. "So I could probably work out a trade and it wouldn't cost much."

"Where does she live?" I told him and he grimaced slightly. It was a pretty nice neighborhood, but it was adjacent to the largest shopping center on our side of town. In fact, it was only a couple of miles from my house, and only one highway exit away from his. I knew full well what he was thinking.

"It's only for a little while," I said. "We won't be able to go out, but at least it's a full-sized apartment and it's furnished. We'll have a real kitchen and a living room and everything. We can cook or order in and actually eat at a table for once. It might be nice for a change," I argued.

He mulled it over for a minute. "Find out what she wants for it," he said finally. "It could be a nice change at that." He smiled suddenly and asked, "But where are we going to put our bed? In the middle of the living room?"

I shook my head sadly. "I sold the furniture, Michael," I said. "To some kid. I couldn't store it, and I didn't know if we'd ever use it again."

"Oh," he answered, looking a little sad himself. Then he picked up his glass and raised it. "Here's hoping that he has as many good times in that bed as we did!"

"Cheers!" I said, clinking my glass against his. I could drink to that in good conscience.

"What about that fluffy white comforter? Did you give him that, too?"

"Nope, it's in my car," I said. "Only it's not so fluffy anymore." It was true. It had developed little pinholes along several of its seams, and tiny feathers were now shooting out of it with alarming regularity.

We both sat reflectively for a moment. I was imagining that the state of the comforter was a metaphor for my relationship with Michael, which also was gradually growing thin and tattered. I wondered what he was thinking.

"It doesn't mean anything," he assured me, rubbing my hand where it still sat cozily wedged between his thighs. Apparently he didn't have to wonder what I was thinking. I suppose somewhere along the line he'd grown accustomed to my inner morbidity.

"It will have to end sometime," I said seriously.

"Probably," he agreed.

"Still – I'm glad it's not now."

"Me, too."

And we smiled at each other and I don't know if it was the lengthy separation or the lighting in the bar, but suddenly I noticed how heavily lined his face had become in the past few years. And somehow it pleased me to have been around long enough to witness that transformation, and I was more proud to know the older man than I had been to know the younger one. And although I knew that I probably didn't look much better, for the first time I was not bothered very much by it. Because whether he felt the same way about it or not, Michael had taken that journey with me as well. I'd given him what was left of my youth, and I was glad that I'd had him with me during my descent into middle age.

"What are you thinking?" he asked curiously.

"Never you mind," I said gently.

Then he looked into my eyes and kissed me on the forehead, and I wanted to welcome him back, somehow, back into my life, and I was about to suggest that we take a trip across town to my office after all when he glanced at his watch and said he had to be going.

"Right now?" I said, sliding my hand further up his thigh and giving him the eye.

He chuckled and the tips of his ears reddened. "I have to go and pick up Meghan from the library. She hangs out on campus studying until I get there."

"Oh," I said.

"Soon, though," he said, reaching over to stroke my breast, very lightly, with the back of his hand.

"Promise?"

"Promise."

And then we went outside, and I watched him drive away, leaving me alone with my arousal, and I wasn't sure whether I should be annoyed that he'd gone without pleasing me, or pleased that he still aroused me, but I sure was looking forward to seeing him again.

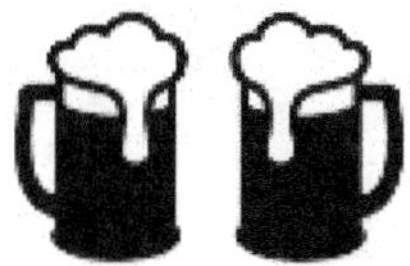

CHAPTER 16

I contacted my client with the condo on the day she was flying out of town.

"Well no, I haven't rented it out yet," she said, sounding puzzled. "Why do you ask?"

"What would you think of me taking it for a while?"

"Oh!" she answered. "But I thought you – I mean, I didn't realize you were looking to move." She must have studied tact in school.

"Oh no, Tom and I are still together," I said quickly. "It's just that I've been getting these terrible allergic reactions at the house. I think it's from his homebrewing."

She'd never met Tom, of course, but the previous Christmas I'd given away growlers of his homebrew to some of my clients, so she at least knew who he was.

"You're kidding!"

"I wish! I don't know if it's the grain or the yeast or what, but if I'm home when he's brewing now, my eyes burn and my nostrils swell up – it's so bad I can't even breathe. In the summer it's less of a problem, because I just open all the windows and that seems to send whatever it is outside. But when it's cold – well, it would just be nice to have a respite once in a while. If it's not too expensive."

Farfetched and self-serving as it sounds, this was actually true. Maybe it was only because he was making larger batches now, but the steam from the boil seemed to fill the whole house, and my lungs right along with it. Since he brewed mostly on Friday nights, it hadn't been much of an issue until recently because I'd had my extracurricular activities to keep me out of the house. But now I was very uncomfortable during brew sessions, and worse, a weird smell constantly seemed to be emanating from the basement. I was convinced that there'd been a nasty spill in a crack somewhere and mold was growing out of control because my nose never seemed to stop running when I was down there.

She gave me a good deal, as I had expected she would, and she wasn't put off by my suggestion that we do an exchange for what she owed me. I told her I'd square up with her on the balance whenever she wanted me to if the rental lasted more than a couple of months. It was an ideal setup for both of us. She didn't have to rent to a stranger she had to worry about trying to kick out whenever she wanted to come back, and I think she was also happy to have some kind of housesitter she could trust while she was away. I even agreed to water her plants, if she dared to let me.

"I'm warning you, though – I've killed every plant I've ever owned. No matter how well I've treated them." This was also true. I'd even managed to destroy a cactus I'd bought on a trip through Texas.

She laughed. "Don't worry; mine are brown-thumb-proof!"

"Hmph," I grunted. "We'll see about that."

And then it was November, and it had been almost two months since I'd been with Michael and I couldn't wait to see him. But he was still shuttling his daughter to and from school, and worse – for me, anyway – because the timing worked out, he was also retrieving his youngest from football practice on his way home, so weekdays were out all together. Just as I was beginning to think we'd taken the new place for nothing, Michael texted me to suggest Sunday afternoon, and I was all over that in a heartbeat. If there was one time when I was still almost always horny, it was weekend afternoons. But even with that, I was too curious about the day and time selection to pounce on Michael the second he arrived. Physically, I mean.

"Why now?" I asked.

"Why not now?" he answered. He apparently wasn't as content to wait, and had transitioned immediately from hugging me in welcome to roughly fondling my breasts without missing a beat.

"No, I mean, why Sunday afternoon?"

"Oh," he said, lifting up my shirt and reaching around me to unclasp my bra. "Kids have a lot of activities on Saturdays now, sports and music and stuff. Sundays they like to hang out with their friends. No time for Mom and Dad."

I would have felt bad for him about being excluded from his growing children's lives except that he was ripping off my pants and pushing me down on the kitchen table as we spoke, and if he wasn't all that upset by it I figured I shouldn't be, either.

Afterwards we went into the bedroom to lie down, and while he dozed I found myself thinking about the kid thing. I didn't have any, so I didn't know, but it seemed as if that's how it must go; you have the kids and there's no time for you and your mate because it's all about the kids, and then eventually they grow up and have no time for or interest in you and that's when you get time for each other again. I didn't believe we could last that long, but if we did maybe we'd have more time for each other, too, as his kids grew up. And then I wondered how Michael and his wife would get along once the children were gone. Would they no longer have anything in common, or would it permit them to renew their passion for each other? If it was the latter, there might not be room for me in Michael's life anymore. But in the case of the former, there might be too much room.

Good God, I thought. What would happen if Michael and his wife ever split up? I might suddenly find myself thrust into a much more important role than I desired. He'd get his own place, naturally. Well, that would be nice – no more teeny apartments. But his kids would probably be living with him half of the time, and then I'd have to stay away, or worse, be Dad's girlfriend. Or way worse, their part-time stepmom. And I didn't know if that arrangement would suit Michael, either. Our relationship notwithstanding, he was a committer just like Tom was. Sure, he had a lover. One, whom he had kept for a period of years now. This was not someone who was likely to be satisfied with a once-a-week dalliance if he had no wife at home waiting for him. He'd have to get a girlfriend to supplement the girlfriend! Oh, it would be a disaster.

Of course, he'd probably had the same misgivings about me and Tom, if he'd ever bothered to think about it. What would I want from him if I suddenly found myself alone? Would I expect him to be my boyfriend, and what would that do to his family? Michael couldn't take Tom's place for me, I knew that. But I would certainly be less miserable without Tom if I still had Michael. And maybe I would want a little more. Evenings can get awfully lonely when you're alone for most of them. Or would I need a new boyfriend to supplement my boyfriend, too?

But of course, I had no reason to believe that there was any danger of Michael and his wife separating. I wondered how they did it, myself. I couldn't understand how a romantic relationship between two healthy people could ultimately succeed without some sort of sexual intimacy. I'd thought a lot about that. To me, fucking had always had been the point of being with someone of the opposite sex. It was great to talk and have values in common and participate in activities together, but those were all things you could have in a relationship with a good friend; they didn't require a lover. It seems to me that sex is the main differentiating factor between a friend and a mate, and I had difficulty comprehending how Michael and his wife could maintain romantic affection toward each other without getting naked every now and again. But who knows, maybe after you've done it enough times, cuddling is enough. Hadn't I said that myself, that Michael and I were spending more time cuddling nowadays than fooling around?

Sometimes I wondered what I would do if the sex went out of my relationship with Tom. I mean, like in a permanent way, if he were injured or something. Would I still want to be with him? Of course I would! But I wasn't sure I'd be able to get by without taking a lover. Oh, wait, shame on me, I already had a lover, and Tom was perfectly functional.

Now, if the situation were reversed and sex were impossible for me for some reason, I know I'd want Tom to get himself another girlfriend, sure I would, just like I'd want him to move on if I passed away. I wouldn't want him to be alone. How would the laundry ever get done? But seriously, as often as I worried that something bad might happen to him and he'd leave me prematurely, I worried equally as often that I'd be the one to drop dead and leave him all by himself. You would think that a good-looking guy with a good job and a great personality would never need to be single, but he'd been alone a long time before he'd met me, too, ever since his last long-term relationship. He simply wasn't the kind who went around picking up girls, and sometimes I seriously wondered how easily he would adjust to being with someone else. Anyway, if the worst happened, I was okay with him finding someone new as long as I remained his favorite until the end of time. He'd better not love her more than me – that was my only condition. Of course, that might be asking a bit much if she was actually faithful to him, which was more than I had been.

I wouldn't say that Michael and I picked up right where we left off, but we did settle into a loose routine fairly quickly. We didn't always meet on Sundays;

sometimes it was Saturdays instead, and sometimes it was more like late morning or early evening. And it was no longer every week; there were plenty that we missed, but it wasn't so bad having flexibility when things came up, such as Christmas and New Year's and his wife's fiftieth birthday. I couldn't believe she was fifty already. She was only a few years older than Michael, and he was only a few years older than me, but suddenly it sounded as if she and I were a whole generation apart. What a difference a few years made when you spread them out in opposite directions!

One of the most significant changes was the end of the overnighters. It had mostly been that way in the beginning, and I supposed I shouldn't let it bother me now, but at this juncture it was a difficult transition. In one way it helped that we'd had some time apart, and were no longer quite so accustomed to things being a certain way. But on some level I think I also expected us to return to normal, and it took me a while to understand that our normalcy had changed. The other great distinction was that we didn't know quite what to do with one another anymore. Our timing was off. We couldn't go out in public in broad daylight, and that meant no meals, no walks, no sitting on the front porch drinking beer, even. Day-time drinking on festival days was one thing; a once-in-a-while decadent luxury. But I had no intention of making a habit out of having an afternoon beer with Michael. I got enough of that at home.

Several times when the conversation ran out we even found ourselves watching TV together. We'd never even had a television set before, but suddenly we needed it. I wouldn't have minded so much except that it reminded me so strongly of what annoyed me most about Tom. Michael even flipped channels in the same fashion, watching some random movie from the middle for ten minutes, and then switching to a worse one and watching that for twenty. At times like those, I believed in karma, because it seemed obvious that this was my punishment for my infidelity. I had not been content with one man, and now I had two who drove me equally crazy with that damned clicker! Of course, I may have inadvertently positively reinforced that behavior in both of them, because I would get so bored watching television that I'd find myself becoming progressively more amorous, even if I hadn't been in the mood before. I'd smother him with wet kisses, roll or climb over onto his stomach, and bump and grind all our good parts together until he voluntarily turned the set off and paid me my attention instead. Tom had developed some immunity to that by now – he knew my mood would probably last until he was done watching television and he could still get his then – but Michael didn't have any resistance yet, and I wiled him away from the TV several times in this way before he caught on to the scheme. It was amusing but a little sad, too. I guess it would have been sadder if I'd ever actually lost the battle with the TV!

I knew that things were changing between us, and I'm sure he knew it, too. I still liked him as much as ever, but the marvelous intimacy, the seemingly limitless passion we'd once had, was finally fading. We weren't spending enough time fucking to be together as much as we were, and we weren't spending enough time just being together to enjoy that all by itself. Yet I felt a certain comfort with him, the comfortable security of being with someone you know well, and who knows you well, and likes you anyway.

I still felt we had that connection I'd sensed when we'd first met, but I also knew that although the bond between us was more than imaginary, it wasn't quite real either. Was it permanent? Was it forever? I could hardly bring myself to ask those questions, let alone answer them. And in some wee portion of my brain, the idea surfaced that maybe this was the driving force behind commitment that was beyond my comprehension. Maybe this was why people really got married, not for the reasons they gave when they got engaged, not for the silly promises they made at their wedding, but to create what Michael and I didn't have, what Tom and I didn't have, a physically permanent union, the assurance of having someone to stand by your side until death forever separated you. They should drop all the loving and honoring and cherishing parts and make the vow simply, "I will be with you." I will be with you. I will accompany you through life. If that was the marriage bond, there would be far fewer divorces. If that was the marriage bond, there would be many more happy marriages.

One Saturday afternoon in February, Michael arrived at the condo in a bad temper because there had been a spill at the brewery that morning – a fluke leak in a holding tank or something – and not only had he had to go in unexpectedly, but he'd lost most of a special batch he'd been laboring over for months. I could only guess how he felt but I knew it must be bad, so I tried to be extra sweet and affectionate, but that only seemed to piss him off more so I stopped. I didn't even dare to ask him if he wanted a beer – although I desperately wanted one myself – and we just sat there silently on the sofa while he seethed, and I realized that I had no idea how to handle him when he was like this. And I also realized that his wife probably did.

Finally I squeezed his thigh where my hand was resting on it and said timidly, "Michael, if you want to just go home, it's okay. You don't have to stay with me."

"What makes you say that?" he shot back. "I'm not pleasant enough for you today?" If I hadn't known better, I would have thought that maybe I'd hurt his feelings.

"No, I don't care about that," I said quietly. "I just thought maybe you'd rather be with, you know . . . someone who really understands you right now. Who knows how to make you feel better."

"You understand me well enough," he grunted.

I lay my head on his shoulder and looked around the condo. It was by far the nicest place we'd ever shared. Yet it was full of its owner's furniture, her pots and pans, her already half-dead plants, her prints of artwork she admired on the walls. In a way it was neat; it was like staying in a hotel. But of course I never forgot that it wasn't really ours, not even for a pretend minute.

I glanced over at Michael, and he was leaning back with his eyes closed. His eyelids were twitching, his brow was furrowed, and even in that seemingly relaxed position I could see how upset he still was.

"Do you wanna fuck?" I said abruptly. I don't know why I said it, except that it's what I would have wanted if I were him and had had a bad day.

He slowly opened his eyes and stared at me in disbelief. I stared right back while he bored into me with those hard eyes and I was afraid I'd really blown it this time. Was I being insensitive? Should we have been talking about his feelings instead?

And then he said "Yes, please!" and inwardly I said, Ha, I knew that was a good idea! And I yanked off my robe and pulled down his pants and got up on him with my butt on his lap and my feet against the back of the sofa and did squats hard around his cock so he didn't have to do anything but hang on. It was a lot of work, and by the end I was so drenched with sweat that he was laughing at me, and I would have laughed too, had I not been so out of breath.

"Thank you!" he said.

"You're welcome!" I answered, and excused myself to go and shower.

I had already washed and was rinsing the conditioner out of my hair when the door opened and there was Michael, completely naked and looking a little sheepish as he stepped into the shower with me. He didn't say anything, but he draped his arms around me and held me there while the warm running water cascaded around us, and for a moment I thought maybe I understood why we kept coming back to each other even though there was no real logic in it. Finally I reached around and turned off the water, yet still we stood, although the air was getting chilly and would soon be uncomfortably so. And then I noticed that something was dripping on my foot and I looked down at it, and then up to locate the source of the trickle, and realized that it was Michael's beard shedding shower-water and we both giggled and I thought, Isn't that nice? I think I made him feel better after all.

As we were drying off, I asked Michael when he needed to be home.

"No particular time," he said. "My wife knows about the spill, so she isn't really expecting me."

"Well, what do you say we go somewhere then?"

He crooked that one eyebrow at me as if I had suggested something highly irregular, which, of course, I had. "What did you have in mind?"

"Actually, I was thinking about the river," I replied.

He looked surprised but not displeased by the idea. "The whole campground will be snowed in," he warned.

"I'm counting on it," I said. "Nobody else will be there, right?"

He agreed, so he drew on his big heavy boots and put on his jacket and then waited patiently while I assembled my layers. My regular socks first, then thick woolen ones over them, then longjohns, jeans, a thermal undershirt, hooded sweater, long puffy coat, waterproof gloves, and a snowcap which I pulled down hard over my ears because I couldn't stand earmuffs. My boots were still drying by the door from the last time I'd gone out so I put them on last, which was a mistake, because it was hard to bend over in the rest of that getup. By the time I managed it I was so hot and sweaty that I was ready for a shower again, and it was almost a relief to get outside. It was one of those days in which the sun shone brightly and it looked like it might be midsummer as long as you disregarded the dirty parking-lot piles of unmelted snow heaped into larger and larger mounds all winter by the snowplows. And sun or no sun, it was bitterly cold, a good day for sitting home and reading a book or watching a movie, not for going out for a walk. But it was too late to suggest a change of plans to Michael, and I liked the idea of getting out of the house. So after a furtive look around, we hurried over to my car, which was closest, not that anyone who did not know my dead-of-winter attire intimately well could possibly have recognized me inside its bulk, anyway. I ran the engine long enough to let our boogers unfreeze and off we went.

The drive was longer than I remembered. When we arrived, the campground was naturally closed to vehicular traffic because the road, such as it was, had not been plowed. However, I glimpsed a few flashes of color amidst the sheafs of white, which told me that even the insane cold couldn't frighten off the even more insane diehards who had felt compelled to sleep out in it. I wondered if they were actually in tents or if they had built little igloos? When I was a girl I'd had a snow toy that formed snow into blocks – the same way you'd fill a pail to make a sandcastle – and the idea was that you could build an igloo with it. I made some real pretty walls, but never did manage to get a good ceiling going, and completing that upper portion seemed crucial if actual winter survival was important to you. I thought it had something to do with the wetness of the snow, but maybe it just took practice.

But Michael and I were not here to count tents or take igloo-making lessons. Actually, I didn't know what we were there for, even though coming had been my idea. But I trudged purposefully across the snow and Michael trudged along beside me, and after a while we came to the river. I had never seen the river in winter in person. Unlike the lake, it wasn't entirely frozen over, and I figured it must be harder for moving water to freeze. Instead it was drifting along essentially as usual except in places where the water was slower or shallower or something, and there you'd find small sheets of ice stretched over its surface, and occasionally one would break loose and come floating downstream with the current. We made a game of digging up small rocks from under the snow on the riverbank and tossing them at the renegade ice patches to see if we could land a stone on one. I was losing eight to two when we finally gave that up. I blamed the fact that I throw like a girl.

Then we slogged our way downstream a little further and came upon a picnic area, empty, naturally, and my legs were tired from tramping through the snow and, well, being older, so I swept the snow off one half of a bench with my sleeve and sat down carefully with my long coat tucked underneath my butt so my jeans wouldn't get wet. I'd cleared enough space for Michael, too, but he preferred to stand and did, directly in front of me, facing me. He put his hands on my shoulders and I leaned forward and circled my arms around his waist and rested my head against his belly. Perhaps the dirty thought was inevitable. Perhaps so was the "why not?" that followed it.

I reached under his jacket and started fumbling with his pants.

"Whatcha doin'?" Michael said.

I glanced up at him. "I'm going to suck your dick," I answered.

And then I had it out and it was too late for him to stop me if he tried, which he didn't. It was surprisingly warm and felt cozy in my mouth, but my lips were freezing cold against it until I got enough in-and-out friction going to make my skin as warm and soothing as his and he was finally able to stop making those shivering noises. And I sucked that cock as hard as I've ever sucked a cock in my life. I sucked it so hard that afterwards I swore I'd pulled a muscle in my cheek because it was sore for days and I'd never had anything like that happen before.

He was breathing nearly as heavily as I was and what I could feel of his bare ass in my hands was hardly even cold anymore when he came in my mouth at last, and after I had licked him clean, he said, "Whew! We haven't done that in a while."

"That's what I was thinking," I said. It was sad but true. Oral sex had slipped quietly out of our sex life in the last several months. I was sure there was a reason for that, but it was hard to remember what it was.

He buckled up again and smiled at me and I smiled back and then he reached behind me and, with a flourish, swept an armful of snow off the picnic table. Half of it fell on my head and shoulders and I yelled in protest.

"Whoops! Sorry!" he said apologetically, then patted the clear spot on the table with his hand while I glared at him. When I didn't respond, he patted harder. "Come on!" he said in an atypically high voice, and that's when I understood that it was the "Here, boy!" pat you'd signal to a lapdog to show it where you wanted it to sit. I didn't know whether I should be offended or amused by that, but since I was in a good mood, I settled on the latter. I stood up and leaned against the table and he politely dusted off the powder he'd flurried me with, and then sat down on the bench facing me and reached under my jacket and unbuttoned my pants.

"You're kidding, right?" I said, but he ignored me, and before I could object again he was forcing me up onto the table and I shrieked because even though my butt was still covered by my jacket, the edge of the table against my thighs was frostbite-inducing. And then he licked me and I yelled again because his tongue was cold and my pussy was cold and I was relieved that the table was constructed of wood because I was worried we might freeze our juices to it if it were made of metal, and this was not a scene from which I wanted to have to be rescued by the fire department. But then there was another lick, and another, and then I wasn't very cold anymore, not hardly cold at all, and I couldn't think of any good reason why we'd stopped doing this because it was so unbelievably awesome that I would have been willing to sit there in the snow until dark if I'd thought it could go on that long. But of course it didn't, and I'm glad now that I did not know then that that was the last time I'd ever have oral sex with Michael because I think it would have been much harder to enjoy that way.

As we were driving home, a memory from three decades before came swimming into the forefront of my mind. My very first real boyfriend. My parents' house was bordered by a small, sparse wood. If you crossed the wood, you found yourself facing the emergency rear exit of a convenience store. That side of the store had an outside stairway with an iron railing leading from the ground level down to a basement that was presumably used for storage. No one ever came out that way, or at least, not that I ever saw. One day this boy hauled me over to that stairway, and we took turns giving each other head. I still remember how he looked down there between my legs, his body slanted because he was kneeling several steps beneath me. And light little drops of summer rain were falling on my thighs and pussy and mingling with his saliva. It was the first time I'd had that done to me. Funny how things come full circle sometimes.

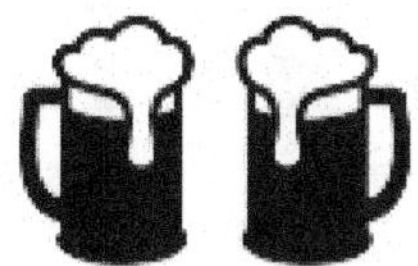

CHAPTER 17

A few weeks later I called my client. Our landlady, I mean. It had been almost four months since I'd heard from her. Her debt to me had already been repaid in rent, and I figured it was about time for me to cough up some cash on my end. I left a message on her cell phone and the next day she called me back.

"Dad's still going strong," she said. "I suspect he's hanging in there because he enjoys having all the kids and grandkids around."

I made my offer about paying the rent but she said not to worry about it. "He always files his own returns, so he doesn't have a tax professional locally. I talked it over with my brother and sister and we'd like to have you do his estate tax return, you know, when the time comes. If you want, we can wait and settle up after that. Are you still planning on keeping the place a while?"

I glanced over at Michael, who had just appeared in the front doorway and was dripping early spring rain all over the foyer, which was thankfully covered with tile.

"A little while longer, at least," I said. I told her I'd send her a list of information she should start gathering regarding the estate. It was best to get a handle on the situation in advance because there were certain items that could potentially receive better tax treatment if you disposed of them before death rather than after. And in any case, estates could be pretty complex to deal with, and getting a jump on assembling the required data while the decedent was still alive could only be beneficial. We agreed to keep in touch.

"Who was that?" Michael said. "A client?"

It was unlike him to be nosy, but I usually didn't take calls from clients on weekends. "Yes," I replied, "The one who also happens to be our landlady."

"Ahh. And did she want some money?"

"Nope. Just some more work."

"Is she coming back soon?"

"Nope," I repeated. "Her dad's still hanging in there."

"Good for him!" Michael said. He appeared reflective for a moment and I wondered if he was thinking about his own parents, who were roughly the same age. Aging parents was another one of those concepts I had difficulty comprehending. My own mother had been younger than I was now, the last time I'd seen her.

"So what's a little while longer, then?" he continued.

My, he really was full of questions today! "A little while longer before I boot you to the curb," I answered flippantly, standing up to hug him as I said it.

He screwed up his face in mock horror, then changed his mind and adopted a gloating expression instead. "You'd better be nice," he said, "Or I won't invite you to come to my convention with me."

"Convention?" I repeated.

He handed me a printout. "They're having it here this year."

I stared at it. It was slowly dawning on me.

"Is this the same convention we…?"

"Yep. They change the venue every year and this is the first time it's been local since then."

"Wow," I said. "When is it?"

He told me. It was months away. "And you know what's really funny? I looked up the dates of the last one we went to, and it's the same weekend."

I looked at him blankly. Why was he telling me this? Didn't these kinds of things usually have practically identical timing year after year? I knew my conferences did.

"You're not getting it. That means it's sort of like our, you know, our anniversary." He was beaming at me like he'd finally remembered when my birthday was.

"So that's when it is, huh?" A number of times I'd meant to look it up myself, just so I would know. I'd never really celebrated any anniversary with any man, but I tried to remember Tom's and mine when it rolled around so I could say "Happy Anniversary!" and kiss him on the cheek and ask him if he was sick of me yet after all these years. Michael and I had never even spoken of such a thing before, and I'll admit I thought it was cute that he was making a big deal about it now.

"Now I know you're not into that kind of thing, and as you know, forced romanticism annoys me as much as it does you." I also habitually boycotted Valentine's Day, a policy to which no man I have dated has ever objected. "So we don't have to exchange presents or anything goofy like that, but I thought it would be fun if we at least went to the convention together."

It would be fun. It would be, only I had to know something first. "Which one is it?"

"Which one is what?"

"Which anniversary?"

"Oh, I don't know," he said. "I don't remember how that goes, I think the first one's paper, then it's tin or aluminum or something, maybe…"

"No," I interrupted. "How many years has it been? That we've been together."

"Four, isn't it?" he answered.

I sat down again because my knees were shaking. Four years. I'd had a lover for four years. I'd been with Tom for ten years and for forty percent of that time I'd had a lover. If I stayed with Michael another two years it would be six and twelve or one-half. Three years more would be nine-fifteenths, three-fifths, sixty percent. I wanted to stop doing the math, but it was keeping my head from reeling. I couldn't believe I'd so thoroughly lost track of the time. Normally I was all about numbers and dates and durations. But that had to be right. I was what, nearly forty-one when Michael and I had finally gotten together, and I was turning forty-five this year. But it was daunting to think about. Maybe I hadn't wanted to know.

"Are you all right?" Michael was saying, stroking my fingers with his.

"A little dizzy," I admitted. "That was kind of a shock."

"We don't have to go," he said uncertainly, "If you don't want to."

"Oh, no, we're going!" I cried.

"You sure?"

"Yes," I affirmed. "In fact, I think it's awfully nice of them to hold a beer convention in honor of our four-year anniversary."

But later on, when we were lying together in bed, the idea wouldn't stop rattling through my brain. I had no intention of talking about it, but I guess it showed.

"Are you sure you're all right?" Michael said again, sliding his arm under my shoulder.

"Me? Oh, yes, fine, fine," I lied unconvincingly.

He squinted shrewdly at me. "This whole thing – about us, I mean, being together so long – kind of weirds you out, doesn't it?"

"A little," I admitted. I didn't know how to say it. "See, in my mind, this is just a fling."

The words were barely out of my mouth before we were both snickering uncontrollably.

"So now let me get this straight," Michael began as I tried to choke back my giggles. He looked perhaps more amused than I had ever seen him look. "We knew each other for what – a couple of years, maybe – before having what was supposed to be a one-night deal. That turns out not to be enough, so we sublet an apartment for several months." I was still laughing. "We follow that up by renting the cottage for a year and a half or so, then we take another year's lease on an apartment together, and finally follow that up with the lovely condominium we find ourselves in today."

He gestured grandly towards our environs and I put on my dignified face and said, "So what's your point, Michael?"

He gave me that one eyebrow and said, "Four years isn't enough. Sharing housing isn't enough. Exactly what will it take to make this stop being a fling for you?"

I'd stopped laughing. It was a good question. I thought hard about how I wanted to answer it, and finally I did. "I don't want it to stop being a fling. Because I can almost justify having a fling. I can't in any way justify having… having another boyfriend."

And there it was, so simple now that I'd said it. He was right, of course. Everything about us smacked of serious relationship. Everything except for the fact that each of us was already committed to someone else.

We were turned toward each other and I was painfully aware of the feel of his hand on my hip, his thigh on my thigh, his head in my hand. I looked at him pleadingly. "How can we have an anniversary when we're not even a real couple?"

He reached up and began stroking my hair. "This is the second-longest relationship I've ever had," he asserted.

"Me, too." My scalp was tingling beneath his touch.

"Well, what's more legitimate than that?" I could almost see him mulling it over in his mind. "Maybe let's not call it illegitimate. We'll call it… non-traditional."

Well, it certainly wasn't traditional. I smiled at him and he smiled back. He was still stroking my hair and I felt caught in the moment unawares, and I almost said it, the thing I knew I could never say, so I cleared my throat instead and waited until the urge had passed before I spoke again.

"What do you think would have happened if we had gotten together in, you know, the usual way?"

"You mean if we'd met sooner, before…?"

"Yeah, something like that."

"Well, I don't know. We might have made a go of it. Except that you didn't want children."

"True," I said. "That would have been a deal-breaker in the long run."

"Yeah. I wouldn't trade mine in for all the treasure in the world." His face glowed with that proud fatherly aspect that transformed him when he was thinking about them, and although it was adorable, I knew it was an emotion we could never share. "Do you still? Not want kids, I mean?"

I shrugged. "I used to worry that I'd get to this age and be sorry I hadn't had any. But I'm not. Guess I just wasn't cut out for it. Probably a little late to do much about it now, anyway."

He didn't respond, but merely lay there, gazing thoughtfully over at me. I would have given him my one eyebrow if I could make mine do that, but instead I had to try to put the irony into the inflection of my voice. "So what you're saying is that it's actually for the best that things worked out the way they did between us, is that it?"

"I don't think that's what I said," he countered.

"Well, see, if we'd hooked up when we were young it might have lasted, oh, let's say, a year. But we waited until we were old, ahem, I mean, older, and you had already had a family, and now here we are coming up on four years together. That's something, right?"

"I guess you're right," he agreed.

"Of course," I went on, "I wouldn't have minded if we'd had more time together when we were young enough to enjoy it."

"Not me!" he returned, sounding surprised. "I'm glad we were older. More comfortable with our bodies. Less drama." He was obviously in the mood to talk, and I was glad to let him. "I guess I've never told you this, but the sex thing – or the no sex thing, I mean – started happening with my wife a few years before it stopped all together. For quite a while it had actually been reduced to special occasions, like our anniversary or my birthday. And for a long time I thought a lot about what it would be like to have, like, a lover. Before I even met you."

"And what did you think?" I inquired curiously.

He laughed. "I decided it would be more trouble than it was worth."

I laughed, too. "How so?"

"Well, I know all the stereotypes about men who have mid-life crises and all that, but I just couldn't see myself hooking up with some hot twenty-year-old, you know?" I did not know. Didn't most men want hot twenty-year-olds? "Not that young women are unattractive, but if I'm going to spend a lot of time with someone I'd rather she were my own age." That I understood. I also felt out of touch with someone who was significantly older or younger, at least in an intimate relationship.

"But then older women are more likely to be looking for something serious," he went on, "And I never wanted to lead anybody on. Younger ones might have lower expectations, but eventually they'd want to move on and get married themselves, and the thought of having to find a new girlfriend all the time wasn't very appealing." I was amazed at how thoroughly he'd thought this out. In a practical fashion that I rather admired.

"And then, you know, the way it's portrayed in movies," he continued, "The other woman always ends up expecting you to leave your wife and family and marry her, or she's a glorified hooker who wants to be kept in style. The whole setup just sounded too complicated. Maybe that's why I didn't do anything about it, but kept my mouth shut and hoped for the best."

I waited.

"But then you came along and you're not like that. You've never expected anything from me. You've never once complained that I don't spend enough time with you because you've always understood that I had to put my family first. You've never asked for money or presents – you even put up your share of the rent, as if you're my equal and not my 'kept woman.' You've never made me think you would ever try to get between me and my family."

I was already blushing. Neither of my men was very vociferous with compliments, and I was unaccustomed to such praise, peculiar as it was.

"Plus, you came on so strong that I never worried about rejection." He grinned unabashedly at me.

I laughed. "I guess I wasn't very subtle, was I?"

"You certainly were not! Which was lucky for me, because otherwise I don't think I ever would have done anything about it." He was gazing into my eyes and still softly stroking my hair, and I thought that this was possibly the most romantic moment we had ever shared.

"You've been good to me, Kate. I couldn't have hoped for better." For a second or two he looked like he wanted to say something else, but all he did was clear his throat and squeeze me gently about the shoulders.

"And now I have a question for you," he continued, and I was grateful he hadn't given me an opportunity to respond to all the nice things he'd said about me because I was sure I would have ruined the moment. That is, I was grateful until I heard the question. "What made you want to be with me?"

I blinked nervously. "I, um, I don't know if I can answer that question, Michael," I said.

"Aw, come on, how come? It can't be that embarrassing."

I shook my head.

"Was it my stunning physique? My sparkling personality? It was the beard, wasn't it!"

I chuckled. "No, I mean, I don't think I know the answer."

He examined me quizzically. "There must have been a reason."

"Must have been," I agreed. "But I don't know what it was."

He shifted his body slightly away from mine. "Were you just looking for a fling?" he asked. Something about the way he said it told me the idea bothered him.

"No!" I yelled. "Of course not!" He had pressed his eyebrows together and was looking even more offended, so I knew I had to try to spell it out for him.

"Michael," I said, "I can't explain why I was drawn to you the way I was. I can't explain it because it wasn't logical or rational; it simply was. I sensed something about you, but my sense, well, it didn't make sense either. I just knew there was something special about you. Something special about the way I responded to you. You know what I mean?"

"Sort of," he said, apparently unconvinced.

"Right from at the start I liked you so much, without really having any reason to. In my mind it was as if I already knew you, knew who you were, knew how you'd be. Wanting to sleep with you was a big part of it, but it wasn't like a superficial kind of lust based on your what you look like. I wanted – I just wanted to be close to you, in every possible way. I couldn't help it. I still can't."

I sighed. He was eyeing me curiously. "It couldn't have happened with anyone else. At first I thought maybe it was me; where I was at when we met. I thought maybe I liked you so much because I was bored; that I just wanted someone to like. But you were so much work, so impossible to get, and it would have been much easier, much less humiliating if I could have simply let it go and found someone else. But that wasn't it at all. I'd never really wanted to stray like that before and I doubt I ever will again. I wanted to because of you, and not the other way around. It's true that there was something missing in my life until you came along. It was you that was missing. No one else would have been worth taking the risk over. No one else would have been worth hurting him for. I needed you. I needed you before I even met you. I don't know what I would have done without you, but I do know that I would not have been anywhere near as happy as I have been."

It was poor oratory but it must have satisfied him, because he quietly resumed stroking my hair, and after a few minutes launched into a speech about where the convention was going to be held, and what its theme was this year, and so on, and I forgot all about whether it was strange to share an anniversary with your lover. It was better than having a lover who changed you in for a new partner before an anniversary could even come around. We were committed to each other. Or as committed as we were going to get.

CHAPTER 18

Spring came and went as it usually did. The snow melted and the rains fell. Tom and I attended the Spring Festival and drank too much. I prepared two thousand pounds of tax returns. I still saw Michael regularly. In May I was still much hornier than I was the rest of the year and I wondered if that would continue throughout my entire life. It was perhaps because of this that I had coerced Michael into seeing me twice in one weekend in the latter part of the month.

"It'll just be a quickie," I promised, late one Sunday afternoon when I suddenly found myself desperately in the mood for him. That was one nice thing about having a place close to my home and office and only one highway off-ramp from his house, too. It made last-minute unexpected desires much easier to fulfill.

"Just drop in for a few minutes," I'd said. But of course that wasn't going to work, because the fact was, it was taking us both noticeably longer to get ready these days, me to become moist enough to be penetrable, and him to become stiff enough to penetrate me. I might have taken his increasing slowness to rise personally, but I really didn't think it had anything to do with me, any more than my decreasing wetness had anything to do with him. I mean, a man can't be expected to spring instantly to attention his whole life, can he? Anyway, it wasn't like a big problem or anything, but nowadays we were rarely able to simply drop trou' and get it on the second we saw each other, and we spent a lot more time making out beforehand than had previously been our custom. And so the minutes had turned into an hour, and now we were lying in bed opening our second beer and I hoped he would stay long enough to finish it because I was getting the urge again, if, in fact, I'd ever actually lost it, and the bonus was that I was already ready, so taking it twice was rather efficient in my book. But Michael was telling a cute anecdote about his youngest child at Christmas at the age of five, and I thought it would only be polite to listen to all of it before I pounced on him again.

"So I lift up the stocking, and it's really heavy, and I reach into it, and pull out a big fancy twenty-two that my wife had put there while she was stuffing the stockings. And Christopher's eyes get all big and round, like saucers, you know, and Miranda comes in from the other room and he runs over to her yelling, 'Mommy, Mommy! Santa brought Daddy beer!' "

I pictured how it must have seemed to the childish mind. Santa really did know everything about everybody! It was a funny story, and Michael was still chuckling over it.

"That's how well they knew me," he was saying. "Even at that age, they knew how mush I liked beersh."

I wondered if I had heard him right. From the way he'd slurred that last sentence, I thought maybe he'd had one too many of those beers he liked so much.

"Shanta bought Daddy bee," he repeated.

"Were you drinking before you came over?" I asked him.

"Nah, nah, I jush, jush…" And while he trailed off into incoherence, I looked closely at him and his left eye was drooping and one side of his mouth was hanging lopsidedly open, and out of some public service announcement or medical show from the distant past it came to me, FAST, and I grabbed his left arm and lifted it and he let it fall back onto the pillow and although I couldn't remember what the hell the "T" stood for I knew I needed an ambulance.

He had stopped moving and although he sporadically muttered something incomprehensible, his eyes stared unseeing and I felt my heart constrict with the fear that I was about to lose him. Forcing down my terror, I ran across the room, snatched up the phone, and dialed 911.

"What's your emergency?" asked the operator.

"It's my – my Michael," I fumbled. "I need an ambulance; I think he's having a stroke." I went on describing the symptoms while he lay there, thinking God knows what, if he even could still think, but I certainly couldn't think about that because then I would panic and I couldn't afford to panic right then. I knew what Michael would want me to do next and I needed to be calm for that. I finished with the 911 operator, yanked Michael's pants up from off the floor, and started feeling his pockets for his phone.

"I'm going to call your wife," I said, sitting down beside him on the bed and squeezing his hand. His expression didn't change.

I found her name in his contacts and dialed it without thinking about what I was doing. I wasn't sure if it was the home phone or her cell phone but since there was only one listed under her name, the latter seemed more likely. He probably didn't have to program his own home phone number. While it rang, I made a contingency plan in my head. There were three kids I could call if she didn't answer. I hoped I wouldn't have to do that.

The voicemail picked up, and I panicked and hung up without saying anything. I could hear a siren approaching and I hoped it was for us. It didn't strike me until later how strange that was. You know how you start to feel anxious when you're coming home and you hear sirens or see flashing lights in your neighborhood, but you can't tell whose house they're at and you begin to dread that maybe it's yours? Now I had the opposite fear. What if that ambulance was for someone else? We needed it here.

While I was scurrying quickly back into my clothes, I decided I'd better call back and leave a message. I hated to give her the news that way, but it might be worse to keep calling and have her see that long list of missed calls when she finally consulted her phone. But just as I prepared to dial again, the phone vibrated in my hand, and it was her ringing me back.

I didn't give her a chance to speak or to ask who I was. "Miranda," I jumped right in, "Michael's sick, really sick. I think he's having a stroke."

There was a brief pause. "Are you sure?" she said, in a pinched, almost squeaky tone.

"No. But it sure looks like one. The ambulance will be here any second." And now I knew it was true because the noise of the siren was resounding through the parking lot below, and soon they'd be hurrying up the stairs to come and take him to the hospital.

"Can I talk to him?" she yelled. It was obvious that the siren was audible even through the phone.

"He can't talk," I yelled back. But then I had an inspiration, and shouted into the phone again. "But I'll put the phone up to his ear and you can talk to him if you want."

I didn't wait for an answer, but leaned over and pushed him onto his back so that his right ear was exposed and I held the phone there and just to be sure I wouldn't overhear anything I listened instead to the thud of boots on the steps and yelled "In here!" when they reached the landing. No one should ever have to listen to a wife's final words to her husband. Except for her husband.

The EMTs signaled to me to move the phone away and I nodded and asked, "Wait, which hospital?" and they told me, so I brought the phone back up to my ear and before I could hear anything I wasn't supposed to, I said loudly, "I have to hang up now," and then I told her which hospital they were taking him to and disconnected her before she could say anything more.

They got him smoothly onto the stretcher in one brisk motion but oh, if you have never seen that done to someone you care about, all I can say is, don't. He suddenly seemed smaller than usual, and utterly helpless, and half-dead already, and now that someone else was in charge a lump swelled in my throat and tears rose unbidden into my eyes and I was terrified, more frightened than I have ever been by anything, and I knew that if he died I would never get over it, ever. But I pursued them down the stairs and out to the ambulance.

"Wait, can I ride with you?" I cried, my foot already fumbling for the ramp.

One of them jerked his head at the stretcher and I took that for assent. I followed them obediently into the cargo area and immediately regretted thinking of it as a cargo area because it made Michael sound like a lifeless thing and not a living, breathing person. I told the whole story while they checked him over, every bit of it, even how at first I'd thought he was drunk but we'd only had one beer, just in case I was wrong and there was something else the matter with him, and then once they let me I sat and held his hand and looked into those unseeing eyes and tried to say calm, reassuring things in case he could hear me in there. He was still wearing only his boxers, but they had covered him with some kind of sheet and I thought it probably didn't matter because by the time she saw him they would undoubtedly have him in one of those gowns anyway and she wouldn't have to wonder where his clothes were.

During the ride we barely slowed and never stopped, and I was eternally grateful that we had taken the condo because it was only a dozen blocks from the hospital they were taking him to, and the trip seemed interminable nonetheless. Second by second my anxiety mounted. I wasn't sure, but I thought there was some sort of deadline in getting successful treatment for a stroke and I wanted to ask the EMTs about it but I couldn't speak and I didn't want to interrupt them in their work either, so I kept silent. And finally we came to a stop and we were at the ambulance bay and I was being pushed roughly aside so they could get him out, and then the driver pointed to where I supposed to go and in the interim Michael's body had vanished and I had a moment of panic because I thought I'd lost him. I ran inside and on my left, a lady was sitting at a desk and she asked if I had just come in with the ambulance and I said yes, so she asked me a lot more questions like his name and address and date of birth and fortunately I could answer those. But when she wanted to know about his insurance I couldn't even guess, and that's when I told her that his wife would be here soon and she would surely know the answers to any more questions they might have. And then I wanted to know when I would be able to see Michael and what were they doing for him, and she looked at me funny and told me there would be no news until the doctor had finished examining him. So I turned around to see if I could find someone else to ask and there he was again, being wheeled down the hall on one of those beds that are designed for that purpose, and he was so completely surrounded by medical people of various kinds that I only knew it was him because I caught a glimpse of that coppery-red hair as they went by. I ran after them and started asking questions but they told me I had to get out of the way so they could treat him and of course they were right so I just stopped and stood and watched the bed being wheeled away. When they turned the corner at the end of the hall, I went back to the lady at the desk to ask her what was happening, but she looked very sorry and said that without the patient's consent she couldn't share that information with someone who wasn't immediate family and that I would have to wait for his wife to arrive.

I had seen a photograph of Michael's wife once, but it had been a long time before, and although I had a picture of her in my head, I wasn't sure I would recognize her in person. She was blonde and of medium build and that was all I could clearly recall. I could have described the mailman at the condo with greater accuracy. I'd seen lots of pictures of the children, though, and I would know them if they were with her. But of course, even assuming I did recognize her on sight, I couldn't simply walk up to her as if we were old friends. I also didn't want to risk having the lady at the desk point me out to her as the woman who had brought Michael in, so I scanned the waiting area for a place to hide, preferably one that was close enough to allow me to hear conversations at the front desk. Off to the left and across from the main entrance two restrooms, a men's and a women's, faced each other across a short hallway. I crossed the lobby quietly and stationed myself in the space between the two doors. I thought that it would be safe there because it seemed unlikely that Miranda would stop to pee when she arrived.

The seating area was now in front of me and off to my right, but was at such an angle that although the room was full of people, the only one who could see me from there was a baby who was hiked up onto its mother's shoulder and was examining the room behind her. Once it caught sight of me, it did not look away. Although I reminded myself that it shouldn't matter because it was only a baby, I grew increasingly uncomfortable under its unwavering gaze, and I made what I hoped was a scary face so that it would turn away, but it just giggled and stared harder. So I tried another, but apparently my scary faces weren't scary at all, because the infant started scrambling to climb up higher on Momma, whether to get to me or to see me better I couldn't tell, but either way I was afraid of the attention, so I shrank as far back into a corner as I could. Then I heard wailing and I guessed that Mom had pulled the fussing child from her shoulder, utterly unaware that she was ruining its entertainment.

And then I was panicking again because now, not only could I not see, but I also wasn't sure I was going to be able to hear what was going on with that kid screaming, and sure enough, somewhere beneath the roar I could now perceive the high-pitched rumble of two women talking, although I couldn't make out a word of what they were saying. I squatted down so I would be out of the line of sight and peeked around the wall, and a chill travelled down my spine because yes, it was Michael's wife, I was sure of it. And now she was starting to walk away from the desk and the baby was screaming even louder and I cursed it, cursed its infantile soul because I hadn't been able to hear anything, and now I would have to traipse conspicuously throughout the whole enormous hospital to try to find them. But apparently the wailing was deafening everyone else, too, because she turned back toward the desk and asked loudly, "What floor was that on?" and the lady shouted back "The fourth!" and I withdrew my curse and made it a blessing instead, because if that stupid kid hadn't been screaming like that they might not have ever spoken loudly enough for me to hear. I cringed into my corner again but of course she didn't even turn her head as she strode briskly down the hall, presumably towards where the elevators were.

I was glad I'd found the restrooms, because by now I desperately needed to expunge my earlier beer. After washing my hands, I counted deliberately to two hundred before I followed in the direction she had gone. I found the elevators but passed them by. The stairway was at the very end of the hall, and I headed for that instead. When I reached the correct landing, I opened the door and peered cautiously out. There was a nondescript older gentleman waiting by the elevators, but that was all. When I reached the corner there was a sign on the wall listing all of the various departments with an arrow pointing to where each one was. From here they all pointed left, so I made the turn and began walking slowly past a long series of rooms with closed doors, periodically punctuated by large waiting areas. I hadn't been in hospitals much. This one didn't reek of antiseptic like I'd always heard they did. And it wasn't particularly depressing, either. There were plenty of staff members bustling about and most of them bore a cheerful, reassuring air that made you feel as if you'd come to the right place for care. The walls were not all white but were painted in a variety of pastel shades, and I supposed that some expert in hospital psychology must have decided that those tones were soothing and perhaps they were.

I couldn't tell what the rooms were like because even though each time I passed one I turned my head and peeked in the window, not much was visible through the tiny pane. I didn't let that faze me because she was the one I was looking for, and she was likely to be waiting outside anyway if they were still working on him. And, indeed, several minutes later I spotted the back of a grayish-blonde head that looked like it might be hers in the central row of hard plastic chairs in one of the waiting areas. I could have continued walking past to get a glimpse of her from the front, but taking a seat here was too good of an opportunity to pass up, so I chose a spot along the wall ten feet behind her and studied the woman in question more closely. I hadn't really noticed what she'd been wearing, but it might have been khakis like this woman wore. The jacket she had draped over the back of her chair was plain and black, and I was pretty sure that was a match, although lots of people wore black jackets.

I was still debating whether I should stay there or make the rounds of the rest of the floor when the question was settled for me by the arrival of a woman who was a stranger to me and all three of Michael's nearly grown children. I'd never noticed before how much they all resembled him. Perhaps the effect was magnified when they were all together. The unknown woman stepped tactfully aside while the kids rushed over to their mother, and hugs were exchanged all around while she quietly gave them an update, most of which was inaudible to me. "… Dad…tests…wait…" was all I got out of it. After a few minutes, the woman approached Miranda, clasped her hand sympathetically, uttered a few soft-spoken sentences, and then began walking back down the hall towards where the elevators were. She must have been a neighbor or some other casual acquaintance who had volunteered to drop the children off once they'd gotten the news and come home. Their other car was, of course, at the condo. So were his clothes and wallet, and with a start I wondered how I was going to return them if he didn't make it.

They all sat down in a row, the daughter on one side of her mother and the two boys on the other, and she extended her arms around all of them at once and they all leaned in towards each other while she stroked their shoulders and arms with her shaking fingers. There was the sound of gentle murmuring and the occasional stifled sob, and I felt like a trespasser on their private grief and I tried not to listen to or look at them. But that was a formidable task, and suddenly I couldn't, couldn't stand to be near them anymore, so I stood up and marched back down the hall and didn't stop until I'd reached the stairwell and closed the door behind me.

I threw myself down on the edge of the landing and rested my feet two steps beneath me, and then I cried, oh, how I cried, because Michael was somewhere in this building but he was lost to me, because I didn't know what was happening to him, didn't know if he would live or die or be irreparably damaged, and didn't know how to control myself in front of his family, which was why I was cowering in a lonely stairway all by myself with my lonely, lonely grief. It was wrong; it had to be wrong for me to be worrying about the man who was a husband and father to them but nothing to me. I had no right even to be there. I was no one, had no title, no rank, no rights nor duties of possession. And now he was in the hospital and no matter how much it hurt me to have to stand on the outskirts, I knew, knew, knew that that's what he would want and I would have left the place all together rather than let his family catch on who I was. If the worst happened, why leave them with that? My final memory of Daddy is finding out at the hospital on the day he died that he had a – a what? I knew the word that fit there, but I'd never thought of it in reference to me and Michael, and now it stung because it so belittled all that we had meant to each other. Mistress. I was the mistress. It was a disgusting, ugly word, and the fact that it was the correct one made it even more so. But of course, the mistress is reviled for just cause. She takes what belongs to another. She breaks up families. And sometimes she even sells her sex, for jewelry and rent money. How could I use that word to describe my relationship with Michael? It was wrong, I knew that, it had been wrong from the start, but it was neither disgusting nor ugly, and if we had just been single people he might have been able to call me something nice like his sweetheart or his darling or his beloved, and it could have been beautiful instead of awful.

I didn't know what to call him, either. Friend, boyfriend, lover – those terms wouldn't do. If there was a masculine equivalent for the term mistress, I'd never heard of it. How had I referred to him to the 911 operator? My Michael. My Michael, not yours, or hers, or theirs, but mine, mine during those precious hours we spent together, and mine during all the other hours I spent thinking about him, and mine during the hours he spent thinking about me. My Michael. The name was a title, his title, the definition of what he was to me, and it was as true and meaningful a designation as wife or husband or girlfriend or boyfriend and perhaps even more so because there was only one of him; could only ever be one of him. The name itself had come to mean something to me.

I didn't know how many minutes or hours had ticked away while I slumped there on the landing thinking about Michael, but after a long while I stopped crying and eventually my nose stopped running and I started to think about going back to see if I could track down how he was doing. I checked my phone and estimated that it had been about two hours since our arrival, so there was bound to be news by now. Not one person had interrupted me in the entire time I'd been in the stairwell, and I was grateful for that. I'd heard a door on one of the lower floors opening and closing a few times but no one had come up this far. And then I remembered that evening in the stairway with Michael at the convention and I smiled in spite of myself. And then I thought of the convention we might not be able to attend this year after all, and the smile fell from my face. It was a good memory, though. I would save it for later.

I stopped at the first restroom I came to and splashed water on my eyes. My post-weeping face was in full effect, and I thought ruefully that at least I would likely be unrecognizable in this condition. When I neared our waiting area, I saw that a doctor was talking to Michael's family, and although I couldn't see their faces, he seemed satisfied, and I hoped that meant that Michael was doing all right. The doctor walked away and they sat back down and I assumed that meant more waiting, but I still didn't want to be near them, so I claimed a seat at the edge of the next waiting area down, and watched the hallway for their departure, since this was the direction they would most likely take on their way out. I desperately wished I had a book, but I knew that was stupid because I probably wouldn't have been able to concentrate on one anyway. So I merely sat and stared down the hall and waited until time ceased to have any meaning and finally I saw them coming so I picked up an automobile magazine from the table next to me and pretended to read it while I listened hard and didn't so much as glance in their direction. As they were passing by me, Miranda said something about monitoring Dad's condition, and that was how I knew that Michael was alive.

When they had passed out of sight, I pulled out my phone and made a note of the time, and then I waited for another thirty minutes before calling the front desk and asking for his room number. I was afraid of getting there before they'd left. The halls were dotted with informational medical posters and I stopped to read every single one along the way. One of them had that handy acronym, FAST, for face, arms, speech, and time. Now I remembered what the T was for; it meant to seek treatment quickly. I was glad I had. I finally made my way up to the sixth floor, but the hallways seemed awfully empty, and I was afraid that visiting hours might be over. But his family had presumably come up to see him, and I was determined to see him, too.

There was a desk and I inquired at it.

"And what is your relationship to the patient?" the clerk asked.

I'm not normally much of a liar, but there was no way I was going to leave that hospital now without seeing him, and I knew his wife had already been there. "I'm his sister," I lied. Let them prove that I wasn't. "Can I see him?"

"Well, visiting hours are technically over," he replied. He was a youngish black man with a deep, husky voice and a delicately shaped face, and I sensed that he was a soft touch at heart.

"Just for a minute?" I pleaded. "I came a long way to get here."

He beckoned to a nurse who was striding briskly by and she leaned down and he spoke low into her ear and then she said, "Right this way, ma'am," and she brought me through a door into a room with two beds. One of them was empty, but the other held my Michael. His eyes were open, and even from across the room I could tell that he knew me.

"Five minutes," the nurse said, but I refrained from kissing her and instead merely said "Thank you," as she left us. As I went over to the bed I recalled that only a few hours ago I'd been in bed with him myself, and I smiled through the tears that were threatening to start again and took his hand. He was pale and connected to a number of machines, but he smiled back weakly.

"Thought you'd left," he said slowly, as if it required a lot of effort.

"I waited to come up until I was sure you'd be alone," I answered. Somehow I thought that sounded better than "until after your family was gone." "Are you okay?"

"Sedated," he said. "Be asleep soon."

"Was it a stroke?" I asked.

He shook his head. "Transient something or other. Like a stroke but temporary."

Relief flowed through me. "So that means you'll be okay?"

"Could be a warning. Sign of a stroke coming."

"Oh!" I said. That didn't sound so promising. "Does that mean you're going to be here a while?"

He almost imperceptibly shook his head again. "Just overnight, for observation."

His eyes were drooping, and I could tell he was about to nod off.

"I'll bring your clothes by first thing in the morning," I said quickly, hoping he would remember that when he woke.

His eyes opened again. "You okay?" he inquired.

"Better now," I said.

"Your eyes," he said cryptically, and for a second I thought maybe I should call the nurse, and then I remembered that I'd been crying and that it showed.

"I might have been a little worried about you," I admitted, gently squeezing his hand.

"I heard you," he said softly. "Heard everything." I wanted badly to ask him what it had been like, what he was thinking about while it was happening and if he had understood what was going on, but his eyes were closed again and it would have to wait. Thankfully, now it could wait.

"You did good," he whispered suddenly. I wasn't exactly sure what he thought I had done well but I couldn't ask him because he was already asleep and the nurse was coming back in and saying I had to leave. So I let go of his hand and kissed him on the forehead and commenced the journey away from the hospital, and I didn't care what anyone said; I found the institutionality of it comforting rather than disquieting, and I was almost as glad to be there as I was to be leaving now that it had served its purpose.

I was halfway through the parking lot before I recollected that I had no car, but I didn't feel like sitting around waiting for a taxi, so I looked up directions on my phone and walked all the way back to the condo. My car was outside, and I longed to climb into it and go home without going upstairs, but I knew I must. My feet dragged on every step, but when I got up to the second floor, there stood our doorway, not ominous or threatening in any way, but as homey and welcoming as it ever was. And then I realized that my keys were in my jacket pocket and not in my pants, and that I'd left the jacket at home and couldn't get inside or into my car without them. I leaned downheartedly against the door, my hand dejectedly jiggling the knob. To my surprise, it opened, which made perfect sense now that I thought about it, because how would I have locked up without my keys? In fact, I thought we'd probably left the door wide open, and some thoughtful neighbor had come by and closed it afterwards, and I was touched by this small kindness. And then I went inside.

It wasn't as bad as it might have been. The bed was mussed and a lamp had been knocked over as they carried him out, but it was unbroken. I thought of what the spouses of murder victims had to come home to afterwards, and I shuddered inwardly. There was no blood here, no outward sign of sickness of trauma; only an empty bed and a pile of clothes on the floor where he'd scattered them before we'd made love. Except for his pants, which were hanging half off the bed where I'd dropped them after digging out his phone. The phone was there, too. I packed it up in a bag with his clothes. If I got back to the hospital early enough, Miranda need never know they were missing.

I wanted to get out of there before I got depressed but I couldn't help myself; I dropped down onto the bed next to where he would normally have lain and wrapped my arm around his shadow but I couldn't hold it; it kept fading away into nothing. I was glad he wasn't dead but at the moment it felt as if he was gone anyway, and everywhere I looked reminded me of him. Standing at the window, making howling noises at the rising moon. Leaning over the refrigerator, smacking his lips as he pulled out a bottle of beer. Making the bed in that careful way he had, all crisp seams and tight hospital corners that I would purposefully ruin the next time I got into it. Holding me in the foyer on his way in or again on his way out, cold from snow or wind or wet from rain or fog or warm from sun or the juxtaposition of our bodies. The condo had become a sad and lonely place, and suddenly I couldn't wait to be with Tom.

It was very late when I got home. Late enough for him to ask me why I was so late and hadn't called. He never asked me those kinds of questions these days.

But I couldn't answer. What would I say?

"What's wrong?" he said.

I shook my head. I couldn't tell him.

He came in closer. "Have you been crying?" I still didn't answer. It was obvious anyway.

Then he took me in his arms and held me tight, and it all welled up again and I was bawling, bawling uncontrollably like that child in the hospital. And although my misery was more severe and less transient than that carefree infant's, it, too, eventually passed, and after untold minutes I was calm again.

And then Tom let go of me and walked away and I feared that I might get upset again, but he returned quickly and he'd brought me a beer and a shot of whiskey, both of which I drank gratefully. He really was a good guy. Then he asked gently, "Do you want to talk about it?" and I shook my head again, and we were quiet and simply held each other for a few minutes. And then he said to my shoulder, "Did something happen to Michael?"

And I wasn't even surprised, wasn't at all surprised that he knew I'd been with my other man, and it seemed a trivial, unimportant thing to worry about now, but I couldn't understand how he'd known it was Michael when Michael and I had made a point the last few years of never even speaking to one another when Tom was around.

But he must have read my mind, because without waiting for my confirmation or denial he explained, "He stopped talking to me several years ago. About the time you started keeping such erratic hours. I knew you liked each other a long time before that. It wasn't hard to figure out."

I swallowed but the lump in my throat stayed put. It even seemed to be growing. "He had like, a small stroke," I whispered. "A transient something or other."

He inhaled audibly. "Is he all right?"

"For now," I answered. "I guess you're more likely to have a real stroke after one of these."

"Oh."

I didn't know what to say next, so I merely stood there while he held me, and again I was grateful to have him, grateful like I hadn't been in a very long time.

When we finally pulled apart, I peered into those warm brown eyes filled with concern, concern for me and whether I was upset or unhappy because my other boyfriend was in the hospital, and I wanted to say something to him, something that would convey what I felt about him, about Tom and Tom alone, the Tom that existed for me outside of and apart from and in spite of Michael.

"Tom, I… " I began, but he interrupted me with a shake of his head.

"You don't need to explain," he said.

"But I…"

"I don't really want to know," he said firmly. "I decided a long time ago to accept it, but I don't need to hear about it. The fact that you could do that – that's a part of you I'll never understand. But I learned to accept that, too." He sighed. "I know I brought it on myself."

It was my turn to shake my head. "No," I said. "It wasn't your fault. You just gave me an opening. I needed… I needed that. I was almost glad you gave me a reason."

He nodded and said nothing.

"I still love you," I said.

"I know you do."

And then he squeezed my shoulders and went and poured us each a beer and we got into bed and he snuggled up to me and I felt warm and safe and loved, and for once I didn't think about whether I deserved that or not. I was exhausted, but in a peculiar way, almost happy, and I went straight to sleep and didn't wake up again until it was light.

CHAPTER 19

I went by the hospital first thing. The ward was still quiet, and I hoped that I could slip unnoticed into Michael's room and drop my bag and run before his wife came to pick him up. But a stout white-haired nurse caught me peeking in through the window, and accosted me as I extended my fist towards the door handle.

"Visiting hours don't begin until 9 a.m., ma'am," she advised me severely.

"Oh, I'm not here to visit. I just, um – here are his clothes," I said, not knowing how to explain, and hoping that she wouldn't force me to try.

"Let me see the bag," she ordered, and I handed it over willingly. She rummaged through it, verbally enumerating the contents as she did so. "Shirt, pants, socks, shoes, cell phone, wallet, car keys. I guess this is all right." Then she paused and raised one eyebrow at me in very much the same way that Michael would have done and said, "No underpants?"

I gulped. "He was wearing some… Guess I forgot to bring an extra pair…"

"I see… And what exactly is your relationship to the patient?" she inquired suspiciously. I gulped again, but there was nothing left to swallow; I'd gone completely dry. She was surveying me even more formidably, and I had this horrible fear that Michael's wife would appear in the hallway while we were discussing this, and I'd have to explain who I was to both of them.

And then a voice from down the hall said loudly, "Miranda!" and I jumped and so did the nurse. I looked wildly around but there was no one else there and then she said "Yes?" and I realized that that must be her name, too. All the same, I was glad to be in a hospital because the way my heart was going, I thought I might need one of those defibrillators they constantly kept charged.

The man who had spoken strode rapidly toward us. He was wearing a different uniform and appeared to be in charge, because he said officiously, "You need to get off the clock. Overtime is not authorized for this week."

"Yes, sir," she answered with a half-smile and a well-faked level of obsequiousness. "Simply assisting a patient's visitor." As he turned away she muttered a number of curse words under her breath, foremost among which appeared to be "dick." Then she turned to me and said "Which one?"

"Excuse me?" I responded, puzzled.

"Which patient?" she asked again, slowly, as if she'd decided that I wasn't very bright. "There are two of them in there."

I peeked again and sure enough, there was someone lying in the other bed now. "The redhead. With the long beard." I don't know why I clarified it. How many redheads could be hiding in there?

It wasn't lost on her, either. "How many redheads do you think are in there?" she sneered, but she took the bag and I watched through the tiny windowpane as she dropped it onto a chair next to the bed, and Michael stirred a little as she did so, and I felt reassured that he would find his things when he woke. But I waited until she emerged, and when she saw me still standing there she said sternly, "You'd better go now, ma'am," and I high-tailed it down the hall in the opposite direction from where she was heading and zipped down the stairs to the parking lot. Which reminded me that I still didn't know what I was going to do about his car. He kept a spare key to it at the condo but I still couldn't very well just drop it by his house – that would be almost as suspect as if it were missing all together. Plus, one of the neighbors was bound to see me leaving it and ask any number of uncomfortable questions, especially if they knew what had happened to Michael. And without having someone drive there with me, I would have had to walk quite a ways through their neighborhood before I could catch public transit, which was not a good way to avoid attracting attention to myself in the midst of the suburbs. I was sure Tom would help me if I asked him, but I couldn't even consider doing that. Help me move my lover's car so his wife doesn't find out about us? It was too cruel to consider.

I went through the motions at work, but in my mind, I thought of Tom often that day. More, in fact, than I think I thought about Michael. He was an amazing man; a strange, peculiar, but amazing man. How many men would have stuck with a woman through all that? Of course, in a way, Michael had, too. Even though he'd been sexually faithful to me, he knew I wasn't to him. Sure, we didn't talk about it, but I was certain he didn't delude himself into thinking that I never slept with the man with whom I spent most of my week. Actually, he probably made a point of not thinking about it at all. But he'd never once judged me for that, for any of it. Although he must have felt that what we were doing was wrong, he had always left me to wrestle with my own conscience; he'd never expressed disapproval of me, never, indeed, seemed to believe it was his place or duty to pass judgment. He never treated me like a tramp or made me feel like one. My two men really were an awful lot alike.

Had the situation been reversed, I'm not sure I would have been as forgiving. In fact, I'm positive I would not have been. If nothing else, my fragile ego could not have tolerated it. I would have interpreted infidelity from either one of them as a slight, an underhanded comment on my growing age or waning attractiveness or sexual competency. I would not have been able to accept unfaithfulness as a mere character flaw; to me it would have been an unbearable insult. Of course, I certainly could not have faulted Tom if he had taken a mistress himself. In some ways I wished he had; it would have alleviated some of my own guilt. But if he had, then where would we be now? How many extra people could you squeeze into a couple before the couple couldn't exist anymore? It was too confusing to think about, and finally I gave up trying.

When I left the office, I headed straight for the condo. I had decided to move Michael's car to the public lot in the nearby shopping center. It wasn't a great solution, but it was better than having a friend, or worse, his wife, come here with him to pick it up. The only thing I was nervous about was notifying him of my plan. What if someone else had possession of his phone? But as it panned out, I'd been worrying all day over nothing. When I arrived at the condo the spare key was gone, and so was the car, and I assumed that Michael must have contrived some plan for dealing with it. When I finally saw him again weeks later, I forgot to ask him about it, and I never did find out what he'd done.

That night I dreamt about him. We were in a rowboat that was headed towards Niagara Falls. We were paddling hard in the opposite direction, but of course the current was too powerful to overcome. When we started going over, Michael said, "Don't worry, I've got you!" but as he stood up to reach for my hand he overstepped, and his face was oddly blank as flew down the falls himself. I fell out right after him and for some reason I thought that if could just catch up to him everything would be all right, but he had vanished into a sea of foam, and now I was in the churning whirlpool, too, and it was hot, and I was surprised because I thought the water here was supposed to be really cold, but instead I was boiling like I was being cooked.

And I woke up, and I'd thrown the covers over onto Tom, but I was still sweating and scared from the dream, although it was fading fast with my wakefulness. I felt feverish and thought, damn, I must have picked up a virus in that hospital, so I rolled over away from Tom, who was still sleeping peacefully, and eventually I went back to sleep, too. In the morning I felt fine, so I concluded that I must have just been frightened by the dream and thought no more about it. Which was good, because there was a chance that I might see Michael again soon, and I wouldn't have dared to risk it if I was going to be sick. I waited a few days, though, before texting him, which was fortunate because it gave me plenty of time to compose the perfect message. I was pleased with the final result.

"When will you be in?" it read. It could have come from anywhere; maybe work, or a bar he frequented, but it conveyed what I meant, nonetheless. The reply I received was equally well-disguised. "Soon."

So then I waited. I wanted him to know that I wanted to see him, but I wasn't necessarily expecting that to happen right away. His family would undoubtedly be keeping close tabs on him, and maybe he would be keeping close tabs on them, too. Although I didn't think that Michael was likely to get swept up in a welter of emotional mumbo-jumbo, an experience like that was bound to make a man reevaluate his priorities. He might even like to take some time to himself for a while. And for my part, I felt really awkward about seeing him now because of Tom. It was one thing when I presumed he knew something was going on and preferred never to formally acknowledge it. But now that it was out in the open, I couldn't see myself lying to him about where I was going when he knew damn well where I was really going. Nor could I picture telling him honestly to his face that I was going to be with Michael, and that I'd see him later. He hadn't spoken of Michael or asked any follow-up questions since the night of our trip to the hospital, and I assumed we were once again supposed to be maintaining silence on that particular subject. Yet in a funny way, I felt closer to Tom than ever. He knew something bad about me, my most shameful secret, something I would never have admitted to any other living person, and he hadn't left me; hadn't lectured me, even. I couldn't understand his accepting it any more than he could understand my doing it. But he'd seen everything now, the worst that I was capable of, and it hadn't altered his feelings toward me. The sense of security that rendered to me was powerful and soothing, and I drew strength from his steadfastness.

It was well that I found it so comforting to be with him. I needed the comfort. The hour had not yet gone by in which I had not been frightened by images from my last visit to the condo, which burst into sight inside my mind with all the seeming randomness and shocking fearfulness of bolts of lightning. Michael slurring his story. Michael not moving. Michael blindly staring. Michael on a stretcher, in an ambulance. Michael vanishing. Michael dead maybe. I would never get those images out of my head, not until one day, perhaps, when they would be supplanted by worse ones. I thought of his wife. She hadn't had to see it, and I envied her that. But she also had not enjoyed the privilege of spending what might have been his final hours with him, and if she'd known that, I'm sure she would have envied me more.

She might still have that privilege. I'd gone online and read up on his condition. It was called a transient ischemic attack and it basically consisted of a brain clot that dissolved on its own and caused stroke-like symptoms for a short time, but no permanent brain damage. I'd read that the symptoms usually resolved in ten to twenty minutes, not more than an hour. That meant that Michael had probably become coherent again shortly after he'd left me. I'd wondered why no one had come looking for me to get my version of events, and I supposed now that what I had told the EMTs was enough. I also learned that someone who has had a TIA has a greatly increased risk of having a real stroke. The incidence was especially high in the first ninety days afterwards. This I could not stomach thinking about. Every time that possibility crossed my mind, I wanted to drive across town and pick him up and bring him home with me and watch him for three months so I could be sure he was all right. Of course I knew that wasn't my job. I was sure his wife and family were doing it just fine. It wasn't my place to intervene. But it was hard trying to give him space to be with the most important people in his life when every day that went by that I didn't hear from him filled me with dread and a desire to call all of the hospitals and, if necessary, the morgue. After a few days of near-insane levels of anxiety, I settled on a compromise. Whenever my worrying got out of my control, I visited his brewery's website. My reasoning was that they would surely post something about the funeral if he died. It was a very small, very gruesome comfort.

Even worse, my newfound fears didn't relate only to Michael. Every time Tom was around and I was brooding over what had happened or might happen I found myself picturing his face where Michael's had been. Tom slurring a story. Tom not moving. Tom blindly staring. Tom on a stretcher, in an ambulance. Tom vanishing. Tom dead maybe. And where would I be when it happened? Would it be some other woman who kept him company in his final moments?

About a week after that day – in my mind I always thought of it as "that day," as if all of the other days were too inconsequential to bear the designation "that" – I awoke at four o'clock in the morning with a fever again. I had always been prone to sleeping warm, but now my sweating was abnormally profuse, and I was actually on the verge of waking Tom up to tell him to take me to the hospital when it finally began to subside. I gave it another hour, but I couldn't get back to sleep, so I got up and started my coffee. While it was brewing, I checked my travel bag of medicines for acetaminophen. I had rarely been ill in my life thus far, but I seemed to recall that it was a fever reducer as well as a painkiller, and I thought it would be sensible to be prepared in case I really was sick. I still had plenty. I poured off the first dribble from the coffeemaker, and then as long as I was doing bag maintenance, I decided also to count up my ibuprofen and allergy pills. I had adequate stashes of those as well. There were also two tampons and a panty liner, which would have been plenty, except that I noticed that the wrapper on one of the tampons was torn. That was odd. That usually didn't happen unless I inadvertently left one in there for months and it got banged around a lot. And that was when I realized that I couldn't remember when my last period was. I'd never kept careful track of it, and now I thought hard. I knew I'd had one in April, because although they were really short these days, they came extra hard and fast and I had been fortunate enough for one to happen this year on April fifteenth. I wasn't going to forget that mess in a hurry. But I couldn't recall having one since, and it was now early June. And May was my horny month; wouldn't I have noticed an untidy interruption?

I couldn't decide whether to laugh or cry. I was an idiot. I had missed a period. Those fevers weren't fevers; they were hot flashes.

I'd been thirty-nine when I met Michael. By then I'd already been dreading this day. I'd spent the two years it took us to get together worrying that it would happen too soon, that I'd miss out purely by virtue of getting old. And then in the four years I'd spent with him, I'd somehow nearly managed to forget that menopause was even going to happen. And even though it wasn't here yet, it was close enough now that I knew I ought to lay out the welcome mat for it, and that made me a little sad.

I was gloomy over breakfast, and when Tom asked me what was wrong. I merely said I hadn't slept well, and that was so commonplace that he didn't even comment. Later that evening I told him what had happened. He wasn't as sympathetic as I might have liked, but at least he didn't treat it like a tragedy. In fact, his attitude was almost reassuring once I thought about it. He didn't seem perturbed by my getting old, so why should I be upset? That made me feel better. But then, he'd always had a knack for making me feel better in unexpected ways.

Weeks flitted away and I still didn't hear from Michael. I wondered if it was still too soon to call him. We had another problem. My client/landlady had phoned me. Amazingly enough, her father was still alive. Her disability leave at work had run out, but she'd found a new job in her old hometown, and had decided to stay there indefinitely. So she wanted to secure a permanent tenant for the condo now, which made sense, given that she was charging me way less than market rate. And she said she'd take care of the advertising and forgive my last month's rent if I wouldn't mind showing the place to prospective tenants, if I had the time.

That wasn't really how I wanted to spend my time, but I supposed it wasn't that big of a deal. It seemed a shame to tell her she had to hire someone specially for such a small job, so in the end I agreed. On the plus side, it gave me plenty of reasons to go over there, which was necessary because now I had to pack and move again. By now, moving had lost most of its charm for me. This place had been so well-stocked with its own stuff that we hadn't needed furniture or anything like that, but because space had been abundant for once, I'd filled it up with extra clothes and a kitchen full of food and even a shelf of my own books for times when I was waiting for Michael and wanted something to read.

Michael had taken my cue and left behind a spare jacket, several sweatshirts, and a pile of T-shirts I found tucked mysteriously under the bed. I wasn't sure if they were clean or dirty, but when I lifted them to my nose they smelled like Michael so I didn't wash them but stuck them on the top of the box with his other things in case I needed a whiff of him again. I spotted them several days later when I was in a melancholy mood and imagined what it would have been like to have found those shirts if he had died that day just a few weeks ago. Burying my face in that pile, knowing that the shirt and the smell was all I had left of him. And I was overcome by the tragedy that hadn't happened and lay down with his clothes and cried as if he really were gone forever. And afterwards I didn't even kick myself for being a sentimental fool.

There were numerous inquiries as soon as the ad hit, but I only had to show the place four times before I found tenants. They were a nice-looking young married couple with no children. I was reminded of our landlord at the cottage and scanned them for rings. They checked out. They would be moving in two weeks later. I called my landlady and told her the good news so she could arrange for the moving company she had hired to come and get her stuff and bring it out to her. That would be a week from now.

And then I couldn't wait any longer; I would have to call Michael and tell him; couldn't risk having him go there with his key and barge in on the new people. It was early enough in the day that I thought he might still be at work and I preferred to contact him when he was there rather than at home. I pulled out my phone and found a text message reading "Is the condo still available?" and I thought that was a little odd because all of the other inquiries had come through my email; I'd only given out my cell number to the serious prospects. But of course, this must have been one of them; someone who'd had a change of heart and wanted it now, but too late.

"Sorry, it's been rented," I sent back. You can imagine my surprise when it buzzed back a minute later and the message I had received read, "So when can I see you then?" I had a moment of amused perplexity wondering what kind of weirdo tries to pick up some lady who merely showed him an apartment, via text message no less, before I realized that this wasn't a prospective renter; it was Michael.

I was sorry I wasn't standing in front of a mirror because if I had been, I'm sure I would have seen my face light up like a firefly's behind. I wrote back that the place would be available for another week. He suggested Friday night. "Yes, please!" I answered.

It was already Wednesday, so I didn't have too long to wait. On Thursday evening Tom went out of town for a long weekend for a bachelor party for one of our friends who had divorced a while back and was now getting married again. I was glad he was going to be away. It meant I didn't have to decide just yet what I was going to tell him when I was with Michael.

Friday flew by in a daze of unbridled, joyous anticipation. I forgot about everything else, forgot about the moving and the hot flashes and even Michael's mini-stroke, forgot everything but the clock, which cooperated very nicely and was pushing me out the door before I was even really ready to leave the office. But I left anyway because although I'd put the pork roast in the slow cooker, there were still the potatoes and asparagus to prepare, and I was not a fast chopper. I hadn't cooked for us much, and since this might be the last time we'd have a full kitchen, I wanted to do it now when we were going to be meeting early for a change. I was so busy at the stove that I didn't notice he'd come in until I felt his arms around my waist and I dropped my spatula on the floor and turned and hugged him like he'd just returned from a two-year stint in Antarctica. Just as I was leaning in for my kiss, I heard the instantly recognizable hiss of liquid boiling over and had to whirl back to the stove, so he leaned over my shoulder and kissed me on the neck, and I giggled because his beard was tickling me. He asked if there was anything he could do, so I put him to work monitoring the sauce for the roast and setting the table and it made a funny picture in my mind, us being so domestic, almost as if we were a real couple.

He had cracked open a beer and was about to pour it when I said sharply, "What do you think you're doing?"

"Having a beer?" he answered cautiously.

"Did you go to work today?" I inquired.

"Yes."

"And did you sample any beers while you were there?" I blinked my eyes rapidly at him.

"Yes, of course!"

"Then I'm afraid you'll have to put that away," I said, snatching up the bottle and stashing it back in the fridge.

"Did you just take away my beer?" he asked, too surprised to be offended. "That was your beer, too, you know!"

"Persons at risk for stroke should limit alcoholic beverages, one per day for women and two per day for men," I recited. "Since you've presumably had at least one full beer already today, you'll want to save your remaining one for later, I'm sure."

"Fine," he said, looking disgruntled. "How about a glass of milk, then?"

"Persons at risk for stroke should limit their intake of cholesterol…" I began, but he cut me off.

"Fine, I'll just have water," he pouted.

"Excellent choice, sir. And would you prefer the tap or refrigerated variety?"

"I'll get it," he said, rising from the table and pouring us both a glass from the pitcher in the refrigerator. "You know you sound just like my wife, don't you?" he said, without seeming particularly annoyed by the fact.

"I always suspected she was a fine woman," I replied, equally unperturbed. I looked him over as he was walking back to the dinette and said, "She must be doing something right. You've lost weight."

"It's all the no beer," he said glumly, and I really felt bad for him. What if one day I had to stop drinking beer, too?

But he cheered up as we ate and he related to me the events of the last several weeks. I was impressed by how not-depressed he was. Me, I was having trouble dealing with the disturbing memory of something that had happened to someone else. He, on the other hand, welcomed it as a timely forewarning.

"What if I hadn't had the attack?" he said. "Then I might have had a real stroke and that could have been disastrous. I mean, I know it could still happen, but now I'm on these medications, and I know what to look for, so I think my chances are much better." As I listened it struck me that there was something incongruous and almost comical in his appearance, and it took me some minutes to figure out what it was. The conversation was meaningful and the man who was talking was mature. Yet his attire reeked of the young and frivolous. He was wearing my favorite shirt, or, I should say, my favorite of his shirts. A burgundy T-shirt, a souvenir from a concert he'd attended three decades before, featuring a "hair band" that had been popular in the eighties. I won't embarrass us by telling you which one.

"Which reminds me," he continued, seemingly unaware of the drollness of his apparel. "How did you know? That day?"

That was odd, I thought. He also refers to it as "that day." My amusement subsided as I told him about the acronym.

"That was lucky," he said.

"Yeah," I agreed.

I guess I didn't sound as if I felt very lucky, because after a pause he asked, "Was it really awful? To watch, I mean?"

"I still think about it," I said shortly, closing my eyes tight to clear out the morbid image that had come into my mind when he mentioned it.

"It must have been scary," he said quietly.

"It was for me," I said. "Were you scared, too?"

"I didn't have a clear idea what was happening. I could tell you were upset, but I didn't seem to be able to do anything about it. And then when you brought the phone over and my wife, she, well, she was a bit hysterical and I only understood about half of what she was saying, but it sounded like goodbye. The kind of goodbye you'd give a dying person. And then I was scared."

"I'm sorry!" I wailed. "It seemed like a good idea at the time!"

"No, don't be upset!" he said. "It was the right thing to do. If the worst had happened… No, don't ever be sorry about that. It was the best thing you could have done. I'm grateful for it. I'm sure she is, too."

By now we were done eating and he began clearing the table and I washed the dishes and updated him on the events of my life over the past month. There wasn't a lot to tell. I explained about renting out the condo. I pointed out the box of his clothes that I had assembled. In a moment of weakness, I even told him how I'd wept like a baby over the shirts. He seemed touched. I guess it's always nice to know that someone cares about you, even if they show it in foolish ways.

When the dishes were finished, I let him pull the beer back out of the refrigerator and we sat on the sofa and sipped at it slowly.

"Have you been exercising?" I asked.

"How do you mean?" he said.

"Persons at risk for stroke should engage in thirty minutes of cardiovascular activity at least…"

He slapped me lightly on the tush. "I haven't been over to see you, have I?"

"Hmph!" I said. "If that's your only exercise, I think we're gonna need to step it up a notch!"

He laughed, but I said, "Seriously, do you want to take a walk or something?"

"Here?" he answered skeptically.

"Oh," I said. "It's a little late to worry about that now." And I told him about coming home from the hospital and what Tom had said to me.

"He knew all along?"

"I wasn't surprised that he knew," I said. "I always figured he must know on some level."

"Okay, I could see where he would suspect there was somebody. But how could he have known it was me?"

"We screwed up. You stopped talking to either of us in public. We'd gotten along too well before that to stop speaking all together. It didn't seem natural. He just put two and two together."

"Smart guy," he said.

"Unusual guy," said I.

"How so?"

"How many other men do you know who would put up with their girlfriend having another boyfriend?"

His eyes glinted. "Just one."

It took me a second to understand whom he meant. I reached over and stroked his bristly cheek with the flat of my hand. He grabbed it and kissed each of the fingers in turn.

"So all of our precautions have been for naught, eh?" he said.

"Well, not for naught, I hope. Your wife doesn't know, does she?"

"Well, she hasn't confronted me about it. It's the things she doesn't say that makes me think she knows. You know, she never asked me who I was with that day. Wouldn't that be a natural question? Who was the woman who called me? At the least, most people would want to say thank you, but she's never even mentioned it."

I mulled that over. "You must be right," I said. "But at least she doesn't know who I am. And it must save her some embarrassment, not being forced to acknowledge it." I explained about Tom, and how I felt really awkward about sneaking around now that the secret was out in the open.

His face fell. "Does that mean you won't want to spend the night?"

"No, of course I do! I mean, I would this time, no matter what, but luckily, Tom's out of town anyway." I hesitated. "But I'm surprised you want to – or that you can, I mean. I would think your family would really want you home right now."

"I wanted to talk to you about that, actually. I do want to stay with you tonight." There was a dreadfully long pause while he seemed to search somewhere inside for the words he desired. "Because I think it's going to have to be the last time."

He didn't wait for me to respond, and I was grateful for that because I needed to catch my breath. "My wife, the kids, they have, they've been all over me. Checking up all the time, making sure I'm still alive."

"That'll ease up after a while," I predicted.

"Yeah, I know. That's the problem. 'Cause right now, this past month, we've all been, well, we're all really close, really happy to be together. It's like a special bond between all of us. I don't want to mess that up. More than that, I want to enjoy it while it lasts."

He cleared his throat uncomfortably. "I've never regretted being with you. You've become like – almost like another family to me. But in some way, having that seems to take something away from my first family. Not because of anything you've done or because I neglect them to be with you, just the idea of it. I can't focus as much on them when I'm thinking about you."

I knew what he meant. I'd rarely lapsed in my affection for Tom, but Michael cast a long shadow, and sometimes I thought we had trouble bridging the invisible gap that it created.

"I never thought I'd have to worry about dying before the age of fifty. But if it happens, there's a certain way I'd like them to remember me. Loving husband and father. Good family man. When he wasn't working, liked to stay home and spend time with his wife and children."

He looked at me pleadingly, and for a fleeting moment I thought he was asking me to let him go. As if maybe there was still a chance that he might change his mind, if only I said, No, please stay with me, stay with me a while longer. But that wasn't the Michael I knew. And then I understood. What he was asking me so intently with his eyes was not to let him go, but to comprehend why he had to go. Not to be hurt by it.

Now or later, it would never be enough. It was time now.

"I always knew it had to happen eventually," I said. It was the me I knew saying it.

He wrapped his arm around me and I leaned up against him and extended my arm around his somewhat flatter belly and thought crazily that at least this way I would never have to see him if he got really skinny, and I laughed out loud at the absurdity of it. And when he asked me what was so funny I told him, because it was the end and I might as well lay all my cards on the table because it was my last play and I had nothing to lose. And he was pleased because he'd always thought I was teasing him when I made comments about his beer belly and didn't understand that I really did find it attractive, although I knew he needed to get rid of it now. And then I told him how much I'd liked him in the beginning, even when I'd thought he was a jerk, and how I'd fantasized about him for weeks and months on end, and how I'd never ever been disappointed with the reality of being with him even though it was very different from the fantasy. And then I told him about my missed period and my hot flashes and how losing my fertility made me feel like less of a woman somehow, and how I'd known that he was the last man that I would ever really, really want and that I'd been afraid of losing out on that because I was getting too old. And I told him that although I was still sad to be older and not younger, that I knew I wasn't nearly as sad as I would have been had I never had him. And then in my mind I finally understood that that was the key to the whole matter, that he was my companion, maybe not for now and ever, but at least for that long torturous walk across the bridge from youth to middle age which we had taken together and which he had made bearable for me. Which we had made bearable for each other.

"What are you thinking?" he asked me.

Since today was the day for spilling everything, I answered him truthfully.

"Something corny," I said.

He kissed my cheek. "Well, I don't think you should be too worried about getting older. I still think you're hot."

"Oh, pshaw!" I said, waving my hand disdainfully at him.

"In fact, I think it could be a good thing for you."

"Really? How come?" I said. Maybe aging wasn't the worst thing that could happen to a person, but calling it a "good thing" was certainly a stretch.

"Maybe if your hormones calm down a little, you'll finally get a handle on that sex drive of yours," he said.

"What does that mean??!!" I huffed.

"Now I'm not saying you're out of control or anything," he continued gravely, "But I seriously had trouble keeping up with you in the beginning. Oof!"

I'd punched him in the beer belly.

"Think of all the extra time you'll have if you subtract out all the humping!" he gasped. "You can take classes, maybe write that book you keep talking about…"

I pulled my arm back as if I was going to punch him again, and he yelled, "Give! Give!" and I withdrew my arms, but turned away from him and put on my fake pout until he sneaked his body around the edge of the sofa and got his face in front of mine again and kissed my wholly unresponsive lips until I couldn't suppress my giggles anymore.

"Whatcha doin'?" I said.

"Taking you to bed," he replied, gathering me up in his arms and standing up slowly under my weight.

"Careful!" I cautioned. "Your back!"

"Just getting my exercise," he assured me, so I put my arms around his neck and let him carry me into the bedroom. I couldn't remember how long it had been since he had last done that. It seemed more difficult now. He set me gently on my feet, sat down on the bed himself, then reached out and held my hands and looked up at me warmly. And even though I knew it was the end, I wasn't so sad anymore because we still had here and now and it was the culmination of years of fond memories that I would carry with me always.

"What are you thinking?" he inquired again.

"Something even cornier," I answered.

He smiled and pulled me gently down onto the bed.

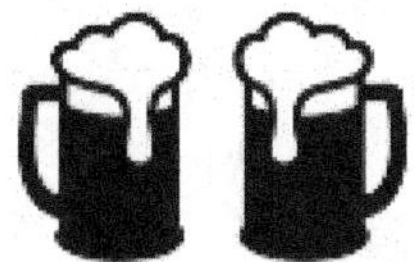

CHAPTER 20

I awoke at four o'clock and for once I was happy about that because it gave me the chance to watch him while he slept one last time. But not for long, because he looked so peaceful that it made me feel peaceful, too, and I felt myself drifting off again before I was really ready to close my eyes to him. When I woke again it was still very early morning, just beginning to get light, but Michael was no longer in bed with me, and I had a moment of panic thinking that he'd left me without saying goodbye. But no, there he was again, sitting on the edge of the bed, and he'd started the coffee I'd prepared the night before and brought me a cup.

I thanked him and sipped it. He was dressed already and I was going to get up, but he insisted I stay in bed, and tucked me in under the covers so tight that I couldn't have gotten free if I'd tried. I'd left the windows open all night to let in the cool evening air and the room was a bit chilly, but it was warm and comfortable there in the bed. And he lay down on top of the covers next to me for a while and held me until I felt sleepy again, and then he kissed me on the forehead and I knew it was time for him to go and I was scared, but in a strange way, happy, too. We looked at each other silently until I couldn't bear to look at him anymore, and then he stood up and it was time.

"Michael," I whispered.

He just smiled and didn't say anything back, so I knew he understood what I meant.

When I woke again it was full morning, and I was alone. But the coffee was still warm in the pot, and the cacophonous harmony of squirrels chattering in the trees outside was drifting in through the open window, and I was all right. I drank my coffee and packed up what was left to pack of the kitchen stuff, and then I went into the bathroom and living room and did the same. And then I went into the bedroom and stripped the bed and wondered for the hundredth time what to do with that massive white comforter that was now past its prime, probably as a result of being wedged into my trunk so many times. I thought it over. I still had no better solution. Back into the trunk it would have to go. But maybe that was okay now. Maybe I'd like always having it with me, but tucked away out of sight. I looked to make sure that Michael had taken his box of stuff from the chair where I'd left it, and he had. In its place there was a single T-shirt, the one he'd been wearing the night before. I put it up to my nose and it hinted to me of sex and beer and I smiled because to me, that was Michael. And then I tucked it into my bag and quietly left the place.

I didn't feel like going home yet, and I thought I'd like to take a long walk or a drive but I didn't know where to go. Then I remembered the lake where we'd spent a weekend what seemed ages ago and that idea appealed to me, but then I thought, no, I'm not going to do that, I'm not going to revisit our old haunts and apartments and places we'd been together that were special to me, to us. So I pulled out my map of the city and its environs and found a state park not far outside of town that I had never been to, and that was where I went instead. It was quiet there, and I walked silently under its trees and thought, not about Michael, but about what I was going to do with my life now.

In the late afternoon I finally went home, and my legs were tired as I tottered up the steps and for once I was glad to be there; it was welcoming somehow. The sun was at the angle in which it bathed our tiny backyard, so I fetched a large towel from the hall closet and laid it out on the grass and then lay down myself with a book and read until the sunshine abandoned me. Then I went inside and fixed myself a little dinner, and ate it sitting on the couch with my fork in one hand and my paperback in the other because, what the hell, I did all the cleaning, so if anybody had a right to spill on the furniture, I did. After dinner I took the book with me into the bathtub and stayed there a long, long while, so that I had to re-heat the tub numerous times by turning the hot water tap on full blast for half a minute until the water warmed around me.

When I finally got out and dried off and went into the bedroom to dress, darkness had fallen both inside and out. I never kept a light on in any room except the one I was in; it was a matter of principle with me. And since I could find my way around the unlit house tolerably well, I rarely bothered with turning lights on as I passed from room to room. But usually there was someone else here in the house with me, and there would be light coming from another room or from upstairs or down, and not this solid obscurity draped like a curtain around our bedroom as I got ready for bed. Or else Tom would be here in the bedroom with me and I wouldn't notice the darkness in the rest of the house. I tried not to notice it now.

I almost made it through the day. I had not had the leisure of reading in bed for a long time, so I poured myself a beer and kept it going with my book, which was pretty engaging, until about eleven o'clock when I finally had to put it down because I'd finished it. It was past time to go to sleep so I turned off the light and relaxed on my pillow, but the house was unbearably quiet and empty and lonely, and for some reason I thought of Tom, sitting here by himself all those nights while I was with Michael, and how empty and lonely he must have felt, too. And then I cried, not for me, not for Michael, but for him, for Tom, for what he had chosen to endure to be with me, and I pitied him so, pitied him for being attached to such a woman, a woman who could have subjected him to that undeserved punishment. I'd thought only of me, of my worries, my fears, my insecurities. Was I attractive, was I old, was

I worthy of love. What about him? Did my infidelity make him pose those questions to himself, too? It was horrible, the pain I must have caused him, and I'd shut it out, shut the effects of it out of my mind because acknowledging it would have interfered with my own selfish desires.

It was bitter, that first night after Michael. When dawn came, I finally rose without having any assurance that I'd slept at all. My brain was foggy but I needed to do something, so I traipsed out to the car and unloaded the remnants of my time with Michael. Sad how the years I'd spent with him could be reduced now to a pile of junk. Spare towels. Spare sheets. Spare dishes. Spare clothes. Spares of everything you needed to make a home with someone. A second home, maybe. Another family.

And then there was his shirt, and I picked it up and clutched it in my hand and it strengthened me somehow; took hold of my mind and heart, and suddenly it came over me that I didn't regret it either, any more than he did, not one bit of it. I wasn't sorry at all, not about my man or his woman or the way we came together or even the way we parted. How could I be sorry about something that had given me so much happiness? The life I'd had before Michael had had little room in it for me, for anything I wanted for me, myself alone. But my life with Michael was all about want, my want, his want, no one else's want, only ours, our want for ourselves and for each other. The wanting had given me purpose and pleasure, and if I had to suffer now for want of him as much as I had taken joy in wanting him, it was a worthy exchange.

And as for Tom, there was still time to put things right. I was not at heart an unfaithful person. There would be no more Michaels, because Michael was, well, Michael. Perhaps that was why Tom had chosen to accept him as a part of my life, because he knew it wasn't truly in my nature to cheat. He had simply come along when I needed him; almost, it seemed, because I needed him.

I couldn't help myself. I put on his shirt, and then lay back down on the bed and slept until noon.

When I woke, I changed into my own clothes and carefully packed the shirt away and hid it in the bottom of my closet. I knew I could never wash it or it might lose its long-familiar smell, so I had to conserve it for when I really needed it. I spent the rest of the day doing housework, and when Tom came home at nine o'clock I welcomed him with enthusiastically open arms.

"Hi, there!" he said, surprised but pleased by my eagerness.

I kissed him. "How was your weekend?"

And while he told me about it I fixed us something to eat, and maybe I even enjoyed it a little, attending to that chore that was such an essential part of our life together.

After dinner we got into bed and opened a beer and lay awake and talked and he didn't seem unhappy, not at all unhappy to be with me. Although he was clearly fighting to stay awake, eventually his eyes started drooping, and I leaned over and kissed him on the forehead and said, "Go to sleep, Tom. You need your rest." And then he was snoring softly and he looked beautiful and peaceful there in our bed, and I wasn't at all unhappy to be with him either.

In the morning I rose early and made breakfast as usual, and after we'd eaten I accompanied him to the garage as I always did to say goodbye.

"What's that?" he said, gesturing toward a large white bundle in the corner near the door.

"Spare comforter," I said.

He snapped his neck around as if he were rattled. "What are you going to do with it?"

"I'm going to get rid of it," I said resolutely. "I don't need it anymore."

He looked at me hard; then kissed me hard and hugged me harder. At last he climbed, smiling, into his car, and I watched and waved as he backed out of the garage, like I did every morning. It wasn't such a bad routine at that.

Towards the end of summer a postcard addressed to me arrived at my office. It bore no inscription, but it had a picture of a pretty nice hotel in another city on it. I tucked it into a file in my desk with the one picture of us that had ever been taken. Happy anniversary to you, too, Michael.

I looked for him at the next beer festival, but if he was there I didn't see him. I looked again the time after that, but by the following one I'd stopped looking very hard. And then one day I heard that he had moved to go and head up a brewery in another part of the country and that was when I was finally convinced that I would never see him again. He was gone.

It's been several years now, that I've been without Michael. I'd like to say that I don't miss him, that I've forgotten him, that I'm so fully contented with my own existence that I never think of him at all. But that would be a lie, because although I don't dwell on him anymore, or even truly wish to have him back, I don't believe I'll ever forget what he gave to me, or the change he made in me. And I think perhaps I meant something to him, too; was maybe a bit more than merely a lover or sex partner, because every year on or about the anniversary we never celebrated, a postcard with no inscription arrives at my office from a far-away city, and I know that Michael is alive and well, and has not forgotten me either. At least, my heart hopes that he is well.

And I? I'm still here, still in the same dull, repetitive life, still with the same job, the same house, and the same boyfriend, but maybe I'm different somehow, because I enjoy it much more than I did before Michael. I haven't strayed again, and I haven't wanted to, because Michael was enough; will always be enough. I wonder sometimes, what would have happened if he'd never left me; if we would have gone on together in our way, or if we would have parted long ago. But had we stayed together, I imagine that my life with him wouldn't be so different from the life I now have without him, a life of quiet, and peace, and contentment; a life of few regrets, or unfulfilled desires, because I've had all that I could have wanted, and more than I deserved. And in the comfort of this tranquil existence, I don't fear my old age as I feared my middle years. Because I've secured a willing partner for that journey, too; one who is well-suited to guide me upon my particular path through the remainder of my life, and whom I hope to guide, in turn, upon his.

OTHER BOOKS BY THE AUTHOR

JUST THE THREE OF US

Three close friends get far too close for comfort in *Just the Three of Us: An* *Erotic Romantic Comedy for the Commitment-Challenged.*

Meet Kathy, a thirty-seven-year-old drifter who's constantly on the move: to new towns, new jobs, and new relationships. Imagine her surprise when she's befriended by lifelong friends Sam and Ted, attractive young men who, though ten years her junior, are far more settled than she thinks she'll ever be. Cheer them on as their three-way friendship succumbs to passion, then passion to romance, and romance to… well, surely it couldn't be love. Could it?

With a well-earned Heat Level of 4+, dialogue guaranteed to make you laugh out loud, and a plot to tickle your most sentimental of spots, *Just the Three of Us* promises an entertaining read for fans of romance looking for a unique take on love and sexuality.

Now available in paperback (both standard and large print sizes) and eBook at retailers worldwide.

Excerpt from *Just the Three of Us:*

Ted lay calmly beside me, his hand resting lightly on my hip, seeming perfectly at ease. His fingers took a few tentative steps down my thighs and warmth flooded into them. I guess it showed because he smiled meaningfully at me. I smiled back, my knees parting subtly in welcoming expectation.

I heard heavy breathing in my other ear. I turned to look and saw that Sam was hyperventilating.

"Are you all right?" I said, stroking my fingers against his chest.

"Are we going to…?" he choked, panting with the effort of speaking. "We are, aren't we?'

"We don't have to," I said uncertainly.

"We don't?"

I put on my bravest face and tried to swallow my eagerness. I felt Ted's fingers pressing into my thigh and disappointment overcame me again. I forced it down. We were friends first, after all. Even if I could pressure him into this, I wouldn't.

"Not if you don't want to," I assured him.

He swallowed and gazed thoughtfully into my eyes. Behind my back, Ted remained silent.

"But you want to, don't you?"

I shrugged away my ardor with effort. "It's not all about me," I said.

I saw him glance over my shoulder and knew he was looking at Ted.

"It's not that I don't want to," he mumbled. "I'm just… I'm just not sure I'm ready."

Ted laughed loudly behind my back, breaking the tension, and I swiveled towards him, startled.

"This is all you've talked about all week!" he roared, rolling his body forward into mine.

"What?!" I said, turning back to look at Sam. He was grinning rather sheepishly.

"Night and day," Ted confirmed, his hand abandoning my thigh and tightly circling my waist instead. "How he absolutely couldn't wait one more minute and couldn't we get you to come over sooner and did I think you'd really go through with it."

"Well, I…" Sam protested feebly, his cheeks coloring as he lapsed again into that sheepish grin.

"So the truth comes out!" I laughed.

"Hey, it's totally different now that you're actually here! I still can't believe…"

"Believe it, buddy!" I interrupted and he gaped at me, surprised by my sudden change in tone. "Now get your butt over here before I lose my temper. It's not polite to keep a woman waiting," I said severely.

"Yes, ma'am!" he said, sliding into me with all of the force and enthusiasm of mud on a California hillside. "Miss!" he hurriedly corrected himself.

"That's better!" I asserted. "Now by the time I count ten, I expect to be in bed with two very handsome and very naked young men. No more dilly-dallying!" I threatened, wagging my finger at them. "One…"

Abruptly they both jerked away from me, and I rolled onto my backside and watched as polo shirts and boxers went flying across the room like kites snapping in a spring breeze.

"Eight," I breathed, but they were already done. They rolled sideways against me where I still lay flat on my back and then snuggled up close to each side of me, their cheeks pink with excitement. I sensed the weight of their bodies pushing against me from my chest to my legs; felt the sweat forming where their skin was pressed against mine. And into each of my hips poked something hard but soft; deliciously promising and hopelessly decadent, and I gulped, uncertain whether to savor the sensation or run away from it.

Maybe I, too, had the tiniest of doubts about this.

THE HANNELACK FANNY, OR HOW I LEARNED TO STOP WORRYING AND LOVE MY RUMP

One weekend a few months after my glorious ass-awakening, John and I went on a road trip. I'd leaned over sideways and lifted my skirt up over my hips so that he could rest his hand on my ass while he was driving. Sunshine was streaming through the open sunroof and my butt felt warm in spite of its near-nakedness. How I relished that sensation now!

Suddenly a truck horn sounded.

"Hey!" I heard a man yell. "Hey, wide load!"

A year before, I would have been mortified. Not anymore.

I turned to look. A semi was travelling beside us. The man in the passenger seat was staring at my bared ass. The driver was leaning over, trying to get a look.

"Like what you see, boys?" I yelled back, jerking my body in my seat to set my rump to rippling.

"WOOOO-EEEE! Shake that ass, mama!"

In that moment, something possessed me. It was as if the beast that had so long been bolted to my bottom had finally broken free of its cage. It wanted out. All the way out.

I unhooked my seatbelt and jumped up on my seat. With effort I wriggled my way through the open sunroof, ass and all. And then I wiggled out of my panties, lifted up my skirt, and showed myself to the world. Every last wobbling inch of me.

"Look at my ass!" I yelled, slapping it hard with my palm. "Look at my ass!"

I was bouncing, jumping up and down in place, and my ass, behemoth that it was, was bouncing, too, the fat landing on the warm roof of the car and then retreating back up to my waist in happy rhythm while I pointed and laughed.

"Look at my ass!"

A young woman's life is changed forever when she discovers what everyone around her has known all along: that a renowned family characteristic has re-emerged in a most unfortunate location – her own backside. Follow her journey from embarrassment to acceptance to unbridled joy as she learns to appreciate the wonders of going through life with the Hannelack fanny. And don't forget to look for my commentary on the real-life inspiration behind this glorious tale of a glorious behind – me!

Short story; 6,000 words. Now available in eBook format.

ABOUT THE AUTHOR

Lori Schafer is a writer of serious prose and humorous erotica and romance. Her flash fiction, short stories, and essays have appeared in numerous print and online publications, and her first two books were published in November 2014. *On Hearing of My Mother's Death Six Years After It Happened: A Daughter's Memoir of Mental Illness* commemorates Lori's terrifying adolescent experience of her mother's psychosis, while *Stories from My Memory-Shelf: Fiction and Essays from My Past* is an autobiographical collection featuring stories and essays inspired by other events from Lori's own life. In the summer of 2014, Lori began work on a second memoir, *The Long Road Home*, during the course of a two-month-long journey across the United States and Canada. She anticipates that it will be ready for publication late in 2015.

Lori's first two novels, *My Life with Michael: A Novel of Sex, Beer, and Middle Age* and *Just the Three of Us: An Erotic Romantic Comedy for the Commitment-Challenged,* will be released early in 2015. She is currently at work on a third novel, a sequel to *Just the Three of Us*. When she isn't writing (which isn't often), Lori enjoys playing ice hockey, attending beer festivals, and spending long afternoons reading at the beach in the sunshine.

For further information on Lori's upcoming projects, please visit her website at http://lorilschafer.com, where you may subscribe to her newsletter or follow her blog for the most current updates on her cross-country travels. You are also welcome to email her directly at lorilschafer@outlook.com with any comments, questions, or suggestions you may have. No requests for advice on your love life, though. She'll give it to you, but you probably won't be thrilled with the results.

Website: http://lorilschafer.com
Twitter: http://twitter.com/LoriLSchafer/
Amazon: http://www.amazon.com/Lori-Schafer/e/B00MC1UI16/
Facebook: http://www.facebook.com/lorilschafer/
Pinterest: http://www.pinterest.com/lorilschafer/
Google Plus: http://plus.google.com/u/0/105878636247618615880/
Linked In: http://www.linkedin.com/pub/lori-schafer/67/30a/b64/
Goodreads: https://www.goodreads.com/author/show/4392104.Lori_Schafer/
YouTube: http://www.youtube.com/channel/UCb5RugrJMSHh6_4hkgHmkMA/

"We Are All Miss America"

BOOK CLUB QUESTIONS

1. What was your favorite part of the book? What was your least favorite? Why?

2. Kate freely acknowledged that she was wrong to have an affair. Could you understand her reasons for doing it anyway? What might motivate someone to do something like that in spite of the guilt?

3. In what ways do you think Kate's decisions were influenced by her age and time of life? Do you think she would have behaved differently had she been older or younger?

4. What role do you think Kate's sexuality played in determining her behavior?

5. Kate and Michael knew each other for nearly two years before finally getting together. What did you think of the way their relationship started? Could you imagine how difficult it might be to make that kind of connection?

6. The book discussed in detail the logistical difficulties that Kate and Michael encountered in seeing each other – the when, the where, even the excuses they made to their significant others. How do these affect their relationships with each other and with their partners?

7. At a number of places in the story, Kate became aware that her position as Michael's lover precluded her from participating in key aspects of his life. Do you think this prevents an adulterous relationship from ever existing on the same level as a legitimate one?

8. Tom and Miranda both pretended not to know that their real-life partners were having affairs. Why do you think a spouse might adopt that position?

9. How would the story have changed if Tom and Kate had had any children?

10. It's common in novels about adultery for the adulterer to be severely punished for his or her unfaithfulness. Were you surprised that Kate was not? How do such situations usually play out in the real world?

11. Were there elements of the book that you thought might be partially autobiographical? What made you think so?

12. How would you classify this book? Is it a romance, erotica, a work of women's fiction, or something cross-genre? For what types of readers would you recommend it?

www.ingramcontent.com/pod-product-compliance
Lightning Source LLC
Chambersburg PA
CBHW081208170626
46811CB00010B/3226

* 9 7 8 1 9 4 2 1 7 0 1 5 0 *